PRAISE FOR *THE MIDSL*

'Ripe to be plucked for a screen adaptation, this mouth-watering debut novel—meticulously researched and crafted—raises the bar in contemporary and historical fiction coupling . . . our heroines are compelling, passionate and admirable.' —*Australian Women's Weekly*

'Given the passion of Kirsty Manning, the ease at which she slips into the quintessential lifestyle of the author, and with another novel in the works, there is no doubt *The Midsummer Garden* will not be the last we see of her.' —*Herald Sun*

'An evocative, lyrical tale of the search for identity by two unforgettable women, separated by history. It's a journey of passion through food, the natural world—and love—towards personal fulfilment . . . A fictional *Eat Pray Love* that all lovers of food and wine will devour.' —Sally Hepworth, author of the *The Secrets of Midwives*

'A satisfying read, bound to delight Kate Morton fans.' —Natasha Boyd, Book Bonding Bookstore

'Behind the beautiful cover of *The Midsummer Garden* lies an equally beautiful tale of two women, hundreds of years apart. Sumptuous food, glorious imagery, and alluring settings—what's not to love?' —Jodi Gibson, jfgibson.com.au

'This is a rich, sensual, and evocative novel, fragrant with the smell of crushed herbs and flowers, and haunted by the high cost that women must sometimes pay to find both love and their vocation.' —Kate Forsyth, author *of The Beast's Garden*

'I absolutely loved *The Midsummer Garden*. The dual time frames, strong female leads, the picturesque locales, the historical grounding and rich food references sold this reader.' —Mrs B's Book Reviews

Kirsty Manning grew up in northern New South Wales. She has degrees in literature and communications and worked as an editor and publishing manager in book publishing for over a decade.

A country girl with wanderlust, her travels and studies have taken her through most of Europe, the east and west coasts of the United States and pockets of Asia. Kirsty's journalism and photography specialising in lifestyle and travel regularly appear in magazines, newspapers and online.

In 2007, Kirsty and her husband, with two toddlers and a baby in tow, built a house in an old chestnut grove in the Macedon Ranges. Together, they planted an orchard and veggie patch, created large herbal 'walks' brimming with sage and rosemary, wove borders from chestnut branches and constructed far too many stone walls by hand.

Kirsty loves cooking with her kids and has several large heirloom copper pots that do not fit anywhere easily, but are perfect for making (and occasionally burning) jams, chutneys and soups. With husband Alex Wilcox, Kirsty is a partner in the award-winning Melbourne wine bar Bellota, and the Prince Wine Store in Sydney and Melbourne.

Her new novel, *The Jade Lily*, is published in 2018.

KIRSTY MANNING

the Midsummer Garden

ALLEN&UNWIN
SYDNEY • MELBOURNE • AUCKLAND • LONDON

This a work of fiction. Names, characters, places and incidents are products of the author's imagination or are used fictitiously. Any resemblance to actual events, locales, or persons, living or dead, is entirely coincidental.

This edition published in 2018
First published in 2017

Allen & Unwin
83 Alexander Street
Crows Nest NSW 2065
Australia
Phone: (61 2) 8425 0100
Email: info@allenandunwin.com
Web: www.allenandunwin.com

A catalogue record for this book is available from the National Library of Australia

ISBN 978 1 76063 244 1

Set in Minion Pro by Bookhouse, Sydney
Printed in Australia by SOS Print + Media Group

10 9 8 7 6 5

The paper in this book is FSC® certified. FSC® promotes environmentally responsible, socially beneficial and economically viable management of the world's forests.

For Alex,

who always points to the horizon and says, 'Go for it.'

It is the Romance of the Rose,
In which al the art of love I close.
The mater fair is of to make;
God graunte in gree that she it take
For whom that it begonnen is!

Roman de la Rose

Chapter 1

Tasmania, April 2014

It was an odd engagement present. Heirloom or not, such gifts were not usually covered in grime and dust. Pip sneezed as she started unpacking four boxes of antique French pots: copper boilers, streaked and mottled with watermarks, so when the soft morning light reflected off the pots and hit the white walls of the tiny worker's cottage, they rippled with rainbows. Some of the pots were so large Pip had to brace herself to lift them out of the boxes. When she pulled off the lids, their blackened insides were etched and lined with age.

The pots had sat at the top of her parents' kitchen dresser, steadfast. They had been there when her mother Mary had shown her how to roll pasta and make batches of apple chutney and, later, when her father coaxed her through her maths, chemistry and biology homework.

'Are you sure you don't want to leave them in the boxes till we get the rest of the cottage sorted?' Jack asked as he bit into an apple.

'Trust me, these pots will make it feel like home,' Pip replied as she stood on her toes to plant a goodbye kiss on his lips. 'Everything will be unpacked today—Megs is going to help.'

Jack almost choked. 'Good luck with that,' he said.

Pip was making a start on her first home with Jack by organising their tiny galley kitchen—a tricky task considering the limited number of pale green plywood cupboards available and the unlimited supply of advice her big sister (who was currently dusting the living room) would dispense freely.

Pip tugged open the kitchen window and glanced outside at the tall row of bushy macrocarpa pines that stood proudly between their old weatherboard cottage and the grand Ashfield House. The Georgian homestead's second storey towered over the trees, cream cast-iron gable and flag mast jutting high into the crisp blue autumn sky. A quartet of wide bay windows looked out across the gentle slopes of the vineyard—neat rows of red, crimson and yellows—to the sweep of the grey D'Entrecasteaux Channel below. Jack's parents lived in the big house and Jack's plan—with Pip's blessing—was to slowly buy them out of the vineyard and move digs across the paddock when they felt ready.

Pip lifted a small skillet out of the box with a grin. Right now she was happy to be moving in to this tiny cottage with Jack.

Jack had proposed last month after a long, windy day helping Pip collect native clam and sediment samples at North West Bay. He'd gently folded a shivering, muddy Pip into his arms and asked her to move in to his simple cottage immediately.

Pip preferred waterfronts to wallpaper swatches and he promised to hold off on the wedding and any new projects until she'd finished her PhD in November. He'd built a shelf on the verandah for her sampling equipment and put up a line of hooks for her dive gear so she didn't have to lug it to and from the university. Anything to help her over the finish line.

But this week Jack had changed his tune. Their plan was tripped up when the Rodgers walked over with the news of a fantastic offer from a consortium of neighbouring vineyards that wanted to buy Ashfield House.

Pip dusted the skillet, held it up to the light to admire the sheen before she plonked it on the benchtop with a sigh. She shivered as a chilly gust slipped through the window. Autumn had tumbled early into winter. Outside, almost-bare fruit trees skirted the sagging verandah. Green Granny Smith apples lay strewn across the lawn, sheltered by a layer of yellowing leaves. The old pots would come in handy for some chutney and stewing. She'd have a full shelf in a single batch!

Beyond the fence, neat lines of pinot noir vines were turning gold. She could see Jack walking between two rows and she took a moment to admire his broad shoulders and the long tanned legs emerging from his favourite navy work shorts. Despite the chill, Jack insisted on wearing shorts to work. He'd do the same in winter, too, when the mornings barely snuck above zero. Pip felt a surge of warmth and love flood through her as she watched Jack stride down to the deep grey water surging up the channel, occasionally tucking a branch back into wire or plucking a leaf that hid a fat bunch of grapes.

She smiled, then let out a huge sneeze, her nose irritated by plumes of dust from the boxes that filled every corner of the kitchen.

As if on cue, Megs came to stand in the doorway, a green surgical mask firmly in place, tsk-tsking and shaking her head as she observed the pots Pip had unpacked. 'This is ridiculous. Some of these pots are bigger than your bathroom. That one—' she gestured from a distance at a large pot with a slight green tinge '—is a cauldron. Are you planning on cooking for a local village fair? What was Mum thinking?'

What indeed? Pip jammed a lid in place. Megs had been married to fellow surgeon Will for four years and their parents had never given *her* as much as a teaspoon. But when Pip had Skyped her parents to announce that she and Jack had finally set a date for their wedding in December and they were moving in together, Mary had sent the pots.

Megs read out the card on the bench beside the box: '*Congratulations, Pip and Jack. I thought these pots were the perfect engagement gift. Something old to watch over you. Love, Mum.*'

'I think the pots are beautiful,' Pip said, removing a skillet from a box. 'I always have. Even if they are a little, um, impractical.'

Megs raised her eyebrows then rearranged the mask more securely over her nose and mouth before returning to her dusting in the living room. Anyone would think the weatherboard cottage was a hazard zone. Pip was glad she and Jack had given the inside a couple of coats of white paint last week after patching up hundreds of cracks in the plasterwork. It made the place feel fresher, despite Megs's paranoia. The smell of paint had been overtaken by armfuls of the blackwood and bluegum branches Pip had harvested along the back fence and placed in stainless-steel specimen buckets to cheer the room.

Pip rubbed her finger around the rim of the smallest saucepan, creating a hum, then leaned against the island bench Jack had crafted from old woolshed floorboards. When Jack had first showed her the pile of wood stacked behind the shed, Pip couldn't imagine how these rough, thick grey slabs could transform a kitchen. But he'd sanded the planks until they were smooth, and then polished them with a bit of linseed oil on a rag until they coloured the deep brown of leatherwood honey. Now, as she traced the lines and curves of the grain absent-mindedly, her thoughts turned to everything she needed to do this month.

She had no time for reading the piles of bridal magazines Megs bought her—finishing her data collection was more important than hunting for a dress. But it was hard to avoid the menu put together by her excited boss, Dan. He'd handed it to her on soup-stained paper during her break at Zest last Tuesday.

'Might have to give me a pay rise, Chef. Can I afford this on a kitchenhand's dime?' she'd joked.

Pip glanced up at the wedding menu sticky-taped to the tired fridge spruced up with blackboard paint:

WEDDING MENU FOR
PIP ARNET AND JACK RODGERS

Canapés

Pacific oysters
Peking duck pancakes, hoisin sauce
Smoked eel crostini with fig paste
Crepes with sugar-cured salmon or ocean trout
Provençal vegetable tartlet with parmesan

Entrées

Pan-roasted blue eye trevalla

Scallops and saffron

Chilled tomato soup

Side dishes

Glazed seasonal greens

Roasted potatoes, rosemary and sea salt

Mains

Crispy-skinned duck breast, spinach, potato puree, mushrooms, port jus

Slow-cooked Ashfield House lamb shoulder with fennel, braised lentils, roasted garlic and rosemary jus

Galantine of chicken and hazelnuts, cress salad, olives, radish, hazelnut vinaigrette

Baked mushroom tortellini with Gruyère

Dessert

Wedding cake plated and served with fresh berry compote and cream

So far, so standard. She hadn't chosen a wedding cake yet—Jack was keen on chocolate mud. Everyone loved chocolate, he argued. She'd annotated the menu, noting changes to local seasonal fish, like line-caught couta or hapuka, and some herbs to dress it up like thyme, basil and fennel. She'd asked Dan to drop the scallops, Pacific oysters and salmon. Barbecued local clams and pipis would be nice for a starter. She could harvest a few buckets herself down near North West Bay. Were clams wedding-ish enough?

Pip glanced across at the big table strewn with waterproof data sheets. On top of the wedding preparations, she had her work to think about. After two and half years, she felt she was poised on the cusp of a breakthrough. The pristine Tasmanian environment and waters were prized for their precious seafood, but they were under threat from pesky invaders, the European clam among them. Pip's project was to identify why this was happening and find solutions to prevent it. She needed to nail down the perfect environmental conditions. Find balance.

But just last week there had been discrepancies in her data and now she'd need to re-test before the winter rain set in. Extra tests meant a funding blowout and delays. Pip was determined to finish on time. Her PhD swam through every cell in her brain and it took far more energy than she cared to admit. Wedding cake would have to wait.

The day before, her supervisor had explained over a flat white and half a blueberry muffin in her spartan university office that funding for environmental and climate change research was being axed.

'I'm sorry. No more extensions, Pip,' said Imogen, blue eyes apologetic.

'But Jack's booked this work trip to Italy—and it looks like we have to try to buy out the vineyard *now*, even though we hadn't planned to do it for ages . . .' Pip looked up at the ceiling and blinked. She didn't want to lose it in front of her supervisor.

'I know, I know,' Imogen said, nodding. She gave a sympathetic smile. 'And you've got a wedding to plan.' Her long fingers picked at the edges of the muffin. 'I've tried talking to the heads, even the dean.' Imogen shrugged and shook her head. 'They just don't know yet which positions will be funded for the next three years. They are making cuts across at IMAS too.' Imogen worked with both the Institute of Marine and Antarctic Studies and the university.

Imogen continued, 'If you want a shot at a post-doc research job, you have to get that thesis in by November. Okay?'

'But—'

'No excuses! You're bright, Pip. Your research is a game-changer. We might be able to clean up this patch of the channel. But I can't do *anything else*—' she tapped a pile of documents with her index finger '—until you prove you can finish. We've already given you extra time because your prelim results were outstanding. There's no more.' Imogen ducked her head and peered over the top of her glasses. Her voice was warm, but firm. 'C'mon, Pip. Just knuckle down and get it done. I understand lab work is tough—God, we've all been there.' She rolled her eyes. 'And Italy's not going anywhere!'

Pip nodded and slumped back in her chair. What kind of future could she promise Jack? There was no guarantee she'd get a job or funded research position once she finished her PhD. *If*. But Jack had other plans for the rest of this year and she needed to collect more data. How would she find time for both?

Even if she and Jack offered to match the consortium's bid for Ashfield House right now, Pip's current employment mix of casual teaching and kitchenhand work wouldn't cover the ridiculous mortgage repayments and her student loan. What about the much-needed repairs for crumbling walls, keystone archways and the oversized cast-iron lace on the verandah? Not to mention new vineyard plantings. Pip felt dizzy—it all felt too rushed, too forced. Too uncertain.

Between her paperwork and the beautiful old pots, there was no surface left on which to put anything. Jack probably thought *she* was an invasive marine pest.

Megs followed Pip's gaze to the floor of the living room, and the stacks of graphs labelled with black marking pen in capitals: LI, HARRY and TAJ. 'What are these?' She pointed to the TAJ pile.

'Honours students. I'm mentoring three to help with their sampling.' Pip loved watching undergrads picking their way through buckets of clams, cockles and pipis, trying to classify each species by the size and hue of the shell, counting basal threads dangling like silk, or holding a limpet up to the light and running their fingers over tiny yellow ridges skirting the shell, marvelling at the perfect grey and white logarithmic spiral of the elephant snail. 'I'm bringing Taj around your way next week, before we have dinner next Sunday. I'm going to help her collect some sediment cores in the intertidal zone—that's the mudflats along the front of your place.'

'Brrrr. It'll be freezing.'

Pip glanced at her paperwork and shrugged. She wasn't outside *enough* since she started writing up the data.

'Pip,' Megs said carefully, 'don't you think you have enough on your plate?' She glanced around the room at the boxes before letting her eyes rest on the piles of graphs again. 'Seems crazy to take time out to help undergrads with *their* theses when you're struggling.' She paused. 'I don't mean struggling academically. Sorry! It's just that you seem to have spread yourself so thin this year. Helping Jack in the vineyard, tutoring undergrads, planning a wedding, helping me with babysitting—which I'm very grateful for, by the way!'

Megs was spot on, as usual. Pip glanced up the hallway to the spare room where baby Chloé was sleeping in a portacot and being watched by her nanny, Eva. No noise. Perhaps they were both asleep.

'Megs, I'm going to finish my PhD. Don't worry—that's top of my list.' Pip swallowed traces of an uneasy guilt as she unwrapped a medium-sized pot—perfect for boiling waxy pink-eye and kipfler potatoes. She held the pot up with both hands to show her sister. Megs shook her head.

Megs was skinny but tough—a sleek ebony thoroughbred compared to Pip's sturdy stockhorse—but these days she seemed barely strong enough to lift Chloé. Recovery from the caesarean section probably didn't help. Their mother, Mary—midwife and maternal nurse—had begged Megs to take some more leave last time she was over visiting from Victoria.

Megs had replied, deadpan: 'Mum, I'm a trauma surgeon. I spend half my time in emergency. Will's the surgeon in charge. I think we've got this.'

Pip had made the mistake of asking Megs last week if she was getting enough sleep.

Her sister's response had been sharp: 'Bloody hell. Not you too! Mum asked me the same thing. Nobody is asking Will if *he's* okay, how *he's* managing with work and the baby.'

It wasn't like Megs to swear. Pip knew better than to push her, but it did seem like she was missing the point. After all, it wasn't Will who'd had the C-section, and he wasn't breastfeeding. He was amazing, doing bathtime, nappy changes and seriously daggy dad-cooing, from what Pip had seen, but still . . .

Pip needed to pop in and visit Megs more often, she decided. Mind the baby so her sister could go for a gentle walk. Or just go out for a coffee. Did Megs drink coffee these days—or was it on the banned substances list? Megs needed sunshine. Sunshine, food and rest. They couldn't be banned, surely?

'Pip! Are you listening to me?' Megs snapped her fingers in front of Pip's face. 'Tune in.'

'I'm listening.' Pip smiled.

'I just think if you want to finish your thesis before the wedding, you have to *prioritise.*' Megs touched Pip's arm and spoke softly. 'Hey, I know you're anxious about this buyout. It's a massive decision. That pressure would give me sleepless nights.' She gave a wan laugh. 'And that's saying something!'

Pip squeezed her sister's hand, moved that Megs admitted to being ever so slightly human.

'But what's this now about you both going to Italy?' asked Megs, snapping back to her stern voice.

'Jack wants to see how they make wine in Tuscany. See if we can apply it here.' Pip was too embarrassed to admit Jack had booked the flights without first checking whether it fitted with her shifting research schedule. Lately, it felt like Pip always had to wedge her life around Jack's plans—as if her doctorate was some kind of hobby.

'And you can help with that how exactly?'

Pip forced herself to keep smiling so hard that her jaw started to ache. 'It's a big commitment. We have to be sure.' She shook her head. She wasn't sure of anything.

Except Jack.

'Do you want something to eat?' Pip asked, to change the subject. Megs and Will ticked off goals like ordinary people did items on a shopping list—uncertainty just didn't exist in their world. There was no point trying to explain her dilemma; Megs wouldn't understand.

She glanced at Megs, feeling churlish, then immediately regretted her bad temper. Her sister looked shattered. Her skin was as pale and translucent as a scallop, her skinny jeans sagged at the back. Someone could probably carbon date Megs at the moment by counting the black rings around her eyes. Pip would make something delicious for Megs. Maybe she could even talk her into having a little rest in the spare room after lunch? She'd put a fresh set of crisp white sheets on the bed just last night, before she ended up sleeping in them—but she didn't want to think about that just now. It was a silly moving-in tiff, that was all.

Pip would insist Megs had an hour's rest today. It was sweet of her to come and help Pip unpack and sort the cottage, but as she scanned the room she saw there were only the pots, a few bags of clothes, three chardonnay boxes of spreadsheets and notes and the snorkelling gear on the front verandah. She would just get these lovely copper pots sorted and then she could fix them all Jack's favourite lunch—a toasted corned beef, cheese and green tomato pickle sandwich. Pip lifted a hefty saucing pot out of the box, but the lid was wedged on tight. She needed to get the lid off to stack the last tiny pot inside.

'Pass me a knife please, Megs.' She propped the pot between her legs to hold it firm and tried to lever the lid with a butter knife, but the blade bent into a right angle.

Pip laughed. 'We've got a stubborn one here. Can you please get me a screwdriver from Jack's toolbox, in the corner over there?'

Megs fetched the screwdriver and handed it to Pip with a slight frown. 'Be careful you don't poke a hole in your hand.'

Pip jemmied the screwdriver under the lid and twisted it from side to side. The screwdriver scraping metal sounded like empty scuba tanks scraping the edge of a dinghy as she hoisted them into the boat. She winced, clutched the handle and tugged.

From under the lid came the scent of stale musty copper, but also the faintest trace of wood. Inside the dark pot rested a scroll of paper about the length of her hand tied with a piece of brown string. Reaching in, she gingerly lifted up the mysterious parcel. Sweet-smelling faded red-pink rose petals and a mummified piece of what looked a bit like wormwood—*Artemisia*—dropped out. It had obviously been pressed flat when it was still lush. But how long ago? Now the feathery fronds had lost their chlorophyll pigments, hardened and turned silver—like the delicate antique French lace she'd been eyeing off for her wedding dress.

Gently, Pip held the plant frond up to the light. The fretwork in this single leaf was perfection, like the curve and swell of a clam shell. Each shape in nature was perfect in its oddity. She lifted the fragile leaf and inhaled the faint bitter woody scent with traces of liquorice—and a lot of dust—before gently placing it down on the wooden benchtop. Her mother had always grown wormwood in her garden at Mount Macedon because the pungent smell rubbed off onto the feathers of the chickens as they brushed past and kept them free of fleas and lice. Sometimes, Mary had even made the girls drink a tea made from wormwood when she suspected they had worms or a stomach ache. But mostly Mary picked handfuls of the silver foliage to catch the light in the glass vases she arranged around the living room.

Pip picked up the scroll, untied the string and slowly rolled it out on the bench. There were a dozen pieces of faded brown paper—surely that couldn't be parchment? It looked seriously old, whatever it was.

'Here, Megs. Look at this.' She held up the brown pages to the kitchen window one by one. Each piece was thick, but translucent. She could see the fibres threaded through it and it reminded her of looking at microalgae in Petri dishes through the microscope.

'This looks like handmade paper. How beautiful. I wonder how old it is?' She turned it over and studied the writing, crisp with ink. 'It's written in French.'

In one smooth move, Megs reached behind the bench and into her handbag and threw Pip a set of surgical gloves. 'Put these on so you don't ruin the paper. We don't want those pages falling apart.'

'I can't believe you carry spare sets of gloves. That's so sad,' said Pip as she snapped them on.

Pip looked at the top page. 'Hmm. I don't think it's a letter. More like some kind of list.' She read the heading, written in an ornate script. The ink had faded and the writing was as curly as an endive but she could just make it out.

'*Eau de rose.* That's easy: rosewater. *Pour faire ung lot de bon hypocras.* I think that means to make a lot of good . . . something. Good *hypocras.* Whatever that is.'

She scanned the rest: '*Cinamonde, gingembre, garingal, vin de Beaune*—that's Burgundy, pinot. I think this is some kind of recipe, maybe for spiced wine. Maybe that's what this *hypocras* is?'

'Maybe.' Megs walked around the bench to stand behind Pip and read, chin resting on her little sister's shoulder. 'We never did anything like that in French.'

'I think it's pretty fair to say you didn't do anything in French.'

'I got an A minus, actually. So yes, a bit of a glitch. Anyway, I work in surgery. People are mostly out cold. No need for French.'

'And people wonder what's wrong with doctors these days.' Pip laughed, shaking her head as she flicked through the pages. The next page had a heading: *Marzapane.* Marzipan? The following: *Crespes.* She was pretty sure that meant crepes when she read the opening line: *Prenez de la fleur et déstrempez d'oeufs tant moyeux comme aubuns, osté le germe—*

'Actually, I think there's some Latin in there. Or Italian. It's a weird mix of French and Latin, I reckon.'

'Here, let me see the Latin. I understand a bit.'

Pip turned and raised her eyebrows at Megs. 'Since when did you study Latin?'

'Medicine. Anatomy.'

'Well then clearly I know more than you; I know plants *and* animals. Zoology.' She turned her attention back to the pages. 'I have no idea where these came from,' she said, holding them up to the light as if she were studying specimens. The paper lit up as if it were full of hairs. It felt robust, despite its obvious age.

She placed the pile of soft, muddy-coloured parchment on the bench and rolled it up again, securing it with the string once more. 'They've had these pots forever but they've obviously never opened them. Otherwise Mum would know about these notes, wouldn't she?' Pip went to a wooden wine box in the corner of the living room and picked through bottles of preservatives, measuring jugs, mesh bags, sieves and probes until she found a new thousand-millilitre specimen jar. 'Anyway, this'll keep them nice and clean until we work out what they are.'

From a bedroom down the hallway, the baby started a desperate cry.

'I'll get her,' said Pip as she put the notes into the jar and then whacked her shirt to remove the dust.

'No! Let Eva get her—you're filthy. What if she's asthmatic? Or has dust mite allergies?'

The crying subsided and two minutes later Eva walked into the room jiggling a placated Chloé, who was swaddled in a pale pink cashmere blanket. Pip ripped her dusty work shirt off so she was just in a white singlet, washed her hands and rushed to lift the baby from the nanny. 'Come here, Chloé. Let Aunty Pip have a snuggle.' She closed her eyes and breathed in the sweet yeasty smell as she tucked Chloé's head in under her chin. She could feel the feathery hair against her cheek and chuckled at the disproportionate slurping as the baby vigorously sucked her own fist. 'Is she hungry? She's making a racket here.'

'Her fist? Pull it out. I don't want her developing an overbite. I might borrow a towel and have a quick shower so I can give her a feed. Eva, would you mind warming a top-up bottle in a saucepan on the stove for me? Use a small one, please, not those crazy things.' She gestured to the old pots with a frown.

'I have a microwave. We also embrace technology in this cottage, you know!'

'No microwaves,' Megs ordered. 'Distributes the heat unevenly so it could burn her mouth.'

'Sor-ry!' Pip said with an eye roll at Eva. Eva gave her a shy smile in return as she headed into the kitchen.

Pip kissed the top of Chloé's head and idly rubbed her cheek against the baby's hair, placing a finger where the fine charcoal hair whorled at the base of the crown. Chloé wriggled like a slug in her swaddling. She took a deep breath and rocked back and forth, trying to swallow the feeling that something was askew. It had been Jack who insisted they set a date for the wedding. Pip wasn't sure what the rush was. Everyone knew they would get hitched sooner or later. But then he'd booked these tickets to Tuscany without consulting her. Pip understood his sense of urgency. He was excited and Pip was desperate to go with him—who wouldn't be? But Imogen had been adamant that Pip would get no further extensions.

What was Pip going to do? How could she support Jack *and* finish her PhD?

Pip consoled herself with a squeeze of little Chloé's sausage calf. Next year was so uncertain. Her research was critical; it was too easy for most people to dismiss patterns of the ocean. Who cared about benthic invertebrates—they were never going to be front-page news, right? But Pip did. She cared deeply about the creatures and seabeds no-one could see. If she quit studying now without proving things needed to change, what kind of channel would she leave for delicious babies like Chloé? So why did Jack make out *she* was the one who was being difficult? That she was dragging the chain, somehow.

Right now, all she knew was she loved Jack like crazy but their plans were a bit at odds. Perhaps she should make some changes to her workload to meet the date of the wedding? That was what marriage was about, wasn't it? Compromise.

The scent of the rose petals and *Artemisia* filled the living room and lingered in her nostrils, the deep sweet tones of treacle and aniseed with an earthy, bitter kicker.

Pip turned around and opened her eyes to see Jack leaning against the doorframe, his shoulders almost filling the space. Head cocked to one side, dark curls tumbling across his forehead, curious blue eyes and an unmistakable grin from ear to ear. How long had he been standing there?

Chapter 2

Château de Boschaud, Midsummer 1487

Andreas was grateful for the warming scent of rosewater against his skin this chilly morning. He tugged hard on the reins to slow his cart as he neared the wrought-iron gates marking the entrance. They were wide open as carts from the village would be rolling past all hours today. The hunched gatekeeper stepped closer to get a look at the face in the low dawn light. 'In you go,' said the old man, nodding in recognition as the young *épicier* removed his hood.

Andreas smiled, nodded and shook the reins to urge his handsome pair of black warmbloods on. He was in a hurry this morning as he wanted to unload with enough time left over to hand over his gift. They mustn't get caught.

The cart moved past an oversized stone barn with square twin watchtowers on his left. He'd heard it said that during the last few bloody weeks of the final Crusades all the womenfolk and children of the surrounding estates took shelter within the thick walls of this barn—huddled in stinking heat as their village was torched and their brothers, husbands and sons were lined up, gutted or hanged. Today, the wooden doors were ajar and several monks in drab brown tunics swept armfuls of damp straw from the flagstone floors and stuffed it through a tiny window into the adjacent hog pens. The stale straw would stifle the scent of dung and filthy animals spreading beyond the barn area during the high heat of the day when the wedding guests arrived. Who wanted to smell dung on their way to the fanciest feast of the year, for battle-weary knight Lord Boschaud, owner of Château de Boschaud, and the fair Lady Rose, daughter of the Duke of Clinchy? It would hardly be a good omen. With a bit of luck, the monks might throw some armfuls of lavender and rosemary in. They would if Artemisia had anything to do with it. He shivered with cold and anticipation.

Beyond the hogs, cages full of roosters, ducks and chickens shrieked to welcome the dawn. They were lucky; their kin would be hanging on hooks this morning, bled, ready to be threaded onto the rotisserie. His mouth watered.

His musings were interrupted as the horses drew close to the château itself. The rising sun hit the granite walls and spread to each corner, making it look as though it had magically appeared in the vast gardens. He could feel the same sun warming his back and he halted the walk of his horses to enjoy the light unveiling the view in front of him. The château appeared far more workmanlike than most along the plateau and he supposed it was originally built to protect and defend Boschaud blood. It was a three-storey rectangular box flanked by two round turrets with the same slate conical roofs as those on the main part of the fort. Between the round turrets, tacked on as though it were an afterthought, was a tall square turret that ranged a little higher, and he could just make out the smallest of windows tucked under the eaves. He'd always wondered what this tiny room could be used for.

He ran his eye once more over the strong lines of the château. It was plain, to be sure, but he wouldn't complain if it were his.

A pair of guard dogs lay sprawled on the wide stone forecourt, taking their fill of the sun before the day started. A blanket of green lawn stretched across to the far boundary hedge. Red and yellow poppies, feverfew, wispy grasses, wheat, dandelion and daisies glistened with dew and swayed in the faint morning breeze—bordered by a circular gravel road wide enough for two carts to pass. Beyond the *strewe*, a handful of monks were crouched low, chattering and swinging hoes to trim the grass from the flagstones leading to the front door. The giant linden tree in the middle of the field had also been given a decent prune. About time. Both lawn and tree had been starting to look scrappy and nobody wanted that on such an important day. Andreas whistled and tapped the small parcel concealed under his shirt. Yes indeed, he thought as he gently shook the reins, today was going to be perfect.

Instead of following the wide path to the front door, Andreas peeled off onto a smaller delivery road that led past the south turret to the terrace outside the kitchen and cold store. He recognised the speciality wooden carts of his fellow village merchants. The *oyer*—the specialist goose roaster from the village—was unloading a dozen roast geese swaddled in linen. Once the yellow cloth was peeled away the skin would be golden, the flesh would be tender and succulent. The lingering scent of cloves and nutmeg meant the fowl were still warm, wrapped beneath the cloth. His mouth watered. He hadn't a chance to down a bowl of green *porée* with a slice of ham for breakfast before he loaded up his delivery.

Beside the *oyer*'s cart was the *boulanger*'s. Hundreds of small white pillowy rolls were layered in deep wicker baskets. Beside them were the less attractive trenchers—piles of stale dry flat bread used for serving food. All were being unloaded by a trio of nuggety lads. Andreas leaned over and picked up a roll, winking. '*Merci.*' He laughed as a scowling face batted away his hand as it reached for a second roll.

The rickety cart of the *oubloyer* stood six feet away. The kitchen had obviously ordered a cartload of thin pancakes from the village to accompany the soups. Andreas didn't know why they bothered. Eating *oublies* was the equivalent of eating parchment. A waste of time. The tethered mule beside him seemed to agree, snorting and stamping his rear hoof in disgust. The tawny-headed *oubloyer* carried the crates one by one into the kitchen and dipped his head in a silent greeting as he passed. Everyone was far too busy unloading deliveries to stop for chit-chat.

A couple of lids had become dislodged from Andreas's terracotta pots during the journey from Châlus. 'By God's blood,' he cursed; he should have taken the time to seal them with wax. He was lucky nothing had spilled from the lips of the pots. Andreas walked around the side of the cart and drew a deep breath of the sweet perfumes before replacing the lids. Inside half the pots was his particular blend of rosewater laced with nutmeg, cinnamon and myrrh. The other pots held sugar and salt. The rosewater—used as a handwash at feasts—was his secret recipe and in demand with all the local châteaux.

His grandfather told him once that a long-dead pater had brought the recipe back from the east after the Crusades. De Vitriaco family lore whispered it was straight from the hand of Ibn Sīnā. Ridiculous story, of course. It was straight from the family business in Genoa. Still, it didn't hurt his trade.

Andreas grinned as the young kitchenhand Jacobus bounded out of the kitchen door towards him.

'Bonjour, Monsieur de Vitriaco,' said Jacobus, nodding. 'You're a bit late. The spice pots need to go straight into the kitchen, but we'd like the pots for the *laver* to go up the stairs to the grand banquet hall. Abbot Roald has instructed me to help you carry them. We'd better be quick. He has his jousting poles out today! The fat bastard has already smacked me twice over the back of the head. He's in a filthy mood. As he conked me with his closed fist he said: *The rod and reproof give wisdom, but a child left to himself brings shame to his mother.* Whatever that means.' The lad shrugged. 'Don't live with my *maman* and I work like a horse. No shame there, sir.' The lad's face was filthy—streaked with ash and sweat—but defiant as he eyeballed Andreas.

'Ah, Jacobus—the good book of Proverbs shredded again. Abbot Roald is *always* in a filthy mood. Why celebrate a wedding and enjoy a banquet when you can make life a misery for everyone? Just because the righteous chaplain has chosen a life without a woman doesn't mean the rest of us should suffer. God won't keep you warm at night.' He chuckled. 'And waking to matins must be miserable. Make sure you find a better way to greet the sun as soon as you are older.' He ruffled the child's hair fondly. 'Let's get a move on, lad.'

Andreas and the runt of a boy busied themselves unloading the cart before loading it with empty vessels for return. By the time they were done the pale linen shirt was stuck to Andreas's back.

'I have to go, monsieur,' said Jacobus. 'I'm the lucky bastard that gets to stand in the *fournier* for the day. Hildegard needs me to help turn the bread sauce and aioli.' He shook his dirty blond head in defeat and Andreas felt sorry for the boy. Jacobus had a rotten sweaty day ahead, standing in the fireplace fanning coals. He felt a little guilty for hoping the child would avoid hanging his head over the sauce pots. In the extreme kitchen heat, Andreas was worried the boy's lice might jump right in.

Before Jacobus turned to run off, he leaned in and whispered to Andreas: 'Artemisia just snuck out via the side gate to get some herbs for her *entremet*. Out under the quince near the pond. Abbot Roald will gut her if he finds her missing from the kitchen for too long. He's in a flap even though Artemisia and Hildegard have been up till late last night turning the sauces and baking the desserts. Please tell her to hurry.' Jacobus turned and dashed through the gargantuan stone archway and disappeared into the kitchen. Andreas was left with the sounds of crocks and pots banging inside and idle horses and mules switching their tails beside him.

He slipped around the curve of the turret and stood on a cart offloaded with oak barrels sitting by the high stone wall. The stamp showed the barrels were from Rivesaltes. Excellent. He preferred a sweet muscat-style wine to begin a banquet rather than the harsher, drier grenache that ripped your head off and often left you legless for the remaining courses. Andreas was pleased Lord Boschaud had ignored his miserly controller of the treasury—Abbot Roald—and unloosed the château's purse strings a little more than usual. It was going to be magnificent.

His eyes roved the length of the stone wall. On the far side he could make out a dark shadow creeping into the walled garden through a side gate and passing via the lavender beds. As the sunlight lifted and she stepped from the shadows of the wall, he could see the faded rose of her rumpled linen tunic. It looked fair against her dark skin and long thick plait. Artemisia was hunched, struggling to carry the large conical wicker basket on her back. He wanted to run over and offer to carry it, but he knew Artemisia would shoo him away like a pesky child. Worse, she'd probably curse him.

Instead, Andreas watched her walk the linden allée and make her way into the heart of the prayer garden. Designed for the monks who lived in the monastery on the far side of the walled garden, the cloister was protected on four sides by shorn hornbeam hedges and divided into four quarts of vines for verjuice and wine, with a large round reflection pond at the centre.

Artemisia paused, tilted her shoulders and let the basket drop to the ground. She then sat on the woven willow bench with her back nestled into the quince arbour. Watching Artemisia dip her head in worship, Andreas hoped her prayers echoed his. He glanced at the sun and started to count the hours until the banquet would be over and they no longer had to keep their secret.

Chapter 3

Tasmania, April 2014

Jack watched Pip standing with her honours student, Taj, bent over and knee-deep in the stretch of tidal mudflats at Stinkpot Bay. He was helping Pip's brother-in-law Will drag the silver dinghy through the blend of fine sand and mud so they could head out fishing for flathead. The hull carved a ribbon behind them as they pulled the boat through the silt to water deep enough to launch.

As Jack tugged the boat into the shallows alongside Will, icy water bit at his ankles and confirmed winter was on its way. To take his mind off the chill, he gazed across at the white caps and beyond to the shallow sweep of mudflats lining North West Bay.

Usually this stretch of foreshore was more sheltered than the main stretch of the D'Entrecasteaux Channel, where the wind gathered pace and whistled and stung like a whip. The tide was heading out and a nor'westerly was picking up, so they'd better get a move on as the days were shortening. Beyond the wide bay, Mount Wellington loomed like a giant elephant with its head in the clouds. It was a rare day lately when you could see the whole mountain and today it had darkened from pale purple to an angry grey. A storm was gathering.

As they navigated the boat through the rocky outcrops, Jack looked back over his shoulder and admired the lines of Pip's tanned legs, her strong thighs as she bent down looking for clams in the sandy slurry. She was wearing faded denim cutoffs and one of his dark green work shirts paired with an old grey polar fleece to brace against the wind whipping across the top of the water. Despite the old clothes and diminishing light, Pip was luminous.

Taj was watching Pip demonstrate how to place the corer into the sediment. From this distance it looked like a leftover bit of grey plastic irrigation piping but it had an intricate pull and had to be placed at a precise depth. Laughter carried across the water surface as Taj attempted to fill a mesh bag and missed. When the last bag was filled and dropped into a twenty-litre plastic drum, Pip gave Taj a thumbs up and then stood and watched her walk to shore. Once ashore, Taj waved goodbye to Pip before getting into her car with the drum and driving off.

When Pip caught sight of Jack, she grinned and gave him an enthusiastic wave using both arms.

'Hold the boat for a minute,' said Jack as he jumped overboard, dashed across the flats to Pip and planted a sandy kiss on her lips.

Pip's nose was icy, as usual. She had no circulation at the tip. Jack reached out and gave it a rub before he snatched his navy woollen fishing beanie off his head and gently tugged it onto hers. Jack tucked in the strands of auburn hair whipping against her face. Pip lifted her green eyes to meet his and thanked him with a happy peck on the lips. The splash of freckles across her forehead, nose and cheeks grew every summer. Each year she joked this would be the one where they merged. He placed both thumbs on the bridge of her nose and ran them across the constellation of freckles on her cheeks, then under her eyes, where dark rings and uncertainty had crept in. He wished he could wipe them away with a swish of his finger. Instead, Jack breathed in Pip's scent of mud, eucalyptus and sea salt, placed both hands on her sturdy shoulders and gave her an affectionate squeeze.

'You're frozen. You should go up to the house with Megs. Have a hot bath.'

'I'm fine. I forgot how it takes a while to get the knack of the corer. Taj nailed it though. She's even taken some samples back to analyse for me, which is nice.'

'Well, you have been out here helping her for two hours on a Sunday morning.'

'What's that got to do with it?' Pip wrinkled her nose in confusion.

'I'm just saying, you've also been really nice to her. Especially when you could have stayed in bed this morning with me!'

Pip tipped her head back and the sun lit up the freckles across her nose. 'Sure.' Her voice had developed a slight edge. 'Well, the samples needed to be done this week. Sorry it didn't fit your schedule.' She gave him a tight smile. 'I'm going to get some clams for dinner. See you back at the house.' She picked up her red bucket and walked away from him—strong shoulders slumped—across the mudflats.

She looked tired, Jack thought. She needed a break. That was why he'd booked their working holiday—he'd assumed she would be thrilled. It would do her the world of good. And you couldn't get more romantic than Italy. He was really looking forward to exploring the region around Lucca with Pip, but she always sighed, changed the topic and left the room when he brought it up. He was trying to make this buyout possible—secure their future. Why wasn't she more excited?

It was Jack's dream to buy Ashfield House and the vineyard with Pip. He'd promised to wait until they were married, Pip had finished her thesis and found work. But this surprise offer from the neighbours meant they had to make the call to buy out his parents now. His hardworking mother, Sarah, had wrung her hands as she told them the news. She'd asked Jack and Pip to 'just think about it'. With the money from the property's sale, the Rodgers could perhaps help Jack and Pip make a start somewhere else.

Max—tall and broad—took up most of the cottage living room as he shifted his weight from foot to foot. 'Son . . .' He shook his balding head and narrowed his eyes with concern. 'I know you and Pip want to buy us out. And we were prepared to wait.' He sighed. 'But this offer—Nicko's had a look at it . . .'

'Fantastic,' said Jack. 'And what does my expert big brother think, perched in his fancy office on the other side of the world? I'd love to know.'

It turned out the vineyard consortium planned to convert Ashfield House into a luxury boutique hotel with a marble-lined bistro and wine-tasting room. Pip and Jack just didn't have the kind of capital to rival such an offer—how could they compete?

So Jack needed to act quickly to make changes. Find some finance. That meant a trip to Tuscany to study how they harvested and crushed the grapes, how long they left the purple skins in the tanks to give the deep crimson hues in the glass, how different yeasts could bring out certain flavours. *When* they took over Ashfield House, he hoped his blend of innovation and old-school Tuscan winemaking techniques would make it sing in the bottle. Better wine. More profit.

How else was he going to sort the finance without his brother's sticky fingers all over it?

'You jump in first, mate, while I hold it.' Will was standing still with the boat propped against his thigh as Jack pulled himself into the silver dinghy. Jack waited until Will settled into the bow before he took off, skimming the boat over the chop. He glanced back at Pip, who was crouching down studying the murky pockmarked sand, poking it with a piece of gnarly driftwood. It made a change from the usual corer she lugged around. Her work and study schedule was as inflexible as the tides, but since she had finished writing up the first part of her thesis she had grown restless. He often heard her pacing the short length of the cottage hallway in the middle of the night when she assumed he was asleep. Or she would roll away from him in bed, pretending to be asleep, when her sharp shallow breathing told him otherwise. She could do with a holiday, that was for sure. He couldn't put his finger on why she looked surprised—and a little cross, to be honest—when he told her about the Italy trip.

Jack grinned at Will, who was sorting out the rods and checking the tackle. 'Better wait until we nudge around the corner, Will. Don't want to put a hook through one of those fancy hands of yours, do we?' He revved the engine some more to prove the point.

'Nothing fancy about my hands, Jack. Honest day's work!'

'Ha! Work? Built that sandpit yet? Chloé's going to have her licence at this rate. Didn't Megs want the garden finished before she was born?'

'I'm working on it.' Will laughed. 'No rush.'

'Yeah, right. Hands like white cushions. Never seen dirt in their life.'

'I'll take that as a compliment *and* I'll clean the squid. Okay?'

'Aye, aye, Doctor! Hope you do a better job on your patients—'

His sentence was whipped away by a gust of wind. Jack took another deep breath, braced himself against the stiff breeze and made a beeline for the open water. He'd never heard Pip groan about sunburn, sleet or icy winds—she never even slept in. Not once. He needed to harden up. Jack had lost count of the mornings Pip sprang out of bed before dawn to beat the tide along this stretch. She dressed for the weather—a seven-millimetre wetsuit, hood and booties in winter and a full skinsuit in summer so her fair skin didn't burn in the harsh Tasmanian sun.

He'd loved it during Pip's fieldwork when she turned up at the cottage well after dusk with a bucket of clams or pipis for dinner—or, if he was lucky, some of the small local oysters or blue mussels. Occasionally she'd dive for abalone at her 'secret site' on a rocky outcrop in the bay, but mostly she didn't like to disturb them. Said the poachers would be all over it if she gave the position away. She'd bash the abalone meat with his hammer and slice it so thin you could see your hand through it before giving it a quick sizzle on his camping hotplate and finishing it with a squeeze of lemon. Magic. She did the same with the oversized scallops when they were in season after Easter—minus the bashing.

They'd down a couple of beers or ciders with a feed, sitting on the wooden deck overlooking the vineyard. Pip would talk at bullet speed, reflecting on her samples, speculating on outcomes. Ask his opinion. She'd throw her head back and laugh deep from her belly as they'd shoot the breeze and he'd try to pronounce the names of different intertidal animals. Polychaete worms. *Anapella cycladea.*

These last few months in the chemistry lab had seemed to sap all her energy though. Just last night she snapped at him for offering feedback on the organic carbon results. He grilled a steak while she was hunched over the kitchen table analysing data, ignoring him. When he'd first built the table Pip had laughed and said it was way, way too big for the tiny cottage kitchen. Now it was her favourite spot to work—she'd staked her claim with a waterglass of rosemary picked from his mum's vegetable garden.

Since she'd gone from fieldwork to lab work, and—he grimaced—*especially* since she'd agreed to the wedding date, there'd been no more lazy nights. She was determined to wrap up her thesis before the wedding—despite these problems with the data and the extra workload it had created. Why not just submit the thesis after the wedding?

He took a breath. It was her degree. They'd get married in the end. Right? And look, it *was* nearly winter—maybe he was just taking it all too personally? As soon as the sun came back, so would the weekends hiking the ridge to Wineglass Bay, pitching the tent and cheeky midnight skinny-dips.

He looked back over to where Pip stood, framed by the light hitting the cliff.

'You right, mate?' Will yelled above the wind. 'You zoned out there for a minute. I thought it was Megs and I who were struggling. Lack of sleep and all that. Wait till you guys have a baby.'

'Don't hold your breath, mate. Pip's hoping for a research gig and I'll be flat chat next year in the vineyard. Building a winery. Looks like we'll both have to take on a lot more projects than we planned for if we want to make Ashfield House work. My bloody brother keeps telling Mum and Dad to accept this offer.'

'So Nicko's not coming home?'

'You kidding? Now he's got the corner office at the great Goldman Sachs you think he wants to get his hands dirty?'

'Like me, you mean?'

'Ha. No, mate. At least you try! Nicko's in New York for good. Besides, Wei would never move out here.' Jack snorted. Now his big brother had a green card and glamorous local lawyer Wei Cohen as his partner there'd be no homecoming.

Jack continued, raising his voice above the wind and the revving motor. 'He sent me this text last night . . .' He fished his mobile out of his back pocket and scrolled through the messages until he found the one he was looking for. '*Jack, mate. You're crazy! I talked to Mum and Dad and told them the offer is too good. Just buy yourself another patch of dirt. I'll help sort you. Call me.*'

Will grimaced. 'That's a bit rough. I mean, I remember when you planted those vines—what? Seven, eight years ago?'

Jack shook his head. 'Took some convincing for the old man to convert from grazing to pinot noir and chardonnay. I mean, he'd never even heard of sangiovese.' He gave a rueful smile. 'I know nothing's ever certain, but I always thought that I—we'd—have a shot at buying them out.'

'I'm really sorry, Jack,' Will said. 'It's a real blow.' He shuffled along his bench seat until he was in the middle, stabilising the boat. 'I mean, how're you guys going to compete with a bloody consortium?'

'Exactly! Not a chance. Nicko hopes they'll get the deposit for a weekender in the Hamptons, I guess.' Jack laughed with a twinge of bitterness. 'I don't care if we stay in the cottage forever and lease out the big place, I'd start a family tomorrow—Chloé's awesome!' Jack smiled then took a deep breath, savouring the salty air. 'Pip wants to get her thesis sorted first. She's freaked out that she won't get a marine research job at the end of all this. As if!'

'Ha! Sounds a bit like her sister. So alike sometimes.'

Jack laughed as he nodded in agreement. 'I won't tell Pip you said that. She'd hate it.'

'She would.' Will grinned. 'Let's get this boat moving before the weather turns, try to catch some flathead. If the wind drops by sunset, I've got the big torch and jig so when we see some squid we can have a crack at those too. Got a couple of good ones last week. Grilled them on the barbecue with some chilli, parsley and white wine. Delicious.'

'Sounds great,' said Jack, staring across at Pip as she sank both arms elbow-deep in the sand. She looked serene in the fading afternoon sun. So why couldn't he shake this uneasy feeling that there was far more than storm clouds on the horizon?

Chapter 4

Tasmania, April 2014

Pip could sense Jack watching her as he launched the boat with Will, but she avoided eye contact. They'd be gone as long as it took to down a couple of beers and she wanted to keep dusk to herself.

She traced the corrugated ripples of sand with her fingertips as she watched for telltale holes and bubbles before plunging her arm deep into the slurry to grab a handful of sand. She spread the clump of sand out with her foot and picked out a few of the caramel butterfly-shaped *Electroma papilionacea* and threw them into her bucket along with the clams and pipis. The sun was dropping, the clouds darkening and gathering pace in their movement across the sky as the crisp evening breeze lifted and stung her cheeks.

Will's dinghy motor roared and echoed between the low sandstone cliffs for a few seconds as the men sped off into open water. She paused to listen for the wind whipping and rustling the eucalyptus leaves on the foreshore. The sharp smell of the gums softened with the heavy air promising rain.

Pip flicked another couple of pipis into her bucket. Last week, after his parents had called in, Jack had gathered her into one of his big hugs and slowly massaged her shoulders as he'd suggested postponing her PhD deadline until after they had Italy and the buyout sorted: 'Surely down the track you can get more funding? I mean, Imogen said she didn't know, right?'

Conflicting waves of electricity and anxiety had pounded her stomach and Pip bit her lip, hiding her head in his grey T-shirt so he didn't see her hurt. Was she going mad? Was a bit of space to finish her studies too much to ask?

Pip understood that Jack's roots spread wide and deep across these slopes overlooking the curves of the channel. He had no intention of being transplanted. But why did he expect Pip to compromise her research—her dreams—to fit his timeline? It just wasn't fair. But what would it take for him to realise that his ambition couldn't always take priority in their relationship?

Nine-year-old Pip stood on the thick green grass carpeting the middle of the old quadrangle at Melbourne University, playing with her yellow yo-yo. Around her, the sandstone archways were smothered with ivy, the air thick with the scent of purple wisteria. It was a perfect pocket of lush garden in the middle of a magical castle. Her father, David, was wearing a cherry red academic gown with olive facing, a large hood and a gigantic smile. He waved a scroll with his microbiology PhD above his head in the sunshine as adults swarmed around and patted his back, muttering about *breakthroughs* and *tremendous achievements.* In the midst of the fuss, David removed his soft black velvet hat with a pretty cherry tassel and pulled it onto Pip's curly mop. The hat flopped down over her eyes so she could barely see, and as she pulled it up her father crouched down so he was at her eye level. They had the same green eyes.

'Pip, my popsicle,' he whispered, 'you are never too little to dream big. Work hard—use that creative brain of yours.' He tapped her head and she giggled. Then his voice turned serious and he squeezed her shoulders. 'Promise me now, my darling, that you'll make your time on this precious earth count. This PhD is for you.'

Pip nodded solemnly before Megs swooped, grabbed the hat and yanked it onto her flawless black bob.

'Daddy, look at me!' cried Megs in her bossy voice. '*I'm* the one who's going to be a doctor. Pip's the seashell collector. But there's no more room on her windowsill for stinky shells!'

Her dad was now the dean of science at the university. How could Pip face the disappointment in those piercing green eyes when *she* couldn't quite get her PhD across the line? She traced her fingers through the sandy slurry, popping icy air bubbles with the tips of her finger as they appeared on the surface.

The splutter of the engine ripped across the bay, masking the sound of waves lapping against the rocks and the shrieks and twitter of the birds in the black peppermint gums beyond the waterfront.

Pip was grateful for the offshore breeze carrying a whiff of eucalyptus and the thick sweet scent of autumn wattles and blossoms. Sometimes, in the heat of the day, Stinkpot Bay could really live up to its name—if the hydrogen sulphide trapped under the sediment was ever disturbed.

She understood the science, but the mudflats were still magic. So many secrets. Vast, ugly and pockmarked when the tide pulled out, mudflats were protected from oceanic swells, giving life to a complex network of fish, molluscs, crustaceans and birds. Some, like the showy spotted handfish and the yellow pentagon of the live-bearing seastar, never ventured beyond the tiny coves and inlets along these sandstone shores.

Her first encounter with this shoreline had been with her zoology professor, as an undergrad. Jim Grant was a jolly man with a pink face smothered in white zinc cream and shaded by a wide-brimmed Mexican straw hat whenever he stepped outside. He had the dumpy shape and texture of his beloved Irish Rooster potato and wore baggy shorts year-round. Despite his genetic unsuitability for working through the searing sun of Tasmania's summer, Professor Grant would show Pip how to find native oysters—*Ostrea angasi*—along the mudflats. With brown shells curved and terraced like a contour map, the natives were easily prised open with another shell. He pointed out areas where the feral Pacifics—*Crassostrea gigas*—were taking over the foreshore and picked over deep piles of middens—mussel, oyster and clam shells—taking care not to disturb the ancient hand-sized tools used by the Mouheneener tribe as they foraged for protein. The local Aborigines recognised patterns of the oceans and mudflats. Symbiosis. She was an introduced species—yet she felt most at home here on the mudflats, in this stretch straddling water and land. Elation coursed through her body. This was where she belonged.

Professor Grant rejoiced at the sighting of a rare local Gunns screwshell and scowled at its invasive competitor the New Zealand screwshell and the equally invasive European clam. His Irish accent would roll over the string of Latin vowels like a fierce swell: *Gazameda gunnii, Maoricolpus roseus, Varicorbula gibba.*

'Philippa,' he would say, 'your generation needs to look at these patterns again. Look closely, my girl.

'Just as the middens tell their story you need to look at *all* the benthic invertebrates—the crabs, the clams and mussels, the seastars. They live in the sediment and they don't much like to move. Study the nutrients in the sediments, count their numbers, pay attention to the dirty imports like me and it will tell you about how this world is changing. Do you know what will happen if the ocean rises by four centimetres?' He would shake his head and dig his toes into the sand and silt. 'Have you thought about that?'

Pip nodded. It was pretty much *all* she thought about.

'I'm staying put.' Jim smiled. 'A few degrees of global warming and Tasmania will be the perfect climate. It'll take more than global warming to get me back to Ireland.' He shuddered theatrically.

Seeking a way to spend more time on the mudflats, Pip had become hooked on Coastcare, and even more hooked on one of her fellow volunteers. She'd been paired with Jack Rodgers for the last two weeks of that summer to count the number of swift parrots that nested around Stinkpot Bay. Swift parrots were easy enough to find. Volunteers simply listened for the high-pitched musical trill that floated down from their perches in a handful of mottled blue gums. They watched for a flash of lime and emerald green with a patch of red under the little beak. These stunning parrots grew fat feasting on Tasmanian blossoms before departing with the cooler winds on the long flight back to Victoria and New South Wales, to snuggle down for the autumn in the more austere ironbark forests on the mainland.

At first Pip couldn't work out why this surfer with dark raffish hair wasn't riding the chilly waves down near Point Arthur. Why on earth was he counting parrots? It turned out he had a minor in biology. How had she not noticed such a magnificent specimen in her lectures? He'd explained he'd done the first two years at Melbourne University on a rowing scholarship. Later, he told her how he'd felt hemmed in doing laps on the muddy upside-down Yarra and yearned for the space and ruggedness of his channel. 'Didn't miss the bloody wind, though,' he'd said, laughing, as he jumped up and down to keep warm, hugging his torso.

Pip eyed the warm swirls of gold and orange in the tall cliff faces as dusk closed in. Her eyes ached. Once the revised tests were completed she could get on with writing up her thesis—the introduction and outline of the methods should be finished. She could meet Imogen's requirements, but Italy would have to wait. Work had to come first this year. As she listened to the waves lapping against a nearby outcrop, Pip catalogued the chapters in her head like a mantra: 'Spatial variation', 'Seasonal variation'—over and over again.

Was that enough research? Could she get it all finished before the wedding?

She turned and glanced out at the darkening waters of the broad channel, scanning the horizon for a speck of silver. The hum of the cicadas told Pip darkness was not far away and with it would come the tide. Her red bucket was half full of the larger local clams, *Katelysia scalarina*, and she estimated she had a couple of kilos. Enough for dinner.

She lifted one of the small, smooth shells and ran her fingers over the waves of yellow ridges and watched the clam clamp tight. Perhaps it was time for her to do the same.

Chapter 5

Château de Boschaud, Midsummer 1487

Artemisia sighed and dropped her head as she tried to find a comfortable position for her back against the contorted branches of the quince winding around the arbour. Her back and feet were sore and she needed to sit a while. Why did they always make these so-called resting spots so uncomfortable? Was God such a miser that he wanted to stick thorns in your side while you viewed His creation? Abbot Roald seemed to think suffering was holy and just. It was different for the ladies of the château, with all their padded dresses and thick flesh around the back and bosom. Perhaps they didn't feel the gnarled woven branches digging through the clothes into them as they sat and finished their tapestries, or prayed. Artemisia was an old maid—even if she didn't know her exact age. She first bled seven long summers ago, so she was every bit the 'hag' Abbot Roald had snarled at her yesterday when she struggled to lift copper pots wider than a hog onto the broad granite bench.

Today Artemisia had a giant ache in her body that was as long as her service.

An orphan, Artemisia had been given refuge at Château de Boschaud by the kind château chaplain Abbot Bellamy when he found her wasted and filthy in the chestnut forest while foraging for early spring fungi. She slept in a bed of straw out in the barn and for her keep she had learned the cook's trade—along with an arsenal of curses—by clinging to the tunic of the ancient, hunched Hildegard. Together they clanged about in the kitchen and roamed the grounds of the walled garden, including the orchards and Abbot Bellamy's precious physic garden. Abbot Bellamy explained to his young ward that tending the garden was the work of monks because God Himself had written in the first Book: *The Lord God took the man, and put him in the Garden of Eden to dress it and keep it.* The abbot gently counselled the monks to follow his planting regime. From November—the season of All Saints—in went the broad beans and the dead sage branches should be cut. Sage, lavender, clary, dittany and mint weren't planted until the moons of February—depending on the frosts. House-leek and salad seeds went into the soil from March to St John's Day, and gillyflowers were planted by St Remy's Day in October—or March for a second season. Sometimes the abbot would join them after his prayers, showing Artemisia how to read the sundial, or suggesting she take a moment on a grassy mound in a sunny corner for her own meditation. He would point out the round reflection pool at the centre of the grid of raised garden beds and tell her how this symmetry—this beauty—was inspired by God's work. Occasionally, he'd pluck a white rose shimmering with dewdrops and pass it to Artemisia with a smile as broad as his precious garden beds. 'A rose, Artemisia, is perfection in the morning. Look how we make the windows in the cathedral. A symbol of life. Love. Perfection. His work. We must give thanks for such divine beauty.'

Abbot Bellamy thrived on routine and encouraged all the monks in his charge to do the same: matins, reading and transcription, gardening and then vespers in the evening. He tended his herbs with love and studied them with precision, often asking Artemisia to pluck them with the dawn when they were fresh so he could draw them on his monastery herbals.

The abbot taught Artemisia to read and write alongside the young heir, Master Boschaud. Together the children would sit in the shady cloisters, reciting their prayers, practising geometry and learning to do the necessary additions and subtractions to the treasury columns the young master would one day inherit. The fair boy with the cheeky grin would lean back with his feet on the desk, swatting flies with his makeshift sword fashioned from twigs and twine, and sneak away to the pond to catch tiny brown tadpoles and fill his velvet pockets.

'I won't always be here, young master. You have to learn your duty. There are many people working within these walls who will rely on you one day when you are lord,' said Abbot Bellamy, tapping the latest treasury numbers on stiff parchment.

The young boy giggled and shot a narrow look at Artemisia. 'I'll have Artemisia. She can do the numbers better than me. You'll help me, won't you?'

Artemisia blushed and looked at the abbot. How could a girl who lay in straw be any help to a child wrapped in velvet? They were roughly the same height and the master's shoulders were wider, but Artemisia felt a strange pull to protect this carefree, freckled boy who spent his days face turned up to the sun, climbing trees and chasing rabbits with his bow and arrow.

The abbot sighed and rolled his eyes at the heavens as the boy reached down and hoisted his little wooden sword. The young master ran off to practise his footwork stabbing imaginary dragons and filthy English knights in the orchard. 'Don't worry . . .' The words trailed over his shoulder in the summer air like a ribbon. 'Artemisia can do it—she'll live here forever.'

Artemisia's skin prickled hot and cold and she closed her eyes and sent her prayer to the Holy Father. She hoped the boy's words were true enough—she was grateful for her bed in the barn and work in the kitchen. It was more than a dirty stray like her could ever have hoped for.

Within a couple of years, young Artemisia was assisting Abbot Bellamy and his failing eyesight, helping to check and balance the weary chaplain's chronicles for the château—including adding up all the orders for Hildegard's kitchen. She could transcribe remedies like the abbot's prized *tizanne doulce*—barley and hulls, figs and liquorice, boiled until the barley burst and strained through linen—for Hildegard to dispense to the monks and tenants.

Of course, her favourite herb was the wild grey shrub in the corner with feathery branches that shimmered on frosty morns yet stood firm and tall in high summer. *Artemisia.* It was the abbot who insisted on her christening. 'A foundling like you will thrive in many *terroirs. Artemisia* is the Mother of Herbs, named for the mighty Greek goddess Artemis. Diana. She will protect you, my child. Have faith.'

It had been two winters now since the monks had hacked at the frozen dirt with their shovels and Abbot Bellamy's body was laid to rest alongside Boschaud kin in the cemetery within the walls. No sooner was he lowered in a linen sheath into the ground and dirt settled than the young Abbot Roald was dispensed from the Benedictine abbey in Limoges. In addition to his general priory duties, Abbot Roald certified all official purchase papers from the château and kept the accounts. Abbot Bellamy had been the château's treasurer, chaplain, chronicler, almoner and apothecary—no task was too grand or too demeaning for the gentle old man. Lord and peasant were treated equally: 'A soul is a soul, Artemisia. God cares nought for your position, child. Only how you use it.' He'd waggle his finger at her and smile. It was hard not to believe him.

Under Abbot Roald, much of the physic garden was ripped out and replaced with grapes, roses chopped at the root and pulled for an extended melon patch. Matins were moved to before dawn, and vespers extended by double. A severe whipping was meted out to any monk or servant who did not attend.

Lord Boschaud, however, had stepped in and given Artemisia and Hildegard special dispensation. Artemisia carried the tradition with Hildegard of preparing the finest feasts of these southern valleys.

'Not the kitchen servants.' He waved his hand at Artemisia. 'I don't want those fires going out. I want to be able to have boar, hare or fowl if I please.' Lord Boschaud blinked his long lashes and wrinkled his nose, and for a moment he was the cheeky child who'd ignored his lessons.

Abbot Roald's mouth puckered as if he had sucked the whole citrus crop. It was not unknown for Lord Boschaud to order his master huntsman and marshal to prepare the stable and the full court for an outing on strict days of penitence—despite the protestations of his chaplain.

When Artemisia looked closer, she noticed rings under the young man's eyes, and a sallow milky pallor to his complexion. The happy, laughing child had long gone, replaced with a broad man whose shoulders were weighed down with chainmail and weary with battle. The burden of providing for all within these castle keep walls was thinning his skin and his sweat was souring. She'd put aside some of the fine green liquorice and make Lord Boschaud a fine *tizanne doulce* and a fresh potage of almond milk with a large dose of sugar when the sun was high.

'You understand me, Chaplain?

Abbot Roald had pinched his lips, nodded at his lord and shot a look laced with the tiniest sliver of resentment at Artemisia. His neck turned purple at the collar to match his robes.

'And one more thing . . .'

Abbot Roald turned his attention back to Lord Boschaud.

'I'd like Artemisia to be in charge of the kitchen records. She can order as she sees fit.'

Abbot Roald blustered, 'But m'lord, if I may object, it's hardly appropriate for a cook—a *woman*—'

But Lord Boschaud was having none of it from the sweaty, doughy new abbot. He held up his hand. 'Silence. Otherwise you can scurry back to that stinking rat hole of an abbey and give charge of the château monastery, the chapel and your fine corner wing in the old priory to another willing candidate. I'm sure they'll be only too happy to issue me with another chaplain from the ranks of priors rotting away there.' He looked the abbot in the eye and waited.

Abbot Roald opened his mouth to speak, then shut it.

'I'm sure others at the abbey are equally equipped to be charged as chronicler? Not just of the records—but to keep charge of the domestic servants and tend to the needs of the tenants while I'm away. Shall I send for one of them?'

Abbot Roald looked down, red-faced.

'I thought not,' said Lord Boschaud.

The lord started to stride away—sword in hand—with his swarthy marshal two steps behind. Then he paused and turned just enough for Artemisia to catch his profile as he ordered: 'And, Chaplain, I'd like you to give the chancery columns to Artemisia after every full moon. I want her to check them—on my behalf.'

Artemisia's head snapped up. But she caught the twinkle in the lord's brown eyes and just for a moment he was the spirited boy slaying dragons and goldfinches among the apple trees. She'd do as he'd asked, of course. Artemisia felt the legacy of Abbot Bellamy wrap around her like a protective blanket. She nodded a brisk thank you to the heavens—just in case.

Artemisia scratched her back against the dark green leaves of the quince and wondered if she was developing a hunch to rival Hildegard's. Her back was tender after bending over benches and copper pots, stirring, chopping and pounding. The wedding banquet preparations had gone on for weeks. There had been no end to her swearing at the poor wee kitchen lad Jacobus and the more deserving Abbot Roald—behind his back, of course.

The cool flagstones of the barn floor where Artemisia slept alongside Hildegard and Emmeline did her no favours, no matter how much straw she tried to stuff under her blanket. Her knees and back were as stiff as the dead every morning these days as she hauled herself out of bed before dawn to stoke the fires. She spread her hands and massaged her thighs for a moment, wishing she had some clove oil mixed with arnica to soothe the aches. She examined her palms. They were flat and broad, the base of the fingers callused. Her hands were as tough as the soles of her pigskin boots.

She took a minute to listen to the water trickle from the mouth of the ghoulish stone lion fountain perched in the middle of the pond and tried to ignore the shrill songs of the nightingales and louder screeches of the yellow hammer. Only the sweetness of the blue catmint blossom and roses cheered her. As the sun rose high for solstice, the scent of pollen would carry through the heat long into the night.

She rubbed her back against the quince once more. The ancients had dedicated the quince to the goddess of love. Perhaps it was the promised sweetness of the cooked fruit that sent the ancients giddy with romance. Perhaps Lord Boschaud had proposed to his Lady Rose in this very spot? It seemed as good a spot as any, she thought, as she eyed the rest of the garden. That was if you ignored the monstrous lion.

The parchments she occasionally smuggled in her apron from the château library revealed Charlemagne had ordered quinces to be planted by the dozen at all the grand châteaux. A folly for the rich. Artemisia thought there was only so much paste and pulp a person could eat. Charlemagne and his people didn't have to spend hours stirring vast pots of the damn stuff with a wooden spoon until the hot sticky pulp turned to paste and their tunics became drenched in sweat. Quince was sweet enough when she sliced a block of the paste for herself to spread on a fresh white roll warm from the oven, but it was hard work. She'd heard stories in the village of cooks from the east blending quince slices in an unusual slow-cooked lamb stew with fenugreek seeds, garlic, cumin seeds, cinnamon, allspice berries and the leaves and root of fresh coriander. Perhaps she'd try that next season when the monks brought the baskets in. She'd need to ask Andreas not only for the recipe, but also to source spices for her if he didn't have them in his village dry store. Like all the recipes shared between Artemisia and Andreas, it would have to be kept a secret. Artemisia had heard some recipes from the east could make the heart beat faster and the mouth dry.

Artemisia bent down to pick handfuls of chives, garlic chives, catmint and broadleaf sage that were clumped around the seat of the arbour. Though the pungent herbs looked as though they had self-seeded, she had underplanted the quince trees the previous autumn in a bid to scare the defiant coddling moth and cherry slugs. She was careful not to crush the pretty mix of blue and purple buds as she arranged the sprigs in her basket to hide the wild strawberries beneath. She was forbidden to walk beyond the garden wall without the abbot's permission. Artemisia had needed a well-enough reason to leave the kitchen and everyone knew strawberries needed to be picked with the dawn.

Abbot Bellamy had cared for Lord Boschaud's subjects when the knight was away for lengthy periods training for battles with the other vassals in the region. The monks who lived in the monastery along the far wall were divided into gardeners, scholars and scribes, and attended their crafts with love and care. This tender delight nurtured within the château walls was quashed with the arrival of Abbot Roald—now the garden was both retreat and prison. With the loss of autonomy of the chancery columns, he'd clawed back control of domestic staff. It wasn't uncommon for chambermaids, monks and gardeners to be queried and slapped if their movements did not suit the abbot. Obedience was the only path to perfection. No mention of love.

It wasn't worth risking his bitter temper on this wedding day. Artemisia was determined to show Lady Rose and Lord Boschaud the love that flourished within these walls. It was the day of St Jean—a day of love and new beginnings for all. Her stomach looped with nerves and excitement. She took a slow deep breath and inhaled the crisp morning air deep into her lungs. Yesterday's eve, Artemisia had crept around the walls hanging hefty fragrant clumps of St John's Wort, yarrow, fennel, rue and rosemary to ward off evil spirits as the sun set itself to sleep. She'd asked Lady Rose's chambermaid to tuck a knotted bunch in a corner of the maiden's room at the top of the turret.

She trusted her pretty parcels of herbs would do their job today.

Artemisia's robe was damp from the morning dew in the fields and if Abbott Roald saw it she would be in trouble. Any transgression in outward appearance—no matter how thin her cloth—was a sign of disrespect for the Holy God. More likely, an excuse for a swift whack between the shoulderblades. Artemisia knew the God that Abbot Bellamy introduced her to would forgive a damp hem in exchange for some juicy strawberries—but that version of the Heavenly Lord was as dead to her as her beloved tutor.

So Artemisia rose with the matins and waited till dawn to sneak past the wall and into the woods to gather the basketful of tiny pink wild strawberries that were hidden under pockets of dark leaves gripping the sunniest spot of the rocky riverbank. She had placed open wicker baskets over the more bountiful spots to protect her territory. She was sick of competing with local rabbits and hares for the pink gems when the colour started to turn. Skin the lot of them, she would—if she could catch them. Now she thought of it, there were plenty hanging in the larder: Lord Boschaud and his visiting hunting party had been ruthless on that front. The wedding had got everyone moving around the castle keep, that much was certain.

So busy, in fact, that she hadn't a chance to discuss with Lord Boschaud some overpayments with liquor and mead deliveries. The columns in the most recent parchments did not add up and when she'd queried the abbot, he had slammed both hands hard on his dark oak desk and banned Artemisia from his formal reception rooms and library.

While walking back through the woodlands, she'd stopped to pick handfuls of wild celery, nettles, goose grass and shepherd's purse. Some hyssop to make a brew for the abbot's weekly purge. Last, a welcome cupful of deep blue violets. Precious, fragile, temperamental violets could be used to soothe anxious souls. Violet broth could also take away a hacking cough. She'd brew a few for Hildegard today as she could not dull the old lady's cough. These unseasonal violets would be a welcome boost to the dried petals, as they would soften the brow and ensure the guests lifted a happy head—rather than an ale-addled head—off their feathered pillows tomorrow. The fresh starlike blue flowers were so dainty that they struggled under the weight of the glistening dewdrops.

Her precious strawberries—so sharp of flavour—would be diced and thrown over salads made from the spinach, mint, parsley and purslane she'd asked the monks to harvest for her under the dew that morning. The monks also needed to pluck the tiny buds and stalky leaves of the summer savoury to sit in her verjuice before she drizzled it over the salad with the poppyseed oil. The savoury would settle bellies prone to the bloat. Artemisia hoped that by combining summer savoury with the rose petals, she was making much more than dressing. She was blending a sprinkle of love and hope for the young fair Rose.

She knew Abbott Bellamy would approve—even if his replacement didn't. Love. Devotion. Lady Rose looked dizzy enough with the pairing her parents had arranged, but Artemisia would see to it the young bride had a touch of the ale, a nip of the Burgundy and a good dose of the salad all the same.

Artemisia had taken a fancy to the highborn lass from Clinchy and wanted her to feel welcome in the garden, not trapped within the high stone walls. She wanted Lady Rose's wedding night to be dusted with magic. In the absence of magic, a little liquor and some absinthe should do the trick. Though truth be told it wasn't the entwined limbs of Lady Rose and Lord Boschaud she was imagining, it was her own with—

She stopped and sighed, dropping her shoulders. Well, no good would come of that now when she had work to do.

Artemisia spotted a couple of the bald old monks hunched over on their knees in the garden bed harvesting the tender baby leaves and petals. She'd need to remind them to pick the rose petals to garnish her salad: red *and* white. She'd had to bang the bell twice outside their segregated cloisters to get them out of bed. Probably all tangled up with one another—or the nuns. There were better ways to start the day than matins, of that much she was certain.

The real reason Artemisia was sneaking around the woods and garden this banquet morn was because she needed herbs that ran wild to garnish her secret gift to the bride and groom. If caught, she'd cut Abbot Roald a thick wedge of the eel and flounder roe pie she'd baked to keep him satisfied. That'd shut the fat bastard up. The clanging of carts being unloaded accompanied by low deep voices coming from behind the wall near the kitchen reassured her that her preparations were running to plan. Andreas was likely close by, unloading his precious spices.

She picked up the basket and made her way back along the allée until she reached the large wooden gate leading out of the walled garden and back to the kitchen.

She almost dropped her basket when she saw Andreas waiting for her on the other side.

'*Bonjour, mademoiselle*,' he said, giving an exaggerated bow. 'I have just unloaded five pots of your requested *épices de chambre*, nutmeg, anise—the rosewater is in the banquet hall, all ready for the wash bowls.'

'Thank you.' Artemisia looked directly into his dark almond-shaped eyes. She longed to brush the wayward curls from his face to get a clearer view. She'd never dare. Not here, anyway. She noticed a flush rising from his collar. His shirt reeked of lavender, rosewater and sweat. One day he would have to tell her what his blend was. She longed to lean against Andreas. She longed to press her face into his chest and drink in his perfume.

'Artemisia, I have brought you something. A gift.'

'*Merci*, you are very kind,' she replied. Artemisia took the small cheesecloth bundle with a smile. The parcel was fastened with a knot. As always, Andreas had threaded a twig of wormwood, *Artemisia,* through the knot. Andreas leaned in and whispered into her ear: '*Mère d'herbes*.'

Mother of Herbs.

His lips were close enough to brush against her hair. Artemisia dropped the parcel into the deep pocket of her stained apron. She knew wrapped inside was a handful of sugared almonds and spices—wedding confetti.

Underneath the confetti, she hoped, lay a much sweeter secret.

Out of the corner of her eye, she saw the red velvet hem of Abbot Roald's robes disappear through the garden gate. A chill rippled through her body. Just how long had he been standing there watching them?

Chapter 6

Tasmania, April 2014

Pip picked her way around clumps of dry spiky bracken and silky native grasses back up the slope and into Megs's shiny new kitchen. The room reminded Pip of the emergency department where Megs worked: all stainless-steel benches and glossy black cabinetry. Thankfully there was no blood on the benchtops, but Pip noted the line-up of stainless-steel appliances. She wouldn't put it past Megs, or Will for that matter, to have a cheeky defibrillator on loan from emergency among the collection. It just didn't seem that strange for a couple of overachieving surgeons. Especially now they had Chloé. Pip chuckled—she couldn't wait to see sticky handprints along those pristine walls.

'Hiya.' Megs walked in and pulled a bottle of chardonnay from the fridge. 'Want a glass? It's good.' She paused. 'Or so Will tells me. I can't have any, of course.' She grimaced.

'Surely a glass won't hurt?'

'Pip! It's hard enough to keep my milk in—I don't need to contaminate it,' she snapped. She covered her face with her hands and took a deep breath. 'I'm sorry. Let me pour you a glass.'

As she took a wineglass from a shelf she continued: 'Chloé is asleep finally, thank God. Eva is out for the night—hot date. Luckily I'm off tomorrow and by some miracle so is Will. We haven't been off on the same day in over a month.'

'Ah, so that's the secret to this fancy clean house.' Pip laughed at her sister. 'You guys are just never home! Or is it Eva?'

'Ha. As if.' Megs yawned widely. 'I'm on constant rotations between emergency, general surgery and ICU. Did three doubles last week and so did Will.'

'That's nuts, Megs. Surely you can go part-time?' It wasn't like Megs to admit that she was feeling pressured. She usually thrived where mere mortals, like Pip, fell apart.

'We're so short-staffed, if I try to take a day off it just means more work for everyone else. I just have to suck it up.' Megs hesitated, as if she had something else she wanted to say, but instead let out a big sigh.

Pip waited, sipping her wine.

'The pair of us have been living in scrubs. Did I tell you how hot Will looks in scrubs?'

'Still? Seriously, Megs. I'm sure there are rules about fraternising on the wards. I watch *Grey's Anatomy*—all those hot surgeons getting it on.'

'Yeah, yeah.' Megs rolled her eyes and gave a weak laugh. 'Inevitable really when you spend a hundred hours a week at the hospital. Great Southern Hospital ain't Seattle Grace though. The place is falling down. I had to gaffer tape up some drips last week. Ridiculous. The poor nurse couldn't believe it.'

As Pip selected ingredients from the cupboard and fridge, she looked across at her slim big sister and admired her black skinny jeans, silver ballet flats and white V-neck tee. Pip wondered if Megs could look any more French chic, with her dark blunt bob and severe fringe. Most days she wondered if they were even related.

Pip set out to dirty the kitchen. She measured out a cup of flour onto the cold steel benchtop, Megs watching with a mixture of horror and something else . . . Pride? Curiosity? She cracked two eggs into the hole, mixed in a dollop of olive oil using her hands and kneaded the floury mixture until she'd made a soft, silky dough. She pounded the ball against the stainless-steel bench. Comforted by the sensation of having her hands deep in the soft, malleable dough, Pip began to unwind.

'So my lab work has stalled. I need to run some more sediment tests but my funding is kaput. Imogen can't renew it. Told me to get my thesis in or it's all over.' She sighed. '*No excuses*—you'd love her!' Pip half laughed. 'Peas in a pod.'

'Hilarious.'

'Jack still wants me to go to Italy. And we have to sort this buyout. But I can't see how I can swing it—not if I want my PhD.'

She paused. Why did everyone expect her to choose between her wedding and her work? Why could she not find her own way? Pip poured her guilt and uncertainty into the dough and folded it over twice, pounding it with the heel of her hand for good measure.

'At least my job at Zest is good.' Pip took another gulp of wine.

Megs walked around the island bench to stand beside Pip and stack the cutlery from the dishwasher into a drawer with quiet precision. Megs looked sceptical. She was eyeing the bucket of clams and the bunch of fresh parsley Pip had picked from the garden on her way into the house. Pip bet that Megs didn't even realise they had parsley growing in their neglected cottage garden.

'Pip,' Megs said, 'I get it. I wanted to pass my final surgical exams before we got married. Will was desperate to travel. *Desperate.* He'd lined up that residency in Germany, remember? He'd already passed six months earlier, but *I* still needed to finish. I didn't want to have to come back and study.'

'So Will waited until you passed your surgery exams,' Pip reminded her. 'But you and Will wanted the same thing. Jack's more settled. He's trying to buy out his parents and then he wants to start a family.'

'Oh! Already?' Megs started. 'I mean, that's great—if it's what *you* want. Is it?'

Pip didn't know how much to reveal. 'Of course I do. I mean, look at Chloé—I could just eat her. It's just . . .'

Megs caught her eye and nodded before finishing the sentence for her: 'You want to put all that study to work.' She put her hand over Pip's, leaned in and said with a whisper, 'I get it, Pip. You're right. You need to finish before you do anything else. Otherwise it will break the flow and you'll never finish.'

'Exactly.' Pip nodded, relieved her sister understood. So why couldn't Jack?

The way he talked about their future, it sounded like a romantic dream. Take over the vineyard. Have a baby. Easy. But what he wasn't factoring in was that she had a doctorate to complete and then, she hoped, a job she loved. But that would all be closed to her if she had a baby and they bought Ashfield House. Jack had said he'd help—take the baby in the pram to work around the vineyard during the day. But how realistic was that if she was breastfeeding?

She'd seen her female colleagues at the Institute for Marine and Antarctic Studies struggle, up all night with a baby, in at the lab during the day, juggling childcare pickups before heading home to cook and clean. It was like they had three jobs. It never stopped.

Imogen had quipped to Pip as she held up a vase-sized takeaway coffee one morning, 'Pip, we should be so proud of all our goddamn education. Now I get to do all the work my dad did plus all the work Mum did too when I get home.' Pip had quietly thought Imogen should review her husband situation, but she was hardly going to rub salt into the wound. Will seemed to pull his weight, and they had Eva, of course. Still, she saw how shattered Megs was. And Megs was the most capable person Pip knew—how the hell was Pip supposed to handle it?

Pip adored Jack. And she wanted it all too: house, career, family. She just didn't have the energy to do anything else properly before her thesis was done. Up until the last week, Jack had agreed with her.

Megs closed the dishwasher and turned to face Pip. 'Have you told Jack how you feel?'

'I've tried. He's a little hurt I don't want to go to Italy. I get it—it's nuts! My fiancé has bought me a ticket to Tuscany and I can't go. Who wouldn't be mad? But I've been working on this data for three years. Three goddamn years. I need to rerun these tests then write up my thesis!' She slumped against the kitchen bench, deflated. 'It's not that I'm ungrateful. It's just that everything I've been working for is about to come to a standstill.'

'I think you're right: Tuscany might be too much this year. Just explain it to Jack—I'm sure he'll get it.'

That was the problem. She *had* explained. And he still didn't get it.

'I'll try to talk it through with him again tonight. I'm sure we can work something out.' She reached out and squeezed her sister's shoulder. 'Hey, thanks,' she said. Opening a drawer, she located a rolling pin then began to roll out the dough. 'Maybe it's just my turning-thirty crisis?'

'Perhaps.' Megs chuckled. 'Speaking of crises, have you seen the beard Will's got going on?'

'Uh huh,' said Pip, nodding. 'What's with that? You can't have blond hipsters. The last Nordic god to have a beard was Thor, I think. Tell him it's gotta go. What's next—a man-bun?'

They both laughed and the tension was diffused.

Pip spread the silky sheets of pasta flat on the benchtop and started cutting rough narrow strips of fettuccine using a paring knife.

The sing-song chime of a Skype call sounded on the sleek Mac perched at the end of the bench. Megs turned the laptop around to face them.

Their mother's smiling face and dark bob—almost identical to Megs's—popped onto the screen. She was sitting at the desk in the office, and their father hovered behind. As usual, his top half was cut off, so all the girls could see of David was a rotund 'cheese-and-wine gut', as he liked to call it.

'Hi, Mum,' chorused the sisters.

'Hello, girls, nice to see you. Have you had a good week? Your father and I have been pickling all the green tomatoes this weekend. I'll bring you some next time I visit. Now how is that sweet baby? In bed by now, I suppose?'

'Yes, sorry, Mum,' said Megs. 'All snuggled up and sound asleep. Chloé's's wonderful—doing all the normal baby things. Eating and sleeping!'

'And what about you, dear? Are *you* sleeping?' Mary was frowning. 'Darlings, you've both got those black rings under your eyes again. Are you getting enough iron? And sleep? Pip, you're not fretting too much about your thesis again, I hope. Get Jack to cook you a steak.'

'Oh, Mum, I'm fine,' Pip lied, then, to change the subject, said: 'So I unpacked those big old pots—'

'Do they all fit in the kitchen, darling?' Mary interrupted.

'Not quite, but I'm working on it. Jack's building some more shelves. But anyway, there were these old French recipes and letters in one of the pots. The lid was jammed on—almost impossible to get off.'

'Oh! I've never seen any recipes. David, have you?'

A thick grey head of hair ducked into the corner of the screen and bobbed from side to side.

'I'll take that as a no,' said Pip. 'Any idea where they could have come from?'

'Hmm. Let me see.' Mary frowned and tucked her hair behind her ears. 'The pots were a wedding gift from David's great-aunt Margot, I think—you remember, Megs: we named you for her, though of course the name was shortened the minute you started preschool. Anyway, Margot was French. But I'm not sure if the pots came out here from France with her. I mean, could they have?'

'They could have come from a flea market,' David grunted.

Mary continued: 'Aunt Margot had some kind of family link to an old château in France. Near Châlus. She used to holiday there in the summer. Remember? We went there for lunch one day when we had that holiday in France. Megs was nine, so you must have been four, Pip.'

'Oh, yeah, I remember that place,' said Megs, nodding. 'An old castle with an overgrown garden around the back surrounded by a wall? Bit of a dump, really.' Megs wrinkled her nose.

'I don't remember it at all,' said Pip. 'You think I'd remember a fancypants château.'

'There were two turrets,' Megs recalled 'A big round one at the front with a staircase in it. At the top was a tiny room with a window. The maiden's room, the owner Madame Boschaud called it. Surely you remember that? They said it was haunted. Maybe that château is where the pots are from. What was the name of the place?'

'Château de Boschaud,' said David.

'That's it.' Megs clicked her fingers. 'I remember now. We stopped in at that café in the town square and had a croissant and Orangina. There were plaques about Richard the Lionheart. He carked it in the town somewhere. Some battle. Died of a stab wound.' Megs cocked her head to one side and gave a cheeky smile: 'Betcha I could've saved him.'

Pip shook her head. 'So back to the old letters. Can you find out where they came from, Mum?'

'I'll try, darling.'

'Thanks. So how about you two? How's work?'

'Oh, lots of lovely juicy newborn babies this week in the clinic. Bonanza.'

Pip looked over at her sister, who was furiously wiping streak marks off the stainless-steel bench.

'And Dad?'

The screen filled with his pink face. 'Good, good, thanks, Pip. Bloody funding battles—nothing new. Up every night trying to get paperwork sorted. I guess it's the same in your department. Heard anything?'

'Oh, I should be okay,' Pip lied again. She didn't want to worry them. 'Will there be enough pickles for me?'

'Plenty. So how are your latest results looking?'

'Sorry,' Pip broke in. 'Gotta go. The guys are back from fishing. Speak soon.' She pressed the key to end the call.

Her worries about her thesis could be left for another day. At least they hadn't asked about the wedding.

Pip walked to the dining area carrying one of Megs's elegant pale blue porcelain platters laden with the steaming pasta, filling the room with the scent of garlic and the ocean. Megs had set the table at one end for a cosy Sunday night dinner. The Danish lines of the furniture were offset with large white plates, balloon pinot glasses and a small jam jar filled with a handful of dainty blue love-in-a-mist that Pip had plucked from the overflowing cottage garden beds surrounding the house. The days of the sweet rambling garden beds dotted with old-fashioned blooms and roses were numbered: there was a landscaper coming next week to give Megs's garden an austere minimalist overhaul to match the sleek lines of the renovated house. The love-in-a-mist would be ripped out and tossed into a skip, alongside the blushing Wedding Day roses, red geraniums, sunny orange and yellow dahlias and the tenacious pink salvias that all fought for airspace and sunshine with the native grasses and wayward bracken. Instead of beds of colour, the house would be surrounded by sleek black slate tiles, with a line of carefully sculpted box-hedge balls of varying sizes. Uniformity and minimalist chic was the brief from Megs. Pip thought it was a shame.

Will, Jack and Megs were already sitting at the table—laughing and pouring wine—as Pip walked in with the food. She placed the platter in the centre of the table.

'Red?' Will asked as she started to dish up the pasta.

'Thanks,' Pip said, nodding.

'This looks amazing, babe,' Jack said. 'Tell you what, you're sure going to show those Italians a thing or two when we get to Lucca. We might have to eat out a heap in the name of research, but I reckon we won't find any pasta that tops this.'

Will piped up: 'Too right. Another wonder dish, thanks, Pip. We'll miss these Sunday night catch-ups. I'll be eating baked beans on toast while you're gone.'

'Hey, that's not fair. Or true,' Megs said as she filled her wineglass with mineral water. 'You'll be eating off the barbie: steak and salad. But you know there's always an alternative—you can just man up and expand that repertoire. I mean, what the hell is that fancy industrial kitchen for? An award?' Megs sounded harsh but Pip knew she was joking. Just.

Pip blushed and stared at her plate. Megs shot her a sympathetic look. Her chest tightened a little.

'What date do you leave?' asked Will. 'You still heading off after vintage?'

'Yes, three more weeks and we'll be done. We'd better pay for those tickets tomorrow. I can't wait. We're counting down the days now, aren't we, Pip?'

Pip looked up from her plate and met Megs's eyes before glancing at Jack. She'd been savouring the silkiness of the pasta, just coated in olive oil with a warm kick of chilli and garlic. She took a deep breath of the fresh parsley while she swirled another mouthful of pasta on her fork, buying time. Jack had put down his fork and was staring at her. So were Megs and Will.

They waited.

Megs spoke first. 'You mentioned needing to get your test results sorted before the funding stopped.'

Pip gulped her red wine. 'Um, yes,' she agreed, grateful for her sister's support. She looked at Jack and took a deep breath: 'Like I've said, babe, I'm not sure if I can go right now. It's not great timing. I have to collect more data. I can't move forward with my thesis until I get this sorted. They won't extend my grant money. It's kinda now or never.' She half laughed, still looking at Jack. He had tilted his head sideways. Pip could just make out a hint of hurt in his eyes. And shock.

'More pasta, mate?' Will to the rescue, as always.

'Yeah, load her up, thanks,' said Jack, now avoiding eye contact with Pip.

'Love this pinot, mate. Is it one of yours? There's no label—what are we drinking here?'

'It's last year's so we haven't labelled it yet. Was a warm one, so that's why it's a bit sweeter than normal. You can almost taste the sunshine, can't you? Another year or so and it's going to be a ripper. Best ever, I hope.'

'I reckon,' agreed Will. 'About time.'

'Oh, well, Dad's a bit of a control freak. I've just got a few different ideas about what we do in the barrel and on the vine. Takes time to change but I'm getting there. Slowly.' Jack topped up his red and took a big sniff before downing half the glass. 'The official offer's in.' He shook his head. 'Nicholas told Mum and Dad to take it. We have to make a decision before we go to Italy. Well, before *I* go to Italy, anyway.'

Megs interrupted to ask: 'Anyone for thirds? I'm going to have to run thirty kilometres tomorrow to lose these carbs. You're killing me, Pip. I bought a lemon tart—used those blackberries you picked for the topping. See, I can do homemade! Better save some room.'

Pip smiled, knowing she wasn't fooling anyone.

Chapter 7

Château de Boschaud, Midsummer 1487

Artemisia carried her basket with one hand and patted her apron pocket with the other as she turned her back on Andreas. It was time to get to work in the kitchen. She had no idea what lay within the cheesecloth and it took every ounce of her will not to turn around for one more glimpse of those sincere brown eyes and loose Genovese curls.

She weaved her way around the carts, avoiding the twitchy tails and hooves of the warmbloods, sidestepping parcels of geese and ducks that were being carried inside by a team of men from the village. She inhaled the sweet scent of roasted meat as her mouth watered and stomach groaned. It would be nettle *porée* again today for the kitchen servants, but perhaps they would get to gnaw some bones and taste succulent scraps of leftover meat before Jacobus took it all to the hog pens. Hildegard was so poorly and Emmeline could do with a bit more flesh on her bones—especially as the young maid would soon take over the running of the kitchen.

Artemisia stroked her pocket as she took a moment to consider the changes afoot. She had told no-one of her plans, preferring to keep them folded and tucked away deep in her heart until the right time.

Instead, she had busied herself teaching sweet, docile Emmeline how to make the weekly orders for the meats, liquor and spices. For today's wedding banquet Emmeline had been placed in charge of ordering the mustard sauces, vinegars and honey from the beekeeper at the bottom corner of the estate next to the chestnut woods. Artemisia had shown her how to mix the verjuice to extend it in summer when the old juice was too weak and the new juice too tart, and how to swap a crushed grape sauce for cherries or sloe berries with the season. When the lord and his stern marshal came back from a hunt, she'd shown the girl how to hang the hares and then stew them, or salt the sides of lamb and beef that came in from the fields. The girl had been taught to write well enough at the church school before she left to work in the fields with her mother at the château harvesting vines, gathering berries and working the vegetable patch while her older brothers ploughed paddocks and felled trees. Then, last autumn, when Artemisia cut back the sage, thyme, catmint and rosemary out in the raised beds alongside Emmeline, she had invited the young maid to shadow her in the kitchen in preparation for the spring and summer of feasts. For this fine wedding for their master, the women shared the writing of the menus, the ordering, preparations and sauces—which in turn had given Artemisia time to focus on her gift for the bride and groom this last moon past.

And now the day had come when she was to present it.

Artemisia closed her eyes and leaned against the stone wall for a moment, feeling the heat through her thin linen tunic.

As she opened her eyes, she recognised the branded stamp burned into the oak barrels unloaded along the wall—Rivesaltes. The wine merchant was nowhere to be seen and as she counted the barrels, she discovered there were two more than she had ordered. This had happened with the last spring harvest feast too and she tutted with annoyance. Artemisia had pulled the jovial merchant up on it last time and he'd insisted that he had delivered the full order for Château de Boschaud and not a drop more. Abbot Roald, the chaplain, had confirmed the order himself, he said.

Artemisia tapped her pocket with frustration and strode to the large plain oak door to the larder to check her record of provisions. As she reached the door, and reached under her tunic for the large iron key strung around her neck with a leather ribbon, she looked down and noticed the large bunch of St John's wort plucked from a nearby meadow on yesterday's eve.

She'd dipped it in a pot of water and left it outside the larder door resting on a terracotta lid. Tiny yellow petals shaped like stars glittered with dew, their centres like fine strands of saffron tipped with orbs of gold. The delicate leaves and stems were the brightest lime. Artemisia smiled—it was hard to believe such a fragile flower could ward off evil. But today was not a time to break the tradition; she needed as much goodwill as possible on this fine day for the wedding banquet.

She shivered with excitement as she straightened out the kinks in her apron with her left palm and allowed her hand to linger on her pocket. There was no place for wicked spirits today. She might smoke a few of the fronds of the fairy-like pink yarrow blossoms she'd placed at the bottom of her basket, releasing bitter, tangy scents from the sweetest cluster of buds.

But first, there was work to be done. She bent down and twisted the iron key in the door and gave it a shove with her shoulder to push it open, being careful not to lose anything from the basket swinging on her elbow behind.

She stepped into the larder and saw a pile of straw linen cloths stacked neatly on the shelf, a row of mid-sized copper pots and skillets and two boilers and strainers. Artemisia wiped dust from a gleaming pot with her elbow and stared at her dark reflection and intense brown eyes. In the low candlelight, her long, raven hair was almost the colour of pepper. She turned her head slowly from side to side as if she didn't recognise this happy face. Her cheeks appeared as flushed as if she'd rubbed them with Abbot Bellamy's favourite climbing red rose. She sniffed her tunic and turned up her nose at her earthy sweat.

Pity she didn't smell like a rose.

Legs of dried ham and beef hung from the ceiling, and the scent of cinnamon, galangal, ginger and anise filled the room. Clumps of dried rosemary, thyme, lavender, bay and sage were tied with twine and dangled like feathery botanical bunting against one wall. A pyramid of a dozen green and yellow melons sat in the corner, ready to be sliced and offered to guests in the garden as they arrived.

Artemisia placed her basket on the shelf and reached for the stash of parchment that recorded all the orders—the ones she always checked off against the abbot's records at the insistence of Lord Boschaud. She blew some stray cumin seeds off them and sat on the biggest melon, bracing her boots against another, to check. As she shifted her haunches to balance, she recalled that almost ten moons ago she was sitting doing much the same dreary task when a man with dark dancing eyes and glowing southern skin had lurched backwards through the door carrying a large terracotta pot . . .

'Oh, *pardon*,' said the stranger as Artemisia stuffed the quill and parchment into her filthy apron pocket. 'I was told there was no-one in here.'

Artemisia nodded warily at him, then lifted the lid of the pot and sniffed—cloves, ginger, cinnamon and ground bay leaves. It was the regular order of ground sweet spice mix from Monsieur de Vitriaco. At least it had been, until the *épicier* died in an overturned cart two moons ago. She raised her head to examine this new delivery man.

The man proffered his hand after wiping it on his pants. 'Andreas de Vitriaco.'

'De Vitriaco?' Artemisia raised her eyebrows.

'Yes. I'm Vincenzo's son.'

'My condolences for the loss of your father.'

She could see the resemblance now; Andreas was a slimmer version, but father and son shared the same smile, shining eyes and the thrilling scent of exotic lands.

'He was a good man. I can see why he was a master of the guild.' Artemisia always paid a fair price for her spices, and not a franc more. De Vitriaco spices came from the best merchants in Genoa and the *épicier's* supply never ran short. He'd never substituted her spice order for a version that had lost its scent—the cloves were always pungent and round, bushels of bay thick and large-leafed, and the cinnamon came in lush folded rolls from the east. She hoped her supply wasn't about to be severed.

The man's eyes darkened for a minute and he sighed. She could smell the faintest trace of rosewater on his shirt.

Artemisia asked, 'And you are—'

'Late with deliveries.' His eyes ran over Artemisia's body before returning to her face. Then he smiled and it was brighter than all the candles in the larder. Artemisia didn't know where to look so she tapped a melon with her toe before noticing her leather boots were full of holes. She dropped her foot and quickly hid it under her tunic.

'Do you regularly keep your diary while sitting on melons in the larder?' His voice was slightly mocking, but his eyes were kind.

'Do you always make deliveries without knocking?'

'Well . . .' He paused. 'I'm not sure!' His tanned skin began to flush. 'You see, it's my first one. I'm the new *épicier* journeyman—I'll be master by year's end. I guarantee it.' He winked. 'I—' He stopped, seemingly distracted by the bulge in Artemisia's pocket. 'So what were you writing? A letter to a lover?' He tilted his head to the side and started to sing:

She ruled in beauty o'er this heart of mine,
A noble lady in a humble home,
And now her time for heavenly bliss has come,
'Tis I am mortal proved, and she divine.

Artemisia could feel her ears burn and she studied the shadows on the far wall to regain her composure. Why did he mock her with Petrarca?

She straightened her back and looked him square in the eye. 'Not that it concerns you. But recipes—and some accounts,' she said with a hint of pride.

Andreas's eyes flickered with interest and unspoken questions before he reconfigured his face to a warm smile.

'Where did a pretty maid like you learn to write?'

Artemisia let her new, strange feeling of curiosity and hope float away under the oak door as her lungs deflated. To this unusual man she was nothing but a servant. A chattel.

'I'm the cook,' she muttered under her breath. Why did this dark stranger make her yearn for something more?

Artemisia smiled. If only she'd known what an auspicious day it was all those moons ago. She leaned against the thick wooden shelf and ran her fingers over the end column until she got to the line she was looking for—Rivesaltes. Her smile vanished. Her records were correct. Someone had changed the wine order again and was pilfering the extra barrels on the side.

It was easy to do on a day when there were so many carts entering the château. With a chill, she realised who was responsible. It could only be him. It would be his word against hers. Who would Lord Boschaud believe? And when should she tell him?

Chapter 8

Tasmania, April 2014

'What the hell, Pip?' Jack's voice strained as he hoisted himself behind the wheel and slammed the door to his rusty white twin-cab. The tired engine spluttered a few times before turning over.

Pip felt dizzy as she looked down for somewhere to put her feet. The floor beneath her in the dusty cabin was scattered with bits of fencing wire, pruning shears, scattered receipts and business cards, an old red Swiss Army knife and a half-dozen metal water bottles. She kicked it all aside with her right foot to make some room. Why couldn't he clean up his ute?

'Look, I'm sorry—I don't mean to sound harsh.' Jack's voice softened a fraction as his dark blue eyes narrowed with frustration. 'But when were you planning to tell *me*?'

'I wasn't avoiding it.' Pip half turned to face him as her voice rose. 'I've been trying to tell you,' she pleaded. 'But you got so excited and then you booked the tickets without checking with me first. And . . .' She took a deep breath as her voice broke and her eyes pricked with tears. 'And I was excited too. I *am* excited for you. For us.'

She hesitated for just a heartbeat.

'You . . .' she blurted out between sobs. 'You haven't been listening.' Pip brushed away the tears with the back of her hand and she could taste the saltiness as it spread over her lips.

The engine revved as Jack pumped the accelerator a little too hard. He crunched the gears and set off down the driveway.

'You know I've been trying to work out how I can fit it all in before my funding hits zero. Why are you making such a big deal about this trip? There'll be plenty more.'

'Because it's important. So are you even planning to come to Lucca? Did you *ever* plan to come meet me when I'm working in Tuscany? We could do some harvesting together. When I'm helping out with the winemaking you can take off on your long hikes—head to Lucca or something. Go check out the food. Or work. Whatever you want.' Jack's voice sounded unsteady. She'd never seen him cry.

'It's just that I was really looking forward to hanging out together. I was thinking we'd go for hikes in the mountains, get smashed in the villages, eat our bodyweight in mozzarella. Maybe some Italian lovin' too—you know? Just the two of us. See what we are away from here.' Jack was pleading with her now.

'I'm sorry. I don't know what to do.'

He shrugged and glanced at her. 'I *see* the pressure. You do a bloody good job of trying to hide it.' He gave a slow, dry chuckle. 'That's always been you—bigger goals than the rest of us put together. I *love* that about you.' He paused. 'But you need to let *me* in too. Will you?'

Pip flushed, unprepared for Jack's stripped-back emotion. It was as if they were sandpapering each other—trying to smooth it over—but instead leaving each other rough, raw and exposed.

Pip lifted her gaze and tried to meet his eyes, but Jack was staring dead ahead, his jaw clenched. He looked like a Roman statue—beautiful yet expressionless. But when she leaned towards him she could see a trail of warm tears running down his cheek and glistening in the moonlight even as his eyes scanned the road in front, checking for wallabies and devils. The last thing they needed was for a scared animal to jump in front of the ute and cause an accident. Her ribs contracted in a surge of—of what? Love? Frustration? Guilt?

When Jack eventually spoke, his voice was strained: 'You have your research. Your PhD. Your teaching. The restaurant work at Zest. I come last at the end of a long list. You shouldn't have to justify spending time with me. You shouldn't need a reason to come to Europe.'

'I don't—I'm not,' she stammered, treading carefully in this unfamiliar territory. She tried to swallow; her mouth felt so dry.

'I . . .' Jack paused and took a deep breath before continuing. 'I'm sorry.' He shook his head. 'I'm sick of being slotted into the convenient after-hours of your life.'

This was unfair. 'That's not true!' she protested.

'Please, Pip.' He held up a hand. 'Let me finish—I want to get past this and *marry* you. I want to be with you all the time. Not just an allocation. Why can't we do this trip together?'

He didn't wait for Pip to answer.

'Look, I get that you want to submit your PhD before you commit to *anything*. You have so much on your plate.' Jack shot Pip a look of anguish. 'I get it, Pip. But what I *don't* get, ever, is whether you actually want to be with me. You know, for the long haul.' He stopped speaking for a moment as he swerved to avoid a pothole. 'What I mean is: why the wait? If you can't come with me now—if you are uncertain—what's the point of waiting?'

They both took deep breaths as Jack waited for her to reply.

Pip turned to face him and both hands hit her thighs to emphasise her point. 'Jack, I've *moved* in. We're *engaged*, for God's sake. We will be doing everything together. But . . .'

'But what?'

'But . . .' she exhaled. 'You're so caught up with trying to make Ashfield House work. And this stupid trip.'

'What's wrong with that?'

'Nothing! I understand. It's *everything* to you. You just keep push, push, pushing and making plans. *Telling* me what's best for us. But what about what *I* want?'

She stopped herself. Pip's words hung between them like a wall.

She reached across to put a hand on his leg, but he flicked it away angrily.

His rebuff made her chest constrict. She asked softly: 'Why can't I just finish what I've started before I take on any new projects? That's all I'm asking for—a bit more time.' It was her turn to plead.

Jack exhaled raggedly. 'I can't do this anymore, Pip,' he said, his voice like gravel. 'I love you. I really do. I think you love me, but . . .' He paused. 'Who would know? You can't measure it so it can't be trusted, right? Is that it?'

'That's crazy.' Her chest constricted even tighter. He sounded resolute and it scared her.

'Is it? Well, are we going to Europe together or not? Am I enough of a reason to come to Europe?'

'That's not fair, Jack, of course I—' Pip stopped. She wasn't prepared for another ultimatum. It *wasn't* fair. She needed time to think.

'Yeah, yeah. You *want* to come but study comes first.' He whacked the steering wheel with his palm. 'So, no. I'm not enough.' Jack clenched his jaw again and locked stormy eyes with Pip for a moment before shifting his gaze back to the road. His tone dropped to a cold whisper. 'Pip, I want to buy Ashfield House now—I'll miss the chance otherwise.' He sighed. 'That's why I have to go to Italy now. It's no junket. I need to know how I can make our wine stand out. We need to make better wine from the next vintage. It's the only way I can make some proper money to service the insane mortgage. So of course I want to marry you *now*. Why wait if we are going to do it all anyway? I just don't see the point. It's you who's uncertain.'

'Jack! You're not being fair. I'm just asking for you to wait a bit—six months, a year maybe—until I finish my PhD. Not forever.' Pip paused. 'Just so I can concentrate and get this project finished, then get some funding to put my research to work. I don't think I'm being unreasonable.'

Jack was still. Unflinching. Pip had never seen him like this.

Jack spoke slowly: 'No, perhaps not. But if you aren't willing to marry me now, you may never be. We both know it's over, Pip. Let's not kick the carcass. I'm done with waiting.'

He took a deep breath before tapping his right index finger on the steering wheel and shaking his head. 'Always waiting.

Always an excuse, Pip. First, you couldn't move in until the fieldwork was done. Now we can't marry until the thesis is submitted. Then there will be work for a couple of years before we can have a kid. But what if you get a promotion? Or some post-doc funding?'

Pip hadn't realised she had been holding her breath until she was forced to heave in air through her nose. She gasped and with it came tears. Surely Jack didn't mean this? He couldn't! She felt frozen with shock.

'We're done. I can't do this anymore.' Jack's voice was icy.

Pip barely trusted herself to breathe—his words were like a hammer smashing an oyster shell.

'Jack, please. Can we talk about this? It's crazy.' She wanted to reach out and touch him, rub her fingers along his forearm until she reached the long faint scar from a childhood break, where the soft hair didn't grow. She wanted to press her head to his chest and feel his strong arms around her. Snuggle her head into his broad shoulder. He was speaking to someone else. Pip was certain of Jack's love—yet here he was, shoving her away.

But Jack shook his head. 'I'm done talking in circles with you.'

Pip began to shake. She didn't want to hear this. Not now. Not ever.

'I'm *crazy* about you, Pip. But it's not enough. We keep having the same talk. The same fight. You even slept in the spare room last week, remember?'

Remember? How could she forget?

Pip had come home from her meeting with Imogen and spread her latest set of results over the dining room table as she tried to recalibrate her methodology. Jack had walked in just before dusk, kissed the back of her head and said, 'Why don't you have a break for bit? Come down for a swim. Or a walk. It's unusually warm.' He tugged at her arm playfully. 'C'mon, Pip. It'll do you good. How long have you been sitting there staring at numbers?'

She'd snapped. 'Aren't you going to ask about my meeting today with Imogen?'

Jack looked puzzled. 'You already texted me about it. Said there was no more funding and you couldn't get an extension.'

Pip raised her eyebrow. 'And you didn't think that was worth calling me back?'

Jacked shrugged. 'It seemed pretty self-explanatory. Bit harsh if you ask me. I'm sure they'll give you one if you really want it.' He walked into the kitchen and grabbed a couple of beers. He walked back into the living room and passed one to Pip. 'Beer?' he said, as if offering lollies to a child.

Pip's ears started to burn and her voice came out sounding brittle. 'You just don't get it, do you?'

Jack looked confused. 'Yes, I do. You're just stressed. Come on, this holiday with me—'

'Stop. Just stop,' said Pip with one hand on her hip and the other held up, palm facing him. 'Get it into your head that I cannot go *anywhere* until I get this thesis done.'

'What, so no swim then? It'll only take an hour. Then I'll cook a delicious dinner for you. What do you want?' Jack grinned.

'I *want* you to stop trying to plan my schedule. *That's* what I want, Jack. You go for your swim. I'll finish what I'm doing here, thanks.'

Jack, looking bewildered, shrugged before putting the spare beer back in the fridge. Then he walked out the front door without looking back.

When he returned an hour later, Pip had put herself to bed early in the spare room. Her blood simmered with exhaustion, despair and rage.

Jack didn't try to join her, apologise, or cajole her back to their room.

Nothing.

Pip remembered it was she who'd extended the olive branch the next morning when the icy autumn morning air chilled her to the bone through the thin woollen blanket. She'd scampered across the hallway to snuggle up with Jack.

And it seemed that now, as then, she would have to be the one to make amends. Jack was done talking. His eyes were firmly on the road. But as much as she longed to breach the wall between them, she knew that this time she couldn't give in.

They spent the next twenty minutes listening to late-night music on Hobart 96.1FM. Anything was better than silence. Ed Sheeran, Keith Urban and Adele crooned broken-hearted ballads the entire way home.

Devastated, Pip slumped low in her seat, not bothering to wipe away the tears streaming down her cheeks.

She was empty, drained.

Eventually, they passed the worn telegraph poles at the front gate and reached Jack's sagging weatherboard cottage in the far corner of the Ashfield House vineyard. The porch light offered a dismal flicker, the only light in the pitch-black paddock.

Jack pulled up out the front and got out. He came around to Pip's side and reached into the back tray, grabbing his fishing gear to pack it back in the shed. Pip wasn't sure where to go. They'd each split into their own protective bubble—she needed to move as far away from Jack as possible. But, maybe, if she could just touch him . . .

As Pip hopped out of the ute there was a clang: Jack had dropped the rod back in the tray. She could just make out his silhouette and the distinct smell of salt and damp earth. Suddenly she felt him close, his hands circled her hips and he pressed her back against the ute. He reached up with his left hand and brushed the hair from her face, pressing his palm to her cheek before tenderly stroking it with his thumb. He brought the other hand up to cradle her head. She breathed in his warm salty breath as he leaned down and their noses touched.

Jack pushed in hips-first and gave her a deep, hungry kiss. Pip's heart jumped and she dropped her shoulders, desperate for him not to stop. She wanted to wrap herself around him and drink him in.

He was pressing her even harder now against the ute. Years of surfing and rowing had hardened his torso and thighs and she shivered every time she ran her hands along the well-defined muscles. She stood on her toes, reaching up to his tall frame, and wrapped her arms around his shoulders, pulling him tight.

'Let's go inside,' he whispered.

Pip's head was spinning. It was over—but her urge to touch him was impossible to stop. Her pulse raced and her skin burned as she followed Jack's heady mix of seawater and soil to the bedroom.

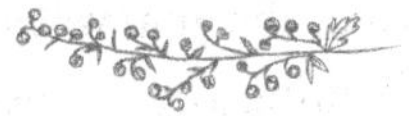

Later, when he had rolled over, asleep, Pip lay her head on Jack's broad chest. She buried her nose deep in his wild curly hair and recalled Biology 101, when a funky young lecturer in Doc Martens had tried to sex up the session with a talk on pheromones. Professor Lett referred to a project at Harvard which said that women were attracted to men based on the hormones and scent they secreted from their glands. It seemed plausible enough to Pip. She could smell Jack's tannins in a line-up any day.

Pip inhaled and then sighed. She was a ship cut adrift from its moorings. Each time she took a breath her heart ached more. Her stomach churned and all her limbs were too heavy to move. She *should* pull away right now. Just get out of bed and walk away into the chilly autumn air. Salvage some pride. But as she rested her cheek on Jack's chest, feeling the rise and fall with each breath—she couldn't leave.

Pip closed her eyes. She wanted to remember Jack's smell. This warmth. His dark curls on the pillow. She nestled into the crook of his neck and wondered how the hell her life had exploded.

It was her fault, of course. This breakup was inevitable. Jack deserved someone who wanted to settle down—whatever that meant. Pip felt clammy with shame. She loved him. Why wasn't that enough for now?

She wasn't sure he was ever going to forgive her.

As if he could read her thoughts, Jack threw a sleepy arm around her, cupped her breast and pulled her towards him. Sticky skin pressed against warm sticky skin as embers crackled in the fireplace. Pip marvelled over how perfectly they fit together. A tightening gripped her chest and she rolled onto her back and stared at a dead fly stuck in a cobweb on the ceiling.

Chapter 9

Château de Boschaud, Midsummer 1487

Artemisia felt the parcel knock against her leg as she moved around the kitchen, but whatever was inside her pocket would need to wait. She dipped her spoon into the cauldron and tasted the thick green soup. It was not too bitter. Today's *porée* was deepened by handfuls of nettle she'd found growing beside the woods, some roasted and crushed fennel seeds, a bouquet garni, and an extra thumb of ginger and some cinnamon flowers smuggled to her by Andreas last week.

Satisfied with the taste, Artemisia unhooked the large ladle hanging beside the pot and spooned the dark green liquid into two deep bowls, concealing a dab of golden butter in each. She quickly stirred the soup in the bowls to melt the butter, giving the soup a glossy finish.

This was the only time today the kitchen staff would sit and eat. All the supplies were unloaded into the larder, the fires burning well and the roasts sealed. The extra servants had been sent upstairs to help the chambermaids and valets set up the banquet room under the close supervision of Abbot Roald. There were long oak tables to be carried from the barn and wide pews from the chapel. Abbot Roald had also specified that two hundred silver goblets lined up on the sideboard be repolished as he had spotted a lone greasy fingerprint. Artemisia had ensured the chambermaids polished the silverware with rags yesterday, but Abbot Roald insisted they were coated with a layer of dust and filth and they be redone so his face shone in the reflection. He'd held a goblet to the light and quoted holy words: '*First clean the inside of the cup and the plate, that the outside also may be clean.*'

His face, spread wide around a goblet, had been hideous.

The sun was creeping above the linden allée and the day was to be filled with banquet preparations. The feasting would begin at dusk and more than likely continue until the sun rose again. The great hall would be filled with lords shaped like wine barrels slumped over tables, blankets and careless maidens.

Emmeline, Hildegard and Jacobus were sitting at the small kitchen table.

'Sit up, Jacobus,' Artemisia barked. 'This will warm you up.' She placed a steaming bowl of soup on the table in front of him.

'It may well kill me.' The boy laughed as he picked up his spoon and tasted. 'I never know what strange herbs you have added to the *porée*. Last week it was—'

Emmeline cut him off: 'Shut up, Jacobus. Be grateful. There'd be no lard and bacon in the soup over the wall. If you don't want it, give your portion to me. I'm starving.' Emmeline meant no harm; she was just overworked today. The girl would see to it that Jacobus would be well-fed and loved, Artemisia was sure of it.

Hildegard grinned, thumped her spoon on the table twice and waved her spoon at the lad, as if to say, 'Eat it up, boy.'

Jacobus Faber had been handed over to the Boschaud estate the year before when his father was unable to pay his tax to Lord Boschaud after a failed crop of wheat on the family allotment. Monsieur Faber was obliged to offer the service of his second son until the debt could be settled. Unfortunately, Monsieur Faber had died when a rotten tooth turned black and sour. The poison travelled down his throat and cut his breath. Jacobus had no choice but to remain in service to the great Boschaud family, thus guaranteeing his mother, brother and sister could continue to live in the nearby cottage and farm their allotted land on the estate until the bill was cleared. Artemisia knew Jacobus would be slaving in this hot kitchen forever.

'Here, eat some bread,' she ordered between slurps of her soup. She was full of wonder at the heat of the black pepper and could feel the warmth spreading down her throat to her belly. She hoped the added ginger and garlic would ward off midsummer head colds as the days grew shorter.

She broke a large chunk of the fine white bread from the loaf and handed it to Jacobus. The boy snatched it with a nod, dunked it into his soup and stuffed it into his mouth. He broke off another chunk.

Artemisia was used to the boy's frenzied eating. The boy's tasks were endless. At sunrise, Jacobus rose to collect pails of water from the wells before chopping and stacking piles of dried chestnut and oak high along the kitchen wall, ready to feed the huge fire that was the centrepiece of the kitchen. Though

Jacobus had the broadening shoulders of a thirteen-year-old, his legs and arms were those of a wiry old man's after a lifetime in the fields. Artemisia was thankful she could fill him with food at least once a day. She always made sure she had a spare loaf just for the boy, warmed alongside the dulled embers.

Their kitchen was hidden at the back of the château, propped against a soaring back turret that acted as a service stairwell to the main rooms. The kitchen itself was small by most château standards—five paces wall to wall. The thick granite wall at the back had a tiny window overlooking the herb garden, allées and the orchard beyond, filled with scores of pears, apples, peaches and apricots in neat rows. The inside wall had a large worn granite benchtop and above it hung rows of crocks, *oules* to hold the *potagers, casses* and frying pans and a series of spits and grills. Beside the bench, in pride of place, was the main fireplace, so large Artemisia could stand upright inside it.

This central fire was the engine of the kitchen. Jacobus had to be sure it never went out.

There was a steel rack as thick as Artemisia's wrist suspended across the fireplace, and from it hung a series of black *chaudrons* with which she prepared all the meals for the house. The smallest of these black pots was her own little *chaudron*. She prepared a different soup or stew, depending on the season, and topped it up daily with herbs and vegetables, a scrap of bacon, lard, tongue, duck fat or some leftover offal.

Today she had prepared a fine chicken stock using the old sod of a rooster—he'd flown at her yesterday morning feet first, scratching, pecking and screeching in a frightening show of his masculinity. Sick of the attacks and scratches, Artemisia threw her apron over him, bound the rooster tight and chopped off his head with the woodshed axe. Jacobus plucked the bird with a promise of some good feeds for the rest of the week. The soup was topped up with Artemisia's favourite herbs: fennel, garlic, sorrel and savoury mixed with ceps and morels harvested from the nearby chestnut forest. All her dreams were poured into this pot—spices from faraway lands that smelled of adventure. She slipped her hand into her apron pocket and stroked the parcel from Andreas. There'd be little time for dwelling on that this morning.

Hildegard tapped the spoon on the table twice to draw Artemisia's attention. Her dear old friend would like some more soup too. Hildegard coughed once with force and took a swig of claret laced with cloves from her mug. She fished in her apron pocket for a rag, lifted it to her lips and started a long hacking fit, throwing her shoulders forward and leaning on the kitchen table with her elbows to brace herself. Artemisia stood and moved behind the older woman, rubbing her back to ease the muscles. She could feel Hildegard's ribs through the thin linen and a telltale rattle deep in the middle of her back. The long cough was back early this year—never had it come before the summer solstice. Hildegard's head hung low in her hands. When she stopped coughing and pulled the rag away Artemisia could see crimson specks of blood on the muslin. There was no mistaking it for the red wine.

Artemisia moved across to the bench where she had steeped the dried violets, plus a few of the unseasonal fresh ones, in boiling water when she had returned from the garden earlier that day. She poured some of the deep purple liquid into a mug and placed it beside Hildegard.

'Drink,' she ordered.

Artemisia saw resignation settle on the boy, Jacobus; he'd lost his grandmother to a cough such as this one, she knew. They were both aware that Hildegard would not see out the coming winter.

The old woman never spoke. With her dark leathery skin, silver hair and wild, sparkling grey-blue eyes, Hildegard had always reminded Artemisia of a witch. A friendly one, mind, but there was something otherworldly and magical about her. Hildegard worked like an ox in the kitchen, making dough, turning sauces, fussing over the pots with her hunched back and hobbling in and out of the larder from dawn to dusk. In the evenings there'd always be a worker from the fields by the kitchen door revealing an ailment: a green hole on the sole of the foot, aching fingers, a red angry toenail or festering eyes from all the grain and dirt flung all day. Hildegard would examine each injury, drain it if necessary using a singed needle the length of her little finger. She'd apply a poultice or send the afflicted one home with a blend of dried herbs they could brew like a tea to sup through the night to reduce the swelling. Artemisia was always nearby, dispensing the salves and acting as translator for Hildegard's hand gestures.

Hildegard had no tongue and most of her front teeth were missing. This made her chin look long, curved and pointy—and even more like a witch's. Artemisia shivered as she remembered Hildegard's bad case of the tooth worm. She was much too poor to visit the booth at the weekly village market where the barber hacked out teeth with pliers and thus it was left to Artemisia to treat her. She would never forget standing behind a kneeling Hildegard, gently pulling the old lady's head against her hard belly for support. She'd had to raise her right arm and smash a granite pestle into Hildegard's mouth to gouge out another rotten black front tooth. Hildegard took her treatment on the wide granite flagstone steps outside the kitchen. Afterwards, she had washed her bloody mouth out with a jug of red wine to dull the pain and seal the wound, gargling and spitting and drinking a bit to kill the rot. Artemisia handed Hildegard a poultice of ground cloves and fennel wrapped in a muslin cloth to suck on for the rest of the evening. Jacobus whispered later that he hadn't heard a sound from the old woman during the whole gory incident. Not a groan.

Still shaken, Jacobus had tucked himself under Artemisia's armpit and through tears lamented that his own father had died of tooth rot. But his father refused to take the short walk through his fields and into the castle keep of Château de Boschaud to ask Artemisia and Hildegard to heal him. He had no time for fancy physicians trained with new lessons in far-off lands, and he certainly had no time to seek the remedies of womenfolk. Teas and herb craft were best left for childbirth. His obstinacy meant that he'd ended up as cold as a stone, dug into a small, unmarked plot at the edge of his beloved field. Worm food. This explained Jacobus's expressionless face and the way he kicked a rock hard when he stomped over that unmarked grave on his monthly Sunday visits to his mother. By God's blood, Jacobus always said, he hoped the heavy chunk of granite hit his stubborn ass of a father where it hurt.

Jacobus finished his soup, licked the bowl and shovelled the pile of mushrooms into his mouth.

'Steady, boy,' said Artemisia. 'Don't want you throwing up the lot on my floor. It's a long day's work before this banquet is over.'

Chapter 10

Tasmania, May 2014

Pip ducked behind the large, swinging door that separated the restaurant from the industrial kitchen, her backpack slung over her arm. She was late and she could hear Chef Dan barking instructions for the consommé to the poor commis, Jean.

Dan looked furious. She was in trouble. Fortunately, he was too busy talking Jean through his instructions for the clear broth to waste time with Pip. She placed a knotted grey plastic grocery bag beside Dan on the stainless-steel bench as she sneaked past.

'Sorry! Nettles,' she whispered. 'I'll make that soup later—the one I told you about that my mum made when we were kids. I'll make it for staff lunch, if you like?'

'It'd better be good, Pip. I'm not having you late because you were out picking some bloody weeds.' Dan's Yorkshire accent boomed across the kitchen. He didn't look up as he spat out the words.

'Can I use some of that stock if there's any left over?' asked Pip.

'Jesus. Anything else, sweetheart?'

'No, I'm good, thanks!'

Pip scooted over to the corner and started unloading her precious booty from the backpack. Woody and sharp aromas filled her corner of the kitchen as she removed unwieldy bunches of fresh mint, rosemary, parsley and chervil that had been yanked straight from a college garden bed on her way past. She tried not to think about the little garden bed Jack had made for her at Ashfield Cottage. Was it empty? Jack had left early for Italy and had sent no word as to when he'd be back. Meanwhile, she was back in student dorms as a tutor until she could find a long-term option.

Pip leaned against the bench as her breath shortened and her heart galloped. She closed her eyes for a moment until her pulse eased and she felt better. By a fraction.

She headed to the large industrial fridge to store her treasure. Then she dug into her backpack and removed an old jam jar filled with brown seed. She shook it and then popped off the lid for a quick sniff.

'Give us a smell,' Dan demanded, standing at her shoulder. He lifted the jar to his nose and inhaled the sweet, musty liquorice scent.

'Mm, fennel seed. Did you roast these yourself?'

'Ah, yes . . . I picked the seed heads on my way home from work last week and laid them out on newspaper to dry. I thought I'd bring you some to try.'

Dan sniffed the fennel seeds again and looked at Pip thoughtfully. 'Why are you here?' he demanded.

'I'm rostered on.'

'No, no, no. That's not what I mean. Why are you working in this kitchen? Why aren't you working part-time in a lab or those stinky mudflats you're always raving about?'

'I . . . I . . . I love working here.' Why was she stuttering? She didn't stutter. 'I don't know. It's just fun to do something different. Creative. I like watching how you put the dishes together.' She hoped he believed her. Besides, there was nothing else left here in Tasmania—not for Pip, anyway. No Jack. Her chest tightened. Was Dan about to give her the flick too?

Professor Grant and Imogen had called Pip to a meeting at IMAS last week to suggest she take some leave. She was struggling to keep on top of her data analysis, and they thought some time off 'may prove beneficial'.

'I told you no extensions,' said Imogen, 'and I meant it. But in light of the cancelled wedding . . .' Imogen paused and tucked a stray piece of blonde hair back into her tight ponytail. 'There's no funding, you understand?' said Imogen. 'No funding extensions without a medical certificate. You're not dying!'

Pip swallowed and nodded.

'Bottom line: we've pressed pause. The funding board at the university has agreed to a suspension.'

'Thank—'

'Stop!' Imogen help up a slender palm. 'Do what you need to do. You are officially on leave from this university.' She pushed her glasses up her nose. 'You *may* be able to reapply to finish in twelve months' time. Don't make us look like fools, Pip. Don't quit now, when you are so close.'

Pip's face burned remembering their concerned faces as they pushed the suspension forms towards her across the desk, murmuring platitudes about *taking some time to regroup*, and the worst—*breakups are always tough on a PhD.*

The forms were already signed—her suspension had already been approved.

Pip hung her head as she listened to Dan speak.

'It's more than that though; you don't just watch.' Dan leaned in close so the whole kitchen didn't hear. 'Every week you bring me something you've grown, or a treat you've collected from the roadside. Or your mudflats. You can follow any recipe I give you. Anything. But it's more than that. You can feel it. You can feel the recipes. The history. You love the herbs. I see you in your corner, sniffing away on a sprig of rosemary when no-one is looking. Collecting your nettles, fennel seeds . . . It's instinctive. You have the makings of a great chef. Come on, Pip.' Dan looked straight into her eyes, still jiggling the jam jar under his nose, before he walked to the other end of the kitchen with a list of loud instructions.

Of course she had considered a change. She needed a job. She wouldn't mind a break from number-crunching to do something creative—maybe travel—but she needed to stick to her plan if she wanted to be a marine biologist. Her research was stagnant, things with Jack were finished. She pulled her phone from her back pocket and checked again. Nothing. Jack wasn't answering her texts or calls since she'd moved out. Pip leaned against the bench for a minute and closed her eyes, remembering the rich smoky aniseed scent of the fennel. She imagined her cheek on Jack's chest, the rhythm of his breathing. His deep earthy smell of the soil and the sea.

It took all her energy just to stand up straight and get on with her work.

She needed to get away from her broken, tattered life, shake herself out of the holding pattern she'd sunk into. She needed a new strategy. A fresh environment and some funds. And then she would work out how to finish her PhD. Somehow.

'Actually, I've been meaning to chat with you, Dan, after service. I, er, I wanted to follow up about somewhere I could work for a bit. I know you worked in Europe. I want to travel for a bit, I think. Get away . . .' Her face burned and she took a deep breath. Dan knew about the cancelled wedding.

The chef patted Pip on the shoulder. 'Well, my best mate Eduardo runs a restaurant in Spain. Google it—it's called Azure, in San Sebastián. He has his own lab for experiments; his focus is molecular gastronomy.' Dan raised an eyebrow. 'If you're interested, I'll shoot him an email. It's pretty hard to get a gig there these days but if I tell him about your science background, he might make an exception. You never know—you might want to start training to be a chef.'

She doubted that. Besides, she was done with labs for the moment.

'And Pip?'

'Yes?'

'If you're late tomorrow, I'll bloody throttle you!'

The lull between the chaos of lunch and dinner service was Pip's favourite time in the restaurant. All the lamb was diced, the John Dory filleted and the Pacific oysters unpacked ready for shucking. She frowned. Why did Dan still insist on ordering this variety? She'd told him about the imported species colonising and upsetting the balance of the estuary ecosystems. He'd listened, but had said it was too hard to find consistent suppliers for the natives. Really, though, how hard could it be?

Pip's herbs were plucked, chopped and bagged, a symphony in green lined up on the long stainless-steel preparation bench.

From the outside, Zest restaurant looked like every other faded, double-fronted weatherboard Federation house in South Hobart. It sat on a tight corner on the lip of a hill that tumbled all the way down to the chilly River Derwent. Like many Federations in Hobart, it faced the wrong direction—south. The only time the sun snuck in was late February. Even then it only briefly touched the courtyard. Dan had placed a worn metal table with matching chair outside so he could enjoy a cigarette in the sun. But judging from his pallor, the sun only hit Dan for a day or so in February too. Chefs weren't exactly known for their exposure to vitamin D.

Inside, Zest was a different matter. The walls were papered with Florence Broadhurst's Japanese Floral print in red and gold. Large round Blackwood spheres hung from the ceiling and the tables were covered with crisp white damask tablecloths. The effect was an atmosphere of both warmth and glamour; Pip could see why the restaurant was a favourite with locals.

And then there was the food, of course. In the five years since Dan had taken over the restaurant, he had established a dedicated following, and not only with locals. Visitors from the mainland often made a meal at Zest the centrepiece of their Tasmanian mini-break, along with a wander around the Salamanca markets to browse the handicrafts and a trip on the ferry from Constitution Dock out to the funky Museum of Old and New Art, known far and wide as MONA.

Now, though, as Dan, Jean and Pip sat around their favourite round table in the corner for their staff lunch, it was Pip's food that was the focus.

'This soup is *magnifique*,' said Jean, who was from Marseilles.

Dan and Jean slurped the soup, tearing off hunks of Dan's specialty sourdough to wipe the sides of the bowl.

'This is grand,' Dan agreed. 'I've heard of nettle soup, but I've never tried it. Where did your mum get the recipe?'

'I've got no idea,' said Pip. 'I think from Dad's side of the family—maybe my grandmother. Apparently there are some family recipes somewhere, but I've never seen them.'

'Where did you find the nettles?' Dan asked.

'They're all along the roadsides. I always make sure that I get them from further up the walking tracks behind my place where it hasn't been sprayed. I used my dishwashing gloves this morning so I didn't get stung.

'But, interestingly, wherever there are stinging nettles there are also dock leaves growing nearby. If you're stung by a nettle, you rub a dock leaf on the sting and the pain goes away. Don't shake your head, Jean—it really works!'

Pip continued: 'My mum's a midwife, and I remember her making batches of stinging nettle soup for a neighbour who was having trouble breastfeeding. Stinging nettles have a substance that helps with lactation.'

'Too much information,' said Dan, wincing.

'Seriously, Dan, it's fascinating,' Pip insisted. 'They are doing lots of research at the moment into the compounds in the leaf. It's used as a tea in Nepal and China to detox the kidneys, help with arthritis, strengthen the heart and beat the flu. Imagine if you could find a way of extracting the elements and applying it for treatment?'

Dan shrugged. 'If you say so—you're the scientist.' He indicated his empty bowl. 'And not a bad cook, either.'

Pip blushed with pleasure. 'And did you notice the yoghurt really smooths it out? The fat takes the bitterness out of it. Makes it delicious and creamy. The one Mum used to make was a bit more like gruel.'

'The fennel seeds were a good idea, too,' Dan said thoughtfully. 'They give the soup a bit of depth. I'd even drizzle a bit of truffle oil over it next time. Not too much, mind, just a drop so you get that warm earthy smell when the bowl hits the table.' He stretched. 'All right, back to work. There's a big lot of pots in there that ain't gonna clean themselves and the floor needs a mop, I noticed. Do a bit of clean-up before you start prep. We'll talk more about San Sebastián and Eduardo tonight, after service.'

Pip took a deep breath and gave Dan a grateful nod. She needed to reboot and San Sebastián sounded like a delicious place to start. Perhaps a working holiday was a good idea? She could use a different side of her brain, be creative. Where was the harm in that?

Chapter 11

Château de Boschaud, Midsummer 1487

Artemisia wiped the sweat from her brow with her sleeve and peeled the tunic from the front of her chest as she stood near the fireplace stirring the *porée* while Emmeline, Hildegard and Jacobus finished their meal. She'd just topped up the thick green soup with slices of dried chanterelles and was watching the yellowish leathery mushrooms expand and turn slippery before being swallowed by the liquid. She'd pulled some hunks of ham and a handful of garlic cloves, fresh hairy nettles and curly parsley to bulk up the soup for the household servants' meal before the banquet. When the kitchen servants were finished, she'd call the chamberlain, the stewards and the chambermaids down to receive their supper.

Next, Emmeline would deliver a tureen and a dozen warm black rolls wrapped in cloth to the monks. They would dine under the monastery eaves in their cloisters shaded by the linden allée. It was a pity she'd added the ham, being a day of penitence and all, but she thought a secret whiff of the hog might bring a smile and a bit of strength to the old withered faces that had tended the garden since she was smaller than the rosemary hedge. Abbot Roald had been pacing the garden walls, leaning over the monks and barking orders, ripping out rows of lettuce should they not be straight, calling them back to finish weaving willow borders by the moon. If hard work and dutiful attention to the sacraments and prayers were the sole path to salvation, then the hunched, uncomplaining monks of Château de Boschaud were well on their way. The monks with the fine use of the quill were no longer used to transcribe the herbal remedies so revered by Abbot Bellamy—Abbot Roald scorned the skills of an apothecary as much as he neglected his duties as almoner. Peasants and servants within the castle keep tended to make for the kitchen door with their apologetic knocks and tentative requests for something healing. Instead, the monks sat under the arches of the cloisters, chronicling the allocated domestic chores of the château, the accounts and sections of the gospel. What was left of the physic garden was left to be tended mostly by the kitchen cooks, and Artemisia was doing her best to keep a transcription of all the remedies and potions mixed by the women for the château's records. Every moon the abbot requested a copy of the menus served at the château, then he would place Artemisia's sheets of parchment between two stiff boards. He'd approve the menus using a red wax seal stamped with his ring with ne'er so much as a grateful nod. Artemisia never risked delaying the presentation of her recipes—the records and library at Château de Boschaud were said to be the best in the Limousin, Abbot Roald the most proficient chaplain in the land. Heaven could not help those who slipped into slothful ways and failed to deliver as he asked.

Today, Abbot Roald would be conducting the marriage rites in the garden, after which he would dine to the left of the couple in the chaplain's correct placement—before other important château officers like the marshal, the master huntsman and the falconer. Artemisia assumed he had a special dispensation from Heaven itself to partake in the boar and caramel geese and duck that would be served at this evening's banquet.

She lifted her ladle from the deep pot and hung it over the thick copper lip as she crossed behind the table to check on Emmeline's *moutarde violette*. The girl had made a fresh batch this morning, seeding all the black grapes and pounding them to make a thick purple paste before blending it with the black mustard flour. Artemisia dipped her finger into the bowl then licked it. The sharp burning flavours of the mustard seed were softened by the grape juice and the skins gave it grip. It would be the perfect accompaniment to the fowl. She reached over to the brown sack of salt sitting on the benchtop and added two pinches to the mustard before giving it a stir and licking the spoon. Much better—the salt balanced the flavours so there was no longer a tussle between sweet and spicy. Piled beside the bowl were a few of the dried mushrooms she'd dropped, so she swept them into the palm of her hand—along with another pinch of salt and a nip of the dark mustard flour, and dropped them into her soup.

As the browning specks lay spinning on the glossy surface and the searing heat from the heavy coals threatened to overwhelm her, Artemisia smiled and drifted back to the cool misty spring day she'd harvested these chanterelles.

Artemisia and Emmeline had walked to the edge of the woods beyond the wall to fill their baskets with the golden wavy caps of the chanterelles. They shimmered like shavings of gold leaf peeking out from brown clumps of decaying leaves covering the shallow roots of the oaks and sweet chestnuts.

Artemisia had promised to supply the abbot with a fresh mushroom pastie after matins every morning during the chanterelle season. His knuckles and knee joints creaked and ached when the evenings started to dip and cool—along with his temper—and the peppery mushrooms eased the start to the day for all.

The pasties were easy enough to make. Artemisia would thinly slice the thick caps and blend them with soft cheese, salt and ground ginger, cinnamon and cloves before wrapping them in thick pastry and sitting them between the warm coals to rise. She always made an extra small parcel oozing with cheese for Jacobus to slip into his pocket when he went out to fetch the day's wood.

This particular morning was chilly, the sky dark and low, and Emmeline and Artemisia had almost filled their willow baskets to the brim with yellow caps, enjoying the mushroom's surprising, teasing scent of ripening apricots. Some caps were the size of Artemisia's palm and she was showing Emmeline how to gently shake the caps so they would pop up from the same spot of damp loamy soil next autumn when she heard the deep thud of hooves on soil and the rattle of a cart drawing near. As she turned towards the worn path that wound between the tall silver beech trees and the sweet chestnuts, she saw a pair of shiny black warmbloods stepping prettily through the forest. Artemisia's heart did a double beat—it was the new *épicier*.

'Good morning, ladies,' said Andreas as he leaned back and pulled the reins to draw his cart to a stop, before removing his felt hat and dipping his head in a gesture far too grand for kitchen servants.

'Monsieur de Vitriaco.' Artemisia dipped her head in return, hiding the curl in the corner of her lips. He was every bit as handsome as she'd remembered from that first day in the larder. His skin was like the finest cinnamon.

'I see you have full baskets. Chanterelles too, my favourites.' He sniffed the cool air. 'And it smells like we are in for more rain. It will be a good season, I think.'

'Indeed,' said Artemisia. The air was thick with the agreeable scent of fallen leaves, damp soil and—Artemisia realised with shock—a sliver of hope. Her heart had never started to flutter, nor had she been left to fish for words with menfolk before. A gust of wind blew through the trees and the ladies were showered in yellow and brown leaves. They both laughed as they brushed the leaves from their faces and wimples.

'And who might this young lass be?' Andreas smiled at the blonde, dimpled Emmeline, who ducked her head and blushed. Artemisia felt her stomach churn a little with jealousy at the maid's silky almond-milk skin and hair. Of course a man would prefer this fair, ripe, plump girl. Still, Artemisia needed to protect the innocent girl from these entitled village merchants who'd have their way then discard her like the seed of a peach. She felt her heart harden just a little.

'This is Emmeline,' Artemisia said curtly. 'She works in the kitchen alongside myself and Hildegard.'

'Aggh, the one with no tongue?' said Andreas. 'Quite the trio you have in the kitchen up at the château.' He jumped off the cart and stretched out his hand, keeping hold of the reins with the other. The horses pulled their ears back and swished their tails. 'Here. Let me take you back to the château. I'm doing your spice delivery now.'

Artemisia swung her basket around and held up a hand to protest.

'I insist,' said Andreas as he clasped the handle of each basket and lifted them into the back of the tray.

Artemisia considered the long trudge back through the sodden fallow fields to the château sitting on the rise in the distance and thought, why not? She had a long day ahead and her weary legs could do with the rest.

Emmeline climbed into the cart first, and as she stepped up Artemisia quickly brushed the twigs and crushed leaves snagged on the hem of the girl's tunic. The linen was thin, and the soles of her boots were worn through so she could see the fleshy pink of her sole. Artemisia bent down to quickly do the same for hers, and noted with dismay the wet band around the hem of her own dull grey tunic. Andreas held out his hand and she lifted herself into the tray with a stiff, 'Thank you.'

Then he swung himself up beside her, and she could see the muscles flex through his pristine white silk shirt and caught the whiff of rosewater as he sat beside her. It was tight to fit the three of them across the wooden seat, and Artemisia could feel the *épicier*'s strong thigh pressing against hers.

Andreas whistled and shook the reins, and the horses took off at a brisk walk. The flat tray was filled with different-sized terracotta pots and they clinked and clanged with every step.

Andreas asked: 'So what will you be making with these fine chanterelles?'

And so Artemisia relaxed just a little and spent the rest of the trip telling him of her recipes, and he chipped in with suggestions of spices. He asked how to make the plain green *porée* so adored in these rolling valleys more interesting. She told him of how she had come to call the château home, and Andreas told her of his student days studying Latin grammar, astronomy and geometry in Bologna, transcribing endless pieces of parchment. When his father was killed his mother, Alba, had called him home to finish his journey to the guild and take over the de Vitriaco spice business. One day soon he would run the guild and shop at the marketplace as his father had before him, and Artemisia had joked that if the price of saffron and ginger were to increase she would call for his dismissal at the village meeting with the burgher. They'd laughed so easily at this banter—shoulders brushing, eyes meeting—that for a moment Artemisia forgot she was a merely a cook. Both knew she wasn't permitted to approach the burgher or attend a village meeting without the written consent of her lord. Or the chaplain. It was unthinkable. Until this misty ride in a cart with a smiling man who had travelled to faraway places, Artemisia had always been grateful for her straw and lavender bed in the barn.

The happy pair almost forgot that sweet Emmeline was sitting there, quiet as a larder cat, as Andreas explained the workings of a clever cart designed by Sienese engineer Taccola that he wanted to have made because it could unfold into a bridge. Together they wondered what exotic place in the Far East the shiny nutmeg traded by the Arabs in Venice came from and whether it would soon drop in price. Andreas asked

Artemisia how she would cook the mushrooms and how she dried them. She found herself so pleased that someone had asked her to share her knowledge that she was happy to tell.

Artemisia felt the fresh breeze on her face and her plaits tumbled and jiggled down her back as they emerged from the woods. They drew to a slow walk and the horses flicked their manes and snorted as they strolled beside the château's high stone wall. Andreas admired the flourish of fierce yellow leaves peeking over the top of the hard granite wall until they reached the closed wrought-iron gates of Château de Boschaud and waited for them to be hauled open by the old gatekeeper.

When they pulled up alongside the larder, Andreas busied himself unpacking the terracotta pots from the back of the cart. Artemisia set Emmeline to work in the kitchen alongside Hildegard rinsing, peeling and slicing the two baskets of mushrooms before laying them on a flay tray to dry out above the coals. Emmeline didn't notice that Artemisia had slipped a few handfuls of the golden mushrooms into her apron pocket before ducking into the larder.

As Andreas brought in the last pots, Artemisia quickly wrapped a tiny parcel with mushrooms and a sheet of parchment with three recipes. The first was for her pastie; the second was a list for a sautée with one pound of wild chanterelles, onion, butter, and a pinch each of freshly ground black pepper, ginger, nutmeg and coriander seed. The third was the recipe for her green *porée* with fresh fish. She also wrote a note:

Dear Mr de Vitriaco,

Please accept these mushrooms and the recipes we discussed as a gift. You may wish to pass them to your cook to prepare.

I am thankful for your kind treatment of young Emmeline and myself and your interest in my recipes.

May I be so bold as to ask for your rosewater recipe?

Your most sincere servant and cook,
Artemisia

(One more request, if I may? One would hate this letter to fall into the hands of Abbot Roald as I shall be up for a severe whipping if caught. Lord Boschaud is away preparing for battle and the abbot is the master of the château in his place. You are most welcome to add the recipe parchments to your own, yet I beg you burn any correspondence.)

She folded the thick parchment, placed the mushrooms on top and wrapped her little parcel in cheesecloth, fastening it with twine. Then she slipped it into her pocket and followed Andreas out to the cart as he carried the last of the empty pots to load.

Andreas leaned over the cart to tuck a pot in the far corner and Artemisia surreptitiously admired the strong line of his back until he finished and turned.

'Oh, sorry, Artemisia. I didn't see you there. Is everything okay with the order?' He frowned. 'I hope I haven't forgotten anything.' He reached to pull his list from his pocket.

Artemisia reached out to stop his hand, and their fingers touched. 'No, pardon, Monsieur de Vitriaco.'

She hesitated as she looked around. If she was caught by the abbot . . .

Her mouth went dry just thinking about it and she felt the slow flush of humiliation spread from her collar to her face. It was too big a risk. She had no right to expect friendship from the *épicier*—she was a servant, by God's wound.

'Call me Andreas, please.' He tilted his head and looked at her kindly as Artemisia drew breath and pulled the little cheesecloth parcel from her pocket.

'For you, sir.' She murmured, too afraid to say more.

'Andreas,' he said, raising his eyebrows as he took the parcel and made to untie the twine.

Artemisia looked around for Abbot Roald. Speaking with the village merchants about anything other than larder supplies was against his rules. 'No, not here. It's nothing. Just—just some chanterelles and some recipes.' She blushed. 'To thank you for that ride. It was most courteous of you.'

Andreas lifted dark eyes the colour of molasses and winked as he pressed the parcel to his chest.

'My lucky day, Artemisia.' He then reached over and tucked it into his cart as he tipped his hat onto his head. 'Until next time.'

Artemisia nodded and gave a half-wave as she turned her face up into the cool air, searching for a break in the thickset clouds to find the sun.

Chapter 12

Tasmania, May 2014

To: maryarnet@bigpond.com

From: parnet@unitas.edu.au

Subject: Extended holiday!

Hi Mum,

I've just handed in some deferral forms for my PhD. My co-supervisor, Jim Grant, will hold my research position. It was his idea—along with Imogen—that I take a break from writing up my thesis. Said it might help me find some 'clarity' when it comes to analysing my data.

Of course I was offended—but it makes sense. They don't have the funding for me to stuff about.

I've been toying with having a break to go travelling since Jack and I separated. I mentioned it to Dan (the chef at Zest you met last time you were in Tasmania) and he suggested I could get some work with his friend Eduardo in San Sebastián, Spain.

Eduardo is somewhat of a BIG DEAL in Spain, the pioneer of a style of cuisine they call molecular gastronomy. Weird, huh? It's kind of a blend of everything I'm good at: science and cooking. So you can be pleased at least that my chemistry and biology will be put to good use! I know you are probably thinking I'm going to quit my PhD. Dad will. Well please hose him down a bit before I get there. I'm not quitting just yet!

You know how much I love my work at Zest. I'll be sharpening up my cooking skills. So make sure you tell Dad I shall not just be wandering the world without a plan. Although, really, what the hell is wrong with that? Most of my mates are.

Anyway, in Spain they forage ingredients daily in the mountains. Who knows, maybe I'll come back to Australia and open a restaurant here? Just kidding!

Dan and Eduardo have assured me that everyone speaks great English in the kitchen. And besides, I speak chemistry!

Just one more thing—I won't be meeting up with Jack in Italy. Better to make a clean break. (I am trying hard to remain good friends. Bit tricky when he won't return my calls.) Megs has kindly agreed to store all my stuff in her garden shed. (It's not like they use it!)

Anyway, hope this letter hasn't set off your ticker, or Dad's. Probably inevitable though. Don't worry, I'll be fine. I'll call you in a day or so to work out dates for my visit.

Lots of love,
Pip x

Chapter 13

Château de Boschaud, Autumn 1486

Dear Artemisia,

I hope I may be so bold as to address you as Artemisia in the written word as I mean for us to correspond insofar as you can manage it. With such a beautiful name, drawn from the great Mother of Herbs and Plato's huntress, it would be a shame to neglect the temptation to use it on another fine maiden.

Let me assure you I took a flame to the letter as soon as it was read. It was your words that warmed me, Artemisia, and I am well pleased, if most surprised, of your command of the quill. Your kindly Abbot Bellamy showed much foresight when he taught you to read and write. You have a mind as sharp as pepper and I very much enjoyed our chat on the cart.

I hope you will allow me another opportunity for such a meeting.

Please find enclosed the standard recipe from Le Ménagier de Paris for making house rosewater, as requested. I assume the recipe has come from his cook, though none is credited. My own father would turn in his grave if I were to disclose the exact measurements of the spices we blend with our de Vitriaco version. It has been our family business for centuries. I may be convinced, however, after some careful negotiation with the head cook of Château de Boschaud.

If I were to recommend a blend for laundering sheets and shirts, I'd consider adding a handful of fresh lavender flowers, two ounces of orris, a drop of musk, three ounces of ambergris, as much civet and four drops of oil of clove. Stop this close, and set it in the sun for a fortnight. Put one spoonful of this into a small basin of water, and sprinkle it over your clothes when folding.

Rosewater brings out the flavours of summer. The sauce for a roast chicken is half vinegar, half rosewater and press (orange juice may be swapped for the vinegar).

To make red rosewater, take a flask and fill it half full of good rosewater and fill the other half with the petals of young red roses from which you shall have cut off the end of the petal, which is white, and leave it nine days in the sun and nine nights likewise, and then pour it out.

Lastly, may I be so bold as to suggest a recipe to sweeten your sheets and your dreams.

Three pounds of rosewater, cloves, cinnamon, sandalwood and two handfuls of the flowers of lavender. Let it stand a month in the sun in a sealed jar. It makes a water of wondrous sweetness.

Your most humble servant and épicier,
Andreas de Vitriaco

Chapter 14

Mount Macedon, Victoria, May 2014

Pip studied the faded black-and-white wedding photo of her parents displayed in a simple wooden frame at the entrance to their house. Mary short and dark, David tall and broad, both with their heads thrown back, eyes creased and mouths open laughing as they were showered with rose petals. Her parents married within five months of meeting on the wide stone steps of the biology department at the university they both attended. Both went on to finish their degrees. Forge careers. Raise a family. Pip's stomach clenched and guilt surged through her body. How had they both been so certain? She loved Jack—so why had he cut her off? Why wasn't she enough?

Her heart ached as she swung open the front door and headed outside to walk up the mountain.

'Jesus,' she gasped, as she was engulfed by the sharp autumn mist. She'd forgotten how cold early mornings were at her parents' place on Mount Macedon. She tugged on her navy woollen beanie, scarf and matching gloves, quietly thanking her mum for keeping these remnants of her schooldays. The driveway gravel crunched underfoot as she turned right and headed up the hill to the spot where she would meet her father and his friend Dom for some pre-dawn mushrooming.

Autumn mornings with their clear soft light were Pip's favourite time of day to be alone on the mountain. She loved to wake early and head out for a few minutes of solitude. Her father was still inside, making an espresso and filling a thermos for another one later up the hill. She had at least five minutes up her sleeve before the men joined her and the hike began. A couple of kookaburras hidden in the bush let rip with their cackling, breaking the quiet.

Pip strode up the Tuscan-style gravel path—crunching with each step—enjoying the scent of her mother's herb beds planted with rosemary hedges and bordered with sage. She paused and plucked a leaf of her favourite broadleaf sage and rubbed the wide soft leaf against her skin before crushing it in her fingers and inhaling the rich, woody fragrance. Out of habit, she also picked a sprig of rosemary, rubbed the oil on her fingers and sniffed. The aggressive scent snapped her out of autopilot. She used to keep rosemary on her desk when she was ploughing through sample maths exams for her VCE and sniff it sporadically when she lost focus. That or lick green wasabi paste straight from the tube! Her mother told her constantly: 'You're mad, Pip—bonkers with your herbs.'

Like she could talk! Mary had planted acres of rosemary, sage, lavender, catmint and about five different types of thyme. She used thick hedges of broadleaf sage as borders around the four raised vegetable squares to keep the white moths off the broccoli and cabbages, and catmint under the fruit trees to attract the bees. For dinner she served chicken roasted in layers of catmint, pork stuffed with chestnuts, sage and lavender, roast lamb and crispy potatoes smelling of rosemary. In the summer, Mary added seasonal plants like basil between the tomatoes to repel the slugs, mints to scare aphids and sprawling borage to sweeten the blackberries and raspberries. She always collected and froze the azure blue star-shaped flowers in ice cubes, which added a fairy-like touch to jugs of water laced with mint and sliced lemons.

Pip started walking again and looked up beyond the canopy of the chestnut grove. There was the familiar dark wall of purple-grey where the giant stands of mountain ash framed the rise of the mountain. A great blanket of mist spilled down the slope and over the gum trees towards the farmland far below.

Though the uphill walk to the meeting spot was only two hundred metres, Pip found herself puffing. She reached the intersection marked with a stand of dusty green blackwoods nicknamed 'Pip's forest' from when she used to ride her bike up here as a kid. Megs sure as hell never made it up there. Her sister didn't really get into the bush. Some of the blackwoods and gums beyond had the telltale sign of charcoal up the trunks. It'd been decades since a fire went through here but Parks Victoria did controlled burns every few years. Controlled burns that sometimes went a bit haywire and tore up the slopes, leaving blackened scars right through the bush.

Pip jogged on the spot to keep warm and clapped her hands together. The sound ricocheted down the slope. She was grateful for this moment of solitude before the men arrived. Autumn mushrooming was a ritual Pip's father David and his mate Dom had had forever. Since Pip was about seven—old enough to walk up the hill in the cold without complaining—they'd included her on this annual foraging expedition. They always went after Anzac Day, when the autumn rains had started, softening the ground underfoot.

Pip's father had met Dom twenty years earlier. David and Mary had just purchased the chestnut grove and had no idea what they were going to do with the fruit of forty mature trees. They had bought the block on a whim: two wrong turns on a Sunday and it was pretty much theirs. The first year David placed an advertisement in *Il Globo*, Melbourne's Italian newspaper: *Pick your own chestnuts. Free to good home!* Domenico Sculli, a retired truck driver who had migrated to Australia in 1970 from Piedmonte, had been coming up from Northcote every autumn since.

'*Castanea*. Food of my people,' declared Dom. He showed David and Mary how to extract the chestnut from the prickly husk by stepping on the ball, causing the chestnuts to shoot out the side. Then he'd carefully shown them how to score the shell: 'Shiny, like your hair, Philippa. It is the exact colour, no?'

He taught Pip to look beyond the bracken and harvest weeds dotted up the mountain. He'd yank the cardoon thistles and steam them like an artichoke: 'Best way to eat 'em. No place for them in these forests anyway, they'll take over, like the sorrel. A weed's just something that's in the wrong place. At home, these are delicacies.' Dom also taught Pip to pay more attention to the native plants that tended to fade into the scrub. He showed her how to harvest the native mountain pepper berry and dry it out on newspaper and also to take the young shoots and seeds of the strappy grass *Lomandra longifolia*. He'd fry them up with the mushrooms or use them in a salad.

But mostly Dom came in autumn for the mushrooms: saffron milk caps; the more powerful, meaty orange pine mushrooms; and the slimy brown slippery jacks.

'Are you sure these aren't death caps?' Pip would ask doubtfully. 'Dad told me they can kill you.'

Dom replied patiently: 'I've told you a million times, Philippa: the ones with the orange gills and hollow stems are pines. Once they are cooked, they are perfect. They'll go beautifully with these slippery jacks.'

Pip glanced inside her basket filled with the dark caps and squashy undersides of yellow. They smelled moist and peaty. She'd adored mushrooms ever since.

Over the years, Dom had shown Pip how to see fungi everywhere: a fairy ring of delicate threads of red toadstools poking through moss, a staircase of brown coral-like bracket fungi clinging to the pale bark of a eucalypt, tiny fluorescent red and pink caps popping from a rotting soil-filled log. She'd learned to look for the telltale holes scratched by wallabies searching for nuggets of native truffles and to watch for the globs of golden jelly bells. The prettier they were, it seemed, the more poisonous.

Megs wasn't interested in cooking at all, she was always off playing with Barbies in her bedroom. Ripping their limbs off and putting them back together. But Pip would stand in the kitchen helping her mother peel warm chestnuts until her fingers were raw. Her mother would freeze the chestnuts in portions, ready to roll into a pork shoulder or stuff into the cavity of a chicken with garlic, sage and rosemary . . .

Pip was jolted from her memories by a giant bear hug from Dom.

Her father beamed beside her, rugged up in army disposal gear and a red sleeveless puffer vest with a thermos sticking out of the pocket. He held out a basket to her: 'You forgot this when you raced out the door, love. You were in a bit too much of a hurry, as usual.' He grinned and handed her the basket and Pip noticed a slight stoop in his shoulders. When had her dad started getting old? In the rising light his curly hair looked silver. It was as if he had aged ten years since her last visit, six months earlier.

'So, Philippa,' Dom said as the trio marched up the hill, 'your father tells me that you are off to Spain soon.' He bent and reached for a slimy brown mushroom. 'Slippery jacks.' He nodded in approval, picked a handful and gave them a vigorous shake before dropping them into his basket. He lowered his voice and leaned in close: 'He's very proud of you. *Sì*—always talking about his clever daughters. Now look here, young Philippa: sorrel, plantain and dandelion. My parents lived off these in the mountains during the war. Try the sorrel. It tastes bitter now, sour, but come back when the new growth is out and the young leaves are sweet and delicious. Add to some salads with beetroot leaf. Nothing is as it seems, young Philippa. Sometimes you have to take a second look. And sometimes what was plentiful one year is missing the next. You have to keep your eyes open, to look for new places. It's a matter of survival for all of us. You know this, *mia cara*.'

Pip nodded, as she put one foot in front of the other. Had Dom guessed she was seeking new places because her life was as soggy and decomposed as the leaf matter they trod on?

Dom's voice was kind. 'You live knee-deep in those murky riverbanks, with festering fish, rotting bones. Yet from the rot we get the beautiful new fish and the molluscs. The sea is filtered and we get new life.' He spotted what he was looking for. 'Ah, here they are: the morel. They too are born from decay. A perfect morsel from death. Different every year. Don't be afraid of new locations, *bella*.'

He placed the mushrooms gently, gills down, in the basket. 'The spores, the spores. The gift.'

'What are you banging on about with my daughter?' David loved to spar with Dom. 'Encouraging her to throw away all those years of study. What a waste.'

'Dad!'

'I agree, my friend, an education is important. The war stole that from me. But the trip to this land—a new land—brought new opportunities. A life we would never have lived in the village at home. Your Philippa is a clever girl. You always tell me so yourself: "That Pip is a clever girl." Beating your chest, tearing your hair out because she does not go point to point like Margot. She is not like her sister. Pip is wild and she needs to forage for a bit. She will have her nose in strange places, to be sure. But we do not get the magic without the hunt, no?'

She grinned. Perhaps she would find the hint of magic she was missing in Spain. Pip could see her father give a dismissive shrug—he regarded academia and research as sacred. There was no use arguing. Her mum, for a change, was the more sympathetic of the two.

They continued up the hill in the cool morning light, raiding clumps of mushrooms as they went. The silence was sometimes interrupted by the thump of an unseen kangaroo pushing off down the slope.

Pip breathed in the damp soil, sodden leaves and pine needles as she listened to her father's heavy steps behind her. David loved his annual mushroom harvest with Dom, and usually he was thrilled whenever she could join them. Perhaps not this year though. Behind her, his disappointment felt as thick and heavy as the fog. Her father had seen many of his PhD students crumble under pressure when they were almost done. He just didn't expect it from his daughters. Perseverance. Take nothing for granted. His words from her childhood echoed in her mind, haunting her.

Pip ducked to miss a branch and heard her dad's breath shortening. Mount Macedon seemed to be getting steeper by the year. They were nearing McGregor's Garden now—really just a clearing in the forest. Pip could see the slim frame of her mother firing up the park barbecue. Like Megs, Mary didn't much go in for a morning of foraging, but she always met them at the top of the mountain for a harvest breakfast. Pip watched as she returned to the car, struggling to pull the old orange cast-iron frypan from the back seat. No wonder she never used the big old copper pots; they were impossible for her to lift. On top she had balanced a block of butter, a bottle of balsamic vinegar and handfuls of parsley, sage and thyme from her garden.

This was Pip's favourite part, when they gathered to fry up the mushrooms. As they sizzled in the pan, the smell filled her nostrils, fragrant with the sharpness of thyme.

Dom held up a bottle of his homebrew red.

'No thanks, mate. It's a bit early. Your reds rip my head off.' David laughed as he sat down.

'Come on, Dad,' said Pip in protest. 'Don't be a party pooper. Mum's having one.'

Mary raised her enamel cup. 'Cheers.'

'Well, your mother can have whatever she likes. But just remember: that red you're drinking has had his bloody feet in it, hasn't it? Don't want his hairy buggers in my wine. No thanks! More than happy to pay my twenty dollars for the privilege of not drinking his foot odour. Top dollar, in fact.'

Dom retaliated. 'Ugh, these tannins in the Australian wines you love. Always sweet, too sweet. Too much heat in the grapes. And sometimes I can taste the eucalyptus, the bitter tannins. It's strange you love them so much.'

'All right, boys, quit your bickering,' said Mary. 'Who wants some of these mushrooms? I've got the sourdough ready—rubbed it with garlic before I came.'

Pip sat at the picnic table and let the banter wash over her. She watched her mother dishing up the mushrooms onto enamel camping plates and admired her girlish charm and the freckles stamped across her nose. She swished the fringe from her face and laughed at some story Dom was telling.

David coughed to clear his throat of breadcrumbs. 'Pip, your mother and I were wondering how Megs is? She just seems so busy lately we haven't had much of a chance to chat. Plus that bloody Skype keeps dropping out.'

Mary shot him a sharp look. Pip knew that one all too well—*be careful!*

'Megs? She's fine,' Pip said. She shifted position on her fixed seat. Why wouldn't she be? she thought resentfully. Her sister had it all sorted: husband, child, an amazing job and all the help in the world.

But then Pip remembered the dark rings under her sister's eyes, how Megs had almost cried with gratitude when Pip had offered to babysit Chloé the week before because it was Eva's day off. 'I think she's pretty tired, though,' Pip conceded. 'She's been working long hours.'

And despite the pressure she was under, it had been Megs who helped Pip to move the last of her things from Ashfield Cottage, carefully wrapping the copper pots in newspaper and placing them in oversized boxes before bundling Pip onto the plane to Melbourne for some TLC.

Pip returned her attention to her mushrooms. The scent of smoke and earth enveloped her and she closed her eyes, enjoying the sweet tang of the balsamic vinegar and the creaminess of the pine mushrooms filling her mouth.

Mary came and put her arms around her as though Pip was still their baby, and they all sat for a minute breathing in the scent of mingling eucalyptus and acacias and listening to the sharp screech of the sulphur-crested cockatoos.

Eventually, Pip spoke. 'I know you both have a lot on at work—and Megs and Will do too—but I know they would love a visit.'

Mary inhaled. 'Are you sure?' She paused. 'I mean, last time I spoke to Megs she snapped at me when I suggested she swaddle Chloé a bit tighter. And she almost bit my head off when I suggested that some people find a dummy handy when they're trying to coax their babies to sleep right through. It stops them wanting to suckle all the time.'

'Mum! Hello! You are a midwife. How many stories have you told us over the years about mothers going nuts over silly things? How they don't want advice when they're having a hard time?'

'Exactly! Which is why I think it's better if I stay away and she finds her own way.'

'Mum, she's just being a perfectionist, beating herself up when things don't run according to plan. But since when was Megs any different? You guys should go.'

'Good idea, Pip,' said David. 'We'll book once we get you on that plane.'

Mary shot him another dark look. Did they think Pip was incapable of that, too? She'd had enough of being managed. Of fitting into other people's schedules. It was time she made her own.

'Great,' she said with a forced smile. She took another sip of Dom's rough red for warmth. She was more certain than ever that she had to get away—to put some distance between herself and Jack, and her stalled thesis. Between family and failure.

Chapter 15

Château de Boschaud, Midsummer 1487

Artemisia moved purposefully across the kitchen to talk to Pierre the *hâteur* about the order of the roast meat on the grill. Now that everyone was back in the kitchen, she had to make sure they stuck to their tasks otherwise they'd trip and end up with the coals. The ruddy fellow had come in from the village specially to turn rows of animals mounted on spits. There were ten long rods with the roasts on the fire and each needed to be turned at a different rate. The kid would be served with a golden sauce, the lamb needed to be basted with parsley, verjuice and salt. The suckling pig was to be stuffed with powdered ginger, soft white cheese, saffron, salted ham, chestnuts and eggs. Over in the far corner, Hildegard had already started making the stuffing in a large pot on the granite bench. Her dark twig-like arms were elbow-deep in the crock, turning the mixture over. Hildegard paused for a moment and pulled one arm out, making a needle with a sewing gesture at Artemisia. Hildegard needed a needle and gut to sew the stuffing mixture into the pig's belly. Underneath the rotisserie were wide metal trays with beet, turnips and carrots that were being glazed by the dripping fat.

Artemisia counted her blessings that she had ordered an extra dozen roasted geese from the *oyer* for the main course. The kitchen was simply not big enough to cook it all at once, and she wanted this banquet to be perfect.

'Why doesn't the old lady talk?' asked Pierre above the din of the pots, nodding towards Hildegard's back. Pierre was new to the village and loved a chat, but Artemisia didn't have time today.

Artemisia took a step towards him and lowered her voice: 'Abbot Roald chopped her tongue out two years ago, when the lord was away on a hunt. Said he didn't want another bitter word coming out of her mouth. Hildegard had suggested he was a glutton and he had taken too much of the roast meats over winter. She thought his humours needed balancing and she suggested a few weeks of bread and nettle *porée*.'

Artemisia paused and looked at the fire as she recalled Abbot Roald's exact words. *Your tongue plots destruction, like a sharp razor, you worker of deceit.* She would never forget the fierce look on his face. If Abbot Roald did the bidding of God, then Artemisia was pretty sure she never wanted to meet her Creator.

'He asked her to poke it out right here in the kitchen and he sliced it clean off with his dagger.'

Emmeline paused in her pounding and grinding of spices and seeds in the giant granite mortar and Artemisia turned to watch her. She squatted with her knees apart, low on her haunches with the mortar bowl wedged between her thighs and her tunic hitched a little to reveal her dirty knees. Artemisia relaxed as the rhythmic thumping of the pestle resumed. Yes, Emmeline was more than ready to take over the running of the kitchen. Hildegard would help, of course, along with the lad Jacobus, but Artemisia felt guilt throbbing and churning like bile in her gut—she would miss them all.

She turned back to the *hâteur.* 'Get on with your work,' she scolded. 'Stop this prying and be getting on with your work now, otherwise Abbot Roald might do the same to you.'

Pierre, looking chastened, returned his gaze to the fires.

Artemisia glanced back at the hot kitchen filled with boiling pots, rotisseries and sweating bodies before stepping into the cool dark larder. The tiny cell was lit only by the dim candle she carried in from the kitchen and placed on the shelf. She bent over and lifted the apron to wipe the sweat from her brow and leaned against a wooden shelf stacked with clay pots to draw breath. Her back ached. The smell of charring meat crept under the closed door and overtook the tiny space. Her face started tingling hot and cold as she reached into her pocket and retrieved the parcel. Artemisia propped it on the shelf to hold it steady as she unwrapped the string, ripping the wormwood from the centre of the knot and tearing back the linen. Underneath, her present was covered with confetti. Sugared coriander seeds rained on the floor and rolled like tiny marbles into every corner as she brushed them aside in her excitement. She'd sweep them up after she had looked at her betrothal gift.

Chapter 16

San Sebastián, September 2014

Pip kicked hard to propel herself through the water as she swam fifty metres offshore. She was midway through her daily laps and it felt joyous. She'd attempted surfing. Many times. Jack had tried for years to teach her. But nothing compared to the feeling of water against your bare skin.

Pip loved the way her lungs filled with oxygen and started to burn as she took as many strokes as she could with each breath. She could feel the steady flutter of her kick. Three kicks to every stroke. She'd always found comfort in the regular rhythm of swimming. The tension and hurt laced through her body since the southern summer seemed to have subsided—one stroke at a time.

This temperamental nook of the Bay of Biscay had become Pip's stomping ground between shifts at Azure. As most residents of San Sebastián laid low and enjoyed the afternoon siesta, she took the opportunity to hit the waves when there were fewer boards to contend with. Today, it was blowing a strong southerly so Pip kept her elbows high and her stroke short to avoid being clipped by the chop in the waves. Some days the chop got so bad it felt like she was swimming in a washing machine. Still, she had not missed a swim since her arrival two months earlier.

Nearing the eastern point of Zurriola, Pip kicked hard to catch the next wave—only ducking at the last minute to avoid a guy who had inadvertently aimed his surfboard at her head. Pip plunged deep into the darkness and felt the water drop five degrees. She shivered in her navy Speedos, cursing herself for not spending some money on a decent wetsuit. It just seemed like a waste of money when she was only going to be in San Sebastián for a few months.

Pip turned to face the shore, floating on her back with her feet forward, arms circling. She considered the city that had been her home for the past two months. It was still a shock to see ornate five- and eight-storey sandstone buildings—the tall, elegant townhouses known as 'Donostia's ladies'—standing shoulder to shoulder along the waterfront promenade. It didn't look like anywhere else she'd been in Spain, and the locals would probably say that was because San Sebastián was more Basque than Spanish; Donostia was the Basque name for the city.

Looking back at the beach, she eyed the breakwater with massive black concrete blocks the size of cars piled high to break the natural sweep of the bay. She'd been surprised to learn from kitchenhands that the sand was all trucked in, was held in place by the breakwater, and that the popular surfing beach was not a beach at all.

The sun was behind her in the bay and her feelings softened along with the light. The sandstone buildings with their slate roofs and curved wrought-iron balconies had a femininity to them—a softness. The ironwork was almost botanical. She felt fortunate to have washed up in such a beautiful part of the world. A beautiful *baroque* part of the world, she amended wryly, recalling her early days in the city.

'Baroque,' Eduardo had barked at her on her second day on the petit four station at Azure. 'Donostia is baroque. We need this to represent Donostia.'

Pip had looked down at the elaborate black piping she was meant to fashion on a chocolate biscuit the size and depth of her thumbnail and wondered what the hell she was doing trying to pipe a wrought-iron balcony onto a biscuit. She had to make one hundred of them, each exactly the same. She was up for the challenge, but she had no idea what the chef was talking about.

'What is Donostia?' she'd whispered to Pedro, the handsome section chef.

'It's the Basque name for San Sebastián,' he'd replied. 'We don't call our city San Sebastián in this kitchen. That name is only for tourists.' He'd said it with an edge, but had winked at her before turning to check on the manchego *macaron* being soldered together by the equally new and hopeless kitchenhand beside her. Pip couldn't help noticing the length of Pedro's dark eyelashes and the smile that reached his dark brown eyes. Best to concentrate on the weird biscuit balconies.

Eduardo may have barked *baroque* at her for days but she'd never paid much attention to history at school and didn't really understand what he meant. The only time she'd heard the word *baroque* bandied about was in her year eight music class. Something about harpsichords and bassoons? Or was it oboes?

Enough of the daydreaming. The tide was coming in, right-hander waves were picking up with the southerly and she could feel it whipping across her shoulders. Pip dropped further into the water to keep warm. She shivered, but suspected it had more to do with adrenaline than the cool water. She started swimming again. It was time to get to shore.

She was feeling excited because she'd been invited to present a dish she'd invented to Eduardo and the entire creative team at Azure tonight, during the staff meal before service. If it was any good, they'd consider incorporating it into the menu. It was the highest honour someone could bestow on a kitchenhand. Pip thought it unlikely she'd succeed, but she'd set out to blow them away with something original. In fact, it was inspired by her daily swim at this very beach. She'd asked Pedro last week for the Basque translation of 'the mighty ocean'. She knew better than to use a Spanish phrase in these parts. So *Abiega Ozeano* it was. She just hoped Pedro wasn't taking the piss—it was nerve-racking enough trying to get the technical elements right.

Pedro had moved her on from the petit four station after one week. 'Too easy for you,' he'd said with a nonchalant shrug and assigned her to the dessert station, where things got interesting. There she'd mastered making *jamon* and egg ice cream using dry ice, diffused a mushroom and balsamic caramel emulsion to drizzle on a plate and dehydrated thousands of paper-thin slices of apples, pears and radishes to scatter across the tops of the ice cream. She'd extracted the compounds from the juice of apples, frozen the liquid to separate the water and then reconstructed the pure juice with gelatine, lichen and yoghurt to make glossy bright green 'apple spheres'. She had also spread long sheets of the local elderflower honey, dehydrated the sheets until they went brittle and turned them into a toffee crunch to act as the 'soil' under the ice cream and apple spheres.

Eduardo and Pedro told her she was not to think of herself as preparing plates of desserts: she was 'assembling landscapes' or 'daily montages'. Eduardo's English was excellent and he talked a lot about nostalgia for the food of his childhood: 'the perfect crisp apple', 'the thickest, creamiest ice cream', 'a sweet red toffee apple at the fair'. Every day for weeks Pip deconstructed Eduardo's Basque dream and rebuilt it on a white plate. Or a sheet of slate. Or a hand-hewn bowl made of ancient oak. This meticulous presentation was so unlike the simple French home-style fare Dan served up in Hobart.

She was surprised and pleased in the first week how much she had to concentrate to keep up. At the same time, Pip couldn't help wondering if simplicity was perfection, why were they working sixteen hours a day to deconstruct it?

While the produce seemed to be the best available locally, Pip noticed the wastage right through the different sections. She had a prime view of the area where they prepped and plated the mains. Species of squid she didn't recognise, mackerel, scallops—the trays were so abundant with shiny seafood that the kitchen felt like a slaughterhouse some days. A side of spring lamb would be butchered from the vertebrae to the top ribs for the tender cutlets, but the backstraps and lower ribs were tossed aside. A prime shoulder of aged beef would be sectioned and cooked in a *sous vide*. All the meats, veals, fresh fish, chicken breasts would be sliced into perfect sections and then cryovaced in plastic. Pip could understand the hype about cooking meat at the perfect temperature, but when she had asked Eduardo about all the food wastage he was dismissive, saying it went to a charity in the old part of town. When Pip asked him the following week why it was necessary to use so much plastic, and if they couldn't find an alternative method to *sous vide*, she was met with stony silence.

The dozen chefs in her section had stopped moving for a moment.

Pip thought she was about to get the sack, but she ploughed on optimistically: 'Eduardo, the oceans are full of rubbish. I see it every day when I swim. Plastic suffocates the fish and this stuff is everywhere. Do you really need to use it?' Eduardo had curled his lip, shrugged his shoulders, then turned and left the kitchen. He'd clearly understood her point, but the perfect slice of veal was worth more to him than the oceans.

Dan would be mortified, Pip thought. She thought back to the thrifty Hobart kitchen and nose-to-tail approach. Eduardo's kitchen took only the best part of each ingredient, and tossed the rest. At Azure, a thimbleful of apple essence was extracted from the local cultivar and the pulp went in the bin. They didn't even compost. Crazy.

'Molecular gastronomy. That's not even a real thing, is it?' she'd needled Pedro one day when all five dessert station cooks were in the test kitchen being shown by Eduardo how to make a strawberry and oak bark emulsion. 'All food is made of molecules. It's not even a proper science.' She'd noticed Pedro stiffen in his white apron and chef's hat, but then he had shrugged and walked away, though he'd turned and winked at her over his shoulder. At least he had a sense of humour about it all—the other chefs were so damn earnest; pompous, even.

Pedro had disappeared through automatic sliding doors into the climate-controlled spice room. After a minute, he poked his head out, and beckoned to Pip.

Joining him, Pip found herself in an oversized larder. The lino floor was bright green, and the stainless-steel racks were filled floor to ceiling with neatly labelled plastic takeaway containers.

She walked over to one wall and started reading the labels aloud: 'Ajwain, akudjura—'

'That's Australian.'

'Never heard of it.' Pip continued: 'Alexanders, alkanet—'

'For red colour.'

'Right. Never heard of that either. Alligator pepper! Should I even ask? Allspice—I've used that before, when cooking Chinese. Angelica, anise, anise hyssop—is there a big difference between the two? Who has two different types of anise?' Pip went on, mesmerised. '*Artemisia* . . . wormwood. I know that one because my mum grows herbs. She plants it near the chook pen.'

'Chook?' Pedro looked confused.

'Sorry: chickens. Anyway, Mum swears it keeps the lice off them.'

Pedro lifted two plastic containers off the shelf. In the first were dried twigs, in the second a ground powder. He said: 'We use this herb to flavour liqueurs. Have you ever heard of absinthe? Makes you hallucinate.'

Pip gave a chuckle. 'It sounds all very Harry Potter.'

He held up a silky silver stem of *Artemisia* and the fine hairs shimmered under the down light. Pip could smell the familiar stalky smoky woodiness—far sweeter than sage—and remembered the old recipes she'd found in the copper pots. She should ask Megs to send her a copy. They were still sitting in the specimen jar, shoved in a box somewhere in Megs's shed. Along with her sadness.

Pedro dimmed the lights a little and when Pip looked up at the ceiling a delicate curled feather danced across the white. Pip watched delicate patterns stretch across the wall—reminding her of wedding lace she would likely never wear. Pedro moved the stem, and it swirled across the roof and green floor, wrapping around her legs. There was no need for *Artemisia*, or absinthe. Pip felt for a moment she was stuck in a kaleidoscope.

Pedro whispered as he watched the feathery strands twirl across the ceiling. 'Artemisia. Mother of Herbs, the ancients used to call her. Strong. Bitter. Beautiful.'

'Why do you have it in a restaurant, if it is bitter?'

'Pip.' He still pronounced it 'Peep' and she found it sweet. 'Have you not learned anything here with us? Food is about nostalgia.' Pedro gave her a disappointed look and switched the light back to full strength. 'A tiny speck is meant to increase appetite, get the digestion happening. Great for a restaurant! And goodwill. Hallucinogenic. Antibiotic. The witches used to say that wearing a sprig would ward off the evil spirits. It is powerful too. Witches brewed it to boost fertility. So you see, something bitter and dangerous can also bring a new life. New perspectives.'

Pip looked hard at the green floor and tried not to cry. Was there something in the thousand containers here in the spice room that could wash away her bitterness? She shivered. Sixteen degrees was way too cold. She left the spice room. Fast.

Pip was starting to feel cold on her final lap of Zurriola, thinking about that afternoon in the spice room with Pedro: green floors, *Artemisia* . . .

She was interrupted by a familiar slicing through the waves over her left shoulder. Dammit! It was too late. Pip turned to hear an angry volley of incomprehensible words bouncing across the water. She tried to duck-dive but the fibreglass surfboard clipped her shoulder and sprang back as the rider fell sideways to pull off the wave and jerk the board back to avoid injuring her. This oceanic collision was all happening too fast. They were both dumped by a right-hander and the rubber cord, board and legs became tangled as both Pip and the surfer tried to figure out which way to the surface. Water filled Pip's nostrils, her ears, and her mouth was bitter with the taste of the salt. Still underwater and feeling like she was in a washing machine spin cycle, Pip opened her eyes, caught a glimpse of light and kicked hard to get to it and push her head above the swell. Her lungs were burning, her ears ached and her legs felt weak. Her shoulder hurt where the surfboard had clipped it. But she broke free of the surface, mucus and water streaming from her nose, trying to catch her breath. The errant surfer was back on his board, paddling away from her with not even a backward glance to see if she was okay. She kicked her legs hard and smacked the top of the water.

The strong taste of salt was so intense Pip couldn't wipe it with several swipes of her tongue and a mouth filling with saliva. Was it possible to have degrees of salt? The blow to her shoulder had made her feel a bit woozy but Pip focused on the idea that the salty water of the D'Entrecasteaux Channel was much sweeter. And softer. She remembered clambering onto the sandstone ledges around Stinkpot and North West Bay, and collecting the piles of salt left there when the water had evaporated. The salt on her tongue right now, at Zurriola, could clear your throat. Like eucalyptus oil. It was *that* strong.

Pip stopped drifting and started a full-throttle freestyle to shore. That's it, she thought. I'm lacking that intense saltiness in my dish. It needs to fill the mouth with dryness, and then the sweetness and vegetables will take it away. It needs to be an assault on the palate. I've been too soft. My dish lacks punch. I've been a complete wuss.

With that realisation, she used a slow six-beat kick and strong steady stroke to the end of the breakwater before bodysurfing to shore.

Tonight, she was going to blow Eduardo, Pedro and the whole Azure team away with her take on Zurriola.

Chapter 17

Château de Boschaud, Midsummer 1487

Artemisia looked at the sugared coriander seeds spread across the larder floor and sighed at the mess. She slipped the gift from Andreas back into her pocket to open later and used the small willow broom to sweep up the seeds. Cleanliness was next to godliness in the abbot's book and she'd get the full purple-grape-faced wrath—and perhaps fist—if he were to burst in now, as he was wont to do on occasion. Usually when she was at her busiest. She looked at the sheets of parchments with the latest orders and accounts and tried to think when the best time to approach Lord Boschaud would be. The payments were due soon—along with the taxes to the royal court—and who knew when he would next take his mounts to battles, jousts and bloody tourneys in the north? She really didn't have time for this today—not when there was a banquet to prepare.

She started to smile. But if not today, then when?

Artemisia popped a few of the sugared seeds into her mouth and sucked as she contemplated her dilemma. Her mind buzzed from the sugar and she started crunching the toasted seeds between her teeth to release the *citron* flavour. The seeds would improve her breath and calm the nervous humours churning deep in her belly. She should tell Emmeline and Hildegard to harvest the untamed fluffy rows of coriander planted alongside companions anise, sweet woodruff and chervil before it overtook the beds. The soft stems were scattered with arms of tiny pink buds straining to reach the sun. The herbs had run to seed early this midsummer and they'd need to put half aside for when the soil warmed next spring, and toast the others above the coals. They should have enough to see them through the autumn before they needed a sack from the *épicier.*

Artemisia sucked on another seed, allowing the sugar to melt on the tip of her tongue. The sugar was infused with a slight liquorice flavour and she pictured the layout of the *épicier*'s tiny family market shop in the village square where brown sacks overflowing with seeds and spices of all hues of yellow and green—turmeric, coriander, mace, poppy, sandalwood, fennel, yellow and brown mustard, black pepper, cumin and caraway—jostled for space on a plain slab of oak to the side. Beside the sacks was a large locked oak box in which the de Vitriacos kept their most expensive spices, like cubeb, mastic, spikenard and sumac. Underneath, a dozen bags of sugar for the candied spices leaned against oversized sacks of ground cinnamon, anise, black pepper, salt and dried ginger. The front of the shop was a simple pop-up wooden awning, polished with beeswax until the cherrywood shone and every ripple and vein could be seen.

Standing at the shopfront every market day beside a large set of scales was Alba de Vitriaco, Andreas's mother, stout of shoulder and breast but with the same caramel skin and ivory teeth as her son. Alba's eyes squinted just a little as if she was always laughing and her crow's-feet spread deep and wide. Emmeline accompanied Artemisia through the cobblestoned alleys of the village every market day. First to the *bouchier*'s lane where the blood ran down the paths, past the stalls with sheep's heads, boars and offal to their man at the far end. Here were the finest legs of hog and sides of beef in the valley. Next was the *boulanger*'s, to confirm supply of the fluffiest white rolls and the harder black bread for the servants and monks. Depending on the season, they may stop for capon, pheasant or quail, or visit the mushroomer for a basket of morels. Friday was the day for fishmongers and Artemisia was sure to get the finest trout and carp—never the chewy dried cod or herring brought from the far north.

On the last market day of spring, she had the fattest of four black eels for the princely sum of four francs wrapped in cheesecloth and curled up at the bottom of her basket as though they were asleep. Lord Boschaud was touring, so these eels were for the sole pleasure of Abbot Roald. He preferred them cooked in the southern style of St Vincent, with pomegranate seeds, orange peel, lemon, rosemary, ground cloves, cardamom and ginger. But as she reached the stall and unpeeled the cloth for Alba to squeeze the flesh, Alba declared she must make *torta di anguille* and set about scooping dried figs, a pinch of saffron threads, pine nuts, ground ginger, cinnamon and black pepper from the sacks until she made a tiny cheesecloth parcel tied up at the corners.

'Here.' She handed it across the counter. 'Make the pastry, cut the eel into two-fingerwidths and boil them a little with almond milk. Add two full handfuls of dark spinach mixed with raisins and a bit of sugar, and soften it with verjuice.'

Alba dropped the spice parcel into Artemisia's hand and continued, 'I'll write the recipe and send it with Andreas.' She looked Artemisia dead in the eye and smiled.

Emmeline coughed and turned to watch the filthy children in rags slinking behind the slow carts that were bumbling over the cobblestones, hoping for an apple, pear or loaf of bread to drop.

The butcher's frail wife, Madame Deniau, sauntered up to the spice stall with her squat maid following behind carrying a squalling baby.

Artemisia and Emmeline nodded and stepped aside for her to make her purchase. Artemisia's stomach started to contract and turn as she yearned to reach out for the chubby child and press his tiny face to her chest to dry his tears.

Alba leaned over the counter and pinched the cheek of the baby. 'And what is wrong with this bonnie babe?' she asked.

'The gums are as raw as a kidney. And just as bloody. Screamed the whole rotten lane down last night, he did.' Madame Deniau sniffed and looked at the sky. 'Anyway, I must be moving. Master Deniau would like another two sacks of the good salt by the morrow.' She started to walk on, stepping past Artemisia and Emmeline without acknowledging them, as if they were stray dogs.

'Wait, Madame Deniau—if I may.'

The butcher's wife turned, her nose twitching in annoyance.

'One moment, Madame de Vitriaco, if you will humour me,' said Artemisia softly.

Alba's eyes twinkled as she raised an eyebrow.

'Madame de Vitriaco, could you please wrap some cloves, salt, turmeric and mace with a little of your dried rosemary and a few drops of the chamomile oil?'

The quartet watched Alba bustle behind the counter and prepare a tiny bundle, trying it up in the softest linen before she leaned over and pressed it to the howling child's gums. The noise stopped at once, replaced with loud suckling.

'*Merci*, Madame de Vitriaco', said the butcher's wife with a curt nod. She turned away once more, indicating with a flick of her head for her maid to follow at once.

Artemisia wasn't upset—she'd had a lifetime of people not noticing her.

Past Alba, Artemisia spied Andreas unloading his terracotta pots from his cart in the back courtyard behind their shop. Purple wisteria flowers hung low over a loggia, and espaliered lemon and lime trees climbed the walls. Balls of lavender and rosemary were tucked in each corner and dark tufts of thyme and marjoram stretched their arms wide across cobblestones. There was a wrought-iron table set for two and for a moment she imagined taking her *porée*—with perhaps a fresh white roll and a slice of ham—for breakfast before she lifted the awning for business.

Artemisia caught Alba's eye and she blushed.

'That was kind of you,' said Alba. 'You were good with the bonny lad.'

'It was nothing,' said Artemisia, swatting the kind words away. She wasn't used to compliments.

'To you, perhaps,' Alba said. 'But deep down every mother wants the best for her son . . .' She gave a knowing smile as an embarrassed Artemisia yanked Emmeline away by the elbow and turned the edge of her foot on a filthy wet cobblestone in her haste.

Artemisia's heart beat with a blend of hope and confusion as she hobbled away from the shop. Could it be that Alba would welcome the likes of Artemisia—a lowly cook—behind the shopfront and in her courtyard?

Chapter 18

San Sebastián, September 2014

Pip jogged up the dim alley beside the low sandstone villa that housed Azure, thankful for her comfortable navy sneakers with inner soles for extra support. The shifts were long and it was a killer if you didn't have good shoes. She'd learned that the hard way in her first week at the restaurant. Working full-time was a completely different kettle of fish to being a part-time kitchenhand and the shoes weren't the only adjustments she'd had to make. As staff, she was forbidden from entering the villa via the grand oak double doors that swung open to welcome the cavalcade of paying guests that swooped in from around the world. They booked months in advance to sample the four-hundred-euro, ten-course degustation menu for lunch or dinner. Her entry to Azure was via a discreet utilitarian wooden door nestled into the stone wall at the back corner of the building.

Pip entered, deposited her daypack in her locker, washed her hands and collected her whites—stiff from the starch—and went through the process of what she now affectionately termed 'scrubbing in' at a long trough. If only Megs could see her now! Hands up, clean from her elbows down, she leaned against the swinging door and entered the prep kitchen.

If the outside of Azure was a soft baroque symphony of sandstone, slate and wrought iron, inside the kitchen was a cross between an operating theatre and contemporary art gallery. In a room large enough to house a twenty-five-metre swimming pool there were five stainless-steel galley kitchens organised in formation, each with two large gas cooktops, ovens and severe overhead extractor fans that would be at home in a factory. Metres of wide benchtops were set in sharp military-style rows with a collection of at least twenty copper pots and pans graded by size suspended above. Pip was sure Azure's prep kitchen was big enough to cater for an airline. There were at least a dozen people, mostly blokes, in chefs' whites standing at each station. Movement for each shift took place in two-metre-square zones. To step outside your zone was a sackable offence, unless requested by the head of your station. The industrial feel was softened by a series of bright red, green, blue and yellow old-style globes draped artfully in the centre of each station using a simple black cord. Dramatic silver laminate splashbacks were indented with a Moorish mosaic. There were high windows to let the daylight stream in (but prevent nosy tourists peeking inside) and bounce around the shiny surfaces in the kitchen, and a lower row of modern stained-glass blocks in apple greens and reds set into heavy wooden doors marking the entrance to the service area.

'You ready, Pip?' Pedro whispered in his deep liquorice voice.

Despite her scepticism, Pip had decided that cooking at Azure was the closest she would get to alchemy. At her time on the *pintxos* station she had seen the local tapas reinvented. There was no sign of sliced baguettes and toothpicks. Instead, bread was sliced to less than one millimetre, drizzled with oil and baked until each round looked like a potato crisp. Once cooled, they were topped with a pickled anchovy, smoked caperberries and miniature quenelles of a sweet red capsicum and garlic sorbet. Or the perfect tiny ice cream cone the size of her little finger, made from malsouqa pastry and filled with the creamiest *Bacalao*—salted cod—and topped with an emulsion of reduced Pedro Ximénez. Or the dish of raw mackerel carved into thumb-sized pieces with the scales intact and a silver glimmer, set into an autumnal mushroom broth with dried thyme and a sprinkle of cinnamon and scattered with the local *zizas*—chanterelles—delicate droplets of glossy pine nut emulsion and scattered with fresh thyme and fern shoots gathered from the nearby mountains.

While she worked to plate up her dish, she felt the sweat gathering on the back of her neck. She bit into a baby carrot and then a bright pink radish and enjoyed the crunch. Sure enough, she could taste the iodine Pedro had spoken about as he picked over a tray of root vegetables. Salty mist that lay trapped between Donostia's beaches and the mountains, hanging in the valleys, infusing the vegetables and concentrating the flavours. It was this blend of saltiness and sweetness that she wanted to capture. It was time for her to plate up *Abiega Ozeano*.

First up, she took one of the limestone tiles on which they served entrees and rubbed it with olive oil till it glistened. She didn't want her dish looking like it was on a dirty floor. She added some Galician seaweed that she'd set in a thin talo batter so it was nice and crispy, some shaved lemon rind and chopped parsley for extra punch. To get some crunch onto the plate, Pip had rolled chunky squares of soft goat's cheese in eggplant and garlic ash and baked it so it looked like Zurriola's jagged shoreline. She leaned in and smelled the smokiness. For her splash of the ocean, Pip painted sheets of obulato, a transparent film made from potato extract, with squid ink. She then baked this until it rolled and went hard and crunchy, and then she plated up her rolling splash of the waves. Next, she placed glossy red spheres of salsa she had made yesterday with a reduction of tomato, capsicum, oregano, red onion and black pepper. Pedro had helped, adding some smoked paprika from the trusty spice room. She'd then let the salsa cool and finished the spherification using some gelatine. She was thrilled with the perfect red globes. Lastly, she scattered translucent slivers of smoked eel, raw tuna and *jamon* on the plate. Then she sprinkled the lot with a fine orange powder made from cayenne pepper and ground saffron. Again, that was Pedro's suggestion from the spice room.

After two hours Pip finished the dish and her whole team was gathered around cheering. Her plain grey T-shirt was stuck to her back and her crisp white apron was now rumpled and stained with black ink and red streaks. She wiped away a piece of hair that had escaped from her ponytail and noticed that she had orange sprinkles on the wisps of hair floating in front of her eyes. She must look a complete mess. Pedro stood at the end of the long bench, pristine in his whites, grinning like a proud uncle. He gave her a wink as she held the plate aloft and walked past the clapping and cheering staff, who had formed a guard of honour, through the swinging wooden doors to Eduardo's table.

It was just past 11.30 pm and she was finishing wiping down her section, polishing the stainless steel so there were no streaks when the sun hit the benchtops at dawn. Her calves ached and her lower back felt a little stiff. Adrenaline was still flowing through her body. Despite the aches and niggles, she felt amazing. And just a little proud. Pedro wandered over with two champagne glasses and a bottle of '04 Pierre Peters, smiling as he poured a glass for them both.

'The sommelier sends his regards. He wants to congratulate you. Eduardo also sends his congratulations. He especially loved the tart crunch of the goat cheese against sweet salsa. The slivers of eel also impressed. The masterpiece, however, was your wave. Genius.' He grinned and held out a glass: 'This was left over from their little party.'

He raised his left eyebrow as he poured the fizz.

'*Salut.*' They clinked glasses and the buzz matched her mood—fine bubbles.

She sent a quick text to Megs with a photo of her dish. *My dish was a hit! Tell my niece I'm a super-chef.*

Pip was surprised to get a response immediately. *Looks amazing! Well done. Only cooking in this house is super-omelettes made by super-Will.*

The emergency meals Pip had filled their freezer with before she left must have run out.

Pip shot back a quick text: *I'll get Dan to drop off some more supplies at the end of the week. My treat. P x*

The reply was immediate. *No need. We'll be fine. Besides I love omelettes and scrambled eggs. Will even added some herbs and parmesan this week. Getting fancy!*

Even from a distance her sister was bossy. Pip replied: *Too late, already ordered it. Let me know when it arrives. X*

She'd send Dan an email with the pics of *Abiega Ozeano* and a bit of news about the kitchen when she was back at her bedsit. Pip was sure he wouldn't mind packing up some veggie-loaded soups and mains for Megs and dropping them off before work one day. She'd send him her credit card details too—and a budget! Perhaps they could work out some kind of fortnightly delivery. Not too much, or it would drive Megs nuts. Just enough to help out a bit while Pip was still away.

Still, it sounded like Will was doing an amazing job making sure there was always a cooked dinner on the table. He must be shattered. Megs and Will were always in sync. The perfect couple. Pip paused, listening to her aching heartbeat.

No, she scolded herself. Tonight she should celebrate.

'Hey, Pedro,' she said, 'do you want to go out for *pintxos*? We could go to that place over at the Gros with the *pulpo*.'

'Sure. Let's take my scooter. It will be quicker and it's a little cold, yes?'

'Fine by me. You got a spare helmet?'

'Of course.' Pedro grinned as they stepped out the side door and the moon cast warm light against the sandstone wall opposite. Caught in the light, Pedro's caramel skin and dark hair glowed.

The evening chill had well and truly settled in for the night and Pedro offered Pip his black leather jacket. It hung slightly loose against her shoulders and she hoisted herself onto the scooter and wrapped her arms around his waist. She snuggled in, telling herself it was to avoid the wind in her face. Pedro felt warm and underneath his light cotton jumper she could feel a tight set of abs. She smelled revolting and sweaty, she knew, but Pedro smelled like garlic, smoked paprika and cloves and she wanted to hold on a little tighter.

Pip leaned against Pedro's back and zoned out as they weaved through narrow alleyways and along cobblestone streets. She felt a rush of excitement, but also uncertainty. She'd produced a beautiful dish and mastered some tricky techniques, but now what?

She didn't notice they'd pulled up outside the bar until Pedro said: 'Wake up, sleepy head. Celebration time.'

She was strangely disappointed the ride was over and she had to peel away from his warm back.

'Let's go,' said Pedro, leaning his scooter against the wall.

They pushed through a tiny wooden door with a thick oak beam set above. It would be difficult to get through that door if you were any taller than Pedro, who was just shy of six foot. Her dad would have to duck. Jack too.

'I'll get us some beers,' Pip said as they entered the crowded, noisy bar. 'You order the seafood, okay? Make sure you get the *pulpo*—and the anchovies, if they still have the fresh ones. And whatever else is running this week. I'm starving.' She headed towards the bar to order the local Gross craft ale she preferred. Such a great beer, such a terrible name. It was almost a challenge to order it!

'Philippa Arnet? Pip, is that you?' said a familiar Canadian drawl.

She turned and saw the big bearded bear who was her former lecturer, Tom Green, in front of her. His gut seemed smaller but he was still a giant. Six foot five? Six? she wondered for the hundredth time.

'Oh. My. God. It *is* you, Pip. I didn't know you were coming to the conference. I didn't see the précis for your paper. This is exciting. So you're finally writing it all up. Got some good data to share with us all, hey?' His grin was as broad as his shoulders and his eyes were sparkling.

Pip could see Pedro leaning over the end of the bar, ordering some food in his native Basque tongue, sending her quizzical glances. 'Hi, Tom, great to see you.' She wrapped her arms around him. Her hands only just met on the other side. Pedro was still staring at her, rather nervously, she thought. 'What conference? No, I've been working here for about two months, I—'

'Oh,' Tom boomed as he cut her off. 'So you're working down at MerCon. How can you not know about the conference? They're hosting it. Who's your supervisor there? Bo? Jean?'

'No, no. I'm not working with a lab. I'm working in a kitchen; I'm cooking at Azure. You know, the Michelin-starred restaurant.' Was she puffing her chest a little?

Over the other side of the noisy bar Pedro raised an eyebrow as if to say, *You okay?* She nodded at him.

'A kitchen? What? Did you say cooking?' Tom tilted his head sideways, confused. 'Like a chef or something? What happened to your PhD?' His face darkened a little. 'I really hope you haven't quit, Pip.' He fixed her with a narrow gaze.

Her happy buzz from champagne and exhilaration was abruptly extinguished.

Tom leaned in closer and whispered in her ear: 'I can't help but think that's a waste of a good brain, Pip. Don't throw it away.' She could feel his warm breath on her cheek and caught a faint cloying smell of smoke and beer.

She glanced again at Pedro, who was still watching them.

Tom followed her gaze. 'So, you ditched that down-home farm boy of yours, I presume. That why you're cooking in the kitchen? Chasing Mr Dark and Mysterious over in the corner there?'

'No, you've got it all wrong.' Why was she being so defensive? What was she trying to prove? She was good at lots of things—it was just that nobody she knew considered them important.

Except, perhaps, Pedro.

'We're out for a drink to celebrate,' she explained. 'I was invited to present a dish and I called it The Mighty Ocean—*Abiega Ozeano.*' She was getting the Basque accent right, at last.

Tom's eyes were already wandering around the room; he fixed on a blonde with long hair. Some things didn't change. Pip knew he'd been married once, in his early twenties, to a fellow lab rat, but it hadn't worked out and he'd moved to a research post in Tasmania. 'As far away from Vancouver as you can get,' he'd liked to joke. 'Best way to get someone out of your mind. Switch countries. Forget about it.'

Pip tried to get his attention. 'So, you should come have dinner at Azure. I can get you a good table.' She would be happy to show him her new hard-won skills.

Before Tom could respond, Pedro approached with a silver jug of beer—damn, she'd forgotten to order the beer—two glasses and a plate of grilled *pulpo.*

Pip introduced the men and explained to Pedro, slowly, that she was talking about her dish. It was difficult to hear over the blaring music and loud voices.

Pedro beamed and half-shouted: 'It was great. She should be very proud. Eduardo, the boss, really enjoyed it. Sent it to Creative to see if they can modify it for the menu.'

'I see,' said Tom, looking Pedro up and down. Whereas Pedro was slender and tanned, Tom was tall, pasty and barrel-chested and sported a hipster beard. Confidence oozed from every pore. Once Tom had finished sizing up Pedro, he ignored him and turned his focus back to Pip. 'So, Pip. This it? Throwing in all that hard work to make bloody squid ink look like water? Years of chemistry and zoology and *this* is how you apply it?'

Pip could feel her face burning with humiliation. She was used to Tom being blunt, but rarely was he so rude. She was feeling a bit clammy standing shoulder to shoulder with everyone squeezed into this tiny bar. The heavy legs of dried *porc Basque* hung in rows from the ceiling and mingled with the charred smells of grilled octopus and mackerel.

To avoid responding, Pip sculled her beer and held out her glass to Pedro for a refill from the shiny jug. When in doubt: scull. At least she could tell her parents her university years weren't entirely wasted. She seethed at Tom's dismissal, but it was nothing she hadn't asked herself already.

Tom must have seen he'd overstepped the mark. He leaned in closer, dropping his voice to a whisper. His hand lingered in the small of her back. She hoped Pedro couldn't see it. 'Come down to the conference tomorrow, Pip. I'll get you a pass. It starts at ten. Let me show you what you're missing.' With that he kissed her cheek, pulled her towards him and hugged her for a moment, pressing his chest tight against hers for an extra beat.

Pip didn't get to answer Tom before he turned and walked to the door, bending his head sideways to navigate the exit, without looking back. She turned back to see Pedro hunched over his beer at the bar, picking at the *pulpo* with a toothpick. Pip felt conflicted. Should she go to the conference and meet up with Tom? Did she still want a marine biology research job? The opportunity at Azure had made her realise she was far more than her degree.

Pedro looked up and met her gaze as she stood slowly sipping her beer, his dark eyes questioning. Her stomach fluttered a fraction. Pip wondered if he was maybe just a tiny bit jealous.

Chapter 19

Château de Boschaud, Midsummer 1487

Artemisia headed out the kitchen door and bounded up the thick granite stairs in the turret that spiralled up to the banquet hall and private chambers. She lifted her tunic and wondered how many more times she would run up these stairs today. Best not to think about it. As she rounded the first turn, she brushed shoulders with one of the new young chambermaids carrying armfuls of silver goblets and asked, 'Josette, isn't it? Can I help you?'

'Yes, Cook, it's Josette.' She looked at the goblets tucked up in her apron. 'Not much more to go, now. But, thank you . . .' Her voice faded.

'Settling in?'

'Well enough, I suppose,' Josette whispered, but her voice broke. She dipped her head to the opposite wall and tried to wipe away the emerging tears with her shoulder.

Artemisia dropped her voice and patted Josette's forearm. 'Make sure you come down later for *porée*, won't you, child?' Then she took two steps before adding, 'I just thought I'd check the final table settings.' She smiled. 'Are they almost finished?'

'Yes, Cook,' the girl spoke softly as she nodded and scuttled ahead up the stairs to join the older maids, like a lamb seeking the shelter of the flock. Artemisia knew that feeling well—it would be hard to leave her kitchen flock.

The excited chatter of a dozen chambermaids drifted into the stairwell as Artemisia neared the entrance to the banquet hall. A maid was standing in one corner with a basket, scattering armfuls of barley, lavender, white lilies, rose petals and rosemary across the floor. The vaulted ceiling echoed with the clanging of silver and pewter trays, goblets and jugs being set on the royal blue velvet table runners Artemisia had laid out last night. She double-checked the placement of the head table for the bride and groom, where it sat on a plinth along the far wall. A giant new tapestry shimmered, illuminated by shafts of light streaming in from the tiny high windows on the opposite wall. Artemisia paused and leaned against the cold stone wall to catch her breath.

The edges of the tapestry depicted thick brown trunks of an oak forest, with a clearing right in the middle. The clearing was filled with a circle of wild young women dancing with their arms linked, heads thrown back, laughing. Some women had their hair loose down their backs, eyes closed and mouth open as if they were . . . Artemisia blushed, but she couldn't look away. Their skin looked luminous, their hair was threaded with gold and copper and she could almost feel the movement. She noticed to one side a trio of musicians accompanying the dance—harp, lute and fiddle. These women were also naked, with rose-tinted lips and glistening skin, almost dripping with sweat. So this was the mysterious tapestry gifted to the château by the bride's kin in Clinchy? Rumours had been circulating for weeks. Apparently there was a sizeable dowry attached to Rose and Lord Boschaud was most pleased to secure it. He had declared proudly on his return to the château after his betrothal that it was his finest hunting expedition yet. So it was only proper this wedding gift hung in pride of place behind the head table for the wedding banquet. Abbot Roald had objected to the removal of the original tapestry, but Artemisia presumed the good Virgin Mary was now rolled up safely in the store keep in the barn area, forever reading on her flowery mead surrounded by roses, lilies, columbines, hollyhocks and peonies. Where the Virgin Mary was nestled safe inside the garden wall surrounded by saints, these dancing nymphs seemed to have found a different kind of paradise. A couple of maids beat the new tapestry with broomsticks to flatten creases. Plumes of dust clouds appeared with every thud and the girls shrieked, giggled and covered their eyes as they whacked.

Artemisia guessed the lower tables set in a U-shape along the vast oak parquetry were for the village merchants and bankers. Where would Andreas de Vitriaco be seated tonight? she wondered.

A chambermaid rolled a red runner down the middle of each table and placed a dozen giant silver candelabras in the centre. It was going to be a magical evening.

A series of quick heavy footsteps paced into the hall behind her and Artemisia turned to see the grin of Lord Boschaud, his face looking tan against the pale velvet hunting jacket he wore. A successful hunt—or even more successful celebration—Artemisia guessed. The lord's proud smile and twitching shoulders reminded her of the excitable child who could never sit still for lessons.

Behind him, with a face of stone, stood Abbot Roald.

Lord Boschaud clapped his hands. 'At last it is up. In good time for the feast. Look at those happy nymphs—a most generous gift from the Clinchys. Wouldn't you agree, Abbot?'

'Well, I—I hardly think—'

'Marvellous!' Lord Boschaud beamed. 'A prize. Spirited. Like my fair Rose—one can only hope.' He elbowed Abbot Roald in the gut with a friendly chuckle. Then he turned on the heel of his boots, raised his hands and clapped them twice. 'Very good. Very good. Much better than that boorish, buttoned-up Virgin. Sorry, Abbot, I know you have your vows but surely on days like this your God must let you have a little fun.' He laughed again.

'One who is unmarried is concerned about the things of the Lord, how he may please the Lord—'

'Yes, yes. I understand all that,' Lord Boschaud said impatiently. 'You're not going to start one of your lectures now, are you, Abbot Roald? Not today!'

Abbot Roald blanched and started speaking quickly. 'Artemisia, may I ask what you are doing standing around watching other people work? Is it too much for me to ask *you* to work? It is, after all, going to be the finest wedding banquet in the south.'

Lord Boschaud looked at her with curiosity and she noticed shadows under his eyes that she'd missed, distracted by his bonhomie.

'Artemisia?' Her master's voice softened a little as he held his hand up to quiet the abbot.

'M'lord,' she said in reply.

'Everything in order for the banquet?'

'Yes, m'lord.' She took a deep breath and stepped towards him. 'I wondered if I might trouble you for a moment this noon.' Artemisia glanced at the reddening abbot. 'I need to clarify something about the wine accounts—'

The abbot coughed and stepped forward. 'No need to waste your time, m'lord. I simply took it upon myself to order two extra barrels, as Artemisia here could not be trusted to order the correct amount.'

Artemisia forced herself to remain expressionless. It was useless arguing now. She'd put it in a letter to Lord Boschaud later today. Even so, who would take the cook's word over the chaplain's?

The abbot opened his palms to Lord Boschaud. 'We don't want the guests complaining, do we?' He shot an angry look at Artemisia over his shoulder.

'Very well.' Lord Boschaud sounded weary—and more than a little bored at being asked to consider such petty matters today of all days.

Artemisia slowly turned to fully face the men and pulled her shoulders back. She too was weary from working eighteen-hour days but knew it wouldn't do to stir the abbot's temper. His jowls were fleshy and his nose the colour of a strawberry from his beloved Burgundy. The brown robe and red cord strained over his great barrel of a belly.

'Pardon, Abbot Roald.' Artemisia dipped her head and looked at the floor. 'I merely await your instruction. The kitchen is on time and we shall be ready to lay the dressers shortly.'

'May I ask,' Abbot Roald spat, 'if you could repeat what these *entremets* are? I want to be sure they are up to the standard I commissioned.' He glanced at Lord Boschaud. 'We have quite a spectacle planned for you, sir.' Abbot Roald stood so close to Artemisia that she could feel his warm fetid breath against her cheek as he spoke.

'Well, in that case I shall see them now.' The lord grinned, revealing a full set of yellow teeth stained with red wine. He yanked a chair from the table and sat down, waving his wrist to indicate that a pretty blonde maid should fill the goblet set in front of him. She rushed to grab a jug of wine from the corner and filled his cup, but in her haste spilled a few drops on his crushed velvet sleeve.

'Plenty of chances to practise at tonight's banquet,' said Lord Boschaud, beaming as he mopped up the wine with the edge of the tablecloth.

The girl grinned at the lord, then quickly averted her eyes and walked away after a stiff nod and stony glare from the abbot.

Artemisia stepped in. 'I shall fetch them now and place them on the dressers, Abbot,' she said.

Artemisia ran down the stairs and a wall of heat struck her as she entered the kitchen. 'Quick, Jacobus, leave the coals and help me carry the features to the hall.' She stepped into the cold store and lifted a tray of coloured jellies dyed with sunflower, lavender, saffron and bay. There was a tray of white swans, another with hand-sized blue peacocks, yellow hares and green pheasants. Some were dressed with their original feathers. All feet and beaks were covered with the finest gold leaf—applied with eggwhite and a goose feather to great effect.

Artemisia stood with her foot in the larder door to prop it open and handed out platters of jellies to each of the maids, with a warning to tread carefully. Next were simple platters of whole fruit—glossy oranges, apples, lemons and limes—with fresh leaves attached. As they were carried up the stairs they glistened in the sun streaming through the tiny windows of the curved stairwell. Artemisia marvelled at Hildegard's handiwork and longed to bite into the bright green apple, but she knew this too contained a secret. Under the shiny glaze of each replica piece of fruit lay a fine duck liver pâté spiced with the slightest trace of orange rind and cinnamon.

The last of the heavy trays to travel up the stairs with the maids were the gold and pewter platters. On these, Artemisia and Hildegard had shaped a series of pastries and pies from rabbit, capon, pheasant, beef and wild herbs. The finest two were a hare with enormous standing ears lying in a bed of sorrel ready to jump and a pheasant tucked under a hedgerow of laurel and hornbeam. She was thrilled that her efforts looked so lifelike.

Artemisia's favourite, however, was the delicate *entremet* of Château de Boschaud and the pastry garden. Weeks in the making and garnished with the fresh plants she collected at dawn, it was her wedding gift for the fair Rose and her groom. She couldn't wait to see the delight on the young woman's face when she set eyes on this pastry at the banquet.

The stone walls were made of marzipan and pastry, coloured with some squid ink so it looked like the local granite. The orchard was laid out in a grid with box hedgerow cuttings onto which Artemisia had carefully placed some blossoms. Artemisia had harvested flowers throughout the spring and summer—preserving the shape and perfume of delicate pink cherry blossoms and the blush of apples and pears in sugar water on trays in the cold store. The potager had neat rows of sprigs of lavender, rosemary, hyssop, thyme and sage. Her tiny fields were strewn with upright heads of baby wheat, barley and calamus. Jacobus—dear Jacobus—had sat up late into the eve for a month shaping the bench seats, alleys and arbours from chestnut prunings. But her favourite part of the *entremet* were the woods and field she'd re-created just outside the wall. She had a blue stream of jelly with watercress, a wildflower meadow and a tiny stand of *châtaigne*—a chestnut forest—under which she had trimmed down some fungi and moss to make a soft stand of mushrooms. As she leaned down, she could smell an earthy mix of moss, marzipan and cinnamon.

It took ten of the house staff to carry her masterpiece stair by stair so they did not crack the base. Or knock it into the curved wall of the stairwell. Or tip it too far sideways. Next time she'd make it in multiple pieces. Her heart skipped a beat and she felt herself flush as she realised the next one she made would be for her own betrothed. She was already planning a sweet little forest with a lake and collection of woodland animals.

Still blushing, she ushered everyone across to the grand oak dresser on the side wall and rearranged the silverware on the wide shelf so her château and garden would sit in pride of place. Rose and Lord Boschaud would have a prime view. She thanked the maids as they slid the *entremet* onto the bench inch by inch before hurrying back to their tasks. Artemisia remained alone beside her garden, leaning in to look at the delicate blossoms and admire the pretty clumps of sorrel, borage, angelica, fennel and wild celery she placed along the outside of the wall. She lifted the roof of the replica château carefully, checking it was still intact. The three rabbits could be inserted at the last minute—she'd have the minstrels create a diversion.

'And what have we here?' asked Lord Boschaud as he walked over to the dresser and leaned over the garden for a closer look.

'It's an *en*—'

'Stop, I can see what it is. It's lovely.' He directed the same lopsided grin at Artemisia he had as a child. There'd always been a lazy kindness about him. 'Did you make this?'

'Yes m'lord, I—'

'Lord Boschaud.' Abbot Roald stepped in front of Artemisia, cutting her view of the master and digging his back heel hard into her toes. 'If you'll allow me to present you with this replica of Château de Boschaud. A small token of my gratitude and respect. The monks and I wish you and your betrothed Lady Rose every happiness.' He gave a little bow and waved his hand with a flourish.

'Well. I'm sure the young Rose will be delighted. I am deeply honoured. It is the work of a master, not a journeyman. At least it would be—if we didn't have Artemisia.' He nodded in her direction, his messy straw-coloured hair collecting at his shoulder. Artemisia felt a blush rising from the collar of her tunic.

'See to it, won't you, that one of my stewards guard this *carefully* before the banquet. I don't want anyone tipping a jug of ale or platter of meat on this *entremet*. Nothing is to spoil Rose's wedding. It is her first, after all.' He took a breath before adding under his breath 'Who knows what could happen at the next battle?' Lord Boschaud straightened himself and looked from the abbot to Artemisia.

The abbot looked like he had sucked a lemon.

Lord Boschaud walked past Artemisia and, meeting her eyes, he said with a broad smile: 'Abbot Bellamy would be proud of you, Cook.'

As he left the room, Artemisia gathered her skirts and grinned as butterflies danced in her stomach. *He understood her gift.* There was joy to be had within the château's walls and the garden. Love and devotion.

Artemisia took a deep breath and straightened her tunic and told herself she was being silly, reading too much into a smile. After all, she and the lord rarely conferred over anything outside the accounts. As long as Lady Rose loved the gift, that was all that mattered.

No sooner had Lord Boschaud's footsteps faded down the stairwell than Abbot Roald swivelled to face her. 'I suppose you think you are very clever. Too clever by half.'

'No, Abbot.'

'Do *not* interrupt me.' The abbot's eyes bulged and his face turned the colour of a beet. 'I see you skulking outside these walls. Slacking off your tasks. Don't think I don't see you. You never come to the chapel for absolution. Or confession.'

'Abbot, I—'

'I said do *not* interrupt me.' Abbot Roald's controlled voice had risen to a boom. The maids turned and looked at Artemisia in sympathy before returning to their tasks.

Artemisia could see Abbot Roald was in a lather. Dark patches appeared under his arms and down the front of his chest. Beads of sweat trickled down his bald head and dripped from his earlobes and nose. Artemisia needed to be very careful; she needed her tongue. His dark vicious eyes narrowed and he grabbed her chin, forcing her head up to meet his eyes.

'You. Defying my orders in the kitchen. Making an *entremet* that was not on my list. It is my job to record all the items for this wedding banquet. And as for that little sneaky attempt about the extra wine . . . I *deserve* it,' he blustered. '*I* run the household. His lordship is never here.'

Abbot Roald stabbed his chest with his thumb. 'I'm in charge around here. How many times do you need to be told?' He dropped his voice and leaned in so his nose was almost rubbing against Artemisia's.

'I'd be very careful if I were you. You have no kin. I see you with that *épicier*, de Vitriaco . . . *I* control all the château's business with the masters of each guild. What business could you have with the *épicier* that doesn't lie under your skirt?'

Artemisia felt clammy as heat spread across her shoulders, chest and head. She wished she didn't colour so easily.

'Yes.' He nodded slowly. 'I have your attention now, don't I?' He pulled his lips back in a sneer to reveal a set of black and yellow rotting teeth.

Suddenly, Abbot Roald took a step back. She watched in horror as he swept her precious midsummer garden to the floor.

She was too shocked to move.

The pastry and marzipan crumbled on impact and a mélange of blossoms and herbs spread across the wide oak floorboards. Artemisia breathed in sharply through her nose, then slid away from the abbot. She gulped down her sobs, struggling to swallow. Abbot Roald yanked her hair with the same arm, and forced her to her knees, pushing her head to the floor—smashing her face into the jelly river. Artemisia lay sprawled across the floorboards—her garden smeared in all directions—as she struggled to sit up. Two moons' work destroyed in an instant. She forced herself onto her haunches.

'Stay there.' He placed his leather boot on her shoulder. 'Clean this up.'

He turned to speak to the chambermaids. 'No-one is to help her,' he ordered. 'Leave. Now.'

Josette gave Artemisia a pained, helpless look—her eyes filled with tears—as she followed the other chambermaids out the door.

Once the women were out of earshot, Roald then turned and kicked his foot deep into Artemisia's belly, the point of his shoe ripping her dress. 'That will teach you some respect. *Pride goes before destruction.*' He gave her a piercing look.

'I'll send a message to Lord Boschaud that the clumsy cook destroyed the centrepiece. No doubt there will need to be a suitable punishment.' Abbot Roald turned on his heel and left the banquet hall.

Artemisia slumped back down onto the floor, gasping for breath and trying to stem the flow of her tears. She was devastated for Lady Rose. She was a chattel, 'twas true enough. But Artemisia had wanted to give her a gift befitting her name. Love. Perfection. Hope. Just as Abbot Bellamy taught Artemisia as a child, she wanted to show Lady Rose that within these walls—and beyond—there was beauty if you looked. Her thoughts hardened towards Abbot Roald. *You like to appear righteous in public, but God knows your heart. What this world honours is detestable in the sight of God.*

She should go downstairs and help Hildegard and Emmeline in the kitchen but first she needed to clean up the mess. Was it possible for her to stand? She tried to rock forward and sit up. She could not even lift her head from the floor, let alone her legs. Artemisia's nerves were as smashed and shredded as the pastry beside her and no amount of violet tea would quell the hot bile churning in her belly. She could taste salt as her tears pooled beside her cheek stuck to the floorboards.

She prayed for the strength to make it through to the evening.

Chapter 20

Camino de Santiago, Spain, September 2014

It was 7 am on a rare Sunday off, and Pip had set off to hike into the foothills that escalated in green waves all the way to the Pyrenees. She was following a well-worn goat track in the middle of a field. There was something humble about it all that reminded her of all those bush tracks she'd hiked with her dad over the years. Narrow trails threading up Mount Macedon, weaving around the towering gums and rogue bracken, grasses and ferns.

Here, in the lower foothills outside Mendiluze, the countryside was cleared and honed for rather intensive agriculture. From her vantage point on the crest where Pedro had parked, she could see wide green stretches of pasture broken up with rows of apple trees and larger chestnut trees.

Pip shook her legs, embracing the crisp autumn mist. The sky was looking pretty dark. What had she been thinking, wearing denim cut-offs? At least she had her trusty woollen hoodie.

Pedro had stopped at her station the night before as she scrubbed down stainless steel with hot water, in a hurry to hit the town for a Saturday night out with her station buddies.

'Hey, Pip. Good job tonight. Heading out?'

'Yep. The Gros. You coming?'

'No, I'm leaving for a hike along the Camino de Santiago near Mendiluze tomorrow. I'm going to do some foraging in the hills before I pop in to the best restaurant in the area.' He raised his eyebrows. 'Tempted?'

'Sure, why not? I've been meaning to do some of the pilgrim's trail. That's what everyone comes here for, isn't it? What time are you leaving?'

'I can pick you up at five-thirty.'

'Ouch.' Still, she was excited about the prospect of a walk. 'Cool, thanks.'

'Bring an overnight bag—and comfortable shoes,' he said, eyeing her filthy trainers. 'We'll do a big walk and I'll show you some of the suppliers and where to get the best herbs. We can stay in the cottage next to my parents' old villa. There's a spare room there for you. I promise dinner will be worth it.' Pip was surprised to see a slight flush on Pedro's face before he turned away.

'Sure, thanks,' she said. 'See you then.'

Pip was still adjusting to the sight of the looming craggy mountain range beyond the foothills capped in limestone. She'd studied the dark shadowy outlines of the Pyrenees when she was doing her laps at the beach at Zurriola. Up close they looked twice as big. Pip wasn't used to tilting her head back to take in a view. It was magnificent.

As she stood gazing at the mountains, the ancient chestnut trees and the trail in front, Pip wondered how her parents were. She pulled her iPhone out and snapped a selfie with the hills as background.

Hiya Dad, Heading on a hike on the pilgrim's trail near Mendiluze today with a colleague. Going mushrooming. Will let you know how it compares. P x

Pedro followed her gaze to the mountains: 'Pretty special, huh? I love this section of the walk, heading into the mountains at this time of year. Should find some good food, too.' He grinned, patting his backpack. 'Right. So before we start, if you hear shooting, don't worry. We'll stop and wait.'

'What for? Someone to kill us?' she joked.

'No. For the shooting to stop.' Pedro laughed. 'It's the pigeons. It's September.' Then, seeing that Pip didn't understand, he clarified: 'They are flying south for the winter. Nice and low—too easy. Hopefully we will have some today.'

'Where? How? Do you have a gun?'

He gave her a look to confirm she was being ridiculous. 'Ah, Pip. Just be patient. We have a long walk ahead. We follow these.' He tapped a worn stone obelisk with a scallop shell carved into it, as if that explained everything.

Pedro strode off in front along a trail cut into pasture before disappearing over a solid wooden stile with another scallop shell nailed to it. They were about to walk through a field full of strange shaggy sheep with fleece to their knees.

'*Idiazabel*,' Pedro called over his shoulder, waving a hand in the direction of the sheep. Pip recognised the name of a sharp crumbly unpasteurised cheese they used at Azure. If she wanted the lowdown she was really going to have to keep up. In the field beyond the sheep she could just make out smaller pastures with semi-circular plywood shelters in each corner and an odd-looking mushroom of straw perched above. In each pasture she could make out a black and pink sow lying down, being suckled by a dozen piglets. All those legs of *porc Basque* dangling along the beams in San Sebastián had to come from somewhere, she guessed.

Up ahead, over the next hill, she saw two people carrying large black backpacks and carrying walking poles.

'They're heading to Santiago, right?'

'Yes, some people walk about seven hundred kilometres. Some even start over the Pyrenees in France. I think it usually takes about twenty days when you join the trail on this side of the border. For some it is just a test of endurance. For others the quest is spiritual. Each pilgrim has their own reason for doing the Camino. My papa always says people walk out their answers. It is just about putting one step in front of the other. Sharing a simple meal with other travellers and a clear sleep in the evenings.'

'That's incredible. Maybe I should do it when I leave San Sebastián.'

Pedro stopped walking and turned back to face her. 'But I thought, you know, after such a positive reception to *Abiega Ozeano,* you'd extend your stay.' He cocked his head to one side and raised an eyebrow. 'You are smart. You have real talent for this new style of cooking, Pip, because you strive for perfection. Isn't that why you came to Spain?'

She paused to sip from her water bottle, uncertain how much to reveal. 'I'm not sure, Pedro. I was failing in the lab'—failing everywhere—'so I wanted to try something completely different. It turns out, I love cooking professionally—I adore it. Although,' she added, 'I think I prefer simple food. The science stuff at Azure just seems . . .'

Pip stopped. She'd already offended Pedro with her opinion of molecular gastronomy.

Pedro shrugged and they started walking side by side.

'The truth is, when I came here, I—well, I was leaving behind a lot. I broke up with my fiancé. Jack. His name is Jack.' She took a swig from her water bottle and kicked a small stone along the path. 'But anyway, I wasn't really sure I wanted to stay in Hobart. Well, I want to finish my doctorate eventually—I'm so close. But my lab work was stalling.' She paused. 'You know when I had those few days off last week, I went to the IMNAC marine biology conference for a couple of days with Tom.'

Pedro frowned. 'The fat Canadian guy we met at the bar?'

A little harsh. 'Tom can be a bit of a clown, but he's a brilliant scientist. He's always been a strong supporter of my research. Anyway, he called last night and he's arranged for a secondment in Paris.'

Pedro shook his head in confusion. 'I don't understand. I thought after the presentation of your dish you were celebrating. That you had decided you wanted to be a chef. Hundreds of people write every week wanting to wash dishes at Azure. For free. And you are going to throw this opportunity away? You don't want to stay in Spain?'

She took a deep breath and glanced at the overcast sky as darkening clouds skated past. Why did every man she liked—especially the darned handsome ones—seem to think they knew what was best for her? Pip replied with a tight smile,

'Well, I do. But I also want to finish my PhD. It's taking forever. I can do some research in France and Tom has arranged for someone to be my co-supervisor. It's an amazing opportunity. I'll be based at the National Museum of Natural History, which means I'll have access to the full benthic invertebrate archives. The shell collections, literature databases—apparently the resources are unbelievable. There's datasets on temperature and other environmental tolerances of *Varicorbula*—I mean, the European clam. Who knows what I'll find?'

'The benth-what?'

'The invertebrates that live in the sediment of the tidal mudflats. But I'm looking at the ones that are not from Tasmania. Those that have moved in and threaten the local environment.'

'Of course. Now I know why you attack your *pulpo* with a vengeance. It is an imposter!' He laughed, but there was an irritated edge to his voice.

'Well, *pulpo* are probably indigenous to this region, so the octopus is fine. I have no idea what's invaded the Bay of Biscay—other than a whole lot of plastic.' She gave him a pointed look.

Pedro nodded, conceding. 'I went once to that museum, as a kid,' he remarked. 'It's in the middle of acres of very beautiful gardens. Jardin des Plantes. I remember a huge entrance hall, several storeys high. It had a glass dome ceiling.' He waved his arms to indicate an extravagant space. 'Anyway, along the middle of this hall was a procession of wild animals. Stuffed animals. They were in pairs, like they were being loaded onto the ark.' Pedro scrunched his nose up. 'There was a giraffe in the middle, looming over them all with huge black eyes. At the front was an elephant with long tusks, flanked by a tiger that looked ready to pounce. Behind the giraffe, all these bears and penguins. It was—how do you say?—creepy.'

'What was creepy? It was just dead animals, like the ones you chop up every day.' Pip was panting now. The sweep of the hills was constant and there seemed to be more ups than downs.

'I have no problem with death; my father was a butcher. It was the pretence. That they were still alive.' He shrugged and took a sip of water. 'But you know, I was only about eight. You do not understand that kind of pretence when you are eight, perhaps.'

Did you ever? Pip wondered.

'Anyway,' she continued, 'it's one of the best research facilities in the world. The maritime section is unbelievable. The resources. I mean, we don't have anything like that in Australia.'

Pedro was expressionless.

'While Tom was there he noticed the Southern Ocean and Tasman Sea mollusc section needed checking and electronic cataloguing. There were some inconsistencies with the database the French shared with IMAS—the institute where I researched in Hobart.'

'I do not understand.'

'I get a gig for three months!' She laughed as she stepped forward, clasped Pedro's fine hands and squeezed them. 'Checking mollusc records and finishing my doctorate. I've been fiddling with the data on my laptop since I went to that conference with Tom and I think I have pinpointed some key patterns. I was so strung out back in Tasmania I couldn't see where I needed to go. But now I can. I'm going to nail it—at least, I hope so,' Pip said a little sheepishly as she dropped his hands.

Pedro nodded in silence and upped the pace. The dirt path ahead was thinning and they had to walk single file. The sun had burned off the mist and she was warming up—it felt beautiful on her back. The hills were so quiet compared with the all-night festivities of San Sebastián. Save for the bleats of a few sheep, the only noise was the crunch of their footfall on the path.

They walked past orchards of apples, rows of gnarly trees with yellowing leaves and branches pruned low for easy picking. In the corner of each orchard stood massive wooden cider barrels the height of a house. Every now and again they would walk past fields with two or three large domes that looked like straw yurts sitting in a corner. Pedro explained this was how the locals stored their hay for the long winters, secured with a simple pole through the middle and a series of sharpened poles shaped like oversized nails, punched horizontally to secure the straw in place. Pip thought they looked a little like the frightening Banksia Men from her favourite childhood story, *Snugglepot and Cuddlepie.*

Pedro squinted, raised his arms and pointed to a dark forested area on a distant hill with a cluster of square white houses topped with sloping terracotta roofs. 'That's where we will finish.'

'It's so pretty. Are you sure that's not snow?' she asked, squinting ahead. She could see sun glinting off the rock cliffs.

Pedro laughed. 'Come on. We've a lot to do before we get there.'

Every kilometre or so, Pedro would stop and lead her off the path into a wood of oak or beech to point out the tiny new growth of the *onddo*—one of the porcini family. She was surprised to discover the most precious fungi—the copper-tinted *onddo beltza*—was almost the size of her foot!

'Here, try some,' said Pedro as he broke one in half. 'They are early this year.'

When she looked doubtful, he ate one on the spot.

'You can carry me to the top if I start vomiting,' she said, laughing.

Into his backpack went some *nìscalo*—red pine mushrooms he ferreted out from under a windbreak—and some chanterelles she recognised from cooking at Azure. In another spot he brushed aside large thistle leaves that looked a bit like an artichoke and plucked the mushrooms sheltering underneath. After harvesting the mushrooms, Pedro then ripped the top fresh leaves of the thistle very gingerly and stuffed them into the backpack too, explaining they would make a delicious soup. And so the afternoon went on as the sun crept higher.

They climbed further and further, passing a village until they came to a small stone villa. Instead of going in the front door, Pedro took her hand and tugged her around the back of the building, where there was a series of stables. Instead of horses, though, each stall was filled with neat woodpiles. Pedro swung his backpack onto the ground and Pip dropped her own.

As she stepped closer to the stalls, she was struck by the irregularity of the piles. Each seemed to be made of a different wood. Some were thick like traditional split hardwood, others slim grey branches. In one stall Pip recognised the mottled silver bark of young chestnut branches and for the second time that day she missed her parents. She admired the twisted branches of grapevines and instantly thought of Jack. How was he doing in Italy? Was he missing her at all? Did he ever wonder if breaking up was a mistake? She closed her eyes for a few seconds. She needed to focus.

Pedro pointed at each stall in turn. 'Oak, chestnut, apple wood, pear, and this is the cherry. This lot here'—he waved his hand at some dark wood—'this is from an old orange grove up the hill a bit. And this birch, very rare, is used sparingly.'

Pip's puzzlement must have been obvious, as he laughed.

'For cooking the meat. Here they use a different wood to complement the flavour of the meat. Now the pigeon is in season, he will only use the apple. For beef, depending on the cut, he may like the sweetness of the chestnut or the strong tannins of the oak. A strong wood for a strong muscle. For the salmon fillets, I think the orange wood is the best. Not too overpowering. And the salmon roe,' he said with a wink, 'you shall have to wait and try.'

'Salmon roe? Are you saying they barbecue fish eggs here? Sounds a bit, um, strange.'

Pedro laughed again and shook his head at Pip. 'Not barbecue—*asador*.'

'Right,' said Pip slowly, hoping that Pedro didn't catch on that she had zero idea of what he was talking about.

'They make the charcoals from the different woods, and then use the charcoal to smoke the meat. Just smoke, a good olive oil and maybe a few herbs. Which reminds me . . .' He bent down and picked up his backpack, urging Pip to do the same.

Pip joked, 'I wonder what eucalyptus would be matched with?'

'I'm sorry?' Pedro screwed up his nose. 'I have only smelled the oil. I'm not sure you could cook with that.' He could be so earnest.

'Um, yeah, it may be a bit strong. But maybe a fillet of kangaroo, or wallaby. Might be a bit too strong with wallaby, but one of the wattles—acacias—might work.'

Pedro smiled. 'Yes, I've heard kangaroo is good. Do you eat it?'

'Well, not often. We should eat more roo than we do.'

Pedro looked confused. 'They are wild, no? You don't farm them.'

'Exactly. Eating roo is like eating your local boar, or the pigeons. Sometimes their population reaches plague proportions and they have to cull—kill them. Why not eat them?'

'I see. Why not indeed? What does it taste like?'

'A little like venison but more earthy. I actually use wallaby mince in my ragout. It's sweeter. Not quite as tough as the roo.'

'I guess all that jumping makes for big chewy muscles,' said Pedro with a chuckle as he touched her elbow and steered her inside a tiny stone lean-to tacked onto the back of a large white villa. 'I think perhaps you have the heart of a Basque. Come, there's someone I want you to meet.'

Pip could feel Pedro's warm hand on the small of her back as he ushered her through the door towards the smell of smoke and charcoal. She was amazed to see the line-up of five impeccable stainless-steel barbecues with a line of extraction fans along the far wall. Between these two planes was a series of complicated systems of pulleys and ropes with grill plates and mesh nets tilted at various angles. It looked far more like the rigging of a racing yacht than a restaurant kitchen. Along the other side of the room ran a bank of new fridges with glass doors and there was a simple stainless-steel bench running down the middle of the room with a dozen pigeons lined up in a row, fluffy brown feathers intact and heads tucked under wings. Lunch.

'Papa!'

'Pedro!' A rotund man with silver hair and a Charlie Chaplin moustache wrapped his arms around his son, kissing him on both cheeks. Then the older man stepped back, looked him up and down, and gave Pedro a poke in the abs. Pip wanted to feel those abs too.

Pedro took off his backpack and fished out large clumps of thyme, oregano and the damp bag of mushrooms. 'Here, Papa, take these. And let me introduce you to my friend Pip. She's the Australian *stagier* at Azure I told you about. The scientist. Pip, I'd like you to meet my father and the second-best cook I know—Telmo.'

'Phht.' Telmo shook his head, tilted it sideways and beamed at Pip. She could see where Pedro had got his charm. 'Scientist, eh? What do you make of Eduardo and Azure?'

'It's incredible. I'd never thought of those textures, those techniques. It's nuts where he gets his flavour combinations. It's art, really.'

'Phht.' Telmo whistled again between his teeth and turned to adjust some rigging and flip a piece of salmon closer to a griller. 'Art. Science. Call it what you want. But it's bringing people back to the region. Producers and craftsmen have work. That's important. I say no more.' He drizzled a touch of olive oil over the salmon and plucked a tiny bit of Pedro's thyme and tucked it under the salmon until it started smoking.

Pip's mouth began to water. The walk had been more difficult than she'd expected and she was starving. Telmo poked the fillet with his finger and then removed it from the grill, sliding it onto a chipped white plate to rest.

'Okay, Papa. Do your best. She may look small, but I've seen her appetite.' Pedro laughed and reached for Pip's hand, leading her through a wooden swinging door to a small table set for two in a dim corner. Gone was the pomp and architectural flourish of Azure. Telmo's was a humble converted stone barn with gable ceiling and terracotta flagstone floors. A huge fireplace—almost big enough for Pip to stand up in—framed with a thick oak beam burned in the other corner, giving the room a warm glow. A sleek grey cat stretched its body out flat along the bricks in front of the fire, baring a white belly asking to be scratched.

Their table was clothed with white linen and dressed with antique silver cutlery. In the centre stood a small jam jar stuffed with sprigs of rosemary and sage. Pip picked up the jar and lifted it to her nose, closing her eyes as she thought of her mother's garden. She placed the jar gently back on the table beside a single tea light.

No sooner had she done this than Pedro nodded at the waiter in the corner and a plate with glossy pink globes of salmon roe was placed in front of her along with a basket of fresh crusty bread. Beside it was a tiny dish of butter and another of large cream salt flakes.

Pedro lifted his glass tumbler to clink with hers.

It was Pip's turn to raise her eyebrows at Pedro. It was unusual to have anything but olive oil on the table in Spain.

He grinned. 'The butter, right? A local guy went over the border to learn how to make it. Those French are good for something. Butter and bread. See, try this. It's crisp on the outside, slightly chewy on the inside. Try it with the roe.'

She wanted to ask the provenance of the salmon roe but decided to do that when they were back in the kitchen. Was it really worth provoking an argument over a nice lunch? It *could* be local. She loaded up her torn piece of bread with a thick swipe of butter, some flakes of salt and a dripping teaspoon of the tiny pink bubbles.

'Oh. My. God.'

Pedro grinned as Pip stuffed the rest of the bread into her mouth.

'Did your dad *smoke* the salmon roe?' she asked as she ran her tongue around her mouth, soaking up the flavour. The balls had burst, like pods of smoked seawater. She washed it all down with a sip of sparkling white txakoli. What a way to start a meal!

When she'd scooped up every last pink globe, running her fingers over the plate to wipe it clean, the waiter stepped forward and removed it.

Returning, he placed a jug of cider in front of them and two beer glasses. She knew this was local—they must have walked past more than one hundred barrels in just less than thirty kilometres today. As Pedro poured them each a generous glass, Pip sat back in her seat and started to tell Pedro about the chestnut grove where she grew up, her parents and her brilliant older sister. She decided to omit Jack. No-one wants to hear a breakup story over a delicious lunch.

The next dish was a plate of pickled elvers, smoked so they had turned from white to grey. Crisp and delicate, she could still taste the salty oil. 'You know,' said Pedro, 'we keep these live under the waterfall around the back in spring and summer, near the vegetable patch, until they are ready to be preserved or cooked.'

'Do you know how amazing eels are?' Pip asked. 'How far they travel to get to the sea? How much they transform to survive?'

'I've heard. They go overland, right?'

'Yes, they metamorphose. They live inland in lakes and dams and rivers for years, and then in autumn they will make their way overland—like snakes—dipping in and out of drains and water systems over these hills and mountains until they get to the Bay of Biscay.'

'You mean the eels can come through the drains in Donostia?'

'Basically they get to sea any way they can. Once they hit the salt water, they change, grow gills and swim thousands of kilometres to the Sargasso Sea. There they have a rave, lay a million eggs, and the elvers migrate back to land.'

'And then the whole cycle starts again.' Pedro shook his head. 'That *is* pretty incredible. And so is your knowledge of all the seafood. We've never had anyone like you working in the kitchen before. I mean, everyone loves the detail, but not everyone understands it like you.'

Pip felt herself blushing, as she nodded and dipped her cider glass at Pedro. She was onto number three.

'Or questions Eduardo!' Pedro returned her salute and took a sip of his cider.

And so they laughed and chatted their way through eight slow courses. Pip tried the local *percebes*—goose barnacles plucked from rocky outcrops on the nearby foreshore—succulent razor clams and huge prawns from the deepest part of the bay. Pedro insisted she sample the pigeon breast and they shared a few caramelised beef ribs. They also had a salad of mixed leaves, as well as white asparagus, turnips, fennel, sweet carrots and beets from Telmo's garden. The ceps and *zizias* were dished up smoked with a touch of olive oil infused with garlic and chilli. The pair washed the meal down with a few glasses of a smooth red Rioja until Telmo insisted they sample 'just a dash' of his homemade Patxaran liqueur. He'd collected the tiny sloe berries from nearby hedgerows and marinated them with a handful of coffee beans and cinnamon in anisette for twelve months. He served it alongside the beet and radish carpaccio and a raw goat's cheese from a nearby farm.

Pip was leaning back in her chair, completely sated, when the chef himself appeared at her shoulder and placed a quenelle of ice cream in front of her.

'Oh, Telmo—that was amazing! Wait until I tell my dad about this place. He manages to burn the chops every time. I'm going to bring him back here for a masterclass. Seriously. And the beets were incredible with the goat's cheese. I'm not sure I have room for ice cream after that incredible meal.' She picked up the plate to hand it over the table to Pedro but he shook his head.

'You must try it. It's Papa's speciality.'

'Okay.' She lifted a spoonful to her lips and was struck by a smoky vanilla taste tinged with rosemary. It was perhaps the oddest—and yet most perfect—vanilla ice cream she'd ever had.

'Telmo, you are a fire god. A genius. I think that was one of the best meals I've ever had in my life. Thank you.'

Telmo grinned. 'I'm just a *parrillero.* There are many men like me who grill meat up here in the villages.' He smiled at Pedro and placed a gentle hand on his shoulder. 'Perhaps when my son has finished with the fancy Donostia food he will come and cook with his papa.'

'You can't afford me, Papa,' Pedro joked, but Pip noticed a wistful glance at the floor. 'Come, Pip. It's dark now. That was a long late lunch! We'll walk up to the *cabaña*. It's not far.' He stood and kissed his father on both cheeks and Pip found herself caught in a bear hug with the jovial Telmo. She managed to extract herself with a promise to return in the morning for a lesson on which wood matched what vegetable and cut of meat. If she could walk tomorrow, that was, she thought ruefully. They had covered a lot of ground that day and most of it was uphill. She had a lovely buzz from a combination of weary muscles and new experiences.

Pedro and Pip stepped through the front door and wandered across a courtyard paved with old flagstones and along a small path that led to a tiny stone cottage attached to a larger villa.

It was a clear evening and Pip could just make out the hint of mountains in the distance. Maybe it was the wine, but the stars look soft and blurry, as if they could warm her hands if she just reached out. She marvelled at how the same sky could look so foreign. Her stars at home under the Tasmanian sky look so sharp and felt a lifetime away. The Saucepan was upside down. Orion. Pedro stepped closer and slipped his arm around her waist, tracing the Milky Way with his free hand.

Pip turned her head to kiss him. His lips tasted of apples, vanilla with a hint of smoke, but his hungry probing was far less innocent. He wrapped both arms around her and gently twisted her body to face his. They hugged—softly, tentatively, before stepping closer and clinging tight.

Pip ran her hand up the back of his untucked shirt, before slipping it underneath and sliding it along the edge of his jeans until she reached a soft line of hair leading to those defined abs. She let one hand rest there for a moment, running her fingers over his muscles while she used the other to pull his body against her.

Very slowly, Pip pulled away to catch her breath, adrenaline pumping, stomach churning with apprehension and excitement. She shouldn't be doing this, should she? She still loved Jack. But Jack didn't want her.

Despite her resolve not to contact him, she'd texted him the day before asking if she could visit him in Italy, but as usual he hadn't responded.

What had she expected? Pip didn't need to read the stars to know she and Jack were over. There was no going back. Not now.

Pip sighed and felt her skin shiver as Pedro traced the line of her cheek and tucked a curl behind her ears, his dark brown eyes shining with desire.

He leaned in for another lingering kiss. Pip trembled as he tugged her light cotton T-shirt and she gave in to her own longing and loneliness, gripping him hard and pushing him up against the wall. His body was a new sensation—fine and wiry like a dancer's—and she wanted to run her mouth and hands over every inch of it. Pedro caressed the sweep of Pip's back under her T-shirt as he pulled her hips tight against his. Fingers tiptoed up her spine, following the line of her sports bra to her breasts. Slipping his hand beneath the fabric, he cupped one, squeezing it like a peach. Then he slowly started to unbutton her shorts. Before she could stop herself, Pip's fingers were fumbling for his belt buckle.

Pip had promised herself before today's hike that Pedro was just a friend. But standing pressed against him, huddled against the chilly mountain air and the stars, Pip thought: Why not?

Electricity fizzed through every cell. She *needed* this.

Pip shimmied out of her shorts, feeling the cool air wrap around her body. Pedro kneeled down to plant a row of kisses up her thigh while running his hands up the backs of her legs.

Then he stood up, locked eyes with her, and took her face gently between both hands. Pedro's brown eyes were dancing with kindness and yearning. He brushed hair out of her eyes, caressed her cheek. How could she resist?

Pip sighed and moved against him, their bodies starting to form a rhythm. Pedro groaned and whispered, 'Let's go inside.'

Pip opened her eyes and stared at the wall beside the bed. The stones seemed to be arranged in no particular pattern; just a hodgepodge of reddish stones jammed together with lime mortar instead of concrete. Her head thumped, the roof of her mouth was dry and it hurt to swallow. It hurt to move.

She didn't want to roll over just yet. Or try to find her clothes. She needed to get her head around what had happened the night before, so she pretended to be asleep.

Pip heard footsteps. Pedro adjusted the sheet and duvet, pulling it over her shoulder to protect her from the frosty morning air. She couldn't bear to open her eyes to look at him. She'd been having such a beautiful evening—then what?

After she and Pedro had come inside, he'd lit the fire and offered her some local absinthe. Her cheeks burned and her skin tingled as she remembered leading him to the couch and stretching out on top of him. They'd rolled around, wrapped together, Pip discovering the sinewy lines of his body, Pedro running his gentle hands—then those full red lips—over her curves as he pulled her closer and closer with each stroke. Kissed her deeper.

Pip shuddered as she tried to extinguish the heat and longing coursing through her veins: last night had been heaven.

Bittersweet.

Mother Artemisia had not been kind. Pip's dreams were torrid, drowned in absinthe. And now here she was, in a tiny mountain villa with a man who wanted to create an eel dish with her, and perhaps a home—and all she could think about was Jack. She wanted Jack's rough hands against her cheek, stroking her thigh. If she closed her eyes, she could almost smell him—soil and salt. She squeezed the pillow with frustration. If she wasn't cheating, then why did she feel so guilty?

She rolled over, irritated. Pedro thought she should be a chef, that she was wasting an opportunity. It was flattering, of course. Pedro was adorable. And that lithe caramel body, those elegant hands—she flushed.

But why did Pedro think he knew what was best for her? In a weird way, this was exactly what Jack had been like before they broke up. Pip lay back on the pillow and took a deep breath as the realisation hit.

All this time she'd blamed herself for the broken engagement—and her broken heart. But really, Jack had forced her hand. He had been uncompromising. She buried her face in the pillow as the truth washed over her. Did he have any regrets? she wondered.

Pedro walked into the room as his iPhone beeped on the bedside table and he checked the message.

'Sorry, I thought it was my phone but it's yours,' he said as he passed Pip the phone.

Love to see you next week. Fine to stay. Have spare room. Jack

Chapter 21

Château de Boschaud, Midsummer 1487

Jacobus said, 'You're the colour of this aioli,' as Artemisia stepped into the stifling heat of the kitchen. She'd been up before the sun all summer preparing for this feast and she felt as faded, old and beaten as the crocks and pots hanging along the wall. When she saw her reflection in the tiny kitchen window, her eyes were red and puffy and her nose raw where she had wiped it with her rough tunic. She glanced down at the glossy surface of the aioli Jacobus was stirring and noticed a speckling of lice and pockmarks where his sweat dripped. She could not muster the energy to scold the boy as he used his wooden spoon to push the lice under the surface and gave it a good mix to be sure.

Hildegard gently ushered Artemisia into a wooden chair. Once seated, she dropped her forehead onto the table. Her shoulders were shaking. Everyone in the kitchen stopped moving—the ding of the rotisserie chains hitting their mark missed a beat. She shouldn't be sitting when there was work to be done, but she was too weak to stand.

Hildegard bustled past her, waving her knobbly fingers at Jacobus to indicate he should get on with it. Pierre nodded and started turning the chains. The old woman took a cup from a hook above the stove and scooped it into a small crock that had been boiling away all day, releasing a sour, putrid smell. Hildegard poked Artemisia in the back and she sat up obediently, wiping her nose with the hem of her tunic. She took a sip and grimaced. Hildegard gave her a soft whack, and she took another sip and wiped her mouth with the back of her hand.

'Holy Mother of God! I need something stronger.' She looked around the room and made eye contact with Jacobus. 'Boy, take a tankard from the larder and sneak out to the barrels where Abbot Roald and the monks blended the honey mead. Fetch me a full serve. And don't be stealing any for yourself. Run now. And if you get caught, I'll whip you myself.'

When the boy returned, Artemisia sat sipping the mead as she sagged back in the chair and tried to ignore the clanging and chatter around her. Her tunic and undershirt clung to her arms and back and she could feel the sweat dripping down her chest. She needed to reset her humours. It was unlikely a drop of mead would do it before she continued with the preparations, but the buzz settled her nerves and broke the back of her despair. There was no time to wallow in the muck of her own pity.

She was pleased enough with the mead blend. She'd pulped Abbot Roald's request of juniper, anise, fennel seed, lemon balm and hyssop in the mortar. He insisted Abbot Bellamy's traditional mead blend for banquets using *Artemisia* and coriander seed was too bitter. In God's eyes, there was no room for *Artemisia*—many men died from the waters, because they were made bitter by this most poisonous herb.

Though she felt giddy her heart still ached. She reached down and patted her pocket—as if solace was curled up with the gift. Her betrothal.

'Boy, wash this tankard please. And don't be getting any more of your lice in the sauce. You'll be fishing for them if I catch you again. I'm heading into the cold store. Pierre, mind the pork. We don't want the stuffing to split.' With that she walked the few short steps to the larder and blocked out the searing heat of the kitchen by closing the door gently behind her.

She struck a match, lit the candle on the middle shelf and pulled Andreas's gift from her pocket. It was a small book, the likes of which she had seen them fashion at the printery in the village on market days.

She ran her hands over the calfskin jacket, then she peeled back the cover to reveal the dedication inked in indigo on the finest white parchment:

For Artemisia,
Mother of Herbs,
With all my love on our betrothal,
Your Andreas

She pressed it to her cheek and took a deep breath. Her Andreas.

She turned the page and felt her heart almost leap from her chest. Spread across the parchment was an indigo illustration of

Artemisia's version of Château de Boschaud—with the walled garden drawn with such texture and shading she could almost feel the granite. She recognised the berry path, the whirl of the maze garden with the circular seat at the centre and all the wicker supports and strut work in the physic garden. The circular orchard was set out, with the finest cherry and pear blossoms, and at the heart was Abbot Bellamy's old rose garden. Bless his soul. Andreas had traced perfect buds spilling over chestnut stakes—but Artemisia's stomach sank. Lady Rose would never have any idea about how the kitchen had toiled to welcome her into her new home. She ran her fingertips in a tiny circle, feeling the slightest indentation in the page until she traced it over to the far corner of the picture where the wild chestnut and oak forest swept off the page. She felt herself blush as she let her eyes linger on the two ghost-like figures entwined in the lower corner.

The image was so faint she almost missed it. There was no mistaking the setting, nor the lovers.

Chapter 22

Tuscany, October 2014

'I was surprised to get your text,' said Jack as he sped away from Galileo International Airport. It was a clear autumn afternoon and the only interruption to the stretch of blue sky across the windscreen was the occasional white speck of a plane.

Pip looked across at Jack's strong hands gripping the steering wheel and glanced at his face. His eyes were fixed on the road. What the hell was she doing here? How could she tell him she wanted him after . . . She pushed Pedro from her mind. No, she didn't *deserve* Jack, not one millimetre.

Pip couldn't stop jiggling her feet as she thought of the sparkling line of stars, Pedro's hands exploring her body. His soft kisses on her neck, his dancing tongue. Her stomach curdled with bitter regret. Pedro was one night. Would Jack ever forgive her if she told him? *Should* she tell him?

She wanted to lean over and stroke Jack's brown arm. But after their awkward embrace at the airport they'd barely spoken as he loaded her luggage into his strange old white car. Flying into Pisa to see Jack was starting to feel like a terrible idea.

'Thanks so much for coming to get me at the airport. I know Pisa is a bit of a trek for you. What is this car, anyway? It's like a hotted-up Peugeot on drugs.'

'Panda. A classic. Four-wheel drive. Fits between the vines. This one's about twenty years old. They never die apparently. Bought it from the English guy who was working at Falgino before me. He was a bit of a sap. The car's cool, though. I love it.'

Jack grinned and patted the dusty black dashboard with affection. Pip looked at her feet, surrounded by a familiar pile of debris. Offcuts of wire, secateurs, yellow leather gloves. Crushed cans of Orangina and a green bottle of Peroni. The go-to kit for a global viticulturist.

'Now about you coming here—I wasn't surprised that you were flying into Pisa, but that you were coming to visit me at all. I thought you were kidding when we broke up and you said you *may* still come see me in Europe. Sure didn't seem very likely, after—well . . .'

Pip jiggled her feet some more and looked out the window as they wound around an entrance ramp to the freeway. She could just make out the familiar silhouette of the Leaning Tower of Pisa a few hundred metres away. 'That's it?' she blurted. '*That's* the tower? It's tiny.'

The white marble tower with its elegant columns and arches reminded her of an elaborate wedding cake decorated with layers of hand-cut fondant. Her stomach flipped and her head ached. What the hell was wrong with her? She pushed thoughts of wedding cakes from her head, focusing on the tower instead. 'It's got scaffolding propping it up,' she observed. 'It's hardly leaning, is it? Have they made it straight?'

Jack laughed. 'They're just stopping it from falling over. Probably repairs.'

'It doesn't look very big. I'm surprised. It's smaller than the pine trees at your place in Tassie.'

'No, it's pretty tall. Just over fifty metres I reckon. It's a bit hard to judge the scale from here but you'll get a chance to see it a little closer as we loop around again to join the motorway to Lucca.' Jack glanced in the rear-vision mirror as he changed lanes and then looked across at her. 'We can stop and go see it if you like. There're always long queues, though, especially at the moment because only a few people can go up at a time.'

'So it doesn't topple over with all the extra weight at the top? No thanks. I'll pass on the queues. I get the gist.'

Jack grinned, shook his head and shot a quick glance her way. She wanted to reach over and brush the curls away from his face. Then lay her head down on his lap.

'You're looking a bit skinny, Pip. Don't get me wrong, you look great, but it doesn't look like you've got much meat on you at the moment. I was expecting a bit of a Spanish doughnut after nearly four months working in a restaurant kitchen. Aren't chefs meant to be fat? Fat and shouty.' He laughed at his own joke. She'd missed that throaty chuckle.

'Like Dan? Not at all. I worked double shifts at least five times a week, and I got into swimming the bay at Zurriola—that's the main surf beach there—so I got really fit. It helped keep my strength up.'

It was a relief to fall into a pattern of familiar banter and catch-up for the next forty minutes as she described San Sebastián, Zurriola and the Camino all the way back to Lucca. No need to mention Pedro. Besides, she and Jack were not together, and what would she say anyway? Instead she described *Abiega Ozeano,* how to make dehydrated apple chips and the seasonal garden landscapes they made on plates.

'Anyway, I'm excited about Paris. Just getting access to that database, growth simulations, sediment samples, toxin samples—'

'Backtracking a bit, aren't you? It would have been easier to train it to Paris from San Sebastián than come here first.' An upward inflection. Was she imagining it or did Jack's voice sound hopeful?

'Probably.' She didn't trust herself to say anything else.

They had now left the smooth five-lane motorway, bypassing the walled city of Lucca, and were heading into the foothills. This road was rough bitumen and the back of the car skidded a bit as Jack navigated the sharp corners. Pip used an elbow to brace herself against the door and wondered if she should put the other hand on her head to stop it hitting the roof. 'I see you still fancy yourself a rally driver. What happens if there's a car coming the other way?' She eyed the crumbling stone wall at the edge of the road. Even though it was clearly ancient—a jumble of random rocks and limestone covered in moss—it looked resilient. Much tougher than this tin can of a car.

'We swerve! There aren't so many cars around these parts anyway. Mostly locals. The occasional tractor. That's trickier. You just reverse back until you get to a driveway, or a wider apron on the road.'

'Of which there are so many, I can see.'

Unconvinced, Pip looked out the window as the patchwork of ploughed fields, purple crocus and grapevines gave way to rugged slopes of dense shrubby forest. The landscape was a surprise—she'd been expecting the rolling fields of sunflowers and olive groves that Tuscany was famous for, but the only groves she had spotted so far were on tiny terraces in front of pockets of houses nestled into the hillside. The terraces were more tightly packed than those in northern Spain. Sheep and chickens grazed on grass in some, while in others she could make out nets lying on the ground. 'What's with the fishing nets under the olive trees?' she said as they looped around another tight corner piled with houses.

'The olive nets? They put on them on the ground and then whack the branches so all the olives fall off.'

'Huh? Of course! I'd love to see that.' She peered over a wall into a vegetable patch cultivated on a terrace beside a crumbling stone lean-to. Was that even a house? It was minuscule. The garden was crammed with rows of dark curling leaves of kale and silverbeet, low sprawling marjoram, a giant rosemary bush and dots of what she assumed were red and white cabbages. She could just make out the straight branches and delicate yellowing leaves of tarragon and a line of soft white and purple pom-poms hovering above. Giant garlic, perhaps? Onions? Along the side was a border of creeping thyme. She could imagine the strong woody perfumes trapped behind the wall. She wished her mother could see this garden. Pip knew Mary would appreciate the blend of artistry and workmanship. She sighed. She must remember to take some photos of this area for her parents. And Megs. Pip assumed there was clean running water here, making this an appropriate holiday destination for Megs.

The garden disappeared with the next turn and the view widened to take in a hillside of towering oak trees. Thick branches were covered in rusty leaves backlit by the sun. Pip felt the heat of the sun on her arm and face, and turned her head to soak up the warmth. Underneath the oak trees was a verdant lawn so smooth Pip could imagine rolling down the hill like a child.

The car slowed and they veered onto a tiny dirt side road. Jack pulled over and parked. Peering out her door, Pip saw the terrace give way to a thirty-metre drop.

Jack, who was watching, grinned. 'Yeah. Better get out this side, I reckon.'

He jumped out and opened the boot while she clambered over the bench seat and gearstick, trying to maintain some dignity. Not so easy in a sundress.

He pulled a wicker basket out of the back and in it Pip could glimpse a corner of focaccia, a salami and a bottle of red. 'Welcome to Tuscany, babe.' He spread an old blanket out on a patch of grass, running his hands to smooth it out and picking out any sharp rocks lurking underneath. Pip smiled and turned to look out at the view.

A wild jumble of hills and valleys, dotted with tiny stone villages and layered with dark forest, spread to the horizon. Jack pointed out the walls of Lucca, which she could just make out if she squinted. The valley seemed blurry and her shoulders slumped as she realised it wasn't fog but a dirty haze. They didn't show *this* in romantic pictures of Tuscany.

'It's magic, isn't it?' said Jack as he unpacked the basket and arranged jars of olives and grilled eggplant, wedges of hard cheese unwrapped from paper and some cold meats.

'Mmm,' said Pip. The smog had knocked a corner off her excitement. 'Shame about the pollution though,' she mumbled.

'Yeah, some days are worse than others. It's been fine, mostly, while I've been working here. It's just these still autumn days where it gets trapped. We need the south-easterly off the ocean. Brings the sea salt right up to these hills and dries out the grapes. Olives too. Here. Taste it.' He handed her a glass of red.

'Thanks.' She took the glass, looked at the dark blackberry colour and sniffed. It smelled of currants, dust and damp earth. The aroma was invigorating. She took a swig and grimaced. It tasted gritty after the smooth Riojas she'd been downing the past few months.

Jack chuckled—a rumble from deep in his belly. 'Sangiovese. Full of tannins. Chockers. Perfect for *cignale*.' He cut a thick slice of salami and handed it to Pip.

Pip raised her eyebrows and took a sniff. Her mouth watered with the rich liquorice scent of fennel seeds.

'Wild boar.' The slice of salami melted on the tip of her tongue. 'Here, put some on focaccia.' He tore a hand-sized chunk of bread and passed it to Pip as she took another sip of the sangiovese. The red wine dissolved the oils and filled every corner of her mouth. It was a rich, silky transformation. She bit into her hunk of focaccia and was surprised at the crisp crust. It was nothing like the soggy focaccias sold in Australian delis. This bread was a little charred on the outside yet soft inside and dusted with salt flakes. It was possible she'd just bitten into the perfect piece of bread.

Jack watched Pip close her eyes, tear another section off the focaccia and stuff it into her mouth. When he'd first seen her he thought she'd looked a bit skinny, sickly even, but now she was sitting in the sunlight he could see the contours of her upper arms, the curve of her calves and thighs. She was wearing a floral aqua sundress. It looked a bit retro, like something his grandma would have worn to a dance. He hadn't often seen Pip in a dress and he thought it suited her. It was nice and snug over her hips and cut low at the chest. He could just make out the edge of a pink bra edged with black lace and realised he'd never seen it before. Pip was usually a Bonds girl. Sports bras were more her thing. Was this new bra, this new look, for someone else? Maybe she'd met someone in Spain. Inevitable really. A smart, gorgeous girl like Pip. All those smooth Spanish blokes would have a crack, for sure. He could hardly blame them. Besides, he'd been the one to call it quits. So why on earth was she here?

She looked strong. Fit. Happier than he'd seen her in ages. Her auburn fringe fell over her eyes and he could see a streak of new freckles across the bridge of her nose. Her face was tanned and she turned and grinned right up at him. He had to stop himself from reaching for her hand and kissing it.

'Nice dress, babe. Suits you.'

He could see her blushing. He wanted to kiss her. Push her back onto his picnic rug. He wouldn't, of course. They both knew before he flew out that it was over and there was no going back. It was pretty clear they had no future together.

Still, he was happy to be friends. They were adults, after all. But he was surprised by the woman sitting in front of him. He was surprised by his yearning.

But nothing was going to happen. After all, there was Valentina to consider.

Chapter 23

Tenuta Di Falgino, Lucca, October 2014

Back in Jack's car after the picnic, Pip was still buzzing from a happy blend of sangiovese and sunshine. She'd loved hearing all about vintage, and Jack had seemed fascinated when she told him about Azure, especially when she'd described how the owner Eduardo had converted a draughty old family villa into a commercial restaurant. He'd asked a million questions about how they located a commercial kitchen in an old site, whether they had punched out walls to make a single large space or whether it was a collection of rooms. Was there an outdoor area? What did they do in winter?

It was sweet of Jack to prepare a picnic—they'd shared so many picnics over the years: shivering on the Friendly Beaches in autumn after hours of bodysurfing, hiking the Overland Track in spring when snow still dusted the rocks and ferns. She shivered a little as she remembered in detail what they'd shared *under* those tattered picnic rugs over the years. Had he been camping at all since he'd been in Tuscany? Pip looked down, concentrating on taking slow breaths through her nose. She glanced across at his boots—his worn dusty Blundstones—and closed her eyes. Told herself she was just tired. She'd had to get up at dawn to get the bus, then train, to the airport. Pedro had kindly offered to drive her. She'd given him a hug at the end of service last night and told him there was no need. Things had been awkward between them since their night in Mendiluze. As he drove her back to San Sebastián the next day, Pedro had had a go at her for choosing to finish her research in Paris. He made it perfectly clear he thought she was making the wrong call—she should be a chef in Spain. They had hardly spoken since. Instead, Pedro presented daily at her station with downcast eyes and clear instructions. There had been no further invitations to the spice room.

She opened her eyes and noticed the hem of her crushed cotton dress had ridden up to the top of her thighs as the Panda bounced and skidded along the dirt roads. Subtly, she tried to pull it back to her knees, and tugged on the end of the dress hard. It looked like she'd need to hold it with both hands to stop it riding up and exposing her thighs and new pink knickers. This was exactly why she didn't wear dresses much. Too fiddly. Not to mention uncomfortable. Her cleavage was flushed. Her cheeks were tingling hot and cold. She glanced over at Jack to check he hadn't noticed all the slipping and sliding and indecent exposure happening over the other side of the vehicle. But his eyes were on the road and his fingers tapping the steering wheel in time to an imaginary tune.

'Okay, here we are at Tenuta di Falgino,' he said as they sped past a pair of twenty-metre pencil pines that Pip assumed marked the front entrance to the estate. Ahead, she could make out a pale gravel driveway lined with low white rosebushes and studded with oversized terracotta pots filled with lemon trees in fruit. Pip sat up and gasped. Her mother would *really* love this driveway.

The garden was terraced flat—a giant green wedge cut from the side of the mountain. How had they excavated such a massive space without earthmovers? It must be hundreds of years old, at least. Older than any building she had seen in Australia. From the lawn rose the villa, softened only by the subtle line of rosemary dancing along the front. The villa was about fifty metres wide with faded blue shutters and a peeling ochre lime wash. A blazing crimson grapevine smothered the bottom storey. Brown, scaly trunks of twin palm trees sat beside the arched oak front door and reached past the wide terracotta-tiled roof, dark green fronds offset by the crisp autumn sky.

'You are kidding,' said Pip as she threw back her head and laughed. 'It's like something out of *Under the Tuscan Sun.* I didn't know people actually lived in places like this. I could get used to staying here.'

'It's pretty special,' agreed Jack. 'But that's not where I live, I'm afraid.' He swerved right off the driveway to a service entrance that ducked behind a stout two-metre bay hedge marking the villa's boundary.

Pip rolled down her window to catch a sniff of the bay—she'd never seen such a large herb hedge before—as they pulled up at the front door of a two-storey ramshackle stone barn. The old outbuilding was built into the back of the large stone wall that surrounded the garden of the main villa. Gnarly grapevines threaded through climbing roses and looked like they were holding together the ancient wall. Pip could just make out a peeling white door with an old cowbell for a door chime and a row of four terracotta pots with a mix of succulents and lipstick-red pelargoniums.

On the other side of the driveway was some kind of small work barn. Bushy clumps of lavender, rosemary and marjoram ran riot. Beyond the driveway was a field that sank into a valley before rising into a steep hill opposite. As far as Pip could see, every surface area was cultivated, with ribbons of vines threading themselves up and over into the horizon. No wonder Jack was here for months. Harvest and vintage would take forever. She turned to him, and he shrugged and raised his eyebrows in an I-told-you-so kind of way.

'Not bad,' said Pip with a smile.

'Right, let's get you inside,' said Jack as he reached into the back seat and grabbed Pip's backpack. 'Jeez, been doing a bit of shopping.' He staggered as he swung the bag over his shoulder.

'Cookbooks,' she explained, blushing.

'In Spanish? Be a bit tricky to follow, won't they? Or did you learn the lingo?'

'Nah. But they have lots of pictures. Got some gardening books too. Make a nice present for Mum and Dad. Remind me to post them when you drop me back at Pisa, okay?'

'Perfect present for your mum. Great idea. I should remember to get something from around here for my folks too.'

'Good idea. Your mum would go nuts over these villas, wouldn't she?'

'Maybe. I reckon she's over big old houses, though. All the cleaning and maintenance. Hard on her hips going up and down that staircase all day, and bending over clipping vines. This winter was her last in the paddock. That's what she *says*, anyway.' He laughed. 'The folks will be happy with a slick city pad after they've finished their travels. They're at a trade show in Singapore at the moment. We still haven't come to an agreement. Nicko's howling like a dog from New York. I'm trying to get the finance sorted. It's not easy.'

Pip swallowed and hung her head.

Jack continued: '*If* I can swing it, Dad will still do some of the wine fairs. All the marketing. He likes the travel. Loves Asia. Thinks it's a rush. Mad about the food. Dumplings, noodles, chewy chicken feet. You should talk to him! It's like a second career for him after all those years on the farm and vineyard. I won't be able to do the travel anyway, if I get this expansion underway. The new winery will cost a bit, might need to buy some grapes in until we reach capacity.' Jack kicked a pebble on the ground and then looked directly at Pip. 'So, yeah, I might be moving into the big house,' he said as he dropped his shoulder and pushed the little door to the barn open. The doorway was so low he had to tilt his head to one side to enter.

Pip stood in the doorway. It was weird to imagine Jack rattling around that big old sandstone homestead by himself. The cottage was so tiny and cosy. And unfurnished.

'Your folks leaving the furniture? Ashfield House might look a bit bare with just surfboards for decoration.'

'I reckon. All that heavy mahogany isn't going to fit in an apartment. And who's going to buy an old twenty-seat dining table with wobbly legs? It'd take twenty men to lift it.'

'Or women.'

'You know what I mean.' He grinned at Pip and beckoned to her to follow him up the stairs. 'You can put your bags in here,' he said, leading her up a small wooden stairwell to a bedroom with a black wrought-iron bedstead and embroidered white cover, so neat. A folded towel lay on the end of the bed.

Jack turned towards the door. 'I'll just camp on the couch downstairs for a few nights. Or a friend who works here has offered me a bed.'

Pip felt awkward. 'No, don't give up your bed—I'm fine to sleep on the couch. Seriously. Besides, the couch doesn't look that big; your feet will dangle off the end.'

The back of Jack's neck was reddening as he dashed out the door. 'I'll leave you to have a wash. Get yourself sorted. Bathroom is across the hallway.' He turned to face her: 'It's really great to see you, Pip. I . . . er.' He paused as if he were grappling to find the right words. 'Coffee?'

'Sure, thanks.' She was tired and wanted to lean into his chest, have him put his arms around her. He looked darker, more tanned—almost leathery. As if his skin had changed tone with the terracotta soils of the region. His scent was unmistakable—soil and sweat—but there was a trace of something unfamiliar too. A musky scent; a sweetness. It was a little unnerving and she wondered what, or who, could be the source.

Pip felt a million times better after she'd showered and washed her hair. She slipped into her favourite jeans and a grey T-shirt and dried off her hair as much as possible with a towel. She ran a brush through it to untangle all the curls and then flipped upside down and back to tousle it up again. She didn't like it too neat and it would curl as it dried anyway. No point fighting it. She added a touch of lip gloss before she went to meet Jack's colleagues.

She walked through the thick oak door that led to the pool terrace of the main villa. A bright red vine snaked around a contemporary steel pergola and behind it was a thoroughly modern pool house made from glass and steel. The strong, simple lines of the new building blended seamlessly with the villa and the twenty-metre old-fashioned concrete-tiled pool. Pip could see Jack hunched over, staring into the opening of the old brick oven, poking it with a metal rod. He had mentioned on the way up that he'd put a leg of venison on as a slow roast at breakfast, with some bay leaves and white wine. Her stomach rumbled even though she'd had a solid lunch.

Sitting at a big wooden table were a small dark wiry man and a tall, luminescent woman who looked a little too much like an Italian movie star for Pip's liking. She blanched. This wasn't Valentina the winemaker, was it? Jack had mentioned her briefly in an email when he described how the vintage worked, but she wasn't expecting . . . Pip forced herself to cut off this line of thought. She and Jack were no longer an item. It was no business of hers what went on in Italy. Besides, he would have told her if he was seeing someone, surely?

Jack came over when he saw her. 'Ciao!' He introduced her to Bruno and Valentina. She noticed Valentina's eyes widen in mock dismay as Jack tried to pronounce her name with an Italian accent.

'Jack didn't tell us he had a beauty coming to stay. Your hair is perfect, like *castagna*. A strong Aussie beauty.' Bruno gestured with a hand and tapped the rickety metal chair beside him. 'Come, *bella*, come sit by me. I'm old and my hands and knees ache.'

He poured her a glass of white wine from an unlabelled bottle. 'A 2013 Trebbiano. It was a good year, my friend.' He leaned over and cut a fine slice of prosciutto. '*Cignale*. Shot it out the back of these hills last year. Smoked it myself.'

Pip cut a sliver. It melted in her mouth like butter. She reached for the knife to cut another slice.

'So Jack tell me you have brains as well as beauty. A scientist. Marine biology. My daughter, Brunella, studies chemistry in Bologna. She is in her second year. Perhaps she will be a scientist too. Work in a laboratory. Maybe in Bologna, maybe Roma.' Bruno held up his purple-stained hands. 'Not like her papa. She's a smart girl.'

Pip glanced at Valentina's dark glossy hair cascading in waves to her shoulders. Her dark skin and eyes, delicately shaped eyebrows and chiselled cheekbones were somehow complemented by the old jeans, work boots and denim work shirt she was wearing. Valentina caught Pip studying her and gave her a wide grin. Sprung, Pip shot back her best attempt at a winning smile. It wasn't like her to be jealous or territorial. Jack had always been attracted to intelligent women who just happened to be stunning. His girlfriends before Pip had included an Olympic rower, a Rhodes scholar and a UN worker in Peru he met while hiking in South America. In typical Jack fashion he had kept in touch with all of them and if they were in Australia they often met up for dinner—with Pip included, of course. Now was not the time to start being insecure. Besides, she and Jack were no longer a couple. They were friends, that was all. With a shock she realised that she too had moved into the 'interesting ex' category. She was surprised by how much that hurt.

'I'm sorry. We are filthy. We came straight from the presses—Jack was so keen for us to meet you. We've heard so much about you.' Valentina looked directly at Pip. 'Can I have some of the *bianco*, please, Bruno?' She waved her wine glass at the old man. '*Grazie.*' Her husky voice was laced with caramel. Her wide dark eyes were bright and looked kind. Who the hell could blame Jack if he fell for her? What hope did Pip have against someone who seemed so sure of herself—and who looked so elegant in a man's work shirt?

Chapter 24

Château de Boschaud, Midsummer 1487

Andreas stood to one side of the circular cloister filled with nobles from neighbouring estates and merchants in their finest silks, velvets and furs in royal blues, reds and greens as they bumped shoulders and sipped sweet wine from silver goblets. The midsummer garden was heaving with flowers and pollen. Guests were surrounded by alternating rings of pear and cherry trees underplanted with tight lavender bushes. He'd managed to find a vantage point away from the crowd from which to view the woven willow arbour that was heaving with climbing cream and red roses, filling the air with the sweet smell of love. He closed his eyes and took summer deep into his lungs, imagining how his own simple wedding would unfold.

He opened his eyes and blinked twice at the ferocity of the midsummer light. The sun had moved long past noon and was stretching higher and higher across today's wide blue sky, and he shifted his shoulders to try to stop his fitted green silk jacket from sticking to his skin. He wanted to remove his stockings and boots, roll up his pants and dunk his feet in the little stream that flowed at the bottom of this slope like he'd seen Artemisia do so often when the wild strawberries started to ripen. If the stewards walked past again, he'd take a slice of the pink or yellow melon to cool his humours under this beating sun.

A handful of boys and girls—coats unbuttoned, stockings drooping around their ankles, gold silk ribbons trailing down the back of their white silk embroidered smocks—giggled as they ran past him. They wove between the gnarled pear and cherry trees, spitting black pips between their teeth with melon juice dripping from their chins, knocking lavender heads with their knees. The oils of the plant lingered in the stifling air long after the children had wedged themselves up into branches in the far corner alongside the hornbeam hedges, scaring away flocks of donnocks and goldfinches that were twittering with excitement.

The children's carefree laughter at the plume of rising birds was drowned out as velvet-clad pageboys dressed in burgundy with sprigs of rosemary pinned to their oversized sleeves marched into the cloister and formed the border of an aisle. They stood like proud footmen down the middle of the circle from the stand of hornbeams at the entrance of the cloister to the rose arbour at the other. From neat baskets tucked under their left arm, the pageboys proceeded to throw handfuls of crimson rose petals and white lilies on the lawn to mark the path for the bride in time to the steady beat of a drum, lute and trio of crooning minstrels. A harpist Andreas hadn't noticed near the arbour began to pluck the strings, rounding out the music and filling the cloister as loudly as any chapel as the crowd turned their heads to watch the entrance of the bride. Andreas couldn't help but feel sorry for the poor pageboys whose once-neat shoulder-length hair was plastered to their heads and limp with sweat.

Through a pair of tall linden trees in terracotta pots walked Lady Rose between her fur-clad parents. She wore a simple V-neck dress with wide sleeves in silk the soft blue of the summer sky and shimmering with gold thread. Her blue lace veil flowed down her back like a waterfall, fixed with a wide garland of unseasonal waxy white orange blossom. The orange blossom must have come from afar with the Clinchy household—or had been sent for from the south—for Andreas had seen none within the walls of this château or surrounds.

Behind the bride walked Lord Boschaud and his marshal, who was limping from the weight of the quarter chainmail and sword crossing his body. Abbot Roald was already standing in the centre of the arbour, deep purple robes matching his fleshy face and jowls, beads of sweat dotting his brow. As Lady Rose placed her small hand on the broad hand of Lord Boschaud, Andreas noticed the dainty blue ribbon and nosegay. He smiled at the tight red rosebuds, lilies, garlic and chives with rosemary tied tight with ivy. At the edges were the telltale feathery tufts of silver *Artemisia*.

The deep, petulant voice of Abbot Roald boomed through the cloister as he asked the assembled guests if there were any objections to the marriage of this noble pair.

As the readings began, Andreas's thoughts ran to last spring, when he had found Artemisia in the picking garden tying a nosegay with a piece of royal blue silk ribbon for the Lady Rose's betrothal ceremony.

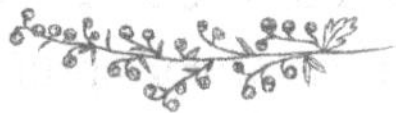

Artemisia was sitting on the grassy mound overlooking the budding apple trees with an under blanket of yellow daffodils. She'd picked a trio of red rosebuds from the bush climbing the nearby gravestone and was weaving them together with violets and tying the bunch together with ivy and finishing it off with the silk.

'Artemisia, please may I join you?' he'd asked.

She had been so absorbed in her posy she hadn't realised he was standing beside her. She looked over her shoulder to see who else was in this area of the garden.

'Don't worry,' he reassured her, 'I just passed the priory and the abbot has taken the monks into the chapel for tierce.'

Artemisia exhaled and busied her fingers as she nodded at him, her lips starting to curve into a smile.

Andreas sat beside her and watched her strong fingers wrap the ivy around the herbs twice more so it looked like thick green twine. She held it above her head and dangled it in the light—the violets and gillyflowers still had a touch of the dew. He could smell the solid garlic and chives and the thick oils of the fresh-harvested rosemary and lavender. They both sat still, admiring the herbs as they shimmered in the sun and swayed slightly in a gentle breeze. The yellow faces of the goldfinches on the fruit branches preened and twisted towards him before resuming their happy birdsong.

'It's for Lady Rose,' Artemisia said with a wistful look. 'They'll be exchanging the rings at dusk.'

'Why don't you make another nosegay?' Andreas suggested. 'For yourself.'

Artemisia flushed and turned away as she brushed the stray leaves and offcut sprigs from her apron. Then she turned to face Andreas.

'And what would I put in it?' she asked playfully.

'Well, chives and garlic to keep the bad spirits away, perhaps a bit of St John's wort for good measure.'

'Naturally. Go on.'

'Roses.'

'Obviously.'

'Lilies for lots of little ones,' he said with a chuckle and reached across to pat her belly. 'And *Artemisia*, of course.'

'Is that it?'

'Why? Have I missed something?' he said, puzzled.

'Well, how about ivy because it sticks deep in the earth, marigolds for the artistic fire, gillyflower for happiness.' She paused and checked them off on her fingers. 'And the iris—for wisdom.'

'I don't think you need the iris.' Andreas held her firm wrist softly and stopped her. 'No-one knows how to blend herbs and spices like you. What a pair we will make. I can take you to Genoa—show you the world.'

Artemisia's dark eyes gleamed like beans as she shook her head. 'Your mother . . .'

'Adores you,' Andreas finished with a smile. 'She's getting too old to run the market spice shop by herself.'

Artemisia's mouth formed a perfect rosebud, as if she couldn't quite believe what she was hearing. 'Oh,' was all she said.

'Let me give you *my* world. Imagine what you could do . . .'

Andreas pulled her onto his lap and wrapped his arms around her strong shoulders. He could smell the rosemary in her shiny dark hair and he buried his face in her plait. Artemisia giggled as he tucked her head under the crook of his chin they both sat watching the pretty goldfinches and wrens squeak and hop from branch to branch in the apple trees. Then he squeezed both shoulders and gently shifted her so he could look her in the eye.

'I mean it, Artemisia. Marry me.'

She snorted and tried to push him away. 'Enough! What nonsense. A cook and a journeyman. It's—'

He put his finger to her lips to shush her and tucked a loose strand of hair behind her ears and back into her plait as he shook his head.

'I've been made master *épicier*. I'm free to take a bride.'

'But not—'

He leaned in and kissed her on the lips to quiet her objections.

'Abbot Roald will nev—'

She leaned back as he kissed her neck and the nosegay dangled from her wrist onto the ground.

'I promise you, Artemisia, by summer you will be a foundling no more. My heart is already yours. I just need to give you my home.' He murmured, 'Artemisia de Vitriaco has quite a ring to it, don't you think?'

Artemisia sat up, smoothed her hair and straightened her white apron over her tunic before lifting her wrist to spin the pretty posy in the sunshine. This time, Andreas noticed the delicate hair-like fronds of the strawberry and the silver tufts of *Artemisia* he'd missed and he sucked in the sharp scent of garlic and chives.

'Artemisia de Vitriaco,' she repeated, turning over the words slowly in her mouth as if it were almost too much to swallow. Then she looked at him and her smile was pure spring sunshine and hope. 'Yes, it does,' she whispered with a shiver as she pressed her shoulder against his.

Andreas touched his shoulder, now covered in the finest emerald silk, as Abbot Roald boomed into the warm air: 'I do pronounce thee husband and wife.' He was looking forward to hearing this pronounced for himself.

Chapter 25

Tuscany, October 2014

Pip stretched her legs, moved her daypack and used the seat in front to lever herself out of the back seat of the rickety old Volkswagen Caravelle. After a few bottles of sangiovese were downed the night before, Bruno had offered to drive the crew the following day up to a remote spot in the Apennines where he used to harvest chestnuts, ceps and morels as a boy. They'd set off after breakfast. The drive was forty minutes from Tenuta di Falgino along a web of narrow roads that spun between terraces on which grapes and vegetables were growing. Pip was blown away by the amount of arable land the Tuscans had made, carving terraces out of the sides of mountains and hillsides, retained by sturdy walls built from random slabs of limestone. It felt more utilitarian and more raw than San Sebastián.

Tuscany had always sounded so romantic. She had to admit there was a charm to the gardens, the pencil pines and the gravel, but up close it seemed like a lot of hard work. Crumbling walls, terraces to be weeded, grapes to be pruned and harvested, olives to be harvested and pressed. No wonder Bruno was so small, hunched and wiry. Even Valentina had stained purple hands and calluses on her fingers and palms. Just like Jack. She had to hand it to the other woman: Valentina was no princess. Pip knew what it was like to work with a team of men. The jokes when they were out diving to forget the wetsuit, the pairing off with the better scuba equipment, the quiet scoffing as she tried to haul her nets up on deck. The complete desire to disappear into work clothes so as to be invisible. The need to collect twice as much data in order to be taken seriously. It frustrated Pip the way the boys helped each other out, using their tinnies to collect specimens whenever they needed. It wasn't even that they were deliberately leaving her out—it was just that they didn't notice her at all.

Pip was last into the vehicle, and so had no option but to sit in the back seat wedged in next to Jack as the front seats were piled with baskets and buckets. Valentina was seated in front of them, but twisted around to chat as they drove. Today she was dressed casually in a scoop-necked white T-shirt, black puffer jacket and denim jeans, and Pip could see the arch of her back, the elegant line from her jaw to the nape of the neck.

Pip's thigh was trapped against Jack's. As Bruno wound his way higher and higher up the mountain in a series of hairpin turns, they were knocked together and bounced on the back seat as the van clattered around each corner at ridiculous speed, honking and overtaking any cars that dared appear in front of them. Pip had pulled away from Jack with each turn, but she noticed he left his thigh pressed firmly against hers. She'd missed these steely thighs. Part of her wanted to reach out and stroke his leg or place a hand on it. But after Jack had offered to walk Valentina home after the previous night's feast she was pretty certain that this wouldn't be welcomed. She'd strained to hear the soft thunk of the thick old oak door closing as he returned home, but she'd drifted off and missed it. Maybe it had never come. The couch had looked unslept on when he made her a morning espresso on the old cast-iron stove.

He'd mumbled, 'Had to help Bruno with pruning the rosemary and bay hedges before we left this morning. I promised. Thought I'd have a massive headache. We ripped the head off a few of those reds, didn't we? I'm good though. What about you?'

'I'm good, thanks. It was really beautiful wine. I can see why you like working here.'

In the van, the shoulder-banging got more intense and Valentina gripped the edge of her seat with both hands to keep from being thrown onto the floor or rammed against the window. The tools—secateurs, wrench, hand trowels—smashed together with clinks and clanks.

'Hey, Bruno. Do you want to slow down, mate? We'll be dead before we hit the forest.'

'*Si, si*, Jack.' The old man waved his left hand out the open window and Pip could see a big yellow sign. 'We are almost there.'

Indeed, the terraces and pencil pines had given way to a thick forest of oaks and chestnuts whose branches formed a canopy across the road.

Bruno steered the van into a car park and pulled on the handbrake. There was no-one else around. 'It is good we got here early,' he said. 'After lunch this forest will be filled with families walking off their Sunday lunch. Come, come!'

Pip was disappointed when Jack took that as a cue to leap up, following Valentina out of the van. Pip could feel the imprint of the pocket of his cargo pants in her thigh and gave it a rub before she got out.

The manicured terraces had disappeared, replaced with rocky boulders, the dappled light of beech trees and towering pines. If she looked up towards the canopy she could see the light while at her feet mist rose from the ground. It was chilly, but the morning light cheered her.

'Here, Pip.' Bruno pronounced her name 'Peep', just like Pedro. She stomped her foot as if to stamp out the memory. She knew she shouldn't feel guilty about her night with Pedro, but she couldn't help it. Not that it mattered. Jack was clearly about to move on—if he hadn't already.

Bruno passed her a bucket and a pair of worn leather gloves then led the way down a narrow track that ran into the forest.

'When I was a child there were bears in this forest,' he said. 'Lots of big brown bears. Wolves too. My parents used to shush me on this trail, so we didn't disturb them. When the leaves are turning, they are looking for food before they go to bed for the winter. My parents, they used to say if I did not behave they would feed me to the bears.'

'That's horrible,' said Valentina, wrinkling her nose. She glanced over her shoulder, as if checking for bears, and her thick ponytail swung in a perfect curve.

'Come, the walk takes about one hour from here. After we find the chestnuts and the mushrooms, I'll take you to

Arrego's.' Bruno had promised lunch at a small bar in a tiny alpine village. Pip's stomach grumbled; the Italian breakfast of espresso was really not working out for her at all. She was starving.

They ambled along the path in single file. Bruno, Jack and Valentina were engaged in a heated discussion about malolactic fermentation. The wines were biodynamic—something to do with sheep manure in cow horns buried in the vineyard during certain cycles of the moon. It sounded dubious to Pip. Surely healthy vines owed more to the nutrients than the rotations of the moon. What next? Sacrificing virgins? Pip found it hard to believe a modern winemaker could believe such rubbish. When she was alone with Jack she'd ask him for the scientific evidence. He had an honours degree in viticulture. Surely he didn't believe this?

Ignoring the conversation, Pip walked at the back, studying the moist soil and moss. She wondered what the average rainfall would be; judging from the proliferation of lichen she estimated well over fifteen hundred millimetres. Her parents' chestnut grove in Mount Macedon was lucky to get eight hundred millimetres in a good year. As she walked through the forest, she saw that many branches and trunks had been chopped right back. In fact, it looked like whole sections of the chestnut and oak trees in the forest had been coppiced. This gave a surprise element, as rows and rows of fine straight branches taller than she was thrust straight up into the air from stumps that looked like they were dead. It looked like this forest had been cultivated for years. She had been expecting wilderness, so this mark of civilisation surprised her.

They walked up and up for nearly an hour, pausing only for sips of water. No wonder Bruno was so wiry—he was a proper mountain goat. Pip did a lot of hiking in Tasmania but Bruno had been at it for a lifetime. It showed. Soon the trees began to thin out, the coppiced rows disappeared and they came to a clearing of grassy meadow and delicate ferns. The mountain environment was so different to Australia, where granite boulders were covered with moss, soft tufts of brown-tinged native grasses and the glossy dark green *dianella*, acacias and bracken dotted the undergrowth, vying for both sun and precious drops of water, their roots spreading like desperate tentacles under the soil. The smooth white and grey trunks of the mountain eucalyptus dominated the snowline. Here it smelled of sweet rotting chestnuts, rich moss and humus.

Pip gazed at the biggest chestnut trees she'd ever seen. The grey trunks, wrapped in moss, were so tall and wide, the branches so thick and magical. The mist was clearing; she could no longer see her breath. They all set about filling the buckets with chestnuts. These seemed bigger, darker than the ones at home.

'Better take a pic for your folks,' said Jack, grinning. 'Show them what a real chestnut grove looks like. Here, stand against the tree there, so they can get the scale. Smile. Perfect!'

'Thanks.' Pip reached for the phone and sent a text.

In the Apennines with Jack harvesting chestnuts. The real deal. Never thought I'd travel around the world to pick chestnuts. Here for another couple of days. Jack says hi. Hope you guys are well. Love, P x

Pip's pleasure dimmed for a moment as she recalled her most recent Skype call with her parents. Mary had just been across to Tasmania for the weekend—Megs was looking a bit worn out, she reported. Mary had suggested Megs take a week's leave just to have a bit of a rest and offered to stay on and look after Chloé. Apparently Megs had laughed and dismissed the idea. A week off surgery meant more work for everyone else, including Will. Megs would *never* see him. Mary had tried to make light of it, but Pip could tell she was worried about her oldest daughter.

'Pip, hello.' Jack was waving his hands in front of her face. 'Here, come and have a look at the huts. These are the old ones where they used to store the fruit that Bruno was telling us about last night. Let's go have a look inside.'

She looked up and could see the others about a couple of hundred metres ahead. Valentina glanced back over her shoulder at them and gave a slight wave when she saw them both looking her way. She then went back to pointing at the mushrooms. Even from this distance Pip could tell from the exchange of staccato Italian that she and Bruno were arguing about the type, and how they should be cooked. Bruno was holding his hand to his lips and waving the other as if he were shaking a frypan.

'Here, let's go inside this one.' Jack pushed open the worn door and led her into a stone hut with a roof made from woven chestnut branches. The windows were just open squares in the wall. The dirt floor, compacted from years of storage and stomping, was dry and firm.

Pip twirled around. 'Wow, this is really something. I should take a photo to send to Dad. Maybe he can build one when he retires.'

'Like that's ever going to happen,' Jack said.

'Yeah, well, he's talking about it. Mum's just doing the one day in the clinic at Sunshine now and they were talking about maybe coming to see me in Paris.'

'Yeah. So the secondment in Paris. National Museum of Natural History, huh? Ooh-la-la—very flash. I heard a fun fact about that place once on one of those quiz shows. Apparently they bought a giraffe from Sudan. No-one had ever seen one before. This is in the 1820s. They put it in the hold but had to cut a hole in the deck of the ship for the giraffe to poke its head through. Poor thing. Then, when they disembarked in Marseille, they had to walk all the way to Paris. With a bloody giraffe. Can you imagine? A giraffe on a dog lead!' He pulled a face. 'The leather straps, the spots, the blue tongue. No-one had ever seen anything like it. The funniest thing, though, is that the giraffe hairstyle became *the* style for fashionable French ladies. *À la Girafe*.' He paraded around the small hut with his hand on his hip, pretending he was a catwalk model. 'Anyway, *that* giraffe is apparently somewhere in the museum.'

Pip felt like her temperature had dropped five degrees. Pedro had also mentioned this giraffe. But she didn't want to think about Pedro right now. 'O-kay,' she said, slowly recovering, 'if I see it I'll take a pic for you.' Why was every breath laced with guilt? She and Pedro would probably keep in touch—they were friends and colleagues. That wasn't unusual. It was just one night—

'I want a selfie with the stuffed giraffe.'

'That's actually a bit sick. The poor giraffe.'

They laughed uneasily and Jack tilted his head on the side. He took a step towards her, and then another. He was inches away from her. She could smell the rosemary. 'I've missed you, Pip.'

She said a touch too quickly, 'But you and Valentina—is there . . . ?'

'Shhhh.' Jack reached out and cradled the back of her neck with a wide hand, and drew her towards him. Her cheek was pressed against his chest, and he stroked her hair with his free hand. Pip started to sob.

'I'm so sorry, Jack,' she mumbled into his shirt.

'Why are you really here, Pip?'

Pip started to sob even harder. She wiped her nose, discreetly she hoped, on his shirt. The green drill felt so comfortable, so familiar.

She knew she could be indecisive but she was sure in that moment that she wanted to be with Jack. Perhaps he was prepared to be a bit more flexible? San Sebastián had given Pip time to reflect, so why not Jack? Despite the mountain chill she could feel her cheeks burning. Plenty of people had long-distance relationships—surely that wasn't beyond them while they sorted out some short-term plans?

She ran her hands down his back and over his bottom, tucking her hands into his back pockets as she used to do. She squeezed. God, she'd missed him. She felt a flicker in her groin and was aware of her back arching a little and her breasts pressing a little harder into his chest. His arm circled tight around her back and slid under her shirt, tracing a line up her spine and lingering just below her bra strap. He unhooked it with a well-honed flick and Pip wondered—as she always did, with a flush of jealousy—just where the hell he had learned that trick. She took her right hand from his pocket and moved it to his head, her fingers sinking deep into his curls. She could feel Jack's hips brush against hers slowly at first and then with a sense of urgency; she felt his knees bend slightly and then they were kissing, a deep, tender, familiar kiss.

Jack inhaled and moaned softly, pulling Pip closer, and she closed her eyes and breathed in his scent of rosemary and sweat as she kissed him harder and deeper—

There was a knock on the door. '*Scusi!* We have finished with the mushrooms and are heading down to the village.'

'Bruno, hello,' said Jack a little breathlessly. 'We're coming—I was just showing Pip the old huts.'

They stepped away from each other. Jack cursed as he hitched up his jeans and tucked his shirt back in. He reached out and squeezed her hands. 'What am I going to do with you, Pip?'

'I want you, Jack.' She stared at him, suddenly feeling small. 'But . . .'

'Are you sure?' the edge of his mouth twitched into a broad grin as he interrupted her. 'As in, you want to get marr—'

'But I—I was with someone else,' she interrupted in a rush. She stepped forward to put her arms around him. 'I'm so sorry—it didn't mean anything.'

Jack's smile vanished. He pulled out of her embrace and took a step back. 'What? When?'

'In Spain.' Pip took a deep breath before lifting her gaze to meet his bewildered expression. 'Jack,' she begged, 'it was nothing—one night.'

Jack's blue eyes flickered with hurt and he blinked.

Neither of them spoke for a few seconds as the wind rattled the thin walls of the hut.

Pip swallowed. 'Please, Jack . . .' She reached for his hand.

Jack flinched and backed away from her towards the door. Then he stopped. When he looked up at Pip briefly, his tanned face was red and twisted. Blue eyes watering. Then he dropped his head to study the dirt floor, drawing a circle with the toe of his boot. When he spoke, his voice was low and gruff. 'So you've slept with someone else.' He paused. 'I hate the idea—' he clenched his fist '—but fair enough. We'd broken up.'

Pip took a deep breath. She pinched her thigh to stop herself from asking, *What about Valentina?*

'Who was he?'

'Just someone I worked with. Pedro. A chef.' Pip squirmed uncomfortably.

'Of course it was,' Jack retorted. 'But—'

'Jack, it was nothing. I mean it.' Pip closed her eyes, trying to ignore the memory of Pedro's fingers tracing her hips. It was Jack's strong hands she wanted. If she could just touch him . . .

She opened her eyes to tell him as much when Jack began to speak.

'Let me finish.' He held up his hand. 'Just so I'm clear. You came here because you want *us* to get back together.' His voice was steady. 'Are you sure?'

Pip took a deep breath and almost wept with relief. It was going to be okay. Jack was going to forgive her—even if she couldn't forgive herself.

'I'm so sorry, Jack. It was silly—it just made me realise how much I missed . . .' She paused and gulped down some air. 'How much I love you.'

Pip took a deep breath and pulled back her shoulders.

'I understand why you broke off the engagement. But I'm ready to marry you, I promise, just as soon as—'

But when Pip looked into Jack's eyes, they were like a wild grey storm. She froze.

'You got your little romp off your chest, but instead of staying here, or coming home, *now* you want to go to Paris to finish your PhD.' He squeezed his eyes closed and inhaled.

The hair on Pip's arms prickled as the atmosphere in the hut turned cold. Jack opened his eyes and spoke slowly. 'So what's changed Pip? You're still saying we'll get married when it suits you.' His voice was hard and mocking.

Pip felt tears running down her cheeks. Her heart was shattering all over again. Jack didn't want to marry her at all. Coming to Italy had been a mistake. Worst of all, she'd misjudged Jack.

'*Nothing* has changed,' he thundered.

'Jack, stop!' Pip cried. 'What about my research? It means more long-term than any stupid house.' She swallowed, immediately regretting her words, even though she spoke the truth. The ocean would be there long after Ashfield House crumbled. 'Don't you want me to be happy?'

'Jesus,' Jack muttered, shaking his head. 'What do I have to do with it? It sounds like you've been doing a pretty good job of keeping yourself happy.' He turned and strode towards the door. 'Who am I to stop you from a date with a giraffe?' he threw over his shoulder as he stormed out.

Pip stood, rocking and crying with her hands on both cheeks as if she'd just been slapped.

Jack felt like he was on fire. He was surprised how much he wanted to rip Pip's clothes off. He'd wanted to do that ever since he'd seen her in that damn dress. And Pip had wanted him too. That much he could tell. But then what?

He shook his head as he walked up the slope, smelling the sweet musky soil with each heavy step. Dappled light streamed through the yellowing leaves as he moved between shadows under the canopy of the chestnut grove. The mottled grey branches stretched high and wide, blocking the sky. The low boughs felt menacing, as if they were laughing at him. It was all so soft and green, the yellows bright and golden. He missed the scrubby grey-brown gnarled tea-trees protecting the waterfront with faded strappy grasses and browning bracken clumped below. The smell of eucalyptus and the crackle of crisp dry leaves when he hiked to the beach, dry white sand between his toes. He missed the endless wide blue sky that could fill with moving white clouds and turn dark and grey within minutes. Standing in the middle of this majestic, damp forest, the cloying scent of chestnuts filling the air, he yearned for his wild rugged waterfront. Salt, sun and sea. He yearned for Pip.

Jack studied a flat red toadstool that was bigger than his hand. There were perfect round white dots on top as if it had been painted by a fairy. So pretty, yet poisonous. Deadly.

Pip had come here to reconcile. Yet she was set on heading for Paris. Why did Pip always put her work first? If she was serious this time, surely they'd work something out? Jack paused, allowing the niggling sensation to creep into his bones that somehow their broken engagement was his fault. Not that it mattered much now. He scratched the side of his neck where he could feel his vein throbbing and kicked the mushroom like a football so it tumbled through the clearing, smashing into tiny pieces.

She'd slept with another man. Moved on.

There was no such thing as a fairytale ending.

Jack wasn't sure what he would do workwise when vintage finished but he might stay on right through winter to see how they worked the land, pruned and then finished making the wine. It would mean an extra couple of months away from home, but the paperwork was probably going to take a couple of months and he wouldn't get this chance again for years as he'd be working to pay the debt. The last few weeks Jack hadn't been certain he wanted Ashfield House anymore. It seemed more burden than blessing. The plan had been to do it with Pip, but now—what?

As Jack stormed up the slope, Valentina looked at him. He could see her eyebrows raised in confusion, and then draw to a squint, her dark eyes flashing.

Last night, after dinner, he'd walked her home to her permanent quarters on the other side of the villa. She had pulled the elastic out of her hair and her thick glossy black hair tumbled down her back and over her shoulders. She was mesmerising. She flicked her head to loosen it and he could smell the sweetness of her rose shampoo. Then she'd stepped towards him and kissed him. A cautious kiss—a follow-on from the very Italian dance of kissing on both cheeks. Then, she'd put her hands on his shoulders and pushed him gently against the wall and pressed herself into him. Jack had felt her silky hair soft against his neck as she'd shifted her slim hips, pressing in against his pelvis. He'd been somewhat surprised. Why now, after all these months? He was confused and a little drunk. Not a good combo. Still, he'd been turned on—it had been ages.

Not like Pip. He couldn't stand the thought of Pip in the arms of another man. Who was this Spanish chef? Was he a better lover? Did they have more in common?

He trod on another red toadstool, feeling it squish flat beneath his boot.

He sighed as he recalled how he'd lifted Valentina's denim work shirt and placed his palm flat across the curve of her lower back, feeling her tremble. Smiling, Valentina had placed her hands on his cheeks and given him another tentative kiss that quickly turned into something far deeper and hungrier. Her black eyes danced with desire, inviting him to come inside. He'd wanted to. Jesus. She was smart. Funny. Sexy as hell. A complete stunner. They'd been flirting all vintage and, if he was honest, he'd been hoping they'd get together. But how was that ever going to work out? Her job was at Falgino. His was in Tasmania. But was that what he even wanted?

As always, it wasn't great timing with Pip. He'd thought she was just being polite when she'd said she would like to come visit him for a weekend. Acting like the old friends they were.

But now it was all getting very complicated.

He glanced over his shoulder to see Pip standing still in the clearing, face twisted towards the light, and was surprised to see her turn and kick a rock against a tree when they made eye contact. Her tanned cheeks were still a little flushed.

Valentina walked cautiously in front of him, buckets full of chestnuts and mushrooms, shoulders sagging. Conflicting waves of frustration, jealousy and lust pounded his heart. *Perhaps tonight.* Would he have taken up Valentina's invitation and gone inside with her if he'd known about Pip and her fancy Spanish chef? Should he have?

Chapter 26

Château de Boschaud, Midsummer 1487

Artemisia ran her hand over Andreas's sketch of her *entremet*, taking deep breaths to slow her heart. She flipped through the pages, noting his skilled likenesses of herbs. She recognised some of the recipes she had been secretly giving him when she stopped by his spice stall in the marketplace. Sorrel verjuice, pottage of old peas, poultry flavoured with cumin. She kept turning until she reached her favourite section—desserts. It was a miracle Artemisia had never had a case of the tooth worm. The rosemary mouthwash helped, of course. For one named after a herb so bitter it only made sense she had a taste for anything with the sugarcane.

She found the recipe for tonight's cherry pudding, noting the correct portions of stale white bread, butter, Bordeaux and cloves had been transcribed. When she flipped to the page of spiced plum mousse with honey she thought her knees might give way. There was no place to sit in the larder, so she steadied herself with one arm.

Last week she had ventured beyond the wall—with the abbot's permission—through the woodlands for part of the early morn to the ancient orchard of wild plums. She knew they were always in season coming into St John's feast and would be a fine course for Lady Rose. The branches had never been tempered with shears and looked like the wide arms of a carnival strongman. She had half-filled the basket when she heard a horse snort and stomp at the ground. She turned to see Andreas dismount from his black gelding and tether it to a low bough.

'You understood my letter, then,' she said.

He held her arms and pulled her close. 'Of course. Our meetings are so rare I had my boy do the deliveries to the east. Here, let me help you finish with the plums.' He removed his cloak and placed it on the ground and then gave the branch above a mighty pull. The ripe fruit tumbled onto the ground and he easily scooped it up and funnelled it into the basket. They did this a few more times until it was full. 'Are you sure you can carry this? I can take it on my horse.'

'And how will I explain that to Abbot Roald when I am out here on my own harvesting plums?'

Andreas picked up a plum and took a bite. Crimson juice squirted onto his pale shirt.

Artemisia stepped towards him with her pocket rag. 'Here, let me wipe it.' She changed her mind at the last minute and instead leaned against him for a slow deep kiss. Andreas tasted of summer and she could feel the heat radiating off his chest. She fumbled with his shirt ties as he shimmied up the sides of her tunic. She felt him leaning against her, pushing her against the smooth trunk of the plum tree. Suddenly he let her tunic drop back and stepped away. Artemisia froze, praying he wouldn't stop.

Slowly, he retrieved his cloak from beside the basket and smoothed it out over the grass. He was careful to remove any twigs and sharp rocks underneath. Then he took Artemisia's hand and led her to the cloak and lay down beside her. He ran his fingers up the side of her leg, tugging the tunic up to her hip as he went. She rolled onto her back and he pushed the linen high enough to reveal her breasts.

'Now these are the wild plums I've been looking for.' He laughed and kissed her again. She could feel the sun against her skin and arched her back to soak it up. She'd need to be having a triple dose of her wormwood, pomegranate, rue and juniper brew to hold off a pregnancy that evening and every morn this week. Perhaps the next. She closed her eyes and drank in the smell of rosewater as his hands explored her body.

Afterwards, Andreas lay stroking her plait with one hand while propped up on his other elbow.

'I've worked out a way we can be married.'

'How? Abbot Roald will never allow it. A master of a guild and a cook? Not likely.'

Andreas smiled and said, 'Emmeline can run the kitchen, can't she? You won't be missed.'

Artemisia laughed and whacked him on the shoulder playfully. 'Thanks very much.'

'I'm serious. I'm going to ask Lord Boschaud for your hand at the feast. He's hardly going to refuse after a bellyful of food and finest ale. Especially on his wedding day. Abbot Roald will be unable to object if the lord himself gives you to me. Neither will the village burgher. I already have your betrothal gift made. I'll give it to you when I deliver the spices. That will be our signal. I'll ask Lord Boschaud for your hand during the *boute-Hors*. After they are served, I'll meet you out by the walled garden, just behind the gate.'

There was a brisk knock at the larder door and Artemisia was jolted from her reverie. She snapped the book closed and pressed it against her chest.

'Excuse me, can I come in and get the sack of sugar, please?' It was Jacobus. 'Emmeline wants me to start sprinkling it over the desserts. Once now then again before we serve it. So it looks like snow.'

'I hate the snow. I don't know why anyone would want it on a special summer pudding.'

She slipped the book back into her pocket. Fancy thinking that Abbot Roald would allow her to present an *entremet* without seeking his approval. Her face burned with shame. At least she had the illustration to remember it by.

Chapter 27

Tuscany, October 2014

Pip was sitting up straight beside Bruno at a rustic chestnut table at Arrego's Taverna, doing her best to avoid Jack. Arrego's was a tiny stone inn—no bigger than a bedroom—carved into the side of the mountain with a terrace overlooking the valley. There were a handful of rickety wooden tables and benches out the front and a cluster of terracotta pots filled with pungent rosemary, thyme, and the vivid red pelargoniums that seemed to bloom in front of every building in Tuscany.

The mushrooming party sat huddled around a corner table inside, hungrily breathing in the cooking smells from the kitchen hidden somewhere behind the lattice swinging door. The scent of tomatoes, roast chestnuts, roasting meats and a buttery polenta filled the tiny room. Jack stood up at the giant slab of rough-edged oak that formed the bar. At its side was a makeshift cheese and *salumi* cabinet with rustic wooden boards stacked beside it. The idea was that customers just helped themselves to thin slices of dried and cured meats, pickled vegetables, portions of hard and soft cheeses and a bowl of smoked almonds while waiting for the dish of the day.

Behind the bar was a frightening black boar head with enormous tusks. It could do with a dust.

'You wouldn't believe it. They've got Castlemaine XXXX on tap here,' said Jack almost under his breath.

The Italians looked blank. Pip said—perhaps a touch too harshly—'What, even the Queenslanders won't drink it so they have to export it?'

Bruno looked from Jack to Pip with narrowed eyes and shook his head in a warning at Valentina. Awkward tension stifled the mood in the miniscule room and Pip felt herself flush with embarrassment. It would be better if she and Jack just didn't speak.

She wished she hadn't come to Italy.

'Ha', said Jack with mock cheer. 'Well I know *you're* not homesick, Pip.'

'What's the other beer?' Pip tried to put on a jovial voice for Bruno and Valentina as she changed the subject, but it sounded brittle.

'A local chestnut beer. Made in the next village.'

'I'll have that, thanks. Call it research for Dad.'

'Righto. Posh local Italian brew coming up. Anyone else want an Australian classic?'

Bruno knocked the table with his knuckle as he and Valentina shook their heads.

Jack sighed. 'Okay. Looks like a jug of the chestnut ale and I'll order a red.'

'Get the Chianti Classico,' suggested Valentina.

Jack returned with Chianti, beer and some small water glasses for the wine.

Arrego, the ruddy-faced owner of the taverna, walked over to greet Bruno with a giant hug. Pip leaned back in her chair sipping the crisp chestnut beer, grateful she no longer needed to talk to Jack directly. Instead she listened to Arrego's friendly banter blowing away the sour air.

There was much back-slapping, kissing and bullet-speed Italian exchanged between the old men and Valentina as she joined the laughter. Arrego was the shape of a wine barrel and reminded Pip a little of her dad. She couldn't help but smile.

A cherubic waiter—Arrego's son perhaps—brought over a plate of charcuterie. Bruno pointed: '*Cignale*—sorry, wild boar, pork and fennel *salumi* and some prosciutto with the pig fed on the chestnuts. *Bellissimo*.' Pip was wondering how many variations there could be of *cignale*. The young waiter returned with a cheese platter and Bruno gestured to a rather revolting-looking cheese, stained purple and wrapped in a rotten brown leaf. It smelled slightly sweet and tangy—much better than it looked. 'Pecorino,' Bruno wheezed, then cut himself a huge chunk. 'Soaked in the lees. Wrapped in vine leaves. Left in a barrel for twelve months. Arrego makes the best.'

'Leftovers from the red grape pressings,' whispered Jack behind her in an expressionless voice before she could ask what lees was. Pip felt his warm breath on the back of her neck and a waft of his familiar earthy scent as he walked behind her chair to seat himself beside Valentina. Even though Pip was disappointed in him, she still longed to rub her cheek on Jack's chest and stay there, or push his shaggy curls back from those blue eyes and long lashes.

Pip noticed Valentina shooting Jack a dark look. Her limbs and chest ached as she recognised the look of a miffed lover. The sooner Pip left for Paris, the better—it was obvious that Jack and Valentina were far better suited. They would make a handsome couple. Pip finished her beer and resolved to leave first thing tomorrow. Make a fresh start on her thesis. Try to repair her shattered heart.

Tired and hungry from their foraging expedition, they tucked into the cheese and charcuterie with relish, washing it down with the sweet chestnut beer. Bruno and Valentina then moved on to a rich Brunello di Montalcino as Arrego came out of the kitchen with some steaming chestnut and lamb soup and more fresh focaccia.

Pip had seconds. Then thirds.

Arrego looked amused. Bruno said, 'Good to see a woman who loves her food.'

Pip looked across at Valentina, who was staring at her bowl, stirring her soup slowly. Every now and again she'd look up and give a half-smile, or a one-word comment to Arrego, but otherwise Valentina seemed lost in her own world.

Bruno's voice was growing louder, and Arrego had produced a collection of vinyl records. The rich tones of Italian opera started blasting across the room. Pip didn't recognise the music but Bruno and Arrego started to sing along. Loudly.

Arrego turned the music up so loud that between the singing and the record it was impossible to talk anymore. Instead, Pip leaned back in the chair and sipped the Chianti that Bruno had insisted she taste.

Jack avoided eye contact like a petulant child.

'"Sempre Libera",' said Bruno, almost to himself, waving his arms in a pretty impressive bout of air conducting.

'La Stupenda. I saw her sing this in 1966,' he continued with his eyes closed.

Pip had no idea who he was talking about. Jack grinned, eyes half-closed, listening to the music.

'You know La Stupenda?' persisted Bruno. 'She's Australian.'

Jack looked at Pip and together they shook their heads.

Pip said, 'Who?'

'Joan Sutherland—La Stupenda,' said Bruno with a grin, pausing in his conducting to take a swig of his red.

Of course! She was an idiot.

Bruno leaned forward to top up his glass. Pointing first at Valentina then Pip, he asked: 'You know this aria, "Sempre Libera"? It's from *La Traviata*. Ah—it is a tale of heartbreak.' He clasped his hand to his heart for dramatic effect.

'It is Verdi's finest opera—about Violetta Valéry, the fallen woman.' Bruno took a sip and closed his eyes to listen.

Jack raised his eyebrow at Pip before he nodded sadly at his red wine. Pip felt her cheeks and the back of her neck burn with shame. It was one damn night . . .

Dame Joan Sutherland's voice soared and trilled like a bird. Higher and higher.

Nobody spoke.

Bruno started to translate—just loud enough to make himself heard:

Free and aimless I frolic
From joy to joy,
Flowing along the surface
of life's path as I please.
As the day is born,
Or as the day dies,

Happily I turn to the new delights
That make my spirit soar.

The song reached a crescendo, Sutherland's rich soprano filled the room and Jack stared at Valentina, who was quietly watching Bruno.

Then he slowly made eye contact with Pip.

Adrenaline flooded Pip's veins. She absorbed the words of the aria, reflecting on her travel, her freedom. Her mistakes.

She'd had her *frolic* in San Sebastián. Cooking grounded her. Pip felt stronger, more balanced. Who knew she'd learn so much about herself while soldering vegetables and dehydrating fruit?

'Sempre Libera' didn't sound like the song of a fallen woman. It sounded like a musical call to arms. Pip *needed* to finish her PhD. She also wanted to work in Paris for a while—*new delights—and* she wanted Jack. Love.

But she couldn't have Jack. He'd made that very clear. It was time to let go.

She clenched her fists under the table because the trilling La Stupenda was right. Pip needed to find a new way to make her spirit soar.

She could start by helping to find some answers—balance—for her little corner of the D'Entrecasteaux Channel. That'd be enough, surely?

Now she was going to finish her work and thesis in Paris and *then* she would look at life back home. It just wasn't possible to find a way forward with Jack. He simply didn't get her.

She glanced at Valentina, who was running her dark eyes over Jack with an affectionate grin.

Pip's skin burned with a strange and prickly jealousy.

Jack tilted his head and broke into a dazzling smile as he met Valentina's eyes.

Pip was far too late, anyway.

Chapter 28

Paris, March 2015

Pip was glad the sun was out as she set out for her daily walk to work. She couldn't think of a much better commute than to walk through one of the grandest gardens of all—Jardin des Plantes. After months of low-hanging grey skies and muted colours, today sunshine danced over the miscanthus grasses cut low, starting to shoot. Towering grey artichoke skeletons sparkled with dew. Layers of gentle green, cream and maroon hellebores cascaded between the large tufts of miscanthus, mulch and dark green groundcover that anchored the perennial beds. Double rows of plane trees—planted with military precision in long avenues—were starting to swell with new buds. In the gardens beyond were soft blankets of blue violets, golden primroses and dancing white snowdrops. It was impossible not to be cheerful.

Pip turned left up Rue Cuvier and headed up past Allée Becquerel so she could do a lap of the wallaby enclosure before work. It was lovely to have a touch of home. The last she'd heard from Jack was a brief email the week before describing winter pruning methods in Tuscany and mentioning a possible trial site for grapes in Tasmania. There was some kind of gala fancy-dress feast that he was attending in May. All the vineyard crew were making a night of it before he went home. It was to be his farewell party—he'd made a great group of friends.

Jack's emails had been polite but distant since her visit to Tuscany five months ago. They hadn't seen each other since. Pip suspected he had moved on, and it was probably high time for her to do the same. And when better to do that than spring?

Pip picked up the pace and skirted the corner of her research building on Rue Cuvier, bypassing the huge wooden front doors and heading to a small back door with her security tag. Inside she took the stairs two at time until she got to the third floor. After the flurry of colour that had greeted her that morning, it was a shame to be back in the austere grey and beige corridors and perched at her little steel desk. At least, if she leaned to her left, she could peek out her window at the patchwork canopy stretching in grids for acres. There was surprising joy to be had in such curated colour, in the unfurling buds of spring.

Pip shared her tiny corner office with another benthic invertebrate researcher, Nadia. The absence of a blue coffee cup on Nadia's desk told Pip she was not yet in for the day. She was probably at a meeting over at LOCEAN. Damn. She needed Nadia's help to navigate the complex password system in the database. She looked at the list of a dozen French passwords in the blue and green colour-coded flowchart sticky-taped to the window and the hairs on her arms prickled. Last time she'd tried to log in, her screen had flashed like she was trying to breach the White House firewall and she'd been locked out of the system for twenty minutes. She'd need a coffee before she risked it.

Pip hung her coat on the back of the door, collected her new green Limoges coffee cup and headed to the staff kitchen.

Ariel, the gruff kitchen lady, was guarding the percolator with the ferocity of a bulldog. It was clear from her demeanour that she would have been equally at home running a women's prison. Pip estimated she must be at least fifty, with salt-and-pepper hair pulled back in a bun so severe it looked like she'd had a facelift.

Ariel swung a blue-stockinged leg into the middle of the floor and put one hand on her hip; the other she held out to Pip.

Pip deposited a euro in her outstretched palm and handed over her cup. Ariel grunted a *merci* and turned to the percolator to fill it. Pip didn't bother to wait for the offer of milk before she sculled the lukewarm coffee and put her hand in her pocket to pay for another. It was damn hard to find a decent coffee in Paris and Ariel's was better than any of the liquid cardboard in the local bars.

'*Non*,' barked Ariel, waving her hand, then she poured Pip a top-up with an unexpected chuckle. It was her lucky day.

When Pip returned to the office, Nadia had arrived and was busy collating two inches of printouts into piles on her already cluttered desk. She was wearing a black long-sleeved T-shirt with *je suis Charlie* printed across the middle. Onto each pile of notes, Nadia was placing a fluorescent pink sticky-note with a number from one to seventeen. It was reassuring to see that despite the mammoth web of databases here in Paris, the filing systems were as rudimentary as at home. A plastic container of couscous and roasted eggplant and zucchini perched on the corner of the desk. Pip's stomach rumbled. She might have to run out for one of the lemon and sugar crepes from the little stall outside the building. Hopefully they would get a chance to sit out in the garden together on their lunchbreak. Nadia always had a secret stash of green metal garden chairs. Chairs seemed to materialise when they sheltered behind the alpine section. On particularly freezing days they sweated it out in the Mexican greenhouse, nestled between rangy cacti and succulents. Pip suspected that one of the gardeners had a soft spot for Nadia. Who wouldn't?

'Sorry, Nadia, can you please show me how to get into the spatial variation section for the benthic infauna? I also need the seasonal variation in the chemistry logs.'

'Sure.' Nadia smiled and fired up Pip's computer, tapping through a succession of blue screens until columns of data starting flashing. While she was bent at the desk, Pip admired her dewy cheeks and dark skin. Her own arms were so translucent they had practically turned blue this long winter. She needed vitamin D.

'Now,' said Nadia when she'd finished, 'I have some good news for you. I stopped by and saw Marie across at the Herbier National and they've managed to carbon date those recipes and drawings you had sent over from your family. She was a little, er, surprised that you risked posting them, to tell the truth. May have used "idiot" and "*Australie*" in the same sentence. Twice!' She grimaced apologetically. 'Anyway, it looks like they date back to the late 1400s or early 1500s. They'll need to run more tests to get any more specific than that.'

'Are you serious?' Pip clapped a hand over her mouth and let out a yelp. She danced a little jig on the spot. 'Wait until I call my sister. She'll freak! She hates old stuff.'

Nadia threw her head back and laughed. 'Yes, well, they are fragile. Marie was relieved you managed to transport them in such good condition. Laughed at the specimen jar. Do you want that back, by the way?'

Pip shook her head and laughed along with Nadia.

Nadia continued: 'Now that they have verified their authenticity, they'd like to consider origination. They've run an initial search through their databases. There doesn't seem to be an exact match for this linen-based parchment. Marie did mention that it was strange that most recipes were French but the paper matches types made in north-east Italy. They polished the parchment with a stone to make it shiny, or something. Very distinctive.' Nadia shrugged. 'Definitely not Germanic. It's a plausible connection, though, as there were strong trade routes over the Alps right through this period. There's also no match for the ink, nor the handwriting. They've also had a look at matching the drawing of the *Artemisia* and other herbs like the rosemary and roses. Nothing—yet.'

'Oh, well I think it's amazing they got the date so quickly. Thanks for chasing it up, Nadia. I know you have a lot on.' Pip looked at Nadia's desk, heaving under the weight of chemistry models.

'Before I forget . . .' Nadia reached into her handbag and passed Pip two specimen bags with brown paper inside. 'They made copies for you. There seems to be two different hands. Some recipes are signed "Artemisia", some "Andreas". It's almost an exchange of letters. It's confusing. They've made a few translations for you. Not many—just enough for you to get a sense of them.'

'Thanks, that's very generous.' Pip held the top bag up to the light, and saw the fine line sketch of the wormwood still had the spiky hairs. It looked like it was drawn in grey lead now it had been photocopied.

'They have kept the originals, and they are going to talk to the main library preservation team for all the herbals. They have thousands, apparently.'

'What's a herbal?' Pip looked over at Nadia.

'From what Marie explained, it's a book made up of documents a bit like this. Herbs, recipes. But they used the herbs as medicines. This may be part of something like that. Or not.' She raised both her palms, and turned back to her desk to get on with work, then swivelled in her chair to add: 'They are also going to take it to the Cluny to get the experts there to look at it. See what else they can find. Often the monks did all the transcription and there may be a record with these names.'

Pip raised her eyebrows and shook her head. Was she supposed to know what the Cluny was?

'It's the Museum of the Middle Ages—the medieval collection. Just up near the Sorbonne.' Nadia turned back to her computer.

'Well, my recipes are in good company, then,' said Pip. 'Thanks, Nadia, I really appreciate your help.'

Nadia turned around again. 'No, no, Pip; you don't need to thank me. You've been so helpful proofreading all my papers and précis for conferences. My written English is so bad. It is *I* who owes you.'

'Let's call it even then. So I'm heading down to Châlus this weekend to stay at Château de Boschaud. There's some family connection there through my dad's side. A great-aunt had some relative there, we think. No-one really knows, because Margot is long dead. She's the great-aunt who gave us the pots I found the parchment in, so I'll take these copies and see if anyone down there knows anything. It's worth a shot. And then I'll go over and see Marie.'

'Of course.' Nadia returned to her work, as Pip took a few minutes to sit down and read some of the translated letters.

Chapter 29

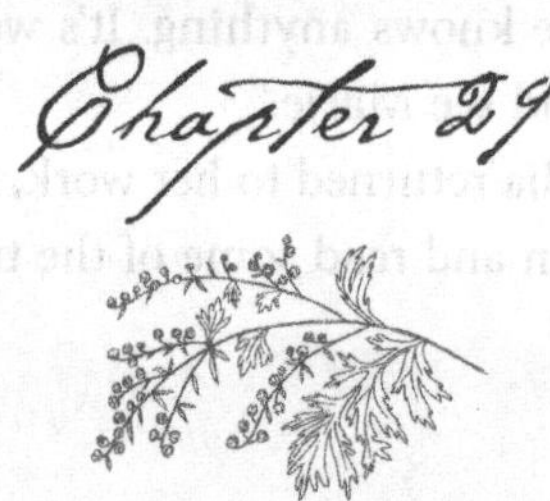

Château de Boschaud, Summer 1487

Dear Monsieur de Vitriaco,

Please find the list of supplies required for the preparation of the Boschauds' wedding banquet next month. I require the main delivery Friday's morn.

My order is as follows:

30 lbs almonds, 6 hulled corn, 8 lbs powdered columbine ginger, 1½ lbs ground cinnamon, 4 lbs ground rice, 6 lbs lump sugar, 2 oz saffron, 1 qr cloves and 1 qr paradise mixed, 1 qr long pepper, ½ qr galingale, 1 qr mace, 2 qr green bay leaves, 1 lb citron, 2 lbs red anise, 3 lbs rose sugar, 1 lb caraway seed and 1 lb coriander seed mixed, 4 lbs black pepper, 10 lbs grain salt.

Thank you for your last letter and the sweet spice combination for your candied orange peel and the spiced apples. I shall serve these items at the beginning of the feast.

I also thank you for your detailed recommendation for the confetti. It has never been used in these parts, but I agree with you that the sugared coriander and caraway seeds and pine nuts in addition to the sugared almonds will make a fine first course with the fruit from the garden and ensure all humours are in good spirits for the banquet. The coriander will assist with the digestion of the last course and the caraway will tie the groom to his bride and encourage love and devotion and ensure the sweetest kisses in the eve.

It is too much, perhaps, to hope that Abbot Roald chokes on the seeds, but perhaps the combination will soothe his bile and take the heat and accompanying anger from his liver. At the very least it may tame his flatulence. It is too much to ask of even your finest quality powder to sweeten the old hog's breath.

I can assure you I am staying well out of sight of Abbot Roald. God himself could not conduct himself to the abbot's standards this week and would be given the same swift kick in the guts or sharp smack to the kidneys to moderate behaviour.

It is my aim to give the new mistress of Château de Boschaud a perfect wedding banquet, and I thank you for your assistance in this regard.

I need also 7 lbs small and large candles and 10 pots of your house rosewater to be delivered to the door the morn of the wedding for wash bowls during the feast, and to launder the wedding sheets and finery.

I trust once you have made a list of necessary items you will burn this letter, as our agreement.

Your humble servant,
Artemisia

Chapter 30

Paris, March 2015

Pip jumped off the 67 bus at the top end of Rue des Martyrs and thanked her lucky stars that her father's colleague, Professor Trigg, had offered her his apartment around the corner from the coolest street in Paris. At the moment he only visited it in the summer with his wife, but they planned to move to Paris for a bit when he retired.

She liked to get off a stop early to walk the few blocks of her favourite street and soak up the *joie de vivre* neatly arranged in the shop windows. This evening she decided to celebrate spring and sunshine by sitting under the red-and-white striped awning at her local deli, Terra Corsa, and enjoy a glass of rosé with a small bowl of tiny green olives infused with olive oil and lemon rind. Baptiste, the owner, delivered them to the table. His skin was as dark and craggy as a Corsican cliff and, despite his crisp white shirt and black vest, he seemed to give the impression he'd just rushed in from a day of foraging catmint and thyme in the mountains. Either that or a surf. She'd recognise the dry, fluffy hair of a surfie any day. She flushed as she thought of Jack.

'*Bonjour*, Pip. You are having some dinner with us tonight? I can put you inside at the big table, if you like.'

'No thanks, Baptiste. No dinner for me tonight. And I'm heading down to Châlus this weekend to see some distant relatives, so I won't be in.'

'I knew your excellent taste had to come from somewhere!' Baptiste twinkled. 'I'll just get you a little slice of *jambon* to sample for the walk home.' He hummed as he headed towards the slicer. The back corner of Terra Corsa had become Pip's second home and she often came in for a late dinner, to skim some work and to hide from the wind and slush right through winter. She'd once told Baptiste about her mother's garden, only to end up in tears. Sometimes, she was so cold and homesick in this city. Baptiste had tutted and given her traditional Corsican recipes like roast chicken thighs with catmint. Her parents would love this place, she thought. Trying new wines. Swapping recipes. She could almost hear Mary's laughter and see her dad studying the wine list and working his way through the cheeses.

Rejuvenated by her glass of rosé, Pip lifted her backpack and headed into the street, past the *poissonière* next door. Trays of fresh oysters, cockles, pipis and clams from Brittany filled the window. She considered the relationship between a sunny day, champagne and benthic invertebrates. Now that *was* something she'd like to crunch the data on in Paris. She laughed. Like Terra Corsa, all the wine bars in the street had glistening shellfish in pride of place in the window. Unfortunately, three hours of analysing samples of the European clam *Varicorbula gibba* and the green crab *Carcinus maenus* suspended in jars of formalin at 15.5 degrees meant shellfish was the last thing she felt like for dinner. Besides, she preferred to bring her molluscs home fresh in a bucket, secure in their provenance, not wrapped in plastic. Spoiled for life with hand-caught Tasmanian seafood whose origins she could specify down to the millimetre, she shook her head.

She missed home. She missed Jack.

This yearning blindsided Pip for a minute. She stepped past the trays of fish and glanced at the queue in the *fromagerie* next door and decided she would skip the brie and chèvre too. Parisians had perfected the art of takeaway. Last night Pip had had paella with mussels, fish, chicken and chorizo mopped up with half a baguette. The night before she'd come from twelve hours straight in the archives so she'd picked up some duck terrine with prunes, cheese and a still-warm baguette. Friday nights were usually her big treat: free-range rotisserie chicken with a few potatoes cooked in the fat underneath and a mesclun salad with exquisite French dressing—just the right blend of mustard, olive oil and vinegar. She could smell it as she climbed uphill. But she'd had a big lunch of a ham and cheese crepe and Nadia shared some of her mum's divine couscous, so she really didn't need the works tonight.

She ducked into the deli and looked at the line-up of orange, yellow, green, red and cream soups in elegant glass bottles—they were so pretty that she'd taken a photo of it and sent that to Megs rather than one of the exquisite rainbow in the *macaron* shop next door. Pip hoped that would brighten her day—Megs adored Paris. When they last spoke Megs had just finished a gruelling night shift and was due back the following evening. Pip smiled to herself—spring colour for her sister was just what the doctor ordered.

Pip needed comfort food, so chicken and leek soup went into her bag, along with a baguette and a tiny lemon tart. Last stop was the fruit shop, with its open green trays of strawberries. It was the wrong season for strawberries; they probably came from Spain. But they were smaller and sweeter than any of the overwatered Goliaths she'd tasted in Australia, so she picked up a tray. Maybe food miles were counted differently in Europe.

She paused for a minute to take in the sweet scent of roses that spilled out onto the footpath from the flower shop. Hundreds of boxes filled with bunches of plump white, red and pink roses. If you wanted to decorate a wedding banquet, you could pull up right now and fill a van. Done. The familiar pang was back, but she leaned over to look at some artful pot plant arrangements of tiny pine cones, succulents, parsley and a dark green featherlike grass. Fairy lights scattered along a grey awning sparkled above.

The patisserie across the road was equally dazzling. Complicated fretwork laced apple and pear tarts, strawberries perched on top of lemon tarts, endless lines of danishes and—Jack's favourite—chocolate mousse. A *croquembouche* sat in the centre of the window. She wondered if it had been ordered specially for a wedding this weekend. Pip picked up her bags and started walking home with her eyes downcast, not even pausing to look at the glossy gems in the window of the *chocolatier.*

The last stop before home was the little épicerie under her apartment building. Mustafa nodded hello and kept counting coins on the counter without looking up as Pip dashed past.

He was used to her crazy midnight chocolate raids. She bought some more coffee beans and at the last minute threw in a couple of dark Lindt balls. Why not? She'd done the Sacré-Coeur stairs twice that morning.

Pip approached the door to her apartment building and reached into her bag for the swipe tag. She swiped. Oops, it was the wrong one; she started digging around the bottom of her bag. Why was it always so hard to find her keys? Jack had always joked she could do an archaeological dig in her handbag. Frustrated, she pulled out her Lee Child novel (for reading at lunchtime if Nadia was too busy) and propped it against the glass door. She also took out her new small makeup bag and a wad of photocopies of the database where sections were missing, which she needed to go over that night. She also had a marked-up ten-thousand-word section of her thesis that Monsieur Leroy had handed back to her today with covering note outlining his thoughts. They were meeting for a coffee next week to go over it. While he wasn't a formal supervisor, he was a global expert in the field and a friend of Tom's from Canada, so it wouldn't hurt to get his feedback before she compiled the final data and results when she got home. Back in Australia, both Professor Grant and Imogen were pleased with the results, so she was very close to presenting her thesis. She did a little skip on the spot and grinned like an idiot. So close!

She'd almost emptied her bag, and she tipped it upside down to see if the key dropped out. It did, along with a couple of stray tampons.

A tenant of the building she'd seen several times—a man of about seventy—gave her a severe look and sneered as he swiped his key and stepped over her detritus. He stopped, pushed on the wooden frame and held the door open for Pip.

It turned out he was a gentleman after all! Pip quickly stuffed her belongings into her backpack and nodded as she walked across the marble-tiled floor of the foyer to the wide staircase with wrought-iron balustrade weaving its way up the spine of the building. She jogged up the stairs to the fourth floor. All those mornings doing the Sacré-Coeur were starting to kick in. She fumbled for her keys—how could she have lost them again?

Once inside, she studied the old oak parquetry floors, floor-to-ceiling bay windows with wooden shutters and the way the foyer opened onto the dining area and sitting room. No corridor wastage. It was one of the grander Haussmann-style apartments and it had been thoughtfully renovated and furnished. Each room must have been over seven metres long; in the centre of the dining space was a ten-seater polished cherrywood table on zinc legs—very cool. She dropped into a black Thonet chair, its feet dipped in fluorescent green, to catch her breath.

She wished that she could show Jack this place. He'd love the way the old building had been given a slick contemporary feel. She'd seen all the sketches he'd been doing for a new addition to Ashfield House when she was in Tuscany. She wondered whether he'd managed to sort the paperwork with his parents. Or if he was planning to go straight home after the gala dinner? The last email she'd had from him was all about trialling a new site with some sangiovese vines in Tasmania. Was he doing this with Valentina?

Flushing, she pulled her laptop out of her bag and checked her emails. Nothing.

To take her mind off Jack, Pip decided to see if there was any information she could find on Château de Boschaud.

She'd spoken to Madame Boschaud and invited herself to stay for this weekend. She wanted to ask Madame about those old letters and recipes. Her mum had also mentioned during a Skype call last week that the château had been trialled on Airbnb. She opened TripAdvisor and hit Google Translate. Even though Pip wasn't a going as a paying guest, the results weren't promising:

We get a yellow card reminder on email, but when we arrived there was no booking. We are taken into a small room, and there was no heating on top of the tower. It was cold and shutters throughout the night with a bang. When we complained, the owner said there was nothing to be done about it as if it were a ghost. Crazy place. Do not visit.

And:

We evacuated the castle without seeing anyone. The rooms are cold, the home has not been done, the food remained in the cabinet has happened since 2011. The beds were not soft. This place is not worth a visit, closed limit for negligence. NOT ADVISE!!! AND ESPECIALLY NOT TO SLEEP!!!!

It was going to be an interesting weekend.

Chapter 31

Château de Boschaud, March 2015

Pip sat in the back of a smart white Peugeot taxi she'd hailed outside Châlus bus stop. She was glued to the window, watching the cinematic cliché pan out before her: soft rolling green hills, clusters of stone buildings with charming wooden doors and fields filled with pretty brown Limousin cattle. It was all so green, the yellows so extreme. The Australian landscape seemed faded by comparison. Faded, prickly and scratchy. But she missed the burning smell of eucalyptus in dry air, blades of native grass cutting her skin as she bush-bashed to the waterfront. The squelch of fine silty sediment through her toes as she walked across the vast mudflats of North West Bay. Hell, she even missed the dull drone of flies in her ears as she collected samples.

Most of all, she missed Jack.

The taxi slowed and pulled off the road, passing through a pair of crumbling pillars. They crunched over white gravel, past a derelict barn on their left. Pip gazed at the old barn with square turrets either side and mentally moved in. She could see the huge wooden rafters through the open double doorway and mentally arranged a mezzanine, gravel courtyard and vertical green garden with automatic watering system. They were everywhere in Paris.

Château de Boschaud sat tall, square and proud in the middle of a wide, flat green park dotted with towering ancient oaks, lindens, pines and chestnuts. The taxi drew to a stop, and Pip got out, paid the driver and took her bags.

A stocky lady wearing a brown skirt, white shirt, brown cardigan and headscarf came out to greet her.

'Philippa Arnet, I presume. It is a pleasure to see you again. You were a just a little girl when you last came here with your family, so you probably don't remember.'

'I wish I did,' Pip smiled. 'Lovely to meet you again, Madame Boschaud,' Pip said, extending her hand.

'Come. It is wonderful to have you here. And family too! What a treat. I'm so thrilled you made contact,' She smiled at Pip. 'Bring your bags. You will have the maiden's room. I insist.'

Madame Boschaud stepped through an arched doorway into a small foyer with parquetry floors and then continued walking through another stone arch on her left. Pip followed with her bags until they reached a turret with a winding staircase. The centre of each wide granite step was worn down with use and Pip wondered how many people had walked them.

When they reached the top Madame Boschaud panted: 'Quite a climb, eh? But I hope you find this room special. Not many people stay up here. It is said this is where the young brides slept before their wedding nights. Others say this is where the lords' mistresses were kept.

'One story says the ghost of a woman who is buried in our graveyard over the hill there still haunts the tower.' She chortled and gave a nonchalant shrug. 'Probably a bit of truth in all of them.'

She pointed at the iron radiator fixed to the wall and looked apologetic. 'It doesn't work, I'm afraid. It is too expensive to heat all the rooms. Only the living rooms are warm. There are no bags of gold coins to run this place. No staff. So we try this new "Air" accommodation.' She shrugged again. 'It is very difficult—' she pulled her cardigan around her '—but we make do.'

Pip looked around the tiny room with walls of whitewashed stone and ancient beams the size of tree trunks overhead. The room had a simple wrought-iron double bed with a navy ticking duvet, a round wooden side table and a small cut-glass vase of erlicheer and jonquils, bringing a burst of colour to the room. The only light streamed in through a window, leaving a bright square the size of Pip's backpack on the opposite wall. The effect was enchanting and haunting in equal parts.

Pip walked over to the window and peered out into the fading light. A garden stretched out from the turret for several acres, enclosed by the thickest stone wall she had ever seen—it was at least as thick as the length of her arm. Directly below she could make out half a dozen cane beds where the shrubs were trained and tied to ornate bamboo scaffolding. In the far corner were the familiar gnarled shapes of apple and pear trees dotted in a grid, and there seemed to be some kind of maze of tall dark hedges spiralling around a circular fountain in the centre. Madame watched Pip studying the garden.

'Yes, that is our walled garden. Very productive. The monks established it and tended it during the medieval times. They lived on the other side of the garden—see the cloister over by the wall?'

Pip examined the long narrow rooms built into the garden wall. Along one side was an avenue of crumbling stone columns. There was a strip of apple-green lawn bordering the cloister, and then a series of raised garden beds—each at least two metres wide—arranged in neat squares. She quickly counted twenty. Each bed looked as if it were edged with wicker baskets—she'd never seen woven wood used as a garden border before.

Her parents would love this garden. She wondered why they hadn't made more mention of it when she told them she was visiting. Even Megs would find it hard not to be charmed by this place, Pip chuckled to herself.

Madame Boschaud came to stand beside Pip and followed her gaze. 'Ah. The physic garden.' Pip must have looked confused because she added: 'Medicine plants.'

She continued: 'Over in the far corner, in the shade, we grow the sweet woodruff, and then in the middle beds there we have savoury, fenugreek, rosemary, rue, iris, sage, bergamot.' She ticked them off on her fingers. 'Lots of mints and the peppermint, lovage and fennel. There are so many, Philippa. You must come see for yourself tomorrow. We will walk the garden together.

'The gardens within these walls had been neglected for so long; overgrown with blackberries and the wretched hornbeam gone mad.' Madame Boschaud tore her gaze from the window and made eye contact with Pip. 'When I came to live here again—almost twenty-five years ago now . . .'

She paused and took a deep breath. Her hunched shoulders dropped a little lower—or was Pip imagining it?

'I decided to restore the garden.' Madame's bottom lip trembled a fraction. A deep sadness passed across her face. 'My legacy, if you like.'

Pip realised with a sudden churning in her gut that she had seen this exact expression on Megs's face several times before she left Tasmania. She hadn't heard from Megs in the past two weeks. Well, not more than a text or two. Hardly anything. She was probably reading too much into it—but her mum sounded worried. Her sister's heavy workload combined with the demands of a baby were taking their toll.

If she didn't hear back from Megs tomorrow she'd try Will. Megs would hate that, of course, but what else could she do? She just wanted to check in and hear Chloé's delicious little gurgle. It was a pity she couldn't squeeze those chubby legs through the phone. She was surprised at how much she ached to see her sister and little niece.

Madame Boschaud was still pointing out the window at the mysterious garden below. 'We've tried to maintain the original shape, but it is difficult. Plants change and die, *non*?'

Madame Boschaud shook her head. 'And we do not have the monks to tend it now, of course. I have some local gardeners maintain it. I do what I can.' Madame gave an apologetic shrug. 'I choose the gardeners over oil.' She nodded at the radiators. 'Far more important, I think.'

Looking at the abundant garden below, Pip agreed.

'How long has your family lived here, madame?' asked Pip.

'Give or take a revolution, since 1104. Richard the Lionheart and his men stayed here. I have some books with a history of the château.' She turned to face Pip. 'I can show you the history of your relatives, if you like?'

'That would be wonderful, *merci*. I also have some old documents—recipes and letters. I mentioned them to you on the phone. The originals are at the Herbier, but I have copies. I wondered if you would be able to tell me if they are from here?'

'I'm not sure if I can help, but I will certainly try.'

'Thanks again, madame. You are so kind, fitting me in at such late notice.'

'It is no problem. And please, call me Gabrielle. We are family, after all. I'll leave you to unpack and freshen up for dinner—the bathroom is one level downstairs. They did not plan for ensuites in the medieval times, *non*?' She smiled. '*Aperitifs* will be in the library at six.'

Chapter 32

Château de Boschaud, March 2015

The first thing that struck Pip about the library was the smell. Orange zest. She glanced around the room and saw several thick candles burning on a long wooden table as well as in candelabras and sconces. The room was lined with floor-to-ceiling shelves of leather-bound books, thick oak ceiling beams and a carved granite fireplace you could park a car in. Leaning over it, Pip could make out a worn crest in the facing of the fireplace.

Ancient floorboards—oak, darkened with age—stretched the length of the room. The southern side of the floor was dotted with a series of squares thrown by the faintest trace of light streaming through the row of windows. The sprawling library could seat at least one hundred and fifty comfortably, she calculated. It would have made an impressive dining room. It still did. It would be the perfect place for a feast.

'Ah, Philippa. What will you take to drink?' Gabrielle had set out an old-style drinks tray with an ornate silver champagne bucket, ice, cut-crystal glasses, olives, lemon rinds and a collection of bottles Pip didn't recognise.

'I have some champagne here, brought up from the cellar.' Pip recognised the hand-painted Art Deco botanical label of vintage Perrier-Jouët Belle Epoque. It was going to be a great night.

'Or,' continued Gabrielle, 'some *liqueur de châtaigne*—chestnut liqueur. You can have it with ice, or in champagne like a Kir Royale. I have some special dry vermouth too—a blend from my friend down the road. It is our little secret.' She leaned in and whispered conspiratorially: 'He has the usual cloves, cinnamon, cardamom, orange peel, juniper, hyssop—but he also sneaks in extra wormwood.'

'*Artemisia*,' said Pip.

'As I said, a secret blend of botanicals.' Gabrielle paused. '*Artemisia*—the most bitter, but aromatic of all herbs.'

'Mother of Herbs,' Pip said quietly, repeating the phrase she'd learned from Pedro in the spice room at Azure.

'Of course,' agreed Gabrielle. 'It's said if you grind and burn marigold, thyme and a twig of *Artemisia*, make it into a poultice and rub your body with it on St Luke's Day you'll dream of your true love.'

Pip grimaced at Gabrielle. 'I might have missed the boat on that one.' Was Jack with Valentina now? she wondered.

Gabrielle raised an eyebrow but didn't comment, saying only, 'Now, Philippa—what can I get for you?'

'I might try a bit of the vermouth. For research purposes, of course.'

'Of course,' said Gabrielle as she poured some vermouth into a wineglass with ice and a slice of orange.

'What do you like to drink?' asked Pip.

'Champagne. I only drink vintage. At my age it's worth enjoying every moment of the *grand vin*.'

'Why not?' Pip laughed as Gabrielle poured herself some bubbles. Pip had to stop herself sculling the vermouth. 'Gabrielle, can we go and visit the person who made this so I can see how they did it?'

'*Bien sûr*,' said Gabrielle. 'It is just across the garden in the old monastery. The monks used to make absinthe and other drinks too, of course.'

Pip shuddered, remembering her last encounter with absinthe.

'Like with this vermouth, they used the local plants grown in the garden, and botanicals like juniper and sloe they foraged from the woods. They would have ordered the spices in from the merchants though. There are no cloves or cinnamon in this climate.' She laughed and pulled her grey cardigan across her ample bosom. 'That's why I burn these candles. They smell like warm places.'

'It smells lovely in here,' agreed Pip, nodding as she had another sip of vermouth.

'Down in the cellar and in the garden we have some of the old clay pots in which they stored the spices—or so the conservators say. Some are in pieces, but others, they will store the spices like the day they were made to carry them. I'll show you tomorrow. They are a distinctive shape.'

Gabrielle outlined the shape of the pots in the air with her free hand.

'Apparently, Château de Boschaud was supplied by one family of spice traders for one hundred and fifty years—and they weren't even French but Genoans, would you believe? According to the monks' ledger, the last abbot who lived here stopped the supply almost overnight in 1487 and the merchants were banished. No reason was recorded. No more *beau* pots.' She smiled wryly. 'A pity.'

Above the stone mantelpiece was a tapestry of rosebuds and on the far wall was an enormous tapestry of some nudes dancing around a fire. The candles flickered and picked up the gold thread and dewy skin of the dancers. If Pip hadn't been standing in a musty old room, she'd have sworn they were teenagers at a full moon party.

Gabrielle followed Pip's gaze. *'C'est magnifique, non?'*

'It's beautiful. Very, ah . . .'

'Sensual? Sexy?' Gabrielle wore a wicked smile as she examined the tapestry. 'The government *conservateurs* uncovered this about a decade ago. It was wrapped in leather over in the monastery. It is thought the last abbot kept it in his room. This would have been in the late 1400s. An unusual choice for a monk, *non*?'

'Very.' Pip nodded and took a sip of her vermouth.

'Indeed, we are lucky to have it. The château's inventory records show it was a wedding gift. There was a grand banquet here in 1487—a wedding banquet for Lord Boschaud held at the midsummer solstice. By all accounts, it was incredible.'

Pip's brain whirred. 1487. She wondered if the fate of the spice deliveries and the mysterious tapestry were somehow linked to this banquet.

Gabrielle walked across to one of the bookshelves. 'We have a manuscript. A record of the menu. And now I think of it, we have recipes, drawings and herbals. They think it was written by an abbot.' She took another sip on her champagne as she walked along the bookshelves, scanning for the manuscript.

'I'd love to have a look at that manuscript, Gabrielle. But before we do, may I please show you these old letters and recipes? My friend has magnified them for me, so we can make out some text. I just wondered if you would recognise them. They came in some old copper pots that my mother gave me, which were a gift from my father's great-aunt but no-one really knows where Aunt Margot got them. No-one thought to ask, I guess.' She reached into her backpack for the recipes and fished them out of the bag in their neat plastic folders and handed them to Gabrielle.

'Ah,' said Gabrielle, nodding. 'Were there some copper pots this big, with handles?' She held her arms out from her body making a circle. 'And so deep?' She indicated with her hands.

Pip nodded. 'And some cast-iron saucepans, and a few skillets. The letters were in a medium-sized copper pot.'

'So *you* now have the pots that were sent to Margot. Your great-aunt used to holiday here in the summer with my husband's papa when they were children. He spoke of them often. Then the northern cousins were all sent here during the war.' She smiled. 'Margot's family went to Australia in the 1920s, after the war. Their home was bombed.' Gabrielle sighed. 'I am just trying to think how she got the pots.' She rubbed her chin. 'I think perhaps they were a gift from my husband's grandparents. They felt sorry for the family. They had nothing of home to take across the world for a new start. Their farmhouse in Douaumont was occupied by the Germans, then destroyed.'

She shook her head. 'To you young people these must seem like silly pots. Impractical. But remember: during the war they had nothing. And Margot's family were farmers. With the pots, they could make *confiture, chutney*—make a summer last right through the winter for very little money. A little taste of home.' She shrugged. 'It's not enough, perhaps, after losing a home. But it's something.' She lifted the spectacles that she wore on a string around her neck and examined the letters, shuffling them, taking time to read and then going back and forth between them.

Finally, she looked up at Pip. 'These were in a pot, you say?'

'Well, there was a small scroll tucked in a pot with the lid sealed shut. I had to use a knife to open it.'

'This is very interesting,' Gabrielle murmured as if to herself. She turned her attention back to the bookshelves. 'We had a curator who came and organised everything; now it is impossible to find *anything*.' She shook her head. 'Aha! Here it is—with the gardening and botanicals section. A little confusing, perhaps.'

'Mmm,' said Pip, sipping on her vermouth. It was divine. Bitter, sweet, floral herbs exploded in her mouth and warmed her throat. She buzzed from top to toe. Fancy her old pots coming all the way from this château! Did that mean the pots were as old as the letters?

'So, this is the banquet manuscript I mentioned. By the abbot.' Gabrielle pulled the manuscript from the shelf, and ran her fingers across the hardened calfskin. She held the cover up to show Pip—pointing out the delicate engraving of feathery fronds.

Pip took a deep breath—she recognised that lace-like pattern.

'*C'est* Artemisia, *oui?*' Gabrielle placed the manuscript gently on the table and opened the pages. The front one was missing. Torn out, judging by the ragged edges.

She tutted to herself. 'Yes, yes. I remember. This is frustrating. A missing front page. It must have been some kind of title, or dedication. Or a gift. Some things stay in the past. Confined to these walls.' She glanced around the library.

'The *conservateurs*, they sent it to a laboratory and scanned the indents on the parchment on the next page. There's a loose copy tucked in the back.'

Pip flipped to the back and pulled out a loose sheaf of A4 paper in a plastic envelope. She unfolded it then read the script:

Pour Artemisia,
Mère d'herbes.
Avec tout mon amour sur nos fiançailles.
Vos Andreas

'Mother of Herbs,' she whispered to herself. That strange phrase again. What did it mean? She dropped into a plump armchair covered in faded yellow silk. A plume of dust fanned out. She sneezed.

'*Santé, ma chére.* Are you all right?'

Pip nodded, biting her bottom lip. Was she? Who was this mysterious Artemisia whose letters ended up in a weatherboard cottage in Tasmania? Were these pages in Pip's lap meant for her?

'Gabrielle, could this Artemisia be an ancestor? Is she a Boschaud?'

'*Non*,' Gabrielle shook her head. 'I have the family tree. I will show you tomorrow. And I don't recall any Artemisia mentioned in the château's archives. It's a most unusual name. But I can ask the archivist to have a look, if you like?'

'Thanks. It's probably nothing—' Pip continued looking at the pages of inky botanical line drawings of rosemary and thyme in the margins of the recipes.

Gabrielle came to stand beside Pip and turned the page. *Fête de la Saint-Jean.* She tapped the page. 'Ah, this means the feast of St John. It would have been very auspicious to get married in the midsummer garden. They think, perhaps, this was a wedding gift, that this Andreas asked the abbot to prepare it for his bride. We don't know why the abbot had it among his possessions. Perhaps this young man Andreas could not afford to pay.'

Pip gasped as she leaned over and saw the faintest sketch of a herb set in the middle of the page: a twig fashioned with leaves and as fragile as a feather. *Artemisia.*

'Ah, this . . .' Gabrielle nodded. 'This part is very interesting.' She sipped her champagne before reaching down and tapping the sketch of *Artemisia.* 'This picture, this engraving, matches the front cover.'

'*Artemisia.* Mother of Herbs,' said Pip. Heart in her mouth, she turned to the next page and scanned the list. What if some of these parchments were by the same Artemisia? Who was she?

Gabrielle placed the letters beside her manuscript so Pip could see the similarity between the two sketches on each copy—almost a little watermark in the corner on the individual recipes. Too excited to breathe, Pip leaned over and turned another page.

It looked like some kind of index, or contents page:

Vin Moelleux, des Salades et des Fruits
Potagers et Brouets
Des Viandes Rôties
Entremets
Desserte
Issue de Table
Boute-Hors

No, she realised: it was a menu.

Quickly she turned the next page and the next. Comparing documents. Her pulse was racing, eardrums thumping, as she carefully turned the pages until she came to the one she was looking for: *Pour faire ung lot de bon hypocras.*

She clapped her hands and laughed. Gabrielle looked bewildered. Pip would need to check with Nadia's contact Marie at the Herbier National, but in her heart she knew.

'It's a perfect match. Your manuscript and my recipes are by the same hand.'

'There is one more letter here at the bottom, signed Artemisia.'

'Maybe the abbot didn't write the book,' suggested Pip.

'Do you think this Andreas did? For his lover Artemisia?'

'Maybe. But what if it was Artemisa who wrote it? Or both Andreas *and* Artemisia, the lovers?'

Gabrielle pursed her lips then broke into a knowing smile. 'Perhaps.' She gestured around the room. 'Who can say for sure what really went on in these rooms?' She tilted her champagne glass at Pip and nodded.

Chapter 33

Château de Boschaud, Midsummer 1487

The *hypocras* would be poured soon. It was unheard of to have *hypocras* at midsummer, but Abbot Roald had insisted she make it so there was no point arguing, though it had been difficult enough. Andreas had been helpful, preparing the spice powder and sourcing the wine from trading partners in the north. It had been almost impossible to stop it turning bitter and sour, though, as there was nowhere to keep it cool in this long week of midsummer.

Artemisia had found it difficult to get the exact *hypocras* blend correct. The recipe dictated by the abbot had failed on her first batch and she'd been punished with a fierce blow between her shoulderblades when he'd come to taste it. Andreas had been in the larder at the time, collecting empty pots and delivering full ones. He came to Artemisia's rescue, distracting and flattering the abbot by saying the chaplain's mead and liquor from the still was as fine a blend as the *épicier* had tasted. Perhaps he would consider supplying this too for the *Issue de Table* on such an auspicious day? The day of St Jean.

The following day, Andreas had walked the linden allée with Artemisia to find Abbot Roald in the garden. The abbot had glared like thunder when she arrived unbidden with Andreas. Blustered about the heat and the blend of his drink. Abbot Roald objected to offering his experiment for public scrutiny. The spirit was too bitter. He could not dull the *Artemisia.* It was far too unbalanced as the herb could not be quelled. Tasted like poison. To be expected, he smirked, and spat on Artemisia's boots.

She flinched and Andreas shot her a warning look: *Be still.* As the menfolk discussed the business of the liquor for the banquet, Artemisia watched dozens of tiny brown wrens—tails held high—skip and twitter as they played hide-and-seek under the leaves of the flowering hedgerow. Her legs ached and her back pinched every time she bent to lift a crock this summer. Droplets of dew glistened with the morning sun and she longed to sit for a bit on the grassy mound overlooking the orchard cemetery where her beloved Abbot Bellamy was buried.

She had much to share with Abbot Bellamy, bless his soul. She had no time for confession—and she was plenty sure Heaven was not saving a spot for her leathery hide. But from time to time she liked to sit in peace on the raised tuft of grass in the corner, tucked under the low canopy of pears and apples. She could see the abbot's grave from her perch, so when the winter's soil thawed and frosts had passed she filled the old clay spice pots with fine damp earth blended with hog dung and gently placed seeds of the gillyflowers deep into the mixture. Come summer, the pink flowers ripened and bloomed like tufts of pink clouds and she'd needed an armful of wattle stakes to make sure they stood proud for her abbot. Just before the gillyflowers were spent, she'd collect the petals and dry them out by the fire to make a sweet wine. She was pleased to see the old red rose she'd secretly rescued from Abbot Roald's burn pile had started to send out shoots and wrap around the base of Abbot Bellamy's gravestone like a warm embrace. Love. Perfection. She sighed and her body felt heavy with grief. Artemisia had sheared the abbot's beloved rose close to the roots to save it, and feared the bare roots may not have survived the relentless blankets of frost and snow this past winter. But for once Luck had favoured Artemisia and she smiled, grateful for the tender green shoots basking against the stone, splayed to catch the sun. It gave her hope. She liked to imagine sometimes that this garden was hers and she was free to do as she wished. One day she would make her own little garden beyond these walls. Soon.

She took a deep breath and allowed the mingling birdsong to fill her head, blocking the low tones of the abbot and Andreas debating quantities of spices and prices. She wondered if they would notice if she wandered down the linden allée to the yew and box maze perched at the end and amuse herself by disappearing deep into the labyrinth. Artemisia loved to wander there every chance she had to leave the kitchen. Which was rare enough. She breathed in sharp woody aromas when she stepped on the clumps of thyme planted along the flagstone pathway. Made sure she brushed against the tall purple flowers of the hyssop popping out from under the hedgerow and gently swaying in the breeze. At the centre of the maze was a fountain where she loved to sit and listen to the soft trickle of water, and remove her boots and cool her feet on a hot day. If she wasn't frightened of the flogging she would surely get if she was caught, she would remove her tunic and float in the shallow green pool, allowing the water to soothe her rough skin. She felt her face turning as crimson as the abbot's rose, imagining Andreas ladling water over her hair and shoulders. She wiggled her toes inside her boots and tried to concentrate on the conversation.

It would be her hide that was whipped if they messed it up.

Andreas said he knew of some botanicals in the woods—juniper, marjoram, fennel seed, aniseed—and could source some others like coriander and a special batch of star anise that would sweeten the drink and give it depth. He would assist the abbot to make the perfect blend. It would be an honour. Artemisia nearly choked as she fought to conceal her contempt.

She leaned down to the third pot of cinnamon sticks, pausing to run her hands down the side. The clay pots used for delivery by the de Vitriaco family were different to the other merchants. They were squat, like a mother's belly ripe with child, with a sweeping curve that tapered towards the lid. Artemisia pulled her tunic away from her chest and started fluttering it to cool her skin. She could feel heat rising and her heart quickening as she recalled Andreas slowly tracing the line of the pot with his finger, up and down like a gentle caress. That was on the day she'd met him in the larder, when he took over his father's deliveries to Château de Boschaud nigh on a dozen moons ago.

Andreas had looked her straight in the eye and winked. The hide of the merchant! She'd never had her head turned by any man in the fields or the carts. What was the point? Her place was here, sweating among the pots and crocks.

As beads of sweat collected at the nape of her neck, Artemisia's hand moved among the cinnamon until she found the recipe from Andreas she was looking for.

To make a lot of good hypocras, take an once of cinamonde, known as long tube cinnamon, a knob of ginger, and an equal amount of galangal, pounded well together, and then take a livre of good sugar; pound all this together and moisten it with the best Beaune wine you can get, and let it steep for an hour or two. Then strain it through a cloth bag so it will be very clear.

Even though she could little change the result, it comforted her to know she had made it just right. Last moon, she had selected the largest two pots and asked Jacobus to help her hoist them onto the hooks over the flame. Both were big enough for Jacobus to bathe in. She may consider asking him to do just that when the feast was over, and throw in some verjuice for good measure to heal the bites and rid him of the fleas and lice that swarmed through his blond curls.

She knew it was madness to move her letters and recipes from pot to crock, but the abbot would beat her if he discovered them. Or worse. This way she could be sure they were kept secret. She took the recipe for the *hypocras*, bundled it with the recipe for rosewater and the spice mix along with some old letters from Andreas, tied them up with the piece of twine and the twig of *Artemisia* Andreas had wrapped her gift in, before placing them in one of the small deep copper pots. It was a useless size. Too small for stews and *confitures*, yet too big to warm a serve or two of *porée*. The lid for this pot had never been a true fit, so she used the end of the meat hammer to jam it into place.

No-one would ever find them there—not unless they knew where to look. She shuffled the unused crock to the back of the shelf with the other fallow pots and prayed on her roses and gillyflowers she didn't forget where she'd put them.

Chapter 34

Château de Boschaud, March 2015

Pip stood with Gabrielle in the middle of an ancient linden alley that stretched like a strip of sunshine right through the walled garden. The sky was low and dark and the spring wind frisky. Tiny bright lime leaves covered with dewdrops caught the dregs of morning light and transformed the garden into a jewel. The birdsong was unfamiliar—softer and more melodic than the relentless high-pitched screeches and squawks of the cockatoos and parrots at home. Everything inside these walls seemed so soft and gentle.

As promised, they had been for an early morning stroll. Gabrielle held the manuscript in her left hand, using her right hand to point, pluck a daffodil, or brush along a box hedge as she walked. The manuscript was opened at a double-page spread showing a line sketch of a model of the garden. An *entremet*. It was the done thing at the time to make pastry replicas of animals, but Gabrielle seemed to think an edible replica of a garden could have been a one-off for Château de Boschaud.

Pip chuckled to herself as she imagined the kind of *entremet* she could have made for Megs's wedding. Sleek glasshouse (toffee), giant black flagstones (dark chocolate), iceberg roses (sugared petals). No plants. She couldn't bear to contemplate one for herself. It felt like pressing a bruise.

Her smile faded and she placed her hands over her face to gather her thoughts for a moment as she recalled the texts Megs had sent in the past month, none of them longer than a few words.

I'm fine.

Just a bit tired.

Going into surgery.

Just out of surgery—will call later.

Or the one that worried her most:

No point Skyping. Chloé with Eva.

Or: *Chloé with Will.*

It was frustrating being shut out but she was going to keep on calling and Skyping until they had a proper catch-up. She needed to cut her sister some slack. Megs *did* go into a bubble at work. But was Pip any different? She had just spent the winter in lockdown identifying differences in sediment readings for various benthic invertebrates in a basement under the most beautiful garden in Paris. She'd only popped her head out for crepes, couscous and coffee.

She leaned against the closest linden tree and stroked the grey wrinkled bark with her fingertips. She closed her eyes.

'You look tired,' said Gabrielle. 'Worn out. You push yourself hard, Philippa.' She was nodding to herself. 'Your body *and* your mind. I can almost feel the winds of thoughts circling in your head. Always thinking.' She tapped the side of her head. 'When we get back to the kitchen, I'm going to brew you a cup of violet tea—it soothes the nerves.' She pointed to the book. 'There's a recipe in here for a violet broth. You have violets in Australia, *non*?'

Pip nodded with her eyes still closed, enjoying the soft spring sun warming her face.

'So, I will email you the translations a few recipes at a time.'

Pip opened her eyes and traced the line of the alley back to the maze they had just navigated. She could still hear the trickle of the water and it soothed her. Using the drawing in the manuscript as a guide, Gabrielle had walked Pip through the different sections inside the wall: the kitchen garden with rows of cabbages, broccoli and lettuces; the immense physic garden she'd spotted from the tiny window above last night; and the berry walk with gooseberries, loganberries and four types of raspberries. No wonder they needed all those damn cooking pots. Maybe Pip should send them back to Gabrielle—they were only gathering dust in Megs's shed at home.

Gabrielle stepped forward and linked her arm through Pip's. 'Come, let me show you my favourite part of the garden.'

They walked along the avenue of trees, passing a small ploughed field before turning left into an orchard. Pip recognised rows of apple and pear trees, a dozen to each row and at least ten rows. The trees had bright green buds and tiny leaves were starting to unfurl. Planted among the trunks of the trees, in straight rows, were lines of daffodils, jonquils and erlicheer in vivid creams, yellows and oranges. It was one of the prettiest orchards she'd ever seen.

Gabrielle smiled at her. 'Very special, *non*? Now come, sit over here with me.' She walked over to a mound in the corner overgrown with grass. Its top had been levelled and a stone bench placed on it to make a pretty garden seat. Gabrielle sat and beckoned with a pat for Pip to do the same.

Pip shivered—the stone seat was as cold as ice and jolted her out of her daze. Dotted between the trees were handfuls of old gravestones tilted on angles, chipped and covered in moss. Some were covered with climbing roses, others crumbling right to the base. Pip noticed the two gravestones closest to them looked less worn. At the base of each were some old terracotta pots brimming with daffodils. Gabrielle caught her staring.

'There are so many of these pots around the garden. I fill them for spring and summer colour.'

Gabrielle sighed at the headstones and opened up the manuscript to the drawing and placed it in her lap. She tapped the orchard area with her fingers twice. 'See, we are here.

'But these two graves, they are new. They are the graves of my husband and son. Jean-Paul and Jean-Charles. Forty years ago an apple lorry took a corner too fast on a narrow lane not far from here. There was nowhere for the car to go.'

Pip opened her mouth to say something but must have looked shocked. Gabrielle leaned over and patted her leg with a sympathetic smile. Pip felt a twinge of guilt—she should be doing the comforting.

Gabrielle's shoulders dropped. 'They tell me my boys didn't suffer. A certain irony, don't you think, that they lie here under all these apple trees?' She gave a wan smile. 'But the Boschaud family has been buried here for centuries. It is what my Jean-Paul would have wanted.

'My son, Jean-Charles, he would be forty-five now. Perhaps with a child of his own.'

She took a deep breath in through her nose and exhaled. 'But it was not to be.'

Resignation filled the air. Pip felt as grey as the sky—no wonder Gabrielle had all these cheery flowers planted. They sat in silence, staring at the trees and flowers.

'I went away for a while, you know? Tried to escape for a few years by travelling, living in Paris. Bordeaux. Lyon. But running doesn't heal the heart. Only time.' She took another deep breath and continued, 'This is my home.'

Gabrielle made eye contact with Pip. 'I try to make my time productive. Do the garden, make chutneys and *confitures* for the local village school—apple, of course.' She smiled. 'This is *my* place now. But when I go, I will be buried here in this orchard, with my boys. Worm food.'

Before Pip could ask, she went on: 'The château is already in the process of being passed to the Haute-Vienne department. I will stay here in my little quarters, but they need to open the rooms and the garden to make some money. There is talk of a café . . .'

Pip reached out to take the manuscript still lying open on Gabrielle's lap. 'May I have another look, please?' She leafed through the pages carefully, then closed it for a second, tracing the dainty lines of the engraving on the cover. *Artemisia.*

Before showing her the garden, Gabrielle had taken Pip beyond the wall, past the cloister and the rooms where her friend brewed his vermouth, right to the edge of the woods. There she identified old oaks, coppiced chestnuts and elms, and explained that she liked to carry on the tradition of wandering the woods with a basket collecting botanicals.

She had opened the manuscript to a recipe and translated: 'Juniper berries, marjoram, fennel seeds.' She turned the page: 'Here is the brew for violets I told you about.

'Now come, I want to show you something.' She led Pip to a clearing with a disintegrating, mossy headstone. When Pip stepped close she got goosebumps. Gabrielle traced the top of the relic. 'According to local legend, this headstone belonged to the girl who haunts the maiden's room.' She shrugged. 'After so many hundreds of years, how can we ever know?'

Gabrielle smiled and her wrinkles gathered in folds around her eyes.

Pip didn't believe in ghosts, but she made a mental note to keep the windows of her room firmly locked. She studied the drawing on the cover again, and this time she noticed two small figures. She squinted for a closer look: were they lovers embracing in the woods? Her skin prickled hot and cold. Was this Andreas and Artemisia—the mysterious owners of her letters?

'Ah, you see the lovers now?' Gabrielle chuckled. 'Sometimes, my girl, it is easy to miss tiny things that are right in front of you. Like this picture—the details are extraordinary, *non*? But we are distracted by the lines of the arbours, the arches of the cloisters, this perfect little circle in the middle of the maze.' She tapped her fingers on the fountain. 'You see the grand oak and chestnuts, the wild plums and cherries over here in the woods.' She leaned in close and whispered in Pip's ear: 'But we miss the point.'

'Which is?'

'Love, *ma chére*. Love.'

Pip must have looked confused.

'The *entremet*, the drawing, the letters—somebody has gone to a great deal of effort for love, Philippa.' She smiled, nodded and patted her heart.

'This garden is me. Look at all this new growth around us. New life.' She waved her hands at the trees and daffodils. 'Each day this garden helps me to piece together my broken heart.'

The wrens twittered in the distance as daffodils rippled under the trees. It felt too intrusive to look at Gabrielle. Too raw.

Pip felt warm tears trickling down her cheeks. She wiped them away with the backs of her hands, but still they kept coming.

'I recognise a broken heart when I see one, Philippa.' Gabrielle wrapped her arms around Pip and she allowed herself to be held. She buried her head in Gabrielle's wide bosom and sobbed. Out it all tumbled: Pip's broken engagement, and Jack's unwillingness to recognise the importance of her research. The night with Pedro that had left her aching with guilt and despair. How everyone in her family seemed to succeed at whatever they attempted—except her.

She paused to inhale the strong perfume of the jonquils and listen to the birds singing in the branches of the apple tree.

Then Pip's voice dropped to a whisper as she unwrapped the tiny kernel buried deep: that her research mattered because it was bigger than her.

As Pip sobbed her heart out, the older woman patted her back and gently pulled away the strands of copper hair stuck to her cheek. The two women must have sat there for a couple of minutes because when Pip pulled away, she'd left a broad damp patch of tears on Gabrielle's grey cashmere sweater.

'I'm . . . I'm sorry,' she stuttered. 'It's not—I don't cry.'

'Shush. You need to be kind to yourself, Philippa. Instead of always this analysing. Give yourself a moment to relax in the woods,' she murmured as she put one hand on Pip's heart. 'Trust yourself—you're a fine young woman.' Gabrielle touched Pip's chest with her fingertips. 'Everything you need is already in there. Don't break your heart—your soul—wondering *what if?* You need to make space for yourself. Hold firm.' She laughed and shook her head at Pip. 'If *you* don't, Philippa, no-one will.

'Clear a little corner in life for your own projects.' She paused. 'Then let love in.' Gabrielle looked over at the gravestones. 'Because life is too wonderful to spend it all alone, looking down your microscopes! You have so much to give.'

Gabrielle lifted the manuscript off Pip's lap, closed it and formally presented it to her with both hands.

'You must have it, Philippa. The letters came with the pots from your great-aunt Margot. And the pots came from the kitchen here from her great-grandmother.

'They are ours. They are yours.'

Pip started to protest as she rose from the bench—the gift was much too generous. 'Gabrielle, I couldn't . . .'

'Shush, Philippa. You are family. I'm old.' She shrugged ruefully. 'Falling apart, like this building. If you don't take it, it will only be gifted to a library somewhere in Châlus. *You* are my family.' She smiled and covered Pip's hands with her own. 'Keep it.' Now there were tears in Gabrielle's eyes. 'You'll know what to do with it.'

Chapter 35

Paris, April 2015

Pip bounded up the stairs from the metro and into Charles de Gaulle Airport. As she emerged into the circular concourse, rows of coffee carts with croissants and other pastry treats crammed every corner. Pip was too nervous to eat. She hadn't touched a morsel since she'd texted Jack yesterday to tell him she was on her way back to Tuscany to pay him an impromptu visit.

It was Jack's last month at the vineyard at Tenuta di Falgino. It coincided with a fancy masquerade dinner—he'd mentioned it in an email, but no invitation had been forthcoming. Not since their moment in the chestnut hut. Pip hadn't heard from him in a couple of weeks and her chest tightened when she wondered what that meant. In two hours she would be on an EasyJet flight to Pisa. She pulled her iPhone out of her back pocket and checked for messages as she walked over to order an espresso.

Still no messages. She'd half-expected that Megs might have sent her a message apologising for cutting her off the night before.

Pip had rung Megs when she got onto the bus in Châlus. Megs had sounded sleepy—no surprises there—but also a little distant, like she wasn't really listening. Her voice sounded muffled, and there was a clicking sound in the background.

'Where are you?' Pip had asked. 'Sounds like you're down a mineshaft.'

'Sorry, I'm expressing—got you on speaker.'

'You at work?'

'Yep,' Megs responded flatly. 'Right now I'm sitting on a box in a storage cupboard. I'm surrounded by old drip stands.'

'Jesus, Megs. Don't you have an office or something?'

'Yeah, right! In emergency? Only the blokes that have been here twenty years get those. My desk is at the nurses' station. I express in here so I don't have to do it in the toilets.'

'Why can't you do it in one of those waiting areas? Some of them have got comfy chairs.'

'O-kay . . .' Megs said slowly in her you-have-no-idea-Pip voice, 'so the families get to see the surgeon with her top off. Nice one, Pip! They think I'm here just to do the prep work and reports until the real surgeons come anyway.' She sighed then briskly changed to subject. 'So tell me, what's up?'

Pip began to pour out her plan to retrieve Jack from the significant charms of Valentina, only for Megs to interrupt her because she needed to go sterilise some bottles. Besides, Chloé had a cold and Megs needed to leave work early to check on her so she really was too busy to talk now. Which probably meant the baby had a slight sniffle, Pip thought. She was annoyed—super annoyed—but checked herself. Her big sister had more on her plate than most.

As Pip scanned the board looking for departure times, a text message came through from Will.

Call me as soon as you get this.

Her heart started racing as she dialled his number. Had there been an accident? She felt sick—maybe Chloé had pneumonia and Pip had dismissed it as a sniffle! She was beyond mean.

Pip's hands were shaking so much she kept misdialling, and then she forgot to add the overseas area code. Finally, though, she got through.

'Will?'

'Pip, thanks for calling me back. It's Megs. She's collapsed.'

'What?' Pip's pulse picked up speed. 'But I spoke to her last night. She seemed normal.' *Normal for Megs, anyway.* 'She said Chloé had a cold. Have they both got the flu?'

'Look, we don't know, yet. She's in hospital—'

'Oh my God. I should come home.' The air was starting to feel thin.

'No, that's not necessary,' Will assured her. 'She's just resting and they're pumping her with fluids, running a battery of tests. Angiograms. CTs. MRIs. Your parents are on their way.'

'What happened?'

'We don't know. She was scheduled for evening rounds in ICU, but called in sick. Sounds like whoever took the call gave her a bit of stick about rescheduling. Apparently emergency was rammed so she was on standby for general surgery.'

Pip knew Megs was *always* needed. 'Jesus. So doctors aren't allowed sick days?'

'Well, it's not like Megs ever took any!' Will continued: 'Anyway, the guilt trip worked because she called the hospital back saying she would head in. The details are sketchy but, according to Eva, Megs was reading some files and expressing milk at our kitchen counter holding Chloé on her hip and then she just passed out cold. Fell to the floor and dropped Chloé.'

Pip gasped.

'Chloé's fine,' said Will. 'I don't think she hit the floor—she landed on top of Megs and Eva managed to scoop her up straight away. But poor Megs has some serious stitches across the forehead and a nasty bump. She was out for almost a minute, Eva reckons.'

'That's it. I'm coming home.' Jack would understand, surely. She needed to be with her sister.

'Look, just wait a couple of days while we run these tests,' Will suggested. 'Then you can make a decision. No point rushing back if she just had a sudden fever. You know Megs, she'll probably be as right as rain by the time you get here.'

The slight inflection in Will's tone was a tell: *he was worried*.

'Sorry, Pip, I've got to go. I'm being paged. I'll call you as soon as I hear anything, okay?'

'Can I call Megs?'

'She's asleep now, and then going for some scans. Try in a few hours.'

'Thanks.'

Pip immediately headed to the nearest airline service counter and pulled her credit card out of her wallet.

'Can you please get me onto the next flight to Melbourne or Sydney? I need to get home. It's an emergency.'

Chapter 36

Tasmania, April 2015

Pip strode down the corridor to the end, where she could see her parents sitting on green plastic chairs. Her mother was bobbing Chloé up and down on her knee, clapping her hands and singing 'Incy Wincy Spider' with the accompanying hand movements. Her father was reading a sheet of paper, scratching his head. At the sound of approaching footsteps, they both looked up. 'Pip!' they said in unison.

'Surprise,' she said.

Her father jumped up and wrapped her in a hug. 'You should have told us when you were arriving, darling. I'd have come to get you.'

Mary, with Chloé on her hip, pushed her husband aside to give Pip a big squeeze, and Chloé wrapped a little sticky arm around her neck. She smelled of apples and milk. Mary passed her Chloé and Pip spun around with her, holding her tight, then glanced at the door to Megs's room. 'Can I go in now? How is she?'

Mary spoke first: 'The nurse is doing a check-up. Just give her a minute.'

Pip returned her attention to her niece. 'God, I've missed this little creature. She's even more delicious than I remember.' She held out a pudgy leg. 'She's doubled in size.'

Mary looked amused. 'It happens.'

'Pippa?' said Chloé.

'Yes, that's right, my little munchkin,' said Mary. 'You are so clever.' She turned to Pip to explain, 'Megs has a photo of you on her dresser.'

'Pa!' said Chloé, giggling as she pointed at David, obviously pleased with herself. 'Gwum.' She pointed at Mary.

Mary shrugged at Pip apologetically. 'Well, grandma is too hard—isn't it, my little petal? Gwum is just fine with me.'

Chloé reached out for Mary and clambered back onto her hip like an adorable chimpanzee.

It was probably the jetlag, but Pip felt giddy. She was so worried about Megs she hadn't slept since Paris. It was a relief to see her parents. She'd missed her family.

'Is Will in with Megs?' asked Pip.

'No. I sent him home for a shower and a sleep. He'd worked a double then slept here overnight with Megs. He was exhausted.'

'You look like you could do with a decent shower!' Pip's dad chimed in.

'David!' She saw her mum shoot him that look she knew so well: *be careful.*

'Thanks, Dad.' Her jeans felt soft, and her skin clammy. She did need a shower, but she wanted to see Megs first.

'What's that you've got in your hand?' She eyed the sheet of paper with a spreadsheet colour coded in blue, yellow and purple.

David handed it to her. 'Here, read it if you like.'

Mary shook her head and eyed the ceiling, blinking away tears. What the hell was going on?

Pip held the sheet of paper up and started to read:

Date

Time

Respiratory Rate

O2 Saturation

O2 Flow Rate

Blood Pressure

Heart Rate

Temperature

Why were they looking at a blank hospital chart?

'Not that side—turn it over, love,' said David. His voice was low and uncertain. Mary sighed and gave Chloé a gentle squeeze.

Pip flipped over the page and recognised Megs's handwriting:

15 April 2015

Dear Dr Thompson,

It is with great regret that I resign from Great Southern Hospital, with immediate effect.

I thank you for all the opportunities and training you have given me over the past four years in ICU and Emergency. I look forward to working with you again in some capacity.

Sincerely,
Dr Margot Arnet
MBBS, FRACS, MS (Trauma)

Pip read it another three times to check she hadn't missed anything, as the nurse slipped out of the room and walked past them.

David scratched his head again. 'Margot asked your mother to hand this in at the nurses' station.'

'It doesn't feel quite right, Pip,' said Mary softly. 'Not after all these years. It just doesn't sound like Megs. What do you think?'

Pip didn't know what to think. 'I don't know, Mum. Has Will seen this letter?'

Mary and David shook their heads.

'Is it—is she eating properly?'

Mary nodded. 'Will says so.'

'Right.' Pip pursed her lips. 'I'll talk to her.'

She opened the door to her sister's room and saw a thin, pale Megs lying in the bed, covered with a neat white sheet, staring out the window. A drip was attached to her arm, and a heart monitor beeped intermittently with blue dots in the corner. She had a bandage around her head.

Pip had never seen her sister so still. She felt the prick of tears in her eyes and took a deep breath to stop herself from crying—Megs would kick her out of the room at the first sign of tears.

As Pip closed the door behind her, Megs turned her head and the corners of her lips twitched.

'You came,' Megs whispered, as if it hurt to talk. 'I made Will tell you not to. Why aren't you in Italy?'

'Because you are in hospital, you idiot. Now. What the hell is this?' She waved the resignation letter in the air. Megs sighed and looked back out the window.

'Are you getting a divorce? Is that it?' Pip asked softly.

Megs shook her head.

Pip exhaled, then thought of something far, far worse. 'Have you got cancer? A brain tumour?'

'Brain damage?' Megs turned back to Pip and gave a half-chuckle as she shook her head.

'You're eating, right?' Pip's voice was escalating.

Megs nodded. 'Thanks to the food you had delivered. And Will.'

'Well, did your brain fall out when you hit the kitchen bench? Why would you resign, Megs?' Pip tickled her sister gently on the arm, trying to lighten the mood. But when Megs turned back to face her, huge tears were running down both cheeks and dripping onto the sheets.

Pip plonked beside Megs on the edge of the bed and wrapped her sister in a gentle hug. 'Ssh,' she said as she stroked her hair. 'It's okay. I'm here. We don't have to talk about it now if you don't want to.'

Megs sniffled and whispered in a trance-like voice so low that Pip could barely hear her, 'I'm so tired.'

'I know. Just have a little sleep.' Pip continued stroking Megs's hair, like she did to Chloé when she was trying to send her off to sleep. 'If you move over, fatso, maybe I can sleep too,' she joked.

'No!' said Megs, a little louder. 'I mean, I'm so tired I can't cope.' Her tears were flowing freely now and there were two wet patches on the pillow on either side of her face.

Pip passed her sister a tissue and Megs blew her nose.

'I'm a terrible mother,' Megs blurted. 'I can't look after Chloé—I can't get her to settle. She won't sleep through the night. I nearly hurt her.'

'It's okay. Will said she's fine. Didn't even hit the floor—although I see you made up for it with that bump on your head.'

'No.' Megs's voice had dropped so low Pip had to lean in to hear her. 'You don't understand—I'm not *capable* of looking after Chloé. It's only a matter of time until I do something wrong.' She faltered and corrected herself. 'Another thing wrong. I—I . . .' She turned away, flushing.

Pip took Megs's hand and squeezed it tight for a minute. They both lay there taking slow deep breaths in sync.

Pip ached with guilt and regret. How could she have missed this—her own sister? Megs had been unravelling right in front of her eyes and Pip had failed to notice. The constant fatigue. Edginess. Missed calls and texts. But Megs was a surgeon and a new mum—that was par for the course, right? Megs was strong; she strode from one success to the next in skinny jeans and heels. Except that here she was: limp, pale and broken.

Megs couldn't stop sobbing.

'Shush now. You have done *nothing* wrong, Megs. Do you hear me? You are an incredible mother. Don't roll your eyes. I mean it.'

'I'm pretending to be a mother. Eva's better than me.'

'That's just not true,' Pip whispered as she gave Megs another squeeze, gulping back her own tears.

'I can't even cook toast. Everything I touch burns or curdles. And that's only if I even *start*. Will does all the food. And there's your deliveries. But . . .'

'But what?'

'The food from Dan just made me feel—' Megs hiccupped '—so embarrassed. Like I'm an idiot.' Megs turned to face the far wall. 'I can't even get through the washing most weeks.' More hiccups. 'I'm such a failure.'

As Megs lay there, hiccupping, her limp body radiated shame through starched white sheets. Pip felt her heart pull and tear as she searched for the right words. 'Megs. This isn't your fault. None of this is *you* talking.' She corrected herself. 'Well, it is, but you need help.' She felt waves of uncertainty crash around her. Could Megs be suffering from depression? Really, they needed some professional advice to work out what was going on. Would Megs even talk to a counsellor? 'I'll call Will now and ask him to come back in. And Mum will know . . .'

Megs flinched.

Pip put her hand over her sister's. 'You don't have to do this alone.' She leaned over and hugged her sister tighter. Megs smelled like antiseptic and soap. After twenty-four hours of flying, Pip probably needed fumigating, but Megs didn't seem to notice.

'I'm right here. I'm going to try to help you work out what is going on,' Pip said gently. 'I'm not going anywhere.'

Megs sighed and wiped her cheeks with the back of her hands. 'I'm glad you're here,' she whispered.

Pip's head throbbed with a mix of frustration and unanswered questions. Every day Megs dealt with crisis after crisis in a methodical, calm and systematic way. Not once did she buckle when her patients and their families depended on her. Why now?

Megs broke her silence, her voice slow and strangely detached as she said, 'Last month when I gave Chloé five mils of paracetamol for a slight temperature, I thought of slipping her fifty mils so she'd sleep right through.' She paused. 'I nearly gave her the whole bottle.'

Pip squeezed Megs harder as she closed her eyes. Her sister wouldn't hurt her own child, would she? She was a *doctor.* Pip's heart lurched—there was something very, very wrong.

'And then, just last week, I was paged straight back to do some emergency paediatric surgery on a fifteen-month-old girl who had come in on the trolley from a car accident—carotid artery damaged,' Megs explained as she wiped her eyes. 'There was no specialist surgeon on duty. The paramedics did a good job, but there was some gastrointestinal bleeding and the toddler was close to bleeding out.

'I—I imagined that it was Chloé lying there on the slab, her soft dark curls pressed flat against the stainless steel and sterile green sheets. All it would take was the faintest twitch of the scalpel, a sudden spasm from the child . . .'

Pip's heart sped up. How long had this been going on? Poor Megs! Why hadn't she told anyone?

'Afterwards, I rushed straight to the bathrooms, kneeled on the floor in my scrubs, leaned over the toilet bowl and dry retched.' Megs began to sob again. 'I can't even vomit properly.'

Pip started to cry too. Big, heavy, unstoppable tears. Megs needed help. Pip needed to go call Will, but she didn't want to leave Megs alone. Not now.

'Then, on the way home after that surgery, a roo jumped out from behind some scrub and I clipped it as it bounded across the asphalt. It bounced up the hill into the forest without breaking rhythm. I was relieved, you know—that I didn't kill it.'

Pip dreaded what was coming.

'But it occurred to me that if I'd just braked and swerved a fraction harder, then *I* could have slammed directly into the telegraph pole on my left . . .'

Pip shuddered as the realisation hit her. Her brave sister was telling her that next time she wouldn't miss.

She pulled Megs tighter and kept stroking her head like *she* was the baby while she tried to work out what to do.

Megs took a deep breath, and when she spoke she sounded slightly more in control. 'Pip, can you call Will, please, and ask him to come in? And when he gets here can you ask Mum to come in here too. Leave Chloé with Dad.'

'Of course.'

'I—I need help.'

Chapter 37

Château de Boschaud, Midsummer 1487

The long midsummer light streamed in shards through the high narrow windows of the banquet hall and the yellow stripes made the room feel a little magical. Andreas eyed the large tapestry behind the head table. It looked as if the naked maidens dancing to the lutes with their heads thrown back might step from their golden threads and join the celebrations. Large leafy branches of elm, chestnut and oak lined the cold stone walls of the hall, which made it feel as if they were feasting in the middle of a forest. Posies of roses, lilies, garlic and tansy lay scattered in the middle of every table.

Andreas watched the po-faced stewards clop across the parquet in clogs to direct the incoming pageboys delivering steaming platters of roasted meats to the tables. The hall was instantly filled with the smell of roast meat, cinnamon, garlic and ginger. In pairs, the boys carried rolled caramelised roasted hog with soft cheeses and garlic spilling from the seams, sides of beef and lamb covered with parsley and rows of hare and capon. A line of pages stepped behind carrying shining silver tureens of aioli, thick brown gravy, piquant cameline sauce and green herbed jellies. As the pages nodded and stepped away from the raised head table, a row of trumpeters started to play. Guests dived towards the platters before a fuming—but largely ignored—Abbot Roald could say the prayers. They tore chunks off the meat with their hands, knives and spoons.

Nobody stopped their chatter and laughter to listen to the music—instead the rowdiness and noise of the room rose to the vaulted ceiling with the sounds of trilling and quavering brass. Burgundy was poured into gold goblets from large jugs and Andreas saw the abbot, sitting to the left of Lord Boschaud, discreetly tap a second goblet for the hapless page to fill.

The bride and groom sat on two broad oak chairs with bunches of sage tied to the top. A touch from Artemisia, Andreas presumed, who wished this fair couple wisdom for a long life. He turned his head towards the sideboard, looking for the *entremet* Artemisia had spent two moons preparing; he'd never seen another like it at all the banquets he'd attended. He was surprised to find it wasn't there. Perhaps she'd decided to serve it after the meats with the jellies and other *entremets?* He hoped nothing was amiss—Lady Rose was in for a beautiful surprise from his clever fiancée. He shivered; he was growing impatient waiting for the time to pass till he could ask for the lord's permission to marry his love.

The bride pulled the rosemary from her sleeves and dipped two sprigs into the goblets, passing one to Lord Boschaud to suck. The groom looked bemused, but did as he was bid.

The marshal stood and, with a flourish, cut a green apple in half with a giant sword. The couple laughed and fed each other the pieces through crossed arms: sharing equal sorrow and happiness. The young couple looked pleased enough with the pairing—their matching milky skin was flushed with excitement and liquor. The lord would be off to his tourneys soon and Andreas sent a quick prayer to keep this young man safe, whatever battles he faced.

Andreas could smell the perfumes rise from where the pageboys and stewards trod on lavender, rosemary and rose petals as they whisked past him. The thick white linen tablecloths were strewn with red wine, splatters of pumpkin soup and orange peel slathered with honey. The velvet blue table runners were twisted and rumpled. The master baker sitting to his left lifted the corner of his cloth and wiped a splash of mead from his chin before taking another sip from his goblet.

Andreas sat at the table with fellow master *corps de métiers* merchants and crafters. Opposite were the jolly village weavers from whom he purchased all his mid-sized willow and chestnut baskets. Next were the coopers, the fishmongers and boilermakers. They all delivered to Artemisia at the château and he wondered what they would make of him marrying the cook. Would they treat her like any other wife of a master? He looked across at the pinched, frail wife of the baker, her waist as slender as a stick of cinnamon, as she surreptitiously wrinkled her nose at the ruddy-faced boilermaker's wife. The bigger woman was drinking her Beaune in hearty swigs and laughing and whistling between the gaps in her teeth. He looked at the strong lines of her arms and thought: *These good, hardworking people will accept my bride.* Artemisia was stronger and smarter than all of them and his heart swelled with pride. Besides, what choice would they have once Lord Boschaud and the burgher approved the marriage?

Chapter 38

Tasmania, April 2015

Pip stood dicing fennel, onions, garlic and cherry tomatoes, scraping them into piles on plastic chopping boards to avoid scratching Megs's stainless steel bench. Mary was beside her, chopping chives, and plucking tarragon and oregano leaves. She'd been fidgety all week around the house when she wasn't playing with Chloé, so Pip decided it was best to keep her mum busy. Mary blamed herself for Megs's fall. It wasn't rational, but Pip understood the guilt. She'd felt it surging through her body, draining her energy ever since she'd cuddled Megs on that stiff hospital bed.

It was lovely to be cooking beside her mum again after so many years. The kitchen was steamy from the large pot of stock boiling on the stove. 'We should be using one of your pots from the shed for this,' said Mary as she sipped her wine. 'There's masses of soup here.'

'I'm going to freeze some portions.'

'Pip, darling, I'm not sure there's any more room in the freezer. They'll be eating out of it all year!'

That was Pip's plan. At least until Megs started to feel stronger.

'Are there any recipes for fish stew in that manuscript of yours? Such a generous gift from Gabrielle. Magnificent. Have you written to her yet, to thank her?'

'Of course, Mum. And yes, there's something called a "*chaudumé* of pike". Gabrielle is sending me through the translated recipes one by one—we're emailing all the time—so I'll be able to use them all.'

Pip glanced up at where she had tucked the manuscript in a plastic sealed specimen bag on the bare shelf. It was three days until the party at Falgino—and then was Jack coming home? Alone? She felt herself blushing as she chopped. He'd seemed surprised and a little doubtful about her spontaneous trip to Tuscany to see him. She hadn't heard from him since she'd had to cancel it, other than a quick call to check Megs was okay—although he had sent a huge bunch of pink and white peonies for Megs.

Jack was drifting away from her and there was nothing she could do about it. Besides, Megs needed her here. That was the most important thing now: Megs's recovery.

Will and her dad had brought back an abalone and a bucket of couta, flathead and squid after their early-morning fishing expedition in the boat, so Mary and Pip made a massive pot of *bouillabaisse*. Mary boiled the fish bones to make the stock and Pip added the abalone offcuts to give it a creamy richness. They'd tipped three-quarters of a bottle of chardonnay into the stock, pouring themselves a glass each as they cooked. As she added the saffron, Pip also threw in some crushed chilli and smoked paprika to give it a Spanish touch.

David walked into the kitchen to get a couple of Cascades from the fridge. 'Beer o'clock. I see you ladies have a wine. Do you need any help? Will's just going to take Chloé down to the rocks to grab some mussels. Thought I might go supervise if you have everything under control here.' He lifted the lid of the casserole dish and had a whiff. 'Superb.' He nodded his head. 'Rightio, I'm off.'

Pip watched her father walk through the newly landscaped courtyard, which was paved with sleek oversized black granite pavestones and bordered with dozens of box hedge spheres planted into steel pots. It was as chic as anything she'd seen in Paris. Tucked in the far corner of the courtyard was a little square sandpit made from old hardwood railway sleepers, complete with a wooden lid to keep the sand dry. Beyond it, out on the flat green lawn, and made from the same heavy sleepers, was a sweet A-line swing with an old tyre on a length of rope. The sleepers framed the clear blue water of North West Bay like a painting. The colour of the sea reminded her of Jack's eyes. For the first time in days, Pip smiled broadly. Why hadn't she noticed this play equipment before? Jack must have built these for Chloé when the old garden was ripped up, before he left for Tuscany. She was sure of it; she would recognise his handiwork anywhere.

Mary followed Pip's gaze and gave her a squeeze. Reading Pip's thoughts, she nodded. 'Jack popped over and helped Will build all this.' Pip thought 'helped' was probably a stretch—the only drill Will knew how to use was orthopaedic.

Mary scanned the box hedges. 'We'll need to get a gardener to come in and clip them to stay in shape,' she whispered. 'I don't dare do it myself in case I muck it up.'

Pip put her knife down on the kitchen bench and put her arm around her mother.

'Mum, you have to stop blaming yourself. Will does too. If *anyone* should have recognised the signs, it was me. I'm her sister.' Mary shot her a knowing look and rubbed Pip's back. 'The good news is that Megs admitted she needed help. We have a diagnosis. A plan.'

'I know,' said Mary, nodding. 'But all the signs were there for post-partum anxiety and *I missed it*.' She started listing them on her fingers: 'Emergency C-section, the milk, the rush back to work, one hundred hours a week. I mean, how can *anyone* function with those hours?'

'Mum, Megs is a freak. That's how! You know all this. The psychiatrist said Megs was suffering from severe post-natal depression. Exhaustion opened the door for PND. And the PND fed her fear of hurting Chloé. And self-harm.' She shivered. 'It snowballed quickly.'

'I know, I know. It's crippling,' said Mary. 'Thank goodness the antidepressants have started to kick in. I know she hates them, but they really *will* give her a bit of a reprieve.' Mary paused for a beat. 'Despite what she said to you last night.'

Pip raised her eyebrows.

'Yes, I overheard, darling.' Mary gave Pip a severe look. 'She *must* take the medicine. And she must rest. The daily counselling sessions will help—they'll keep her on track when she is trying to fob us off.' She shook her head and muttered to herself, 'My own *daughter*? I screen people every week.'

'Mum. Stop!' Pip turned to face her mother with her hands on her hips. 'You're here now, that's what counts. Megs is doing way better after just a week. She *wants* to get better.'

'Yes, I suppose you're right,' said Mary as she lifted the lid of the pot and scraped in the onion, tomatoes and fennel along with the pieces of fish.

She wiped her hands on her apron and gave Pip a squeeze. 'Thanks, my darling. I'm very proud of you.'

Pip blinked away tears as she headed out of the kitchen. 'I'll just go check on Megs. See if she's awake.'

Pip walked up the stairs and knocked on the bedroom door.

'Come in.'

Megs was sitting up in bed watching something on her silver MacBook.

'You're supposed to be resting,' Pip scolded. 'Doctor's orders, remember?'

'So it turns out I'm a terrible patient!'

'What are you watching?'

'*House of Cards*.'

'That's a bit—'

Megs interjected with a slight giggle: 'Depressing? Turns out I'm not as screwed up as some people.'

'You're not screwed up. Rundown? Yes. Ill? Sure. There's a big difference.' Pip smiled. 'Besides—' she nodded at the computer screen '—they're not real.'

Megs laughed again, though it sounded a little wobbly.

Pip climbed onto the bed beside her sister and pulled the woollen navy throw over her knees. 'Dinner will be about an hour. Dad and Will are down at the rocks with Chloé.'

Megs sat upright. 'Did they take solid shoes?' she demanded, her voice suddenly high and anxious. Almost immediately she subsided back onto the bed. 'Sorry,' she whispered. 'I'm doing it again, aren't I?'

'That's okay. Chloé's fine. And *you*, my big sister, are going to feel better once you get some decent rest.' Was that just wishful thinking? 'For once, you will take professional help.'

'The drugs are good. Who knew?' Megs coloured as she rested her head on Pip's shoulder. 'Thanks, Pip,' she said softly.

They sat there for a minute, watching the starting credits roll over images of Washington D.C. moving across the screen. Megs hit pause and turned to Pip. 'Have you heard from Jack?'

Pip shook her head, eyes still fixed on the screen. 'Not since he sent the flowers.'

'Will spoke to him last night.'

Pip turned to face Megs. 'And?'

Megs sighed. 'And he's not coming home next week. He's got some more work in Italy.'

Pip felt like all the oxygen had been sucked from the room. So *that* was why he hadn't responded to her texts. He'd moved on. She hugged her knees to her chest.

'You need to go, Pip.'

Pip mumbled into her knees, 'It's too late. He's with Valentina.'

'What? No! He would have told Will, I'm sure.'

'Maybe. Maybe not.' She shook her head and looked at her sister. 'It's hardly important right now.'

'What do you mean, *not important*? You want to spend the rest of your life with this guy and that's *not important*?'

'This is a pointless conversation. I'm staying put.'

'Great.' Megs sighed. 'You going to move in for the whole year?'

'Sure! Why not?'

'Because I have Will. He promised to look after me in sickness, remember? Despite that dirty hipster beard, he's very conservative like that.'

'Megs, honey, I'm not sure he sees your PND as a *duty*.'

'Okay, but you know what I mean. We've got this. Together.'

'Well, thanks very much,' said Pip, a bit confused about where this conversation was going. Maybe it was the drugs talking?

'Pip, you've been amazing this week. I have enough food to feed a space station for a year. You've come to the appointments with me. You made me a plan with Will and Mum. Hell, you've even written some lists. "Mental Health Goals"!' Megs patted her on the shoulder. 'I'm not sure how much more of you being the big sister I can take. Seriously! It's like I'm living with Mother Teresa all of a sudden. The tipsy, carnivore version.'

Pip laughed. 'I like this bossy gig.'

'It's scary how good you are at it. But right now, you need to go pack your bags and book the next flight to Italy. You'll kick yourself—*I'll* kick you . . ' Megs paused, clearly registering Pip's hesitation. 'Don't think for a minute that I don't want you here—I do. But this week has made me realise how deeply I love Will. He's my bone marrow.'

'How romantic,' said Pip, deadpan.

Megs ignored the comment. 'I mean, who else are *you* going to find who loves mucking about in mud as much as you if not Jack?' Megs gave Pip a big hug. 'He loves you. How could he not?'

It was Pip's turn to get a little weepy, but this time they were warm, happy tears. She squeezed Megs back.

'But what about you? And Chloé . . .'

'Mum, Will and I have already worked it out.' Megs was firm. 'I'm feeling a lot better, but Mum's staying on for a while with Dad.' Megs paused as if she was trying to decide how much to reveal.

Finally she said slowly, 'You know, it was Jack who came up with a place for Mum and Dad to stay. His folks are overseas and he's arranged for Mum and Dad to stay in their new cottage at Battery Point for a few months. He's had the cellar stocked, the beds made, a cleaner sorted and a spare set of keys cut. They move in Monday.'

Pip remained silent. She was covered with goose bumps and she pulled the blanket tighter around her. Jack had done all this from Tuscany? He hadn't even contacted her. Adrenaline was flooding her veins, but she sat motionless. His kindness was overwhelming. Half of her wanted to go see him, thank him—the other half was terrified to leave Megs. What if . . . ? Megs's black thoughts and self-harm daydreams had kept Pip awake into the early hours every night since she had been home. Tina, Mary and Will all said these were reasonably common symptoms of PND and that in time—with the right support—they would disappear. But how could they be so sure?

'And the resignation letter?' she asked.

'Burned. I took three months' leave and then I'll look at going back part-time.'

'Oh, well done. Best of both, hey? Just make sure your version of part-time is not eighty hours a week!'

'Well, I won't be doing *anything* until my shrink gives me the go-ahead.' She looked sheepish. 'It's—it's weird. I feel kind of relieved when I see her. Tina's got my back. She's worked in hospitals; she's the *only* person who really gets how hard it can be.'

Pip let that pass.

Megs continued. 'Tina went into private practice when she had her first kid; the hospital atmosphere was toxic. So competitive, so—so—' She fished for the right words: 'Blokey. Ruthless.'

'That's awful,' said Pip realising—perhaps for the first time—how much pressure her sister was really under at work. Tina sounded like a great find, thought Pip as she bumped shoulders with Megs.

'So, stop arguing with me. I have masses of support. We'll Skype every day, I promise. You just have to brace yourself for a few teary calls.'

'Like I've never done that to you!'

'At least I have some happy drugs.' Megs pointed at Pip sternly. 'Go pack. This is the last time I'm putting you on a plane.' She reached out and put her arm around Pip and whispered, 'Thank you.'

Up close, Pip could see the colour was returning to Megs's cheeks and her eyes looked white and clear. She was starting to look much more like her sister.

'Thanks, Megs. I'll go book the ticket right now.'

'Get out of here,' said Megs with a broad smile and a gentle push.

Chapter 39

Château de Boschaud, Midsummer 1487

Artemisia closed the door to the larder to escape the clanging and banging and chatter ricocheting around the kitchen. She removed the wimple and took the hairpins from her hair to cool her head and wiped the sweat streaming from her brow and chest. Her linen undershirt and tunic stuck to her back and she hitched her skirts up and tucked them into her belt. She stretched her arms above her head as she considered the platters of marzipan sweetmeats they were preparing to be carried upstairs. The smell of sugar, almonds, cinnamon and cloves filled the room and she opened an eye to check the trays were still intact. Jacobus was known to sneak in under instruction from the kitchen servants. She could hardly chide the lad—there was so little sweetness in his life a little missing marzipan wouldn't hurt anyone. She grinned. She enjoyed the rhythm of pounding the sweet dough and plumping it into tiny cushions the size of her thumb.

Andreas had been helpful supplying the recipe for the *nuçato* last week. He suggested it as an addition to the *Issue de Table* when she ran through the final orders for spices last week. Claimed it was an ancient lucky charm for his people in the south, over the Alps. An aphrodisiac, he whispered. Her heart was beating fast and she placed her hand on her chest to steady herself. She took a deep breath.

Convinced the chatter had risen and reassured by the level of clanging, Artemisia slid down to the floor and heaved out a terracotta pot of sweet spice mix from behind another. As she lifted the lid, she was hit with the powerful blend of dried ground bay, cloves, ginger and cinnamon. Her hand dived into the pot and she retrieved the note Andreas had passed to her on his final delivery before the morn of the wedding:

Dear Artemisia,

Here is the nucato *I suggested.*

Take honey, boiled and skimmed, with slightly crushed walnuts and spices (ginger, black pepper, cinnamon, cloves), boiled together: wet the palm of your hand with water and spread it out. Let it cool and serve in small pieces the size of a cherry. Or you may use almonds or filberts in place of walnuts.

I am confident our betrothal will be accepted by Lord Boschaud. Let us meet by the gate, as planned.

Your Andreas

She pressed the note to her heart, filled with longing. The hair on her arms felt charged as she realised chatter in the kitchen had ceased. There was only the melodic bang of pots as they were emptied and washed. She slid the letter deep into the spice pot, replaced the lid and pushed it back into alignment as the door swung open and Abbot Roald's shadow filled the frame.

'Just checking the trays are all in order, Abbot Roald,' she said as she untucked her skirts, hoping he didn't notice as she remained in the shadows.

'And are they?' He sniffed the air and took a step into the small room.

Artemisia used the back of her ankle to make sure the pot was in exact alignment. 'Yes, sir.'

'Very well then, go instruct the maids to come and fetch them.'

'Yes, sir.' She had to step sideways and press her back against the shelving to squeeze past his bulging stomach without touching it. As she was almost past, he leaned forwards—his belly spilling against hers, her back wedged hard and burning against a shelf.

'No nonsense, Artemisia. No mistakes. I am watching you every second. It is my reputation at stake,' he whispered.

She twisted her neck to avoid his stink and glanced back down at the pot. The lid was dislodged, and a tiny corner of the letter was sticking out. Her stomach churned and bile boiled as she watched the briefest flicker of his eyes to the shelves where she kept her kitchen records. Perhaps it was just a blink. It was too dark for him to see. She needed to calm herself.

Artemisia took a deep breath, gathering strength from her spices. 'Of course, Abbot Roald. As you wish.'

She could feel his eyes boring into her back as she stepped into the light and let the banging and crashing of the kitchen wash over her.

Only one more course to go.

Chapter 40

Tuscany, May 2015

The taxi wound up the hill past the ghostly silhouettes of pencil pines lining the road to Tenuta di Falgino. Pip took a deep breath and straightened the navy silk dress crushed across her thighs. The chill had numbed the side of her face pressed against the window, but the rest of her skin felt on fire. Half her cells wanted her to go forward, the other back.

She pulled her mobile phone out of the front pocket of her backpack and there was a return message from Megs. *Good luck. Call me ASAP to let me know. I'm good BTW. M x*

As the car slowed to take the final few hairpin turns it stopped and pulled over to the shoulder of the road to give way to a series of trucks.

'Ah, see: Carnevale di Viareggio,' the driver said, tapping his window with excitement.

A series of oversized papier-mâché effigies slowly paraded past on the back of floats lit up by the full moon. The taxi driver had his window down in an instant, filling the car with biting air and upbeat jazz as he yelled out, '*Bellissimo! Bellissimo!*' and started clapping his hands in time to the trumpet melody. It looked like a barnyard Mardi Gras: the first float had an oversized red-crested black hen with wings flapping, the next a purple Indian-style bejewelled elephant. The floats were flanked by pedestrians dressed as lion-tamers, peasant girls, monks, priests and a wall of Venetian masks with pale faces and ribbons of tears. They waved as they walked past and the taxi driver turned and shouted at Pip: 'Ah, *bella*. This *carnevale* is for all of spring. They take this parade into the town and then we have the fireworks later.'

Pip wondered if the fireworks could possibly compete with this rollicking crowd. A giant clown with pink hair, a bow and arrow and a giant red nose drifted by on a float, accompanied by a dozen mini-clowns dressed in multi-coloured jumpsuits, tumbling and cartwheeling down the road in time to the beat of four huge drums. Behind it came a huge gothic bride and groom dressed in black, tongues out, eyes red and googly, grey hair being whipped around by the wind, only held down by the pointy sequinned witches' hats. A row of dead brides, witches and demons carrying straw brooms swarmed around the taxi, smiling and chanting in Italian. They kissed and hugged and high-fived the taxi driver, who now had his whole torso hanging out the window, his face beaming.

Pip couldn't help but smile too. 'What is it all for?' she asked.

'*Carnevale?* It used to be for celebrating the lowering of taxes. Boring, eh? Now, we do it to mark the end of winter and to celebrate spring—hope.'

He climbed back into his seat as the noise wound its way down the hill. 'I go join after I drop you.'

She glanced at her watch. It was 8 pm; the celebration dinner would have started by now.

The driver continued up the hill.

As they turned into the driveway of Tenuta di Falgino, Pip started to grow anxious. Would Jack be pleased to see her?

She paid the driver and walked across the terrace, the gravel crunching under her feet. When she reached the main villa, Pip stood outside and eyed the heavy old oak door. She took a deep breath and composed herself, counting from one to ten. Below the door seeped the soft warm smell of wood smoke, roasting meats and rosemary.

Adrenaline flooded her veins—it was time to go inside. Pip looked down and adjusted the plunging front of her new navy evening dress so it didn't gape and show the edge of her bra. She'd spent way too much on it—but she needed every bit of chic she could muster this evening. She smoothed the dress over her hips, and smiled.

Pip pulled the herbal from her backpack and traced her fingers over the engraving of *Artemisia*, as she had done so many times this week. Nadia had confirmation from the Herbier lab that the letters, recipes and the manuscript were written not by one but two hands. The drawings, sketches and title pages had used one type of ink, the recipes another. The scientists concluded that it was this mysterious Artemisia who wrote the recipes. Pip had already known that instinctively; now she had scientific proof.

She heard laughing behind her and three drunk witches staggered across the terrace arm in arm, swinging bottles of beer. They nodded at Pip, and pushed open the door.

Pip stepped into the warmth and light after them. Acrobats were swinging from the ceiling, the sound of a male baritone singing opera was blaring from all corners, red and white ribbons crisscrossed the ballroom. Tables were set in rows, clad with red-and-white-checked cloths. Judging from the collection of half-empty carafes and discarded beer bottles, the feast was well underway.

Waiters dressed in peasant costumes—long brown tunics and wimples—weaved through the crowd, carrying huge terracotta platters of veal and chicken, bowls of cheesy polenta and jugs of red wine to the tables. Pip scanned the room full of jugglers, ghouls and weeping clowns, looking for a face she recognised.

Bruno approached on her left and pulled her into a hug.

'Ah, Philippa. I am surprised to see you. Let me look at you.' He stepped back and admired her dress, nodding. 'No fancy dress for you. Me neither,' he said with a vigorous shake of his head.

Pip smiled at his rumpled white shirt, black linen pants and red bow tie. He was a sweetheart and it was a relief to see him.

'Come. Have some wine. Drink.' He handed her a glass of red. '*Salute*.' They clinked glasses. 'Now we find your Jack.'

Pip took a hasty gulp of wine.

'Ah, I see him. Over there. Go, go, go!'

Jack was standing with his back to them in the far corner. She could see the line of his broad shoulders in his navy jacket. He wasn't one for dress-ups either. She smiled. Beside him, with her hand on his forearm, was Valentina in a red velvet Grecian-draped gown. Her black hair was loose and glossy, fanning down her back. Pip could feel her face burning and she turned away and took another gulp of her wine.

'I'll take that,' said Bruno, grabbing the glass. 'Now you turn around, *bella*. Go do what you came here for.'

The opera had stopped, and in its place was a poet at a screeching microphone who was reciting in Italian with much sighing and sweeping hand gestures.

Bruno whispered in her ear after a line or two: 'It is Dante. A poem about the lover and love.' Then he gave her a gentle push in the small of her back.

Pip crossed the room, accompanied by the sighing and singing. She walked right up and tapped Jack on the shoulder. 'Jack.'

He turned slowly, Valentina's hand dropping from his arm. 'Pip?' He looked shocked, then beamed as if the smile was going to rip right off his face. 'Pip,' he said with force and scooped her into a big hug. He still smelled of salt and the earth.

Over his shoulder Pip could see Valentina, who looked equally astonished. 'Oh! What a surprise, Philippa.'

Jack twirled around for a moment, and then put her down. 'But I don't understand . . .'

'Can we help you? Is everything okay?' asked Valentina, placing a proprietorial hand on Jack's shoulder.

'What are you doing here, Pip?' He looked around the room. 'How did you even get here?' He sounded hesitant. 'Are you alone?'

'Yes. Jack—'

'Is it your family? Is there another emergency?' interrupted Valentina.

Pip opened her mouth to speak, then closed it. How did Valentina know about Megs? Just how close were she and Jack?

'Are you all right?' asked Valentina kindly. She stepped towards Pip and reached out a hand to squeeze her shoulder.

Pip's heart was beating loudly in her ears. She wished they would just let her speak.

'I spoke to Will,' said Jack. 'I thought you were in Tasmania.' Pip couldn't tell if he was pleased to see her or not.

'I know, it's crazy, right? I didn't hear from you, and . . .' She shouldn't have come, Pip thought miserably, looking at their concerned faces. She had no business being here. She should have stayed home with Megs.

Jack went on: 'How's Megs doing? Will seems to think she's going to be okay. They are going to get some help. Together.' He shot a sympathetic expression at Pip. 'Poor Megs. I can't imagine the energy—just trying to hide it from everyone. It must be awful: all that work pressure, the house, looking after little Chloé.' He shook his head.

'Megs does everything in double time,' he explained to Valentina, who nodded. Jack pulled his shoulders back and his deep blue eyes met Pip's.

Pip blinked.

Valentina looked from Jack to Pip, narrowed her eyes for a moment, then turned to speak with someone at the next table. Pip had to hand it to her—Valentina had class.

Jack was still staring at Pip and a blush started to creep up from his collar. He scratched the back of his neck and glanced at his shoes. Jack spoke softly to his feet. 'I spent a bit of time with her. Megs. I just helped them with a few bits and pieces around the place. She just seemed so stressed about the landscaping.' He shrugged.

'I know, I saw. Very impressive.' Pip's voice came out a little harder than she'd intended. 'Why didn't you tell me?' She was confused.

Jack took a deep breath and whistled. 'It was really no big deal. Besides, you were working all the time. I'm sorry, I didn't mean . . .'

Pip cut him off. 'I know what you meant.' She offered him a half-smile. She wished she had sculled some more red. This wasn't going well.

'Jack, I . . .' But her voice was lost as a burst of Puccini blared from the speakers and a gaggle of busty peasant brides pushed past them, screeching with laughter.

'Sorry, what?' said Jack, leaning down so his face was almost touching hers. 'I can't hear you. Let's go outside.' He took Pip's hand and led her out through the door.

It was only when they were outside that Pip realised she was still carrying her backpack. So much for her attempt at glamour.

But Jack's eyes told a different story. 'Gorgeous dress, babe,' he said admiringly. 'You look stunning. Though cold.' He took his jacket off and draped it over her shivering shoulders and backpack. But—' he took a deep breath '—I still can't believe you came here. I thought the whole thing was over. For good.'

'I wanted to thank you for looking after my family. Sorting that place for Mum and Dad. But I—I shouldn't have come. It's crazy, I . . . I'm sorry,' she said in a small voice, looking at her feet. 'But I want to show you something.' She lifted her head and met his gaze as she fished in her backpack for the manuscript. When she found it, she put the bag on the gravel and handed the book to Jack.

He studied the engraving on the front cover, running his fingers over the lines of the herb before he opened the front page: *Fête de la Saint-Jean*.

'Whoa. What is this?'

'You know the French recipes and letters I found? The ones in the pots Mum and Dad gave us for our—' she swallowed '—our engagement present?'

'Ye-es,' Jack said. 'They're in your sister's shed.' He sighed, looked down and kicked the gravel. When he spoke again, he sounded hopeful. 'What about them? What's so important you had to come all the way over here in person?'

Pip swallowed. She *really* should have had another glass of red. 'This is a book of recipes for a wedding banquet. A medieval one. Look at the dedication at the back.' She put her hand on his arm. 'Please, Jack,' she said softly. 'It's important.'

Jack flipped to the back of the book and found the loose sheet in its plastic sleeve:

Pour Artemisia,
Mère d'herbes,
Avec tout mon amour sur nos fiançailles.
Vos Andreas

Pip watched him hopefully as he read.

At last Jack looked up at her, a grin spreading across his face. Then he lowered his head to read the dedication again. He closed the book. 'Is this what I think it is?' he teased.

'Um, well . . .' Pip hesitated, then bumbled on: 'The Herbier National has confirmed the letters from the pot and this manuscript were written by the same hand. They think a former cook at Château de Boschaud—Artemisia—wrote it, and that Andreas illustrated it and had it bound. It's calfskin. Very expensive. A cook wouldn't have been able to afford that.'

'It's incredible,' agreed Jack as he stroked the cover and traced the lines of the herb.

'There's no record of Artemisia being married though. She died single. But look at the dedication—it's an engagement gift, or a gift to a lover, surely?'

'Perhaps.' He was still looking at the book. It seemed an age until he raised his head to meet her gaze. His eyes were shining.

'I want to—I want us to be together,' Pip said nervously. 'It's a gift for you. An engagement gift.' She drew a breath. 'I want to marry you.'

Jack looked at her, clearly stunned.

When he didn't speak, she rushed on to fill the awkward silence. 'I want to prepare a banquet,' she said. 'Like Artemisia. *For* Artemisia. I want *us* to prepare a banquet.' She stepped forward and placed her hand on the book. 'I mean it. I want to be with you. Forever.'

Still, Jack said nothing. He just stared at her, his brow furrowed.

'Are you still—will you . . .' She stopped. 'What I mean is, will you marry me, Jack?' Pip could feel herself blushing as the skin on her chest and neck tingled hot and cold.

They stood in silence, the words hanging in the air between them. The muted sounds of singing spilled under the doorway and somewhere in the darkness an owl screeched.

Jack stepped in close. 'I have something to tell you too.'

Pip thought she might just throw up—he was going to tell her he was with Valentina now. She'd come all this way, and it was too late. Mortified, she stared at the gravel.

'I settled on Ashfield House this week. I bought out Mum and Dad one hundred per cent—even Nicko came around in the end and helped me find the best terms. I'm in debt forever!' He took a deep breath then reached out to grasp her shoulders gently. Looking into her eyes he said, 'Pip, when your thesis is finished—when you've sorted your work . . .' He took a deep breath and started again. 'What I mean is, when we are settled back in Hobart, would you think about . . . I—I just love you to bits. You're amazing. I don't want to do it without you. I *can't* take on all these projects without you.' He stopped and sighed.

Pip waited, her heart racing.

'I won't make *any* plans without first discussing them with you. I was wrong to push you to marry me before you'd finished your own project. And Ashfield House—it was a crazy ask. I tried to shoehorn you into my life. But your research is important. You're the brains trust, that's for sure—that's why I fell in love with you in the first place.' He paused and grinned. 'That, and the fact you're pretty handy at fishing!' Jack took a breath and let his shoulders fall, before locking eyes with Pip. 'I'm sorry. But what do you say . . . are you in?'

Pip flung her arms around him, her heart dancing with relief and happiness. 'Of course I'm in, Jack! A draughty Georgian homestead needing a stack of work and a partner up to the gills in debt? How could I resist? Besides, where else are we going to find a kitchen big enough for those damn copper pots?'

Jack leaned down to kiss her and she felt warm from head to toe. 'Now let's go get you out of that lovely dress . . .'

'Wait. Do you—do we need to speak to Valentina? Won't she be wondering where you are?'

'Maybe,' said Jack, teasing again. He draped his arm around Pip and pulled her close. 'There's nothing between us.' His voice was clear and honest. 'We're colleagues. That's all.'

'But—'

'Pip! There's nothing. I won't lie to you—Valentina's gorgeous. There were a few moments when *maybe* there could have been more. But she's just been through a bad breakup. Sound familiar? It would have been awkward working together. Less complicated to stop at friends.'

Pip thought of Pedro walking past her prep station, staring at his shoes, and flushed.

Jack gave her a squeeze. 'The *only* unfinished business I had was with you. I couldn't get you out of my head after your visit. Thought the only way to cope was not to get in touch for a while.'

'Well, Valentina seems pretty awesome,' said Pip.

'She is,' said Jack, nodding. 'Super smart.' Then he leaned down and whispered in her ear, '*But she's not you.*'

Chapter 41

Château de Boschaud, Midsummer 1487

In the banquet hall, a smiling Abbot Roald placed a hand on Artemisia's shoulder as if he were a kindly grandparent. Leaning in, he said in a harsh whisper: 'Lady Rose requests that you go up to her chamber and fetch her a vial of her special oil. The *épicier* made it laced with gold.' Then he hissed: 'You thought I didn't know, hmm?'

Artemisia froze. Surely he hadn't found the letter? Or perhaps he'd found her records that proved his lying and cheating?

Abbot Roald continued, louder this time to make himself heard over the banter and music filling the room: 'She demands it be placed in the bridal chamber—at once.'

Artemisia flinched. 'Begging your pardon, Abbot,' she said, 'but would it not be better for one of the chambermaids to fetch it? My place is down in the kitchen.'

Out of the corner of her eye she could see a duo of troubadours juggling a set of pewter wine mugs as a third played a jolly tune on his fiddle. The crowd was laughing and clapping in time to the music and Lord Boschaud banged his tankard on the edge of the table, missing the beat every time. Artemisia couldn't help grinning as she noticed the shy smile of Lady Rose, who seemed entranced by the spectacle.

Abbot Roald noticed her studying Lady Rose and raised his voice. 'Do not argue. Do you wish to be whipped?' As he was speaking, Abbot Roald turned his head, nodding and beaming—the picture of benevolence—at Lord Boschaud and his bride.

Artemisia thought she might throw up.

'I shall go after I put down this platter of *boute-Hors*, master,' she said.

His threat worried her. Once the last dish was served she would need to find a way to make her escape.

From his position at the end of the table, Andreas watched with relief as Artemisia walked away from the repulsive Abbot Roald and headed towards him. She placed a silver tray of roasted cardamom and anise seeds in front of Andreas, avoiding eye contact. Andreas reached out for a handful of the still-warm seeds. He crunched them between his teeth then lifted the edge of the now-stained tablecloth to wipe his lips. With six courses behind him he needed all the help digesting he could get.

He longed to tuck the dark curl that escaped from Artemisia's wimple behind her ear. He longed to lean close and smell the rosemary she washed it with. He knew she had written this secret into the parchments along with so many others. But she turned and glanced at him, urging caution. Then she slipped out of the room and he saw her turn right to go upstairs rather than downstairs to the kitchen. He wondered what task she had been assigned.

The lead troubadour—clad a in green velvet vest and pantaloons with gold trim—stepped forward, shushing the crowd with a wave of his arms. After a dramatic pause, he began to recite:

It is the Romance of the Rose,
In which al the art of love I close.
The mater fair is of to make;
God graunte in gree that she it take
For whom that it begonnen is!

The revellers cheered and clapped as he raised his voice slightly and thrust his hips at the blushing Lady Rose. If the opening lines were anything to go by, they were all in for a treat. While Andreas could skip Chastity, he was looking forward to the stories of Jealousy, Beauty and Chance. With a bit of luck the narrator would skip through to the plucking of the rose from the garden. Andreas shrugged and found a pewter jug among the mess on the table, poured himself another *digestif* and leaned back to enjoy the act. This was going to take a while. In the meantime, he would watch for an opening to approach Lord Boschaud.

Andreas was halfway through his brew when he saw Abbot Roald excuse himself from Lord Boschaud to oversee work in the kitchen for the next course. He paused in his drinking and sat up when he noticed that instead of heading downstairs, Abbot Roald had turned right to follow Artemisia up the stairs.

Chapter 42

Paris, May 2015

To: maryarnet@bigpond.com
From: parnet@unitas.edu.au
Subject: Engagement

Hi Mum and Dad,

Sorry the Skype just dropped out while we were on the train back to Paris. Couldn't wait to share the news. Megs and Will sound pretty stoked. I'm so happy.

The plan is for me to stay and finish my PhD. I'm close. Should take another two months, I reckon. Jack is going to stay for some of that time, but then he has to get home to work in the vineyard. Earn some $$$$!

He is building a new winery, with a view to including a casual bistro. I'm going to ask Dan to consult, and of course I'll help with the menu. We want to use local sustainable produce. Line-caught fish. As much stuff foraged and grown ourselves as we can manage. Maybe we can employ Dad and Dom!

It will be tricky to balance all these jobs, but please reassure Dad that this time I think I have the formula just about right!

If all goes to plan, we want to host the wedding there in 12 months.

Tell Dad I've accepted that research associate job at IMAS. Dr Philippa Arnet coming right up in late 2015.

Lots of love, Pip (and Jack) x

To: parnet@unitas.edu.au
From: maryarnet@bigpond.com
Subject: Engagement

My dearest Pip,

We are thrilled for you.

How remarkable that the pots I gave you for your engagement to watch over you as you made your own home would lead you all the way to the other side of the world.

And then back again.

What to say to my darling Pip? I remember the first time I held you to my chest, skin to skin, and you looked up at me with your curious little green eyes, pulled your tiny pink fist out of your mouth and stared at me. No tears. (Margot cried, well, like a baby!) It was as if you were saying, 'Here I am.' And then you rolled your head back and tried to look around the room. I'll always remember how strong you were. How quiet and focused. I thought it unusual for a baby at the time. Now I have delivered thousands, I can be certain that you are one of a kind!

From the very beginning you were a curious little girl. Always asking questions, sitting on the benchtop, stirring the cake mixture, rolling the dough for pasta and bread. Licking the spoon—always licking the spoon.

In the garden you'd pull along your little yellow Tonka truck full of bulbs if I was planting daffodils, seeds if I was in the vegetable patch. You never cared much for weeding—but then again, neither do I.

Your father and I could not be more proud of you. You are strong and determined and I wonder where your studies will take you? I know in my bones it will not be the well-trodden path chosen by your father and Margot. But that's okay, my darling. You need to learn to trust your instincts. You have always preferred the obscure tracks running around the side of our mountain here. The stolen moments perched high in the branches of our tallest chestnut tree.

My Pip, with the wild hair. Remember that it can be hard to pin you down for an answer sometimes. You will need to be flexible. Embrace change.

Be kind to yourself.

You already have an engagement present and it turned out to be more special than we ever imagined. But I wanted to send you a list of the herbs I had in my wedding posy. I have a feeling it may suit you—and you can make it yourself!

—White roses for love (Wedding Day, of course)

—Rosemary for remembrance

—Lavender for devotion

—Thyme for strength

—Mint for warmth.

Let us know when you plan to come back to Australia and we will meet you at the airport.

Big hugs and love to Jack,
Mum xxx

Chapter 43

Tasmania, March 2016

Pip glanced inside her basket filled with dark caps and squashy undersides of yellow. She breathed in the crisp air and noted it was cool for early autumn. Unusual. Rain had drizzled across Tasmania since Christmas, and tiny colonies of mushrooms had popped up early in unexpected places. She hoped they would last right through autumn; mushrooms could be so fickle. Pip took another deep breath and inhaled pine, eucalyptus, salt and, yes, excitement. Her nose and throat tingled as her lungs filled. Jiggling the wicker basket to make sure the spores fell onto the ground, she kicked some damp pine needles over the spot. Just in case. Her father's old mushrooming companion had taught her well. She was looking forward to seeing Dom today. Gabrielle was already out early with a basket and a list from Dan, picking herbs from the walled garden. She'd jumped at the chance to be a part of the wedding when Pip emailed the invitation and was keen to take her first trip to Australia.

Though it was only March, Pip could see her breath. She knew the chill would lift soon, when the sun was high enough to burn skin not smothered in sunscreen. She watched the damp mist drift up from the carpet of pine needles underneath the giant macrocarpas and looked out across the rows of vines that ran all the way down to the channel. The dull fermenting acid of the pine needles mingled with the sharp scent of the native blue and white gums. She could just catch a scent of the salt lifting off the mudflats with the morning breeze.

'Brrr. It's bloody cold, Pip,' said Megs, stomping her feet to keep warm, and hugging her belly. 'Why do you always get up this early? Ever heard of cereal?'

'Had to collect the clams before the tide came in. You have a good excuse not to get out of bed,' said Pip. 'You sure you're not too tired?'

'I can't believe you thought I would miss *anything* today! Chloé and I have been dancing around in our dresses for weeks.' Megs threw her head back and laughed and it sounded like sunshine.

'C'mon, I think we have enough of everything now,' said Pip. 'Carry that other basket. I've got work to do.'

Megs sighed, reached down and hoisted the deep wicker basket onto her forearm. She lifted the damp tea towel to look at the tiny green berries rolling around the bottom of the basket. 'What have you got in here?' she asked.

'Native cranberries,' said Pip. 'Sweet and sour. I'm putting them with the blackberries and watermelon I picked yesterday from the garden—I thought it would make a great starter. I'll serve the fruit on big platters, with a boozy cranberry sauce and you eat with your fingers. Lick the sauce off. Like honey. Except with port. Delicious.'

Megs raised an eyebrow at her younger sister. 'Eating with our fingers, hey? Sounds very medieval. Are we having jousting and juggling between courses?'

'Actually, I have seven courses planned,' said Pip as she led the way back up the hill towards Ashfield House, perched high above the D'Entrecasteaux Channel. 'It's a full-on banquet. I got the idea from the wedding manuscript Gabrielle gave me at Château de Boschaud. We'll start off with some dry fizz that Jack makes here at the vineyard. It's a new style he's trialling, among others.'

Pip waved a hand at the lines of golden pinot leaves trellised all the way down the hillside to the channel. As the sun lifted, the mist and glistening dew would burn off, and they'd be able to see almost all the way to Bruny Island. She could hear the drone of a tinnie in the distance. The couta were running early this year and Jack had mentioned he might throw a line or two out this morning with Will and her dad for an hour—just to check. She'd bumped into him at dawn, heading out to the vineyard with his cordless drill and a pocket full of screws. It was hard to tell exactly what he was heading out to fix—he'd mumbled at her through a mouthful of nails and kept walking at full pace up the hill. No doubt there was a row of vines loose, or a gate had come off its hinges somewhere. She grinned. So typical of him to fix it straight away, even before he went for a fish with the boys.

'Thanks for all your help these past couple of days, Megs. I know Dan is really grateful too. If surgery doesn't work out, you can always get a job here.' Pip squeezed her sister's shoulder.

There had been many tears over the past few months as Megs started piecing together her new normal and weaned herself off the medication with the help of her counsellor. Part-time work. Day surgeries only. Light exercise. Scheduled date nights with Will. In other words—baby steps. Pip was in awe of how brave and strong Megs was, even when she looked deflated and tired.

Today, though, Megs was buzzing with energy.

'I might take you up on that. Just look at this place. Not bad.' Megs jogged up the wide flagstone steps towards the Georgian house, swinging her basket. They walked along the terrace until they reached the new conservatory built onto the northern side of Ashfield House—two storeys of glass walls with an elegant industrial steel frame that had been treated so it turned a rusty red.

'It's so beautiful, Pip—like a contemporary art gallery. You are both so clever.'

'Well, it was Jack's idea. He needed a big new winery so I suggested if he was purpose-building something so beautiful it should be multi-purpose!'

'Good thinking.'

Pip passed the old turpentine hardwood door. It was hard to believe it was complete only a little more than ten months since Jack had knocked up some sketches on the train from Lucca to Paris.

A handful of staff was busy setting plates and cutlery. The clatter of china and laughter filled the room. She loved the way Jack had given this room such a sharp contemporary edge with soaring steel beams, but made it feel warm using the louvre windows ripped from the old garden shed. From the six-metre-high ceilings dangled long red cords with giant old-style globes at irregular intervals, and Jack had fashioned lightshades in warped cylinders using some rusty old fencing wire. The brick wall was affixed with oversized smoked paprika tins printed with bright Spanish cartoons sprouting a mix of succulents like pigface, Echeveria and cacti.

Pip looked across at the big old big pine dresser she'd had shifted from the homestead's kitchen. She'd asked Jack and Will to move it into the conservatory to house the copper pots. They looked perfect in their new home. Her home. She smiled.

A door burst open and high-pitched shrieks and giggles streamed inside. Chloé ran up and wrapped herself around Pip's legs, trying to hide from Mary, who was giving chase. The child clung to Pip, howling with laughter.

Megs looked over at the dresser, her eyes sparkling. 'You got the pots sorted.'

'Yeah, well, I didn't think I should ask you to help again.' Now Megs was back at the hospital part-time, Pip watched her like a hawk to make sure she didn't overdo it. Her sister was a brilliant actress, it seemed.

'Pots, pots,' Chloé repeated. Pip idly stroked the toddler's back.

'What's this?' asked Megs, picking up the leather-bound book sitting on the dresser. She opened the cover. Mary came and put her arms around Pip's waist and rested her head on her daughter's shoulder. They all stood silently as Megs flipped through the pages until she came to the title page with the heading *Boute-Hors* and some line drawings of rosemary and *Artemisia*:

Pour faire ung lot let bon hypocras
Dele mele bullito co le noci, detto nucato
Pour fair orengat

Megs flipped back to the cover and ran her fingers along the engraved herb and placed it back on the dresser, giving her sister a quizzical look.

'*Artemisia*,' said Mary and Pip said in unison.

'She was also known as Mother of Herbs,' Pip explained, adding: 'I think that's what we'll call the bistro when it opens. Seems right.'

Pointing to the herbal, she said, 'It's also where I got the inspiration for this.' She pulled a crumpled piece of paper from the back pocket of her jeans and smoothed it out on the dresser beside the book:

Wedding Menu

Spicy popcorn

Bruny Island wagyu tartare, tarrago emulsion

Ostrea angassi

Smoked new season pink-eye potatoes, sauce of whey, garlic, samphire and elderflower

Broad beans, violet artichokes, burrata curd, green juniper oil

Steamed Venerupis clams, anise hyssop dashi and Bellota

Lightly steamed line-caught Tasmanian hapuka and mushrooms cooked over charcoal

Artemisia's smoked eel, poached rhubarb, laver and pickled hawthorn blossom

West Hobart lime posset, iced fig leaf and lovage kefir, caraway and dill shortbread.

'Popcorn?' Megs exclaimed. 'Who ever heard of popcorn at a wedding banquet. What kind of starter is that?'

'The salty snack kind,' replied Pip.

Megs laughed. 'Is there any dish these days you don't add herbs or spices to? I mean, I've heard of salt, butter and maybe honey on popcorn. But spices? Sounds mad to me.'

'Just wait until you try it,' said Pip.

'I think it sounds delicious,' Mary interjected. She bent down and hoisted Chloé onto her hip, nuzzling her neck. 'Almost as delicious as you, my darling.' Chloé squealed with delight as Mary pretended to nip her neck.

'Everyone loves a salty snack in summer with beer or bubbles,' said Pip. 'And it's healthy and not too filling—the guests will have plenty of room left for my feast. It's going to be the best wedding banquet ever.' Pip hesitated. 'I hope people get it. I emailed it to Pedro for a squiz. He's been great with ideas for the menu—even sent me a couple of recipes he's trying now he has taken over the kitchen at Telmo's. It's great having him to bounce ideas off for the kitchen. Dan loves it too. We've got—' she looked at her watch '—eight hours. Better get cracking.'

Pip eyed the conservatory. There were old canteen tables and bench seats from the shearers' quarters, round mahogany tables from the formal areas of Ashfield House, a repurposed scouring table from the woolshed covered with glass and a few square laminex café tables. The restaurant could easily seat a hundred people.

Megs was studying the room too. 'I wouldn't be surprised if Jack designed this place with his own wedding in mind,' she remarked. She wrapped her arms around Pip's shoulders. 'This is extraordinary, Pip. What are the tablecloths?' She leaned over and ran a hand over a soft, grey pile.

'Wool. Bit of a nod to the Rodgers' farming heritage. I didn't want plain white starched tablecloths, and we found these old blankets over in the shearers' quarters when Jack was looking for furniture and fittings to repurpose for the restaurant. You know what he's like—why buy something if you can make it yourself?' She smiled happily as she looked around the space.

The dull of the grey blankets was lifted with bright mismatched plates of Wedgewood and bone china they had pulled from the homestead dressers and whipped into service. She and Jack had filled boxes with antique French glassware, crockery and cutlery from the Clignancourt markets in Paris and shipped them home. It seemed fitting to have glass jars of herbs and flowers scattered among the silverware.

Cut crystal wine glasses bounced light around the room, dazzling in the glow of clusters of tea lights. At the centre of each table was a collection of plain water glasses stuffed with sprigs of rosemary, parsley, ivy and white roses. Alternating glasses were filled with the blue hues of lavender and catmint.

'Smells like a florist—or an apothecary,' said Megs as she closed her eyes and took a deep breath.

Pip leaned over the table to tie a couple of loose strings around the medieval-style posies lying on a silver tray for guests to take home as a gift. Earlier this morning, as the trio sat around the breakfast table making them, Mary explained to Pip how on her own wedding day she'd gathered the posy of herbs and woven it with ivy to represent fidelity and strength—it was impossible to rip from the soil once it was planted. Mary had giggled in her girlish way and said she'd made a buttonhole for David too. It had seemed to do the trick for her parents. Mary suggested hawthorn and holly, but Pip insisted on some native yellow wattle, kelp, a sprig of sweet *Kunzea* and green strands of *Lomandra*. Megs had simply laughed and said, 'What are we, rabbits? I've never heard of herbs and salads for bouquets.'

With the strings secure, Pip turned to Megs. 'Hey, Megs, that's the herb we were talking about. The one in the manuscript—*Artemisia*. Wormwood.' Megs looked to where Pip was pointing at the grey-green row of shrubs glinting with dew and unfurling up to the top of the old brick garden wall.

'It's the base of our vermouth. We grow a lot of the ingredients here.' Pip gestured to the walled garden outside and started checking them off on her fingers: 'Wormwood, of course, rosemary, marjoram, coriander and fennel seed, juniper and sloe berries, and the rest we harvest when it is in season along the foreshore. Some of the gum pollens, the samphire seeds, mountain pepper.

'I can't tell you the rest, otherwise we'll have to kill you. Anyway, it changes depending on the season and what we can get hold of. It's fun. Jack already had the leftover white wine and we bought the vodka from a local maker. It's our little experiment. I create the formula and source the native botanicals; Jack makes it work in the bottle.'

Megs laughed and laughed. 'Is that a number from your French recipe book?'

'Gabrielle tasted it last night and gave it her blessing!'

A long trestle table was being set up near the entrance and the staff chatted and laughed as they set out rows of gleaming champagne flutes and cocktail glasses.

Megs raised her eyebrows at Pip. 'Cocktails? At a wedding? Dangerous!'

'Of course! There's the Sloe Gin Sling and the Artemisia—of course—using our vermouth. C'mon, let's get cracking,' said Pip, on the move again. 'We have a lot of cooking to do. Actually,' she paused, 'before I forget, I just have to pop down to the cellar for a minute. I want to show you something. Mum, can you please find Gabrielle in the garden? It's important.'

Chapter 44

Château de Boschaud, Midsummer 1487

'Give it to me,' hissed Abbot Roald.

Artemisia glared with her chin up and removed the parchment parcel from her apron. In the distance she could hear the nightingales warbling—trapped in their wicker cages—and wondered when they would be presented to the bride. She looked out of the tiny window and saw that the midsummer sun was still high. Below she could see the green leaves of the berry walk where the stalks of gooseberries, cranberries and raspberries all stood lashed to their chestnut props. From high in the turret, the green allée looked beautiful set against the orchard and rows of hornbeam hedges. Serene. She took a deep breath, calmed by the scene of the garden stretched like the bright quilt spread across the maiden's bed.

She turned back to answer the abbot. 'No. It doesn't concern you.'

'I said *give it to me.*' He stepped closer and for the second time that day Artemisia recoiled from his septic breath.

'I will not. It is a gift. Private. It does not concern you.'

'*Everything* in Château de Boschaud concerns me. *Comprendre?* Including this.'

He pulled Andreas's letter from his pocket and waved it in the air. Artemisia closed her eyes. When she opened them again he was holding kitchen records—he must have stolen them from the larder.

'*I say to you, a servant is not greater than his master.* Those are the words of God. Are you above God, Artemisia?'

'No, Abbot,' she whispered.

'Pardon?' he boomed.

'I said no, Abbot,' she repeated, louder this time.

He thrust the parchments into the orange flame of the bedside candle and she watched them ignite. As the flames licked his fingers, he dropped the burning pages to the floor and stamped them with his foot until there was nothing left but embers and ash.

'So you see, Artemisia, a cook is no match for an abbot. I will not have a *nobody* like you running to Lord Boschaud with your petty woes. *I* run this place, and I am in charge. So what if I keep a little wine and supplies on the side? *I deserve it.*'

'Lord Boschaud will find out. He's not a fool. Even if I don't tell him—he'll know.'

'Ah, but with the records gone, where's your proof?' Then he snarled: 'I will not allow you to use your records to send me back to Limoges in disgrace.'

'I wouldn't—'

Abbot Roald held up his hand. 'No, Cook. You won't.'

She realised there was little point in arguing. She couldn't win without evidence and that was now lying in ashes on the floor. Her shoulders dropped as she pondered this problem. *Soon I'll be married, and Lord Boschaud will take the word of my husband. No-one would call a master of a guild a liar.* Their word was their business.

'So back to this little book.' He waved the letter in the air and Artemisia saw the bushel of St John's wort hanging above the bed. Her luck would hold tonight—she would wager on the head of St Jean.

'Why would you not seek *my* approval for marriage? Instead, you sneak around like a dirty whore behind my back. I saw you in the walled garden this morn with the *épicier*.'

'No, Abbot. Andreas—'

'I don't care what the merchant says. You belong to the château. I command the servants and the monks. You should come to me *before* you approach Lord Boschaud.' He sniffed in frustration. 'You and that Hildegard. Always wanting exceptions. The lord will not release you. I will not release you. You belong here. That book in your hand—it belongs to me. Give it to me. Now.'

Artemisia slowly stepped along the wall. 'No.' Andreas was downstairs asking for her hand and it would be granted. How could Lord Boschaud refuse on such a day? She was willing to come and help Emmeline and Hildegard with banquets, if that's what it took to live with Andreas above his spice shop in the village.

She pressed her gift to her chest. Wife of the *épicier*, master of the guild. She imagined a fat child swaddled tight at her chest as she took orders and weighed spices at the counter, slipping the francs into a leather pouch slung low around her hips. 'I'll not be handing this over.' She took two steps towards him, 'Now, *pardon*, I must get back to the kitchen. They'll be wondering where I am.'

As she said it, Roald's right fist slammed into her chin, throwing her against the cold granite wall. Artemisia dropped the parcel and he kicked it across the wide oak floorboards to the other side of the room.

Artemisia began to move towards it, determined to retrieve her betrothal gift. She wasn't leaving Château de Boschaud without it. By God's blood, she wasn't going to let the foul abbot bring a flame to it.

He swung his fist again and connected with her jaw a second time. The loud crack of bone breaking filled the tiny maiden's room.

The room began to spin. Warmth trickled from her nose and mouth and she tasted the sweetness and salt of her blood where her lip was split. Artemisia struggled to stand upright, her hands clutching at the thick stone windowsill to pull herself up. Both cheeks throbbed. Her palms were sweaty and her breath was short and sharp with fear.

She just needed to get down the stairs to Andreas. Then she could leave.

The warm twilight air that just an hour ago had filled her with warmth, love, hope and the sweet perfume of summer blossoms had turned cold and clammy. Artemisia leaned her head right out of the window so she had a full view of the berry patch, the cloister billowing with roses, the walls, the dark hornbeam and the rolling hills beyond the wall. Comforted, she took a slow, deep breath.

Roald wiped the sweat from his brow with his sleeve and straightened his purple robe. He stood blocking the narrow doorway to the stairs. He reached out and snatched the parcel from the floor and his fat sausage fingers struggled to untie the string.

Artemisia flinched as she watched his pudgy fingers run over her precious bound manuscript. He sniffed the calfskin, and said. 'Expensive. Too good for a servant,' before he pulled back the cover and flipped through the sheets:

Pour faire ung lot let bon hypocras
Dele mele bullito co le noci, detto nucato
Pour fair orengat

Artemisia watched him rub the parchment between thumb and forefinger, paying heed to the thickness and the fine handiwork of the sketches. Rosemary, coriander, crocus, catmint. He turned leaf after leaf, frowning and admiring out loud the accuracy of the drawings, the delicacies of the feathering in the ink and reading the herbals. She was proud of Andreas—now the abbot saw what a fine, talented man Andreas was he would hand over the parchments, to be sure.

She sighed with relief and allowed herself a tiny smile despite the thumping pain in her jaw. It was going to be okay. She still had her tongue.

Abbot Roald turned to the front of the manuscript and paused to read the dedication from Andreas. He sucked hard through his teeth and his eyes narrowed as he read the words aloud. '*Pour*—'

Artemisia put her hands over her ears and closed her eyes as her head pounded and ached. She didn't want to hear the words of her lover from those repulsive, wine-stained lips. She inched along the wall, biding her time to snatch the book and run downstairs to freedom.

Abbot Roald snorted and sneered, then tore out the page. Artemisia dived towards him and tried to snatch it out of his raised hand. She kicked him in the shin, but Abbot Roald scrunched the parchment into a tight ball then lobbed it out of the window. She'd have to run down and find it the minute she left the tower and then she could return it to its rightful place.

Artemisia kicked Abbot Roald again and tried to wrestle the book from his hand but he shoved her against the wall and tucked the book down the front of his robe.

Sounds of exuberant dancing, stomping, clapping and wild screeching wound up the stairwell as the guests partnered up and joined the troubadours celebrating and swirling around the hall. The stamp of happy footsteps against oak echoed through the château. Even if she were to scream, no-one could hear her. She was trapped. Not a soul knew they were here in the maiden's room.

Artemisia looked at the St John's wort clumped with rue, rosemary and yarrow and realised it might not be enough to keep the bad spirits away. Her blood tasted bitter and she tried to swallow. She rested her upper body against the windowsill, and felt the cool breeze smelling of hope and freedom stroke her cheek. She would be out of this maiden's room before the song was over, she vowed. Tomorrow she would breakfast in the de Vitriaco courtyard with her fiancé under the wisteria.

Gathering all her strength, she tried to duck and run past the abbot, but he smashed her eye socket with his fist. Before she could slump to the floor, he reached down and grabbed her feet. Her petite frame was easy to lift and within an instant she was balanced on the sill, half hanging out of the tiny window.

Artemisia struggled for a shallow breath, her eyes closed. Her pulse quickened and she started to wriggle and kick. She could see the patchwork of her walled garden five storeys below.

'No! Stop! Release me, you swine.'

'You want me to release you?' asked Abbot Roald, lifting her feet higher.

Artemisia scraped her hands and arms on the outer walls as she tried to brace herself against the wall and window frame with all her strength.

She spat at the abbot as she writhed and twisted to free her legs, still clinging to the wall. One good kick and she would be free.

A nightingale shrieked and beat its wings against its cage.

With not much more than a shove, Abbot Roald grinned and tipped Artemisia over the ledge and out the window like a sack of flour.

Chapter 45

Tasmania, March 2016

Pip dropped her shoulder to shove open the worn Tasmanian oak door and jogged down a dozen flagstone steps into the cellar. 'Careful, they can be slippery,' she said over her shoulder to Mary, Gabrielle and Megs. 'Better let Chloé walk, Mum. Hold her hand.'

The temperature dropped ten degrees as they descended. The tiny room felt dank and lifeless, but Pip could smell traces of cinnamon and ginger. She flicked a switch and a dusty globe swinging from a beam bathed the sandstone walls with warm light.

'Why are we here?' Megs twisted her head and looked around the room. 'What the—?'

'Patience,' replied Pip. 'Now come here to the table, look under this sheet.'

'Bit old for magic tricks, aren't you?' Megs said as Pip peeled back the faded floral bedsheet from something perched on an old wooden wine box. Then she took a step back and let out a long whistle. 'Pip. That's . . .' She poked it with her finger. 'Is this what I think it is? Is this *edible*?'

'Yep, sure is. It's an *entremet.* It's my tribute to Artemisia—there's a sketch of one she made for the wedding feast.' Pip smiled at Gabrielle, who looked as if she might burst into tears of joy.

Gabrielle stepped forward and patted Pip's hand. 'We know—thanks to Philippa here—Artemisia wrote that manuscript. We have evidence. And her Andreas did the illustrations. Perhaps they were lovers—I like to think so,' she looked up and gave them all a naughty grin. 'But we will never know for sure.' She shrugged. '*C'est le vie.*'

Pip added, 'The conservators have no idea how this Abbot Roald managed to get the book, but they *think* he ripped the page out and passed it off as his own.'

'Swine,' said Megs.

'Exactly.' Pip nodded. 'So I made a version to honour her. I mean, look . . .' She gestured to the *entremets.* 'I'm ridiculously blessed.' She looked up and grinned.

Mary came and put an arm around her. Chloé cuddled Pip's legs.

'It's just my crazy way of saying thank you. For everything . . .' Pip choked on the last few words, emotion getting the better of her. She took a deep breath and ran her hands through her hair.

She turned to Gabrielle. 'I wouldn't be standing here if it weren't for you.'

Gabrielle tutted and pulled her grey cashmere cardigan tight across her bosom as she blushed. She patted Pip's hand. 'It's magic just to be here, no? To walk your garden. To see a family wedding. *C'est très special.*'

Megs leaned in under the swinging light bulb, studying the replica of Ashfield House. Pip hoped everyone would recognise the walled vegetable garden, tennis court and the rows of vineyards. She had even re-created the grey choppy waters of the D'Entrecasteaux Channel.

'Is that wall *gingerbread*?' asked Mary in awe as she stared at the replica two-storey Georgian homestead.

'Yep, I cut it in blocks so it looks like the sandstone.'

'I love the lavender lined up along the wall and tennis court. Feel that moss on the tennis court. It's so soft. How gorgeous. The garden beds in the veggie patch are—is that a sliced carrot retaining wall?'

Pip nodded. 'Yes, they're meant to be sleepers but I ran out of gingerbread. I've used dehydrated olives and pine nuts for the soil, and pared baby carrots, celeriac, radishes and turnips so they are teeny-weeny. Can you see them planted in there?' She pointed out the tiny feathery tufts in neat rows. Megs nodded and Chloé took a hand out of her mouth and stroked the moss, cooing.

'And now I just have to add a few things.' Pip reached into her wicker basket and pulled out a handful of tiny pink and green native cranberries. 'I'm just dotting a few of these in a line—two lines, actually—to make a berry walk.' She grinned at Gabrielle, who mouthed a silent *merci,* with the slightest nod.

Pip passed Chloé a handful of the berries and lifted her up above the table. Her voice softened as she pointed out where to place each berry: 'Here, darling. Make them straight. That's perfect.' She congratulated the toddler with a kiss on the top of her head.

Megs watched Pip pluck tiny green leaves. 'What's that stuff?'

'Fennel, dill, carrot tops and beetroot leaves. Plus the native samphire, spinach, some *Poa* grass and a few wattle buds.'

'I see,' said Megs, even though she clearly didn't.

'Had to do this bit at the last minute as the leaves would just get too droopy.' Pip lifted the leaves and folded the purplish beetroot leaf into tiny rosettes as if she were doing origami. The tiny lettuces were planted in neat rows down the middle of the vegetable patch.

'Is this pine?' Megs asked as she lifted some dark feathery twigs from the basket and sniffed.

'Sure is. These are some little branches from the giant macrocarpa pine between the main house and Jack's old cottage. They're massive, but they stop the crazy winds up the river hitting the house.' She placed them in a protective row down the side.

Pip reached down to her mushroom basket, collected a handful, folded them into her apron and pounded them against the wall. The crushed mushrooms smelled like sweetened dirt. 'And now for the finishing touch.' And she spread the crushed mushrooms along the bank of the channel: 'The estuary.'

'No good cake should be without standard mudflats!' Mary giggled. 'How did you make the channel appear so stormy? It looks freezing—you got that bit right.'

'Jelly, obulato and squid ink.' Pip shook a plant with wide green leaves. 'Samphire and sea celery—they're natives. Got them down by the shore this morning. Great with fish or in a salad. I'm going to use them a bit in the meal today,' she said as she shredded and sprinkled it along her faux waterfront.

Gabrielle raised her eyebrows and gave a clap. 'Bravo, Philippa. *C'est magnifique.*'

The sharp tang of eucalyptus cut through the stale air and lingering softer spices as Pip crushed some gum leaves in her hands and laid them along the foreshore, adding a few stands of twigs to make it look suitably scrubby. Pip preferred the parts of the Tasmanian coastline where it remained wild.

She had a feeling Artemisia would approve. It was the perfect wedding present for Jack.

Chapter 46

Tasmania, March 2016

Pip stood with her family outside the walled garden waiting for the wedding service to start. She closed her eyes for a moment and rubbed her cheek against the old sandstone wall. The day's sunshine warmed her skin, her bones, and she smiled. The twilight air was thick with the scent of catmint, lavender and *Artemisia*.

When she opened her eyes, rows of golden vines threaded down the slopes to the billowing tufts of dry native grasses and bracken at the water's edge. Her channel. The grey water surged and licked uneven rocks covered with lichen. The tide was coming in and further along the foreshore her mudflats would disappear for the evening, blanketed in roving currents. The channel was starting to cool, and by winter the deep waters would be far warmer than the surface. She'd swim the length of North West Bay with Jack, keeping her body submerged, watching her breath unfurl across the broad winter sky.

'Look at you: the dreamy bride,' said Megs dressed in an elegant sky-blue knee-length silk shift. Her parents stood behind, beaming. David was in traditional black tie and the buttons on his shirt were straining at the belly. Pip hoped they'd make it through the evening. She leaned over to smell the white Wedding Day rose in his buttonhole and got a noseful of fluffy yellow wattle instead. At least the ivy was holding it all together. Pip readjusted it so no-one could see the squashed bits.

'You look beautiful, my darling,' said Mary, stepping forward in a navy beaded flapper-style drop-waisted dress with a slit up one leg.

'Jeez, Mum. You look about twenty-five. Ever heard that rule about not upstaging the bride?'

'Oh, Pip, don't be ridiculous,' said Mary as she smoothed out Pip's shawl. 'This has turned out well—much better than a veil.'

'Sure has, Mum. Thanks.' Mary had whipped up the shawl from a remnant of French lace Gabrielle had brought over from the storerooms of Château de Boschaud. Something blue.

'Right, I think we're all set then.' Pip ran her hands over her dress, feeling every bit the bride. It was funny; she'd never dreamed of a big fancy wedding, but now it was here she couldn't stop shivering with excitement. Or perhaps she was just cold and should have gone with the long sleeves?

Her dress was plain and simple: cream silk, strapless, fitted bodice with an A-line skirt that billowed a little at the ground. She'd been reluctant to look too bridal, flouncy and fluffy—her only request was for comfort. Mary and Megs had come up with the design to show off the shawl and she'd left them to it. She wanted to be comfortable as she raced between the party and the kitchen, checking that Dan and his team were okay.

'Okay, here's the salad. The only thing missing is the parsley,' said Megs as she passed Pip her bouquet.

Pip held it with straight arms out from her body, turning it in the fading light. It looked and smelled like home—a loose bunch of rosemary, catmint, white roses, broadleaf sage, lavender and some native mountain pepper and eucalyptus leaves. Edging it all like the finest silver lace were a few sprigs of her beloved *Artemisia*. Mother of Herbs. She lifted it and sniffed. Not a hint of bitterness. Just a strong woody, earthy scent, in tune with the eucalyptus and balancing out the heady sweetness of the herbs. And perhaps with time, Pip hoped, it would represent fertility. She lifted the posy and let the silvery fronds brush her nose for luck. Was she the only scientist who still believed in a little magic?

Megs looked at her watch. 'Quick, Mum, I'll walk you to your seat.' Megs flicked the catch to the old turpentine door leading into the walled garden and pushed. Nothing.

'Sorry. It's heavy,' said Pip. 'Put a bit of muscle into it.'

'Rightio,' said Megs as she dropped her shoulder and shoved the door open. 'Now that's what I call a door—see you on the other side,' she said with a laugh as she linked arms with Mary and led her up the gravel walkway to her seat.

Pip turned to face her dad. 'All good?'

Her father tipped his head on the side, smiling. He fished for a tissue in his inner pocket and dabbed at his eyes.

Pip gave him a hug.

'Pip, my popsicle,' he said as he stroked her tamed hair sitting flat to her shoulders. 'I'm so proud of you. Your extraordinary research. Jack. This place.' He stepped back and held up his arms as he looked around in awe. 'You're a remarkable young woman.' He placed both hands on her shoulders and Pip remembered the day they stood together at his graduation when she was a child. 'You always surprise me, Pip.'

'Thanks, Dad.' Now she was the one blinking back tears. She touched her fingers to her eyes, hoping the mascara would hold. Then she took a deep breath, squared her shoulders and took her father's arm.

'Let's go.'

Jack watched Pip walk with her father through the old arched doorway in the wall and blinked back tears. Her auburn hair sat thick and loose on her shoulders, offset by the blue lace shawl she was wearing. She looked up and her green eyes locked onto his, before she wiggled her nose and broke into an enormous grin. He blew her a kiss.

The crowd of about a hundred chuckled, full of goodwill and champagne. They'd been enjoying the last rays of afternoon sun, waterside views from the terrace and a generous dose of 2014 vintage bubbles. Jack saw his parents beaming. Mary nodded encouragement and Gabrielle seemed to be laughing and blushing at old Percy Thompson from next door. Behind them, Nicholas and his sleek partner, Wei, nodded and raised their glasses at him in a silent toast. They looked quite the pair of New Yorkers—Nicko with his slicked back dark hair and white tux, Wei with her plunging neckline beneath a white tuxedo jacket and a whole lot of chutzpah. They'd just bought an ultra-modern penthouse in Brooklyn, all lights, glass, steel and slate. Jack wondered what they thought of Pip's revamped walled garden.

The grey gravel had been replaced with an earthy terracotta stone topping. In the far corner, a square of planter boxes made from old railway sleepers was brimming with herbs and vegetables. Pip's prized *Artemisia* hedge billowed and shimmered like giant silver feathers in the afternoon light.

Pip walked down the aisle she'd designed—two rows of twelve waist-height terracotta pots planted with mature olive trees. Clumps of blue lavender and catmint made a pretty ribbon underneath, filling the walled area with perfume and the faintest drone of bees. Billie Holiday's 'Summertime' started to play and Jack beamed at Pip. It was his favourite song.

Will leaned over and patted him on the shoulder. 'Ready, mate?'

'Ready?' Jack repeated. 'I'm the luckiest man in the world.'

David and Pip finished the walk down the aisle and Jack reached for Pip's hand, eager to begin. He mouthed: '*You look beautiful.*' Pip blushed.

The celebrant stepped forward and cleared her throat.

'We are gathered here today . . .'

Chapter 47

Château de Boschaud, Midsummer 1487

Andreas skipped around the corner of the southern turret and gave a whistle as he swung the chestnut gate open to the walled garden. The solstice eve was warm and the sky wide and bright. Festivities in the banquet hall were well underway, with the music from the troubadours and harpists swelling out the windows and filling the grounds of the castle keep.

Andreas hummed along to the music, filled with a happy buzz. He'd enjoyed a couple of jugs of Abbot Roald's mead and a pretty Burgundy. Lord Boschaud had granted permission for his marriage to Artemisia, though not without some ribbing. He suggested he might like to take a chambermaid and a couple of monks next time.

Andreas stood admiring the linden allée with gold shimmering leaves. What a fine evening this was. None better for a formal engagement. He couldn't wait to lift her into the cart and take Artemisia back to his home where Alba had prepared a room for her until they were wed in front of the burgher at noon tomorrow.

There were new linen sheets washed with lavender and rosewater with a silk coverlet embroidered with daisies. Alba had gone to the attic and unwrapped her own lace veil from Genoa and hung it in the sun with a spray of lemon.

But where was Artemisia?

The last he'd seen, she was heading up to the tower at the bidding of Abbot Roald. But surely preparations of rosewater and libations for the bride would be finished by now?

She was probably sharing the news of her departure this eve with Emmeline and Hildegard. Artemisia would miss them, of that he was certain. He could spare her a few minutes, he decided, as he tapped his foot with excitement.

He rubbed his chest and enjoyed the softness of his fine new silk jacket, imagining Artemisia rubbing her soft cheek against the smooth cloth. When they were married at the village church tomorrow, he would present her with a velvet pillow made in peacock blue on which to rest her head. She would make a fuss of course, say it was too extravagant. Insist her tastes were simple. He'd expect nothing less from his Artemisia. But soon he would share his world with her. He stirred at the thought of her lithe, dark body entangled with his. He pictured her strong hands massaging rosehip oil and cloves into his shoulders.

A gust fluttered the leaves and he stepped into the square cloister divided into four equal sections planted with grapevines and the fountain at the centre. The trickle of water was refreshing. He sat for a moment on the edge of the pool.

The midsummer air was thick and warm with lavender and roses, gentle and sweet. It was perfect time to share happy news with his fiancée. *Fête de la Saint-Jean*—the day of new beginnings and new life.

Andreas rose and straightened his jacket.

A nightingale started to sing somewhere beyond the hedge. He wondered when the cages would be carried inside and the birds released to sing for Lady Rose.

He smoothed his hair as he gave a whistle, then stepped out past the hornbeam cloister towards their meeting point.

Chapter 48

Tasmania, March 2016

Pip and Jack were standing outside the winery in the moonlight, picking at the remains of Ashfield House crumbled on the silver platter. A series of floodlights hit the soaring rusted steel wall and cast a warm glow across the pale gravel terrace. There was no cloud cover and the day had been hot, but the evening had brought autumn's familiar blanket of crisp salty mist. Pip watched the outline of each breath as she wrapped her blue shawl tight around her shoulders. The tiny crystal beads Mary had stitched onto the centre of each embroidered flower—love-in-a-mist, cornflowers and roses—sparkled when they caught the light.

Through folding glass doors they could hear the six-piece wedding band belting out Vance Joy's 'Riptide' and the happy tones of the ukulele drifted high across rows of golden vines out to the velvety black ribbon of the channel.

Jack was standing in his dinner jacket with his bow tie pulled undone and the first couple of buttons open. Pip leaned in for a hug and pressed her cheek against the pleats of his white formal shirt where she could feel his heat. The starched cotton failed to button down his earthy scent.

'Sign of a good wedding cake, Pip,' said Jack as he broke off another piece of gingerbread wall and demolished it. He gave a broad smile and his eyes were glinting with pride. 'The cake really blew everyone away. And your speech—Spain, and Gabrielle's garden, this mysterious Artemisia. Describing your past couple of years as a nautilus shell, a . . . a logarithmic spiral.'

'*Spira mirabilis.*'

'Anyway, best cake ever—'

'*Entremet.*'

'*Entremet.*' Jack let the word linger in the air for a moment before he reached into his tux jacket and pulled out a small parcel.

Pip stepped back, surprised. 'What's this?'

'Call it a wedding present.' Jack handed Pip the parcel, which was wrapped in cheesecloth. It was knotted at the top and she saw it had a twig of *Artemisia*, tied with some bracken and acacia threaded through the topknot. She shook her head and laughed at his clever riff. In a way, uncovering the mystery of those random letters hidden in the old pots had marked a change for both of them.

Pip unwrapped the cheesecloth and saw a small book bound with soft tan leather. She flipped open the book to a random page and saw the curling script of her mother's hand on scraps of paper stained with drops of olive oil. Mary's lasagne recipe. The next page was smeared with cinnamon—butter cake. And so on. She flipped through the pages looking at recipe after recipe filled with memories of birthday cakes, graduation dinners and Sunday lamb roasts.

Pip looked up at her husband with tears and she pressed the book to her cheek. 'Where did you get these?'

'Megs and your mum put the recipes together. It was their little project while your mum and dad stayed in Tasmania last year.'

Pip raised her right eyebrow.

'Okay, okay,' he said with a laugh. 'So it was Mary's project. She started writing down and testing her favourite go-to recipes for Megs; she thought it might be helpful. Then, when Will told me about Mary's recipes, I asked to make them into a book.'

He paused and gave his cheeky lopsided grin. 'I offered to make one for Megs too. She graciously declined!' Jack let his full belly-laugh rip and Pip giggled too.

'I made a special copy for your parents—I gave it to them this morning. With a massive thank you.'

'What for?'

'You. Being great in-laws. Just because . . .' He blushed and shrugged.

Pip closed the book and ran her fingers over the engraved herb and recognised the feathery form. Wormwood. *Artemisia*. She flipped over to the back cover, and there were embossed tiny spindly leaves of her own favourite herb: rosemary. How did he guess?

She traced the spindles with her fingers and, as she tipped it over, pressed rose petals and bracken leaves dropped onto the ground.

'Oh, I forgot about that. You missed a bit.' Jack laughed.

She opened the book to where the rose petals had fallen out and saw a thick section of blank pages.

'I thought you could start writing your recipes down. Now we have the bistro, maybe you'll want to do a cookbook. Or a gardening book. Or both. You know, all about all your herbs and spices. And plants. And fish. And benthic invertebrates.' He beamed. 'Plenty of room for recording sediment data.'

'Perfect,' Pip said and stood on her toes to lean in and place a slow, tender kiss on his lips. She opened up the front of the book and saw Jack's wayward scrawl. He really should have been a doctor. She squinted to make out the words:

For my beautiful wife Pip,
Marine biologist, PhD, forager, cook and Mother of Herbs,
With love on our wedding day,
Jack xx

'Jack! It's—it's amazing,' said Pip as she reached up and ran a hand through his curls, before she kissed him. 'Thank you,' she whispered.

'There's something else I want to show you,' said Jack. He tucked the book back in his pocket for safekeeping, took Pip's hand and led her down the steps towards the vines. Pip lifted the hem of her silk dress so she didn't trip, exposing her white Converse trainers as she skipped down the steps. Jack shook his head at the shoes and chuckled as he placed his hand on the small of her back.

'Jack, I'm not sure we should . . .'

He threw his head back, laughing. 'As desperate as I am to get you out of that pretty dress, that's not quite what I meant!'

'Oh,' said Pip, half disappointed. 'Then where are we going?'

'It's a surprise.'

He squeezed her hand as they followed the top row of vines along the contours of the hill until they reached the highest point of the vineyard where it overlooked the water. She turned and watched the water lapping at the sandstone rock pools. A pair of wedge-tailed eagles made the most of the moonlight reflecting across the water and rocks as they soared over the channel. They were probably heading to their nest.

Pip and Jack kept climbing the hill until they reached Pip's favourite part of the property—a saddle about fifty metres below the peak. It overlooked neat vines tracking across the slope before flattening out to the low dense scrub, bracken and grasses along the waterfront.

One side of the saddle tumbled into wilderness, but on the other she could see Ashfield House rising off the terrace, shrouded in mist and protected by the proud row of macrocarpas.

Nestled into this sheltered area was an extraordinary wooden sculpture. It unfurled down the slope like a medium swell heading for shore. As Pip stepped closer, she gasped—Jack had built it using leftover boards from the shearing shed. Pip traced her fingers along one of the fifty or so overlapping horizontal grey hardwood planks, noting how the slight shift of angles and planes connected to make a continuous fluid form. It was hard to tell where the landscape ended and the wood began. The piece stretched up to the sky at the far end, plunged into the soil at the lowest point then reached out to the water at the far end.

Jack lay down on the sculpture, his head propped up at one end and Pip did a double-take—Jack's sculpture was a daybed built for two.

'Here.' Jack patted the area beside him.

Pip hitched up her dress, clambered onto the seat and stretched out. The wooden wave hugged every curve.

'Thank you, Jack,' she breathed. 'Only you could build something this . . .' She hesitated, searching for the right word. 'Magical . . . organic . . .' Neither of these was adequate. 'It's perfect.'

Jack brushed away her compliment. 'Well, what do you give a girl who thrives elbow-deep in soil, mud and silt?' He cocked his head to the side, and grinned. 'And who loves being in the mighty ocean? I figured a set of steak knives wasn't going to cut it.'

Pip laughed at his pun. 'Megs and Wills already got us a set anyway.'

She leaned her neck against her wooden headrest and slowly turned her head towards Jack. His eyes were the colour of midnight. She closed her eyes and found his lips, twisting her hips towards him.

'Mmm, now that was worth knocking up a bench for,' he joked. 'What comes next?'

'Don't even think about it. If I wanted to get out of this dress—which I don't—I doubt you could do up all these buttons in the dark afterwards.'

'Not even a quick dip?' he asked, glancing towards the water.

Pip shook her head. 'Tomorrow,' she said firmly.

'Damn.' Jack smiled and clicked his fingers.

Pip could hear the high notes of Ed Sheeran's 'One' drifting out from the dance floor. 'Besides, we have to get back to the wedding—what are people going to say when they see us walking back up to the house through the vines?'

Jack propped himself on one elbow, keeping the other hand resting on her hip. 'Who cares?' He tugged at a strand of her hair. 'So I thought at the end of each day, when you come back from the lab or one of your test sites and I'm done in the vineyard, we can come sit here and have a yarn.'

'With a glass of wine,' said Pip.

'Or bubbles,' Jack suggested. He rolled away from Pip, reached under the seat and produced an unlabelled bottle of sparkling wine and two glasses.

Pip clapped her hands. 'Because I haven't had enough today.'

'I thought we should have a cheeky glass of Ashfield House's finest before we head back.'

When Jack had finished pouring, they lay back on their seat and Pip watched the offshore breeze dance and skip across the channel, leaving patches of ripples illuminated by the full moon. The air was tinged with eucalyptus and sea salt. Pip shivered and felt the hairs on her forearms stand on end. Jack draped his jacket across her and tucked the corners under her body, leaving one arm free to sip sparkling wine, the other clasped in his.

'Cheers—thank you,' said Pip as she let go of Jack's hand to rub the tip of her right index finger back and forth across the lip of the wood, exploring the differences in the textures. She and Jack were as different as two grains of wood could be, but they'd finally found a way to complement one another. She felt a tiny hole where a rusty nail once lived and marvelled at the seamless overlap between the old planks.

Chapter 49

Château de Boschaud, Midsummer 1487

Andreas straightened his velvet jacket as he brushed past the hornbeam hedge and out of the cloister. His pace quickened as he hastened to his meeting point with Artemisia.

The stars glistened. The midsummer garden's maze of glossy hedges and the heady scent of roses and catmint spurred him on. The garden heaved with abundance. The evening felt laced with magic.

He'd wrap his arms around Artemisia and celebrate the joyous news.

Perhaps he should stop to gather a posy for his bride?

No. He'd had enough of waiting.

The instant he stepped into the berry walk Andreas spotted Artemisia.

His heart stilled. *She wasn't—*

Artemisia was strewn across the gooseberry bushes like a sheet thrown out to dry. Arms and legs disjointed, neck snapped in half like a goose prepared for a feast.

His knees buckled and he dropped to the earth. Clutching his stomach he roared, 'Noooooooo!' Artemisia was dead.

How?

It had something to do with Abbot Roald. Andreas just *knew.* He'd seen the abbot follow her up the stairwell.

Andreas forced himself to stand. Artemisia was the strongest person he knew and he wouldn't sully her memory with his own weakness.

Heartbreak and fury flooded his veins and he sprinted down the gravel path to reach her.

'Help me!' he screamed as he ran. 'Help!'

Andreas cared not if it ruined the wedding banquet—his life was over the minute Artemisia had drawn her last breath.

He scrambled through the prickly gooseberry bushes. Branches tore at his shirt and scratched his hands and chest but he felt nothing. He kicked through the bushes, stomping them flat and snapping the branches until he reached her. He gently lifted Artemisia's broken body from the bushes and cradled her in his arms. Her still-warm skin smelled of cinnamon, galangal and cumin—the blend of his own sweet *chambre des épices.*

He dropped his head onto her chest and wept.

Jacobus helped one of the monks and Andreas carry Artemisia's body from the walled garden out to the spice cart. It was a burden too heavy for any child, but Jacobus had insisted and

Andreas relented. Artemisia cared for the child and had talked to Andreas of paying his tax debt once he was of age. She wanted to buy his freedom so he could grow to adulthood outside the château. It was as if her own bright future gave her cause to secure freedom for those she loved.

The task of embalming her body with herbs would fall to Hildegard and Emmeline. With the lord's permission, they would travel to the village with him tonight and set Artemisia's battered body gently on a table in his spice storerooms. Abbot Roald refused to permit Artemisia's body to enter the chapel. His mother would allow Artemisia to be buried in her wedding veil. Andreas would prepare a vial of lavender and rosemary oils with a touch of *Artemisia* and gold leaf. Strong. Bittersweet.

Because Artemisia was Andreas's betrothed, she was his kin. Andreas alone was responsible for her burial. The filthy Abbot Roald would not agree to her body being consecrated within the château's walls—the only home she'd ever known—as Artemisia had committed the eternal sin of taking her own life. Not even Lord Boschaud could overturn this religious decree.

'I can't make head nor tail of it, sir,' said Jacobus. 'Artemisia's cheeks had never had so much colour as these past two moons.' The child's narrow chest heaved. 'It—it don't smell right to me.'

Andreas ruffled the child's golden curls, too choked up to offer any words of consolation.

Abbot Roald had insisted she be buried outside the walls. An orphan—a servant and common cook—had no place in the cemetery at Château de Boschaud. None. In any case, Andreas thought a small mound beyond the wall in the chestnut forest was perfect for his Artemisia. From death would come life. Her blood would feed the earth—the herbs, the mushrooms she so adored. She would be free to rest and roam as she pleased.

Jacobus took the torn page he'd found crumpled beside Artemisia's body from his pocket. He squinted to make out all the words in the moonlight, then held it out to Andreas. 'Monsieur de Vitriaco, sir, I—I found this.'

Andreas closed his eyes and groaned, for he didn't need to read the words he had written for his lover:

For Artemisia,
Mother of Herbs,
With all my love on our betrothal,
Your Andreas.

No good could come of this now. 'Here, child.' Andreas batted away the page. 'Be off to the kitchen with you. And toss that scrap of parchment into the coals simmering under the cauldrons with some yarrow and garlic. And rose petals. Make sure you don't forget, Jacobus. Run now.'

It was time to let Artemisia's spirit rest.

Chapter 50

Tasmania, March 2016

Jack could feel the wash from Pip's kick beside his head as she overtook him on their homeward lap of the bay. He adjusted his stroke and stretched out to try to catch her. No chance.

After ten more strokes she slowed, and rose to stand shoulder-deep in the water. As he swam up behind her and stood, she turned and wrapped her arms around his neck, her legs around his waist, pressed her chest against his, clinging tight. He could feel her heart beating and her gasping breath settling into a steady rhythm. Her body felt warm as the wind skimmed the water's surface, whipping his face. He wondered if he could convince her to pull off her navy Speedos as the evening swell started to build around them. When her breathing settled, she let go of his neck and lay back in the water, floating like a starfish.

'Beat you,' she said. 'Again.'

Pip's auburn hair fanned out around her head like seagrass. His wife was beautiful. They hadn't told anyone they were staying put for their honeymoon. He scanned the wide arc of the bay, taking in the canopy of the eucalypts, walls of sandstone and the mudflats that spread like corrugated iron all the way to shore. Greying clouds were moving in fast, obscuring Mount Wellington. The bitter scent of eucalyptus leaf had mellowed and sweetened. He took a deep breath, drawing the soft, humid air deep into his lungs. A storm was gathering, but Jack didn't care a bit. He and Pip could hunker down together at Ashfield House, warm and dry, until it blew over.

He gently poked Pip in the stomach until she was fully submerged.

Pip came to the surface, spluttering. The chill of the wind stung her face and she dived under again, blowing a trail of bubbles. When she floated to the surface a second time, she paddled back to her husband and gave him a slow kiss. His lips were warm. He cradled her head in his hand and pressed his lips close to her ear and whispered: 'I'll beat you tomorrow, babe.'

'Let's find some clams for dinner and go home.' She started swimming with brisk, short strokes to shore.

The mudflats had drained and lay raw, pockmarked and exposed. Jack brought over a red bucket, and Pip squelched ankle-deep in muddy sediment until telltale bubbles popped near her feet. She started digging a small hole with her fingertips before plunging her forearm into the sandy mud up to her elbow. She emerged with a large handful of silt, and when she smoothed it across the surface she plucked several clams from the haul. She looked up and smiled at Jack. 'Couple more of these and I'll be done.' A gust of wind hit her back and she braced against it.

As she paused, she looked up at the shadows falling across the rugged sandstone escarpment, the orange hues fading to a soft grey. Beyond the foreshore, the khakis and browns of the soft scratchy native grasses and spiky bracken rippled and folded like waves as the onshore wind gathered. The scrubby saltbush held firm—stoic even—studded among stands of rough-barked peppermint gums. She scanned for the pale, smooth bark of the rarer blue gum and heard the high trill of a swift parrot. As the high note pierced the low steady evening hum of flies and cicadas, she caught Jack's eye and smiled. Not long now until the parrots jumped on the back of the cool winds and drifted to the mainland for winter. A cycle that refused to be broken.

When Pip had half-filled the bucket she picked up a decent-sized clam, tracing the soft ochre lines where the triangle curved down to the lips of the shell before placing it back into the bucket. Jack lifted the pail with one hand and reached out for Pip's hand with the other as they dropped their heads and shoulders and stepped head-on into the gusty nor'westerly with the sun falling behind them.

Acknowledgements

When I showed my twelve-year-old son Henry the draft cover for *The Midsummer Garden,* he pointed out that my name was way too big: 'Because, Mum, it's not like you did the whole book yourself. You had a lot of help!'

No truer words were spoken.

Three cheers to my very thoughtful agent, Clare Forster, at Curtis Brown Australia. She's read far too many drafts and has always been wise counsel—not to mention a fabulous dinner companion. Thanks also to Dana, Benjamin, Fiona and the team at CB for their enthusiasm and professionalism in dealing with my queries and contracts.

Annette Barlow is a brilliant publisher and, now, a wonderful friend. She has an astute, warm and loving way of engaging with both text and author and this novel is a thousand times better for it. The very clever (and patient) senior editor Christa Munns and copyeditor Ali Lavau completed this Allen & Unwin editorial dream team and I am so very, very grateful for all their hard work. Indeed, the entire team at Allen & Unwin—Robert Gorman, Tom Gilliatt, Karen Williams, Caitlin Withey, Lillian Kovats, Andy Palmer, Tami Rex and Andrew Brown—embraced this concept enthusiastically from the outset and I am thrilled my story found such a vibrant, warm and professional home. Thanks also to Nada Backovic for the dreamy cover.

Pip would still be floundering in chemistry and biology 101 without the generosity, guidance and stiff fact-checking of Tasmanian marine biologist Dr Karen Parsons. UTAS associate Sophie Bestley was most generous with her descriptions of her time working in research at LOCEAN, Natural History Museum, Paris. Any mistakes and misrepresentations are my own.

Jennifer Walker wrote an article in *Quartz* in November 2015 called 'There's an awful cost to getting a PhD that no-one talks about'. From my interviews with many PhD students in general, threats of funding cuts and fear of failure are an all-too-common scenario for these high-achievers.

A huge shout-out to my fabulous, clever and discerning reading buddies Fiona Laird, Peta Heine, Sue Peacock and Kate Daniel. A book only comes to life when there are readers. You all took the time to read sections (or all of it) and talk about it many more times than you probably wish to remember! Also thanks to my beautiful (and very patient) mum, Carolyn Manning, who scaled rocks when camping in the outback to get emails of drafts and was always on the end of a phone line when I needed it. She always said I'd write a book! (So did my dad, who always read to me and told magical tales when

I was young.) Thanks to my beautiful, clever and very special sister, Prudence Hannon, for the fashion advice, champagne and 'detox meals'.

My extended Wilcox clan always provide adventures galore on the Tasmanian waterfront (or any waterfront!), along with amazing meals invariably involving something they've caught. They are all non-stop inspiration.

A special thanks to my incredible, upbeat reading and writing buddy Sara James Butcher. The writing journey is so much better with amazing friends like you.

There are many people in the publishing industry who saw an early draft and were full of enthusiasm and feedback. I'm deeply grateful to each person.

In late 2014 I undertook an online creative writing course with Penguin Random House Writers' Academy UK. It was liberating, and gave me the tools to try my hand at fiction. Barbara Henderson, my online tutor, told me my premise was compelling enough for a novel. She said, 'You must have faith in this idea—I really think it's going to work.' (I kept the email!) She pushed me outside my comfort zone to write more than 3000 words. Closer to home, Kate O'Donnell was a very patient and professional writing mentor and sounding-board. Her deadlines and advice helped me finish the first draft. Bravo!

Tony McNamara, writer and director extraordinaire for screen and stage, read an ugly early draft and gave me three simple but key tips. Hooray!

Tasmanian chef (and keen surfer) Jahan Patterson Were was very generous in multiple phone interviews, sharing his experience living and working as a chef in Spain.

Zest, Azure, Telmo's (indeed the whole village and region of Mendiluze) and the Gros are fiction (as are all the dishes).

Thanks to Magda Debiec and bar owner Gerald Diffey for sharing their Basque experiences with me. A shout-out to my husband, Alex Wilcox, who has the best job ever and is always willing to share his travels and meal highlights. He took his research in Spain very seriously indeed!

The Gardenist, Michael McCoy (www.thegardenist.com.au), was super-helpful on the botanical front, checking flowers, seasons and so much more. Any horticultural mistakes are my own.

Former cardiothoracic surgeon and current CEO of One Life Live It (www.onelifeliveit.net.au) Dr Simone Ryan has publicly shared her story of resigning on the back of a hospital chart. She has gone on to help people keep healthy at work. All characters are one hundred per cent fiction, and the circumstances of Megs's resignation bear no resemblance to those of Dr Ryan's.

If you or someone you know may be suffering from postnatal depression, visit PANDA: Perinatal Anxiety and Depression Australia (www.panda.org.au).

Pip's and Mary's bridal bouquets are replicas of my own wedding bouquet, but I got the original inspiration from Christina Hindhaugh's *The Great Herb Tour*, a book I worked on many moons ago (still one of my favourites).

Alison Pouiliot gave me some essential mushroom tips at a fungi workshop held in the magnificent grounds of Ard Choille Heritage Gardens, Mount Macedon.

Finally, all my love to my family. Thanks to my lovely Henry, cheeky Charlie and darling girl Jemima Artemis for the laughs, delicious dinners, help in the garden and dispensing cuddles, chocolate and daisy chains to keep me going. And to Alex—for everything. Big love. x

Resources

The complete list of sources consulted in the writing of *The Midsummer Garden* is too long to detail here. Below is a list of essential resources.

The following books were useful for research:

A Brief History of Swearing, Melissa Mohr; *The Medieval Cook*, Bridget Ann Henisch; *Medieval People*, Michael Prestwich; *A Study of Cooking Tasks, Methods, and Equipment in the Renaissance Kitchen*, Chris P. Adler; *The Royal Horticultural Society New Encyclopedia of Herbs and their Uses*, Deni Brown; *The Complete Book of Vegetables, Herbs and Fruit*, Matthew Biggs, Jekka McVicar and Bob Flowerdew. Two divine websites useful as background for both the chateau and a medieval garden were www.chateaudebrie.fr and www.prieuredorsan.com/jardins/jardins-a.html.

Snippets plucked from original sources include: *Roman de la Rose (*by Guillaume de Lorris in c. 1230 and Jean de Meun in c. 1275); Francesco Petrarca (1304–1374), *She Ruled in Beauty*; Giuseppe Verdi, Sempre Libera from *La Traviata*; and the *Bible* (in order of appearance)—Proverbs 29:15, Genesis 2:15, Matthew 23:26, Psalm 52:2, 1 Corinthians 7:32, Proverbs 16:18, Luke 16:15.

Some recipes (for example, *tizanne doulce*, rosewater, violet broth) and gardening snippets were drawn from a book out of copyright: *The Goodman of Paris: A Treatise on Moral and Domestic Economy by a Citizen of Paris*, c. 1393, translated by Eileen Power, 1928. (Originally published by George Routledge and Sons Ltd in 1928 and in 2006 by The Boydell Press, Woodbridge.)

Other medieval recipes were mentioned with the kind permission of University of Chicago Press: Odile Rendon, Françoise Sabban and Silvano Serventi, *The Medieval Kitchen: Recipes from France and Italy*, translated by Edward Schneider, the University of Chicago Press, Chicago, 1998. (Originally published as *La Gastronomie au Moyen Age: 150 Recettes de France et d'Italie*, Èditions Stock, 1993.) The recipes referred to include: *hypocras*, *crespes*, green *porée*, spice mixtures, mustard, green *porée* for days of abstinence, roast kids with sauce of gold, parsley studded lamb or mutton, stuffed suckling pig, confetti, eel and spinach torta, san vincenzo's day grilled eel, *entremets*, *chaudumé* of pike, marzipan sweetmeats (*caliscioni*), cherry pudding, spiced plum pudding, *nucato*, candied orange rind, poached pears in spiced syrup, grilled mackerel.

Original language material reproduced from *The Medieval Kitchen* (above) was originally sourced from the following texts:

For the *hypocras* and *crespes*, *Le Ménagier de Paris*, edited by Jérôme Pichon. Crapelet, Paris, 1846; reprinted Slatkine, Geneva, 1970.

For the roast kid, suckling pig, eel and spinach torta, *marzipane* and *caliscioni*, Maestro Martino, *Libro de Arte Coquinaria*, edited by Emilio Faccioli, in *Arte della Cucina, Libri di Ricette: Testi sopra lo Scalco, il Trinciante e Vini dal XIV al XIX Secolo*, Il Polifilo, Milan, 1966.

For the *nucato*, Francesco Zambrini, *Libro della Cucina del Secolo XIV*, edited by Gaetano Romagnoli, Bologna, 1863; reprinted, Forni, Bologna, 1968.

I heard the anecdote about the Sudan–Paris giraffe at the Muséum National d'Histoire Naturelle at Geelong's Word for Word Festival in 2015, in a talk given by *QI* researcher Molly Oldfield. You can read more about it in her spectacular book *The Secret Museum*, Firefly Books, New York, 2013.

The recipes for rosewater were based on the following resources: Jadwiga Zajaczkowa, 'Making Medieval Style Scented Oils and Waters', 2008 (http://www.gallowglass.org/jadwiga/herbs/oil&water.html); Jeanne Rose, *Herbs & Things: Jeanne Rose's Herbal*, chapters VIII, XVII, XIX, Putnam, New York, 1972; *The Goodman of Paris: A Treatise on Moral and Domestic Economy by a Citizen of Paris*, c. 1393, translated by Eileen Power, 1928; 'Sixteenth-Century Sweet Water for Linens', *Bulleins Bulwarke*, 1562, quoted in Eleanour Sinclair Rohde, *The Scented Garden*, 1931.

Lastly, the fruits on p. 163 were inspired by Heston Blumenthal.

COMING IN MAY 2018

The Jade Lily

KIRSTY MANNING

In 2016, fleeing London with a broken heart, Alexandra returns to Australia to be with her grandparents, Romy and Wilhelm, when her grandfather is dying. With only weeks left together, her grandparents begin to reveal the family mysteries they have kept secret for more than half a century.

In 1939, two young girls meet in Shanghai, the 'Paris of the East': beautiful local Li and Viennese refugee Romy form a fierce friendship. But the deepening shadows of World War Two fall over the women as Li and Romy slip between the city's glamorous French Concession and the desperate Shanghai Ghetto. Eventually, they are forced separate ways as Romy doubts Li's loyalties.

After Wilhelm dies, Alexandra flies to Shanghai, determined to trace her grandparents' past. As she peels back the layers of their hidden lives, she begins to question everything she knows about her family—and herself.

A compelling and gorgeously told tale of female friendship, the price of love, and the power of hardship and courage to shape us all.

ISBN 978 1 76029 479 3

Chapter 1

VIENNA, 11 NOVEMBER 1938

It was against Papa's newest rules to look up, but when Romy stared along Wipplingerstrasse, shards of glass dangled like broken teeth from heavy wooden frames. Pretty shop windows had turned into scary *Tatzelwurm* monsters overnight. The wide, grand street was a sea of dark coats—black, brown, navy and grey—weaving desperately between ornate stone buildings.

None of the adults knew where to go.

Some were trying to sweep up glass. Crowds gathered and swirled, chattering, crying and screaming. Black cars honked in the teeming street. Instead of waiting for their path to clear, some cars ploughed into crowds without slowing, forcing people to leap out of the way.

With her father grasping one of her wrists and her mother the other, Romy was dragged through the chaos like a small child, though she was twelve. Still, she made no noise except for the glass crunching under her boots. She tried following Papa's rules, avoiding eye contact with any of the heads above the coats. Instead, she concentrated on the feet of her older brothers, Benjamin and Daniel, who walked an arm's length in front.

Romy glanced sideways from under her navy beret. The smashed and battered doors had scraps of paper pinned to them, flapping in the breeze.

Wehrt euch! Kauft nicht bei Juden!
Defend yourselves! Do not buy from Jews!
Keine Juden!
No Jews!

There were twice as many signs as yesterday. 'Why do they keep putting up these signs?'

Papa looked at her with tears in his eyes and shook his head without breaking his stride. 'Herr Hitler hates Jews. I fear nothing will be the same while the Nazis are in charge of Austria.'

'But I don't understand why the Führer hates us. Why—'

'This is not the place to talk,' Papa said, cutting her off. 'The streets aren't safe . . . Hurry. Remember the rules, Romy.' Papa usually had an answer for everything, but today he looked as lost as Romy felt.

She stumbled on an overturned chair as Mutti tugged at her arm. The Bernfelds just needed to get home.

Three blocks behind them, all that remained of their synagogue were charred bricks, grey tiles and still-burning wooden planks collapsed beneath the debris. The synagogue's library of rare books and manuscripts lay in a pile of smouldering cinders on the footpath.

They weaved between piles of rubbish. Romy coughed—her throat burned and her eyes stung. The air was heavy with the smell of smoke and gasoline and it hurt to breathe. She wished her parents would slow down. She had a nasty blister on her heel from her new patent leather boots, and her thick, double-breasted peacoat with the shiny gold buttons—such a treat last week—scratched her arms and rubbed the back of her neck.

From the corner of her eye Romy saw Papa pat the inside top pocket of his own coat, which bulged with their passports. They had walked miles to the British consulate to plead for visas.

'I studied at Oxford for my doctorate. I taught surgery in their hospital for a year. We all speak English. Does this mean nothing?' Papa had demanded.

The consular official with the mousy hair and gold pocket watch was apologetic. 'We have our orders, I'm afraid, Dr Bernfeld. Britain has strict immigration policies. There is a waiting list for visas. No exceptions. Not even for specialist skills.' He swallowed and looked at his shoes as his ears turned pink. 'America has the same rules. Even Palestine won't take any more boatloads at this moment, I hear. I'm terribly sorry . . .' He shrugged and raised his palms helplessly.

Papa nodded, put the passports back in his coat pocket and turned away to grab his brown felt hat off the desk.

The official coughed. 'You know,' he said, 'there is somewhere you don't *need* a visa.' His voice dropped to a whisper as he leaned towards the family. 'Shanghai. You . . .' He hesitated.

Mutti blanched and shook her head.

'It might be worth . . .' His voice faded.

Papa shook his head and muttered, '*Danke*.'

Romy thought Mutti was going to crush her hand as she whipped her out of the office, heels clip-clopping across the parquetry.

Mutti had barely slowed down since they had left the consulate, but as they approached Romy's favourite café she hoped they might stop for afternoon tea. She opened her mouth to ask then remembered Papa's rules: *No speaking.*

As they marched past the café Romy peered in at the dark wooden bar and saw gentlemen in dark suits sipping their coffee and reading newspapers, ignoring the mess and chaos outside. She pictured herself and Mutti sitting at one of the small marble tables, a dainty coffee cup in front of Mutti and for Romy a dark hot chocolate piled high with cream. It was their ritual after her Saturday afternoon piano lessons. Romy suspected Herr Bloch tolerated half an hour every week out of loyalty to her brothers. Daniel played in a jazz band at his university and Benjamin had applied to study at the prestigious Wiener Staatsoper—the state opera—before the new government said he wasn't allowed. Last week her stumpy fingers had stretched themselves to a D-major arpeggio without stopping, plus passable opening bars of Mahler. Herr Bloch had applauded and said, 'Bravo!'

As the Bernfelds approached Herr Bloch's piano shop through the bitter smoky haze, Romy strained to see the gleaming black baby grand perched in the window. Instead, twisted ebony piano legs dangled through broken glass.

'Look!' said Romy, pointing with alarm. Herr Bloch was being dragged out by his hair to join a handful of middle-aged men on their hands and knees, picking up the glass and scrubbing the street clean. A pair of blond soldiers threw Herr Bloch onto the ground, but as he righted himself the smaller of the two soldiers swung his military boot into his stomach and sent him sprawling onto his back.

'Halt! Bitte hören Sie auf!' Stop. Please stop!

Romy's head swivelled as Benjamin stepped off the footpath and reached out to help Herr Bloch sit up. Papa cursed as Daniel followed his older brother. Romy held her breath as Mutti squeezed her hand. The boys were going to be in big, big trouble when they got home.

One of the soldiers walked over to Benjamin and Romy stiffened, then relaxed as she recognised him; it was Franz, a baritone from Benjamin's choir. There was obviously a misunderstanding with the music teacher and Benjamin would be able to sort it out with his friend. But when Franz looked across at Benjamin the smile didn't reach his eyes. Nor did he greet him with a handshake. Instead, the soldier flipped his long rifle upside down and whacked Benjamin in the head with the butt.

Years later—when she was an old woman—Romy was still trying to forget what happened next, but the memory was seared into her brain.

Benjamin and Herr Bloch were knocked sideways onto the cobblestones. Blood dripped from their ears, down their chins. Mutti let out a high-pitched scream and all around them the crowd fell silent. Romy's breaths were shallow, filled with the smell of sweat, smoke, piss and fear, as the soldier lifted his rifle to his shoulder.

A shot.

'Benjamin!' Romy's skin turned cold and clammy as part of Benjamin's forehead and ear exploded. Warm blood splattered her face. She moaned.

Another shot.

Herr Bloch's limp body fell onto the cobblestones.

Beside her, Mutti collapsed to the ground. Daniel lunged forwards to run to Benjamin but was grabbed around the neck by Franz.

Romy stood frozen. Her brother—was he—?

Benjamin was dead.

Papa was howling like a wolf as he tried to claw his way through the crowd to reach his sons, but he was held back by a wall of shoulders. There was a crack in the air, more rifles fired, and this time everyone crashed to the footpath. Romy felt her knee grind into a shard of glass and let out a cry.

A hand pulled her out from under the person sprawled half on top of her, and she crawled across to a freezing stone wall between shopfronts and leaned against it.

Papa was on his haunches, cradling his head in his hands. Mutti was trying to sit up but was having trouble breathing. Romy remained still. Empty and in shock.

She held her breath as the soldiers lined up all the young men in the middle of the street.

Romy began to cry. Surely they weren't going to shoot Daniel too?

The leader waved his arm, and three covered trucks pulled forwards and all the young men—including Daniel—were instructed to climb in. As Daniel clambered onto the truck, he looked over his shoulder at Mutti and Papa, his eyes full of fear.

'Daniel!' Mutti screamed.

Papa reached for Daniel, but all at once their neighbour, Herr Gruber, was charging through the crowd towards them. His face was drawn and pale as he put both his hands on Papa's shoulders.

'You must go, Oskar. Now! For Romy and Marta. They will kill you too. Leave Vienna. Austria has lost her mind.'

Papa shook his head. 'I—Benjamin. Daniel. My boys . . .' His voice was cracked and broken. 'I won't leave them,' he croaked. 'I—I can't.' He bowed his head and began to sob as, around them, people started to help each other up. Some avoided looking at Papa, as if his misfortune might infect them, while others shared teary glances filled with sympathy.

Mutti crawled towards Papa and they huddled together, sobbing and rocking back and forth.

Herr Gruber bent down. 'Let me help you,' he whispered. 'You *must* get over the border. We should leave at once.'

Romy's skin was clammy and her heart was beating too fast. Her knees throbbed where they had been cut. She felt faint. Then darkness . . .

When Romy awoke, her face was buried in Papa's neck as he carried her along Wipplingerstrasse. Her mother—ashen-faced—walked close behind them, a protective hand on Romy's shoulder. Her head throbbed with each of Papa's steps. Crunch, crunch, crunch. Were they going home or leaving?

Romy peered over her father's shoulder. It was evening now, and a flickering yellow horseshoe was lit up by one of the few unbroken lights in the street. A faded picture of a chimneysweep dangled over the awning. Beneath it—in cheery green and red letters—*Geh nicht am glück vorbei.*

Don't let luck pass you by.

Chapter 2

MELBOURNE, APRIL 2016

Alexandra smiled and nodded at the palliative care nurse, Sally—who was busy writing on charts—as she tiptoed into Oma and Opa's grand sitting room. She caught a whiff of something woody; it was vaguely familiar but she couldn't quite place the smell.

Opa was propped up in a hospital bed. When she'd arrived home last night Alexandra hadn't recognised this withered man with the sallow face. The rhythmic whistle of the oxygen machine and the tiny beep of the heart monitor screen filled every corner of the room, nearly drowning out the tick of the mahogany grandfather clock.

Alexandra stared at walls of screens all day, watching for the faintest nudge in the graph—a variation—that told her to swoop on gold in Shanghai at breakfast and trade it in London by lunch. She spent eighteen-hour days under fluorescent lights searching for volatility. Hunting numbers. Alexandra didn't need to study the beeping screen to know her beloved opa's number was up. She'd been home for twelve hours but she was yet to see him conscious.

She shuddered. Perhaps she was too late?

Alexandra sank into the cushions of the old peacock-blue armchair by the fireplace and traced the curve of the arms, circling the rough patches. Hessian stuffing poked through threadbare velvet and the springs had gone in the base. She shivered and sneezed—so typical of her to pick up a bug in transit. She rubbed her cheek on a cushion. So many hours spent in this very chair snuggled onto Oma or Opa's lap for Aesop's fables and Grimm's fairytales and—as a teenager—curled up with a textbook, practising endless algebra and algorithms with a lead pencil.

The house—Puyuan—was a red-brick Edwardian nestled behind a picket fence weighed down with pale pink climbing roses. Wisteria scrambled up the verandah posts and dangled from the iron lace trim, its blue flowers spent. Oma's sitting room, with the bay window overlooking her precious garden, had lost none of its grandeur with age, though paint peeled from the deep grey-blue walls and wide skirting boards, and the large cream plaster ceiling rose could do with patching. The floor-to-ceiling bookshelves on the far wall were spilling over with books on herbs, Chinese medicine, history and photography. Crammed between books at every angle were political memoirs, British thrillers—le Carré, Forsyth—and five decades of French *Vogue*.

Alexandra gulped back tears as she replayed her hurried departure from London. She'd left her Sloane Street apartment for Heathrow and was on a flight to Melbourne within hours of Oma calling to say the tumours had come back and spread into Opa's organs, bones and bloodstream. Her grandmother's voice had lost its customary calm. Instead Alexandra could hear the deep, low tones of sadness and resignation.

When she'd finally emerged from customs in Melbourne twenty-four hours later, Oma and her friend Nina were standing with their shoulders pressed together in the arrivals hall, one dark and wiry, the other broad and soft. Alexandra allowed herself to be swallowed by their hugs, closing her eyes and breathing in traces of gardenia from her Oma's neat bun and the smell of fried garlic and smoked paprika that always accompanied Nina's kisses.

'*Danke* for coming so quickly. I know with the move . . .' Oma's voice had a new quiver.

'Oh!' Alexandra leaned down to press her cheek against her grandmother's as she stumbled over her suitcase. 'Opa—is he still . . .?'

Her grandmother lifted a tissue and dabbed her eyes as she nodded. 'He's waiting.'

Nina laid a gentle hand on Alexandra's shoulder. 'Your opa's still conscious. Just. He's been asking for you. Come. I'll take your bags.' Nina wrenched the trolley from Alexandra's grip with surprising force for a nonagenarian, insisting on pushing her bags.

Alexandra threaded her arm through her grandmother's and asked quietly, 'And you, Oma? How're you? It must be hard.'

'I'm fine, *liebling*. All the better for seeing you,' said Oma.

Alexandra shifted in the old chair as her Samsung vibrated in her back pocket and she pulled it out. Another text from Hugo: *Call me back. I'm sorry A.*

She deleted the message, resisting the urge to put a permanent block on her ex's number. She wasn't prepared to forgive him, but there was a tiny part of her that didn't want to say goodbye. She was an expert in analysing risk, predicting outcomes, but she had failed to see how exposed her own heart was.

Never again.

She slid the phone back into her pocket without so much as a glance at spot prices on Bloomberg. The market could wait.

She stood and threaded her fingers through Opa's and squeezed gently, as if she could send some of her own energy surging through their joined hands. Oma would say she was channelling her *qi*. Alexandra grinned; perhaps the apple didn't fall so far from the tree after all.

'Li . . . Sophia?' Opa rasped as Alexandra crouched bedside him. He reached up and tried to touch her jade pendant. She shivered and cleared her throat.

She glanced over at the photo of her parents on the marble mantelpiece above the fireplace. Once she'd been a smiling, clapping toddler with glossy hair, dressed in crimson overalls and a stripy turtleneck as she sat on her mother's knee. Her father Joseph, tall, broad and fair, stood to the side with a hand resting on Sophia's shoulder. Her mother was wearing a blue denim sundress with a strap falling from a tanned shoulder, the jade pendant nestled at the top of her cleavage, and she was laughing with Joseph, gazing into his blue eyes. Alexandra's stomach clenched as she stared at the photo, trying to remember this fierce love. It was her sole memory of her parents.

Opa barely mentioned Sophia Shu to Alexandra by name. Oma merely shook her head and smiled when she spoke of 'her gift'. Their clever child adopted from China. Cherished. Like Alexandra.

Opa strained forwards, peering to get a closer look at her face.

'Li?' he repeated.

'Opa, it's Alexandra,' she said, stroking his cool hand with her thumb, noticing how spindly it had become. His muscles had wasted away, and with them his strength and his memory. Alexandra had never heard either of her grandparents mention a Li.

'Oh.' His head dropped to the pillow with a weak smile. Then, confusion. 'Your job in Shanghai?' he asked faintly.

She paused. Was he lucid? 'Shanghai can wait,' replied Alexandra as she adjusted the drip line so she could perch on the edge of the bed. She could hardly tell him she'd delayed her transfer to Shanghai to spend as much time with him before—

She blinked away tears.

'Shanghai waits for no-one, my dear child.' He patted her hand and pushed out a deep belly chuckle, followed by a coughing fit. Between coughs he said, 'You should—' More coughing. 'Li. You won't find her . . . You look so like her, you know.'

Like who? Alexandra wondered. Did he mean her mother? Her heart sank. Her grandmother had warned her Opa was not making any sense. He'd forgotten her parents were long dead, killed in a car accident just weeks after the photo on the mantelpiece was taken. Alexandra was pulled from the wreckage by a paramedic, the back of her head sliced open like a peach. She traced the smooth scar at the nape of her neck, hidden by long hair. Some days it burned and puckered when she touched it, but most days she felt nothing. It was a grafted void.

As her eyes clouded with tears, she looked up at the blurry crystal chandelier and watched the rainbow of light swim across the ceiling and wall. This grey-blue room was home. Her grandparents were her anchor. And now she was losing her Opa. She squeezed his hand again and rubbed his other arm, trying to warm his skin and ease his pain.

Opa spluttered and wheezed. 'The spitting image. Your grandmother . . .'

'Shhh,' said Alexandra as she looked to the nurse for help.

'Your grandmother—Romy.' Cough. 'She was the strongest of us all. The three of us—'

More coughs. Opa's shoulders shook so hard Alexandra thought he might burst a lung.

The nurse jumped up and came over to rub Opa's back as he continued hacking. Alexandra stepped back to give Sally room. 'Can we give him something?' she asked helplessly. 'Water, medicine?'

The nurse ignored her, focused on her patient. 'There, there, Mr Cohen—Wilhelm. Nice deep breaths . . .'

'I'll fetch Oma,' said Alexandra, glancing out the window to where her grandmother was gardening.

'No need, love. It will pass in a sec. Besides. she'll only get her smoke going, or stick some more needles in his ankles. None of it helps much. Not at this stage.'

Alexandra's head thudded as she realised what the smell lingering in the room was: moxa. Alexandra pictured Oma waving dried sticks of Chinese mugwort over Opa's head, under his nose, then lighting the ends for an instant before blowing the smoke softly and pressing it straight onto pressure points on his ankles, wrists and neck. She giggled just a little—no wonder Sally was bewildered.

Sally raised an eyebrow at her and bustled over to the other side of the bed to tap the drip. 'Hydration and morphine. Your grandfather's on the good gear—aren't you, Wilhelm?' The nurse articulated her words slowly and clearly as if Opa were in nursery school.

'Opa . . . will he?' Alexandra hesitated. 'This coughing—do the drugs actually stop the pain?'

'They certainly do. We're doing everything we can to make sure he's comfortable.'

'Is there any possibility . . . I mean, this cancer . . .' She looked at Opa, who had lapsed into unconsciousness once more.

Sally shook her head. 'I'm sorry, love. But he knows you're here. Apple of his eye, you are. Talks about you non-stop.'

The nurse rolled Opa gently onto his side without waking him. She looked back over at Alexandra: 'So you just arrived from London? You must be jetlagged. I hear it's shocking this way, coming home.' The nurse was friendly and businesslike—rubbing Wilhelm's back as she spoke to Alexandra.

Alexandra nodded. Her legs ached and her body felt like she'd been run over by a truck. Last night she'd stepped off the kangaroo-hop flight clammy with a cold and a barking cough despite using the nasal saline spray with a hint of eucalyptus she'd picked up from the pharmacy in departures. The smell made her homesick. But it turned out a whole ocean up her nose couldn't stem this cold. No sooner had the taxi pulled into the driveway than Oma rushed Alexandra straight into a deep warm bath filled with cinnamon. The steamy bathroom smelled like Christmas. Alexandra smiled to herself as she absent-mindedly rubbed her jade pendant. Opa might be dying, but Oma still fussed over Alexandra. Some things never changed.

'Your grandmother tells me you're some kind of financial bigwig over there in London.' Sally eyed Alexandra's navy Stella McCartney yoga pants and gold-trimmed hoodie. 'Sounds very flash.' She grinned.

Alexandra shrugged. 'Not really. I trade commodities. Precious metals. Copper, gold, zinc, nickel, aluminium . . . but mostly I just trade paper,' she joked.

'I see,' said Sally, looking momentarily confused before breaking into a shy smile. 'I guess you'll never have to worry about topping up your superannuation.'

Alexandra was too embarrassed to respond—her job seemed pointless today. As she watched Sally soothe her Opa, rearranging the white sheets around his legs and up under his arms so he wasn't irritated by the scratchy hems, it seemed to her that Sally was the gold in this room.

'There you go, Wilhelm. Just have a little rest for a minute or two and then you can have a catch-up with your granddaughter. Gorgeous creature she is.' The nurse winked and picked up a thriller sitting on a chair in the far corner.

Alexandra sat back down in her comfy chair and pulled a woollen throw over her legs, wishing she could roll back the years. She didn't want Opa to go. Not yet. Not ever. But she hated seeing him like this.

She picked up the soup Oma had made her before ducking out into the garden. It was still warm. She held the cup in her hands for a heartbeat before taking a sip and savouring the familiar rush down her throat, heating her stomach. It was the taste of her childhood colds: dried black bean paste with crushed garlic, ginger and chives.

Alexandra shifted her gaze back to the window and watched as Oma wandered around her vegetable garden chomping on a green bean. Along the back fence was a thick bay hedge. In the middle of a blanket of thyme stood a row of trees. A gnarly Meyer lemon, limes and a tiny ginkgo. These were underplanted with waves of lilies, budding peony stems and purple clouds of flowering garlic and chives floating among blue monkshood.

Alexandra had missed the chaotic colour and whimsical combinations of Puyuan's garden. When was the last time she'd had her fingers in soil? She stretched out her manicured hands. They were so smooth—as if they belonged to someone else. As a child, Alexandra had loved to work alongside Oma and Opa in the garden and the kitchen, climbing the old oak tree, shelling peas, staking tomatoes and cramming her mouth with the tiny ones before they popped and sprayed down the front of her t-shirt.

She took another sip of soup and felt the ginger warm her throat.

Oma's silver hair bobbed among the long rows of tomatoes. The staked rows were about the same height as her grandmother. Oma plucked the leftover red and green tiger tomatoes from the vines, not stopping until she'd filled the wicker basket slung over her forearm. Then she picked handfuls of the purple and deep green basil huddled under the tomatoes. Alexandra's stomach rumbled as she realised Oma was out picking lunch.

Alexandra closed her eyes and listened to the rhythm of the oxygen machine, beeping monitor and grandfather clock. Then she prayed.

When she'd finished in the garden, Romy walked into the kitchen, dropped her basket onto the wooden bench. She popped two tiny red tomatoes into her mouth; they were still warm from the autumn sun, and the sweet juice and seeds exploded, filling her cheeks.

She had mountains of coriander, so she put the leaves and stems into the blender with a glug of olive oil, a handful of almonds, three cloves of garlic and the juice of half a lemon to make pesto for today's lunch. Alexandra certainly looked like she could do with a good feed, and the coriander would be a bit of a wake-up call for her system—helping to fight any lurgies still lurking from the flight. Any leftover paste could go in the freezer.

Romy found she was eating less and less these days, so she pulled the curly green leaves of bok choy out of the basket and gave them a rinse, leaving them in the colander to dry. Just before it was time to eat, she'd steam the leaves and make a dressing of basil oil, chilli, Sichuan pepper and a dash of maple syrup. She'd have a small bowl of greens, instead of the pumpkin and water chestnut risotto left over from the night before.

Nina had joined them for dinner after they'd arrived home from the airport, helping herself to a second serve of the risotto. Some things never changed.

'Is this pumpkin from your garden, Oma?' Alexandra had asked, clearly trying to be bright and cheery as she divided her meal into neat piles on her plate.

'Yes. It'll strengthen your spleen and rebuild your *qi*. The thyme is good for your lungs.'

Nina rolled her eyes at Alexandra in solidarity.

'Well,' Nina exclaimed in her cutting Austrian accent, 'you're fortunate you missed the sautéed lamb kidneys your grandmother forced on me last week. Dished up with orchid stems and shiitake mushrooms.' She winked.

'It's good for your lower back and knee pains,' Romy protested. 'Good for longevity. Look at you—strong as an ox.' She marvelled at her friend's golden skin, full blonde bob and one of her endless parade of sequinned kaftans.

'*Ach*,' said Nina, 'Perhaps it gave me more energy. It certainly gave me more—' she paused as she hunted for the right word '—vigour? Ardour? Old Mr Thompson from my book club certainly appreciated it. I gave him my best Anaïs Nina.'

Nina shimmied her broad shoulders and chuckled as Romy narrowed her eyes and shook her head, exasperated.

Alexandra choked on a piece of pumpkin.

'They're going to throw you out of your apartment in the retirement village if you keep up that sort of carry-on,' Romy said sternly. 'What about the warning letter last week?'

'Psscht. We're old. Not dead.'

The women fell silent. For some minutes, the only sound was the clatter of forks against blue china bowls.

Then Nina reached out and took a hand of each of the other women. She lifted them both to her mouth and kissed first Romy's then Alexandra's. 'Sorry. It was thoughtless of me to make such a joke. I'm here. Lean on me, okay?'

She sighed and looked at Romy, her serious brown eyes pleading. 'It's my turn.'

Romy ran her hands over the fresh mint leaves and raised them to her face to take the scent deep into her lungs. She'd brew up some to help with her granddaughter's sore throat.

She was worried about Alexandra. The minute she set eyes on her in the arrivals hall—the dark rings under her eyes, gaunt cheeks, hunched shoulders—Romy thought of her own mother standing at Brenner station, icy winds stinging her cheeks. Fleeing Austria to begin a new life in Shanghai.

Bereft.

What was Alexandra fleeing? There was the break-up of course. She'd always felt Hugo and Alexandra were two lonely souls who had lashed themselves together like a hastily constructed life raft. Romy always wondered if Alexandra chose Hugo not so much for his mathematical wizardry and companionship, but because she was simply tired of being alone.

Nina, bless her, had noticed too, raising her eyebrows behind the girl's back as they'd loaded her bags into the taxi the night before.

There was pressure, of course, being the only child. Romy's time in Shanghai weighed heavily on her. The need to be *enough* for both parents. It was a burden Romy had always tried to hide.

But here she was—their only grandchild—home in time to watch her cherished grandfather die. Wilhelm and Alexandra had always been quite the twosome over the years, playing tennis, poring over spreadsheets, swapping share market tips.

Romy had made a point of loosening the ties of their circle of three and was accepting when Alexandra chose to pursue study, career and then love overseas. Yet it was hard to watch her move so far away.

But time had a way of pulling back the past. The family—the life Romy and Wilhelm had created in this vast, baking, lucky country—was about to end.

Romy wiped the tears from her eyes, raised her arms and stretched her back, taking in the smell of herbs filling the kitchen.

What was going on with Alexandra? Her usually glossy hair was limp, dull, and there was a tinny optimism, a false bravado, to her smile. Her brown eyes flickered to one side when she spoke, and there was a constant twitch to her legs. She had a cold, yes, but this was something else. A dangerous energy was flooding her robust body.

A lifetime of burying her own uncertainties had taught Romy to recognise the signs.

Chapter 4

BRENNER PASS, AUSTRIA, 15 NOVEMBER 1938

Romy tugged the collar of her blue coat so it sat high at the nape of her neck. She was too frightened to take it off. Not until they were out of Austria. Beside her, Mutti and Papa shifted in their second-class seats as their narrow carriage rolled on its tracks through the tight turns of the Brenner Pass. When they had reached the Brenner *Bahnhof*, Papa had instructed Romy to pull her hat low, hold his hand and not make a peep as they quickly changed trains for Italy. *She must follow the rules.*

Mutti laid a reassuring gloved hand on her daughter's leg to stop her swinging it and kicking the seat in front. Romy was frustrated and fidgety after sitting for six hours with nothing but a slice of beef sausage, a bread roll and half a hard-boiled egg passed back by the kindly old lady with the eye patch from the seat in front. She leaned against the glass to look out the window and catch a better view of the mountains.

She'd never been this far south and Romy wanted to remember every second. The grey sky was filled with swirling snowflakes and the mountains were covered with pine forests. They shot up so steeply Romy couldn't see the peaks, not even when she pressed her cheek to the icy window and tilted her head to look up. She'd always dreamed this narrow pass would be magical—like something out of her fairytale books. With each click of the track, black shadows appeared and disappeared. Her numb ear pressed hard against the window and the jagged mountains seemed to hiss *you can't come in here.* The countryside of her dreams was cold and forbidding. She felt lost.

The old diesel engine bellowed and huffed as it pulled the carriages along the tracks, through the snow. Forests gave way to hamlets dotted with small stone houses as they crept closer to the Italian border. The carriage, which had been full of nervous chatter for the past few hours, fell silent as the brakes started to squeal on the wet tracks.

When Romy was pretending to sleep with her cheek on her mother's soft brown woollen suit, she had heard the adults' desperate whispers, as fluttery as the snowflakes. *Would they be allowed to cross into Italy?*

The night after Benjamin was killed and Daniel was taken away, Herr Gruber had forced himself through the queues and chaotic crowds to the gates of the Chinese consulate. The gates were guarded by half a dozen Wehrmacht soldiers, but their friend heard a rumour that the Chinese diplomat Feng Shan Ho was issuing visas under the bistro table at a café next door as he took his afternoon coffee. Alas, the café was closed for the evening, but as he was leaving Herr Gruber saw a black consular vehicle approaching the gates. Taking a risk, he thrust the Bernfelds' passports through the open window of the car. Feng Shan Ho stopped the car and took the papers with a tip of his hat. No words were exchanged lest the soldiers overheard. The next day at noon, as he took his black tea, Feng Shan Ho slipped a yellow diplomatic envelope under the bistro table to Herr Gruber.

Three days after Kristallnacht—the night of the broken glass—Mutti had told Romy they were going to Italy to catch a boat to the other side of the world. To China. Though it was rumoured you didn't *need* a visa to enter Shanghai, Herr Gruber insisted the Bernfelds get visas—just in case there were problems crossing borders. They'd sail back just as soon as the Führer no longer governed Austria. Or, when Daniel joined them, they would apply to move to America. Because who wanted to return to a country that had told them they were less than nothing?

'It will be soon,' Papa promised. 'Now the world knows about Kristallnacht, they will put a stop to this madness.' But Papa's voice had lifted with uncertainty.

The night Herr Gruber bought the Chinese visas, he had instructed them to pack two small suitcases of practical clothes. Thick shoes. Best coats.

'Take ten Reichsmarks only in your wallet,' he'd instructed Papa.

'Ten?' Papa objected. 'That will not even buy the coffee and some plum jam *Liwanzen* at the station.' He tickled Romy under the chin but his smile was forced. 'They will have us leave Austria like beggars? After all we have done? Why—'

'Hitler is a fool,' Herr Gruber interrupted. 'No-one will take Reichsmarks. They're worthless. Take my camera and sell it in Shanghai.'

Papa shook his head. 'You could be shot for helping Jews. You should come with us.'

'My place is here. I need to keep the school running. The children didn't start this war.'

'You're a good man.' Mutti paused in her sewing and turned a tear-stained face to their neighbour. 'Herr Gruber, why would you risk yourself to help us?'

'We all bleed the same colour, Frau Bernfeld.' The teacher blushed as if he realised too late the memories his words might summon. Benjamin . . .

Romy watched Mutti concentrate fiercely on each stitch as she sewed her grandmother's pearl necklace and her own diamond engagement ring into the lining of the collar of Romy's coat.

Herr Gruber turned and patted Romy on the head. 'Your daughter has always been a good student. Like her brothers.' He paused. 'I'll go purchase your first-class tickets for the next boat from Genoa.'

'That's too extravagant—' Papa raised his hands in the air then dropped them, exhausted.

Herr Gruber reached over and gently squeezed Papa's hand. 'Trust me. It's the only way. You can convert your ticket at the port in Italy, cash them in for second- or third-class before you board. You can't get money out of Austria. You'll get caught and it will be confiscated. You'll be punished . . .'

Mutti touched a gold button on Romy's coat and whispered a prayer.

Daniel had been transported to a concentration camp at Dachau, Herr Gruber had discovered. Herr Gruber wasn't entirely sure what work Daniel had been assigned, but said he would do his best to find out. He had contacts in Germany, and it might be possible to get some release papers using the Chinese visa once the Bernfelds had reached Shanghai.

Mutti's eyes had flickered with hope, before dimming like a broken lamp.

The train's steam whistle blew and the train shuddered, and Romy rocked against her parents as they pulled into Brenner station. The carriage doors were flung open and several Wehrmacht guards with guns invaded the cabin and stood in the aisle, ordering all the passengers off. Papa reached for their suitcases and, petrified, Romy tugged at her collar.

Mutti shot her a quick reassuring look and narrowed her eyes as if to say *don't touch*. A guard shoved Papa in the back with a gun as he stumbled onto the platform, following the crowd to the next platform where the smaller train for Italy sat with the engine running.

A guard yelled: '*Juden. Emigranten. Da drüben.*' Jews. Emigrants. Over there.

Papa ushered Romy and Mutti away from the queues for customs to where a nervous circle of weary passengers stood shivering, despite their fur coats and leather gloves. They all had their felt hats pulled low, as if trying to make themselves inconspicuous.

The rest of the train's passengers had their passports inspected and stamped, but the circle of Jewish passengers were surrounded by more guards with guns and ushered away from the train.

The remaining passengers—those without a large red 'J' stamped on their passport—clambered onto the waiting train with their luggage, casting furtive looks over their shoulders. Some appeared cold and defiant, others apologetic. The engine blew three deep whistles before chugging away from the platform and into Italy.

A man with a grey beard and a narrow face yelled out to one of the soldiers: 'Stop! What about our tickets?'

He was answered with a swift knock in the back of his head with the butt of a rifle. He fell to the ground, unconscious. The guard who had hit him took the man's suitcase and threw it to another guard, who took it inside the station.

'Anyone else have questions?' The guard smirked. 'Line up your suitcases on the platform and open them—*now*!' he barked.

Papa placed their two small leather suitcases on the platform and flicked open the lids, baring Mutti's silk petticoat and three pastel cashmere jumpers. Mutti tucked Romy under her arm, like a hen with her chicken, and Romy could feel the individual pearls pressing into her neck. The guards rummaged through each suitcase, tossing out silver candlesticks, jewellery, cutlery and any other valuable that could be sold or melted down. The bitter wind roared up the valley pass, stinging their cheeks.

Shivering, Romy looked through the white lace curtains into the platform café where a fire burned in a neat black hearth, making the apricot walls glow with warmth. There were round marble tables just like in the café on Wipplingerstrasse. She longed for a hot chocolate. Would they be allowed to go inside to get out of the icy wind when the inspection was over? She groaned as she spotted the sign on the door.

Juden verboten. Jews forbidden.

Her stomach gurgled and her mother tugged her closer.

They were poking through Papa's suitcase. A watch, a stethoscope and Papa's gold-and-black fountain pen—a gift from the medicine department in Oxford—were extracted. His medical textbooks were ignored. Papa pursed his lips, but said nothing. Romy swayed on her feet. Why weren't they allowed to sit on the wooden benches under the station signs? It was so unfair. The next gust of icy wind threatened to knock her over.

'Close them.' The guards pointed at the suitcases and everyone rushed over to reclaim their own.

'Place your suitcase in front of you and stand up straight until the next train.' The guard raised his voice as he pointed his index finger at the straggly line of weary travellers. 'Do not move. Do not sit down.'

Romy crossed her legs; now she needed to pee.

The guard looked at his watch. 'The next train to Genoa will be in exactly three hours and fourteen minutes. If you Jews—' he paused to spit before continuing '—so much as blink in the wrong direction then you will not board that train. Have I made myself clear?'

'Yes, sir.'

Papa spoke clearly and looked the guard in the eye.

The man raised his arm and shouted, '*Heil* Hitler!'

'*Heil* Hitler!' the other guards repeated with a stomp of their black boots as they saluted in return. Then they swivelled on their heels and marched down the platform in neat pairs into the café.

As the door to the coffee shop swung open, the scent of baked apple, cinnamon and coffee wafted across to the passengers before being whipped away by the wind.

Romy tried to stand perfectly still by focusing on a single spot. It was a trick she'd learned at ski school when they were learning to balance on one leg. She stared hard at a sodden brown leaf being lifted and tossed against the iron track. As she concentrated, she felt a warm trickle slide down the inside of her stockings. But she didn't even flinch.

Chapter 5

SHANGHAI, 5 FEBRUARY 1939

Romy stood gripping the dark handrail of the SS *Conte Verde* as they entered the Yangtze River; the choppy brown river would lead them to their new home in Shanghai. Mutti stood beside Romy, pale-faced and lost inside her elegant camel coat. Underneath the coat, the waist of Mutti's pleated brown skirt sagged on her hips. She turned and forced a smile at Romy. Pressed against her left shoulder, Papa stood grim-faced, hunched over the rail in his double-breasted herringbone coat, felt hat pulled low over patches of hair that had turned white in the month they had been at sea.

Papa reached out and squeezed Romy's shoulder, leaning down close to whisper in her ear: 'Be brave, my *liebling*. We'll write to Daniel and he will join us soon enough.'

That morning, the luxurious ocean liner *Conte Verde* had left the endless expanse of blue sea after four weeks. For the most part, the passage had felt like a holiday cruise, and Romy and her new friend Nina spent hours exploring every corner of the ship: card games in the women's parlours, watercolour classes and book salons in the palm-cushioned tearooms, beauty lounges where women read magazines and had their hair set high and lips painted red for formal dinners, a dark-panelled whisky lounge for the gentlemen after dinner. When the ship reached the equator and the almost unbearable thick treacly heat of the ports of Bombay, Colombo and Singapore, the children spent the days on board swimming and splashing in the pools, shrieking and whooping as their mothers sipped soda or cocktails, served with mint and lemon on silver trays by friendly Italian waiters in white gloves.

Now, the *Conte Verde*'s bow was slowly nudging its way along a murky river with the texture of goulash. There were more than five hundred passengers aboard and it seemed most were crowded onto the trio of top decks. Necks straining, mouths open in disbelief.

Sharp salty air had been replaced with smoke, filth and the unfamiliar cooking smells of fish and meat. Some passengers held handkerchiefs over their mouths, others wiped tears from their eyes. With each chug of the engine, Romy felt a pang in her stomach. As the unfamiliar smells settled in her hair and over her collar, she gulped down her losses, her fear and uncertainty, to concentrate on her new surroundings.

All along the shoreline were flat fields, with terraces carved into distant hills. The countryside was so unlike the neatly fenced slopes of Austria that Romy didn't know what to make of it. Every now and again the layers of lurid green were interrupted by a cluster of factories coughing dirty smoke to the horizon. Surrounded by these larger industrial buildings were funny little brown houses with dark roof tiles that curled up like waves at the edges. Mutti put her arm around Romy, pulling her close with a long sigh. Romy had to agree: this countryside was the strangest sight.

'Rice paddies,' said Papa as he pointed to the shore. He turned and gave Romy an encouraging smile. 'I have a feeling we'll be eating quite a bit of rice while we're here.'

Romy bent over the rail to get a closer look as the ocean liner forged its way up the river. Every spare patch of water was filled with tiny wooden boats, red and cream wing-shaped sails flapping as they crisscrossed the river. Some boats just managed to skim in front of the *Conte Verde*'s bow, causing the captain to lean on the foghorn in frustration. One boat that sailed past was so loaded up with barrels it looked like it might sink at any moment. Another had its open deck piled with green melons, the next had rolls of fabric lined up as if they were a tailor's shop. Other boats carried brown hessian sacks of glossy rice, tiny pearls that winked and caught the light.

Romy heard crying and looked down at a little wooden sailboat with a crimson sail skimming the waves at the bow. A squawking toddler with red cheeks was strapped to his mother's chest. The child grabbed a handful of navy fabric and pulled it aside to expose her breast. Romy couldn't help but stare; she'd never seen a bare breast before. The toddler opened his mouth wide as if he were going to bite the nipple right off, before using a hand to nudge the dark purple circle into his mouth. He tucked his head under his mother's chin, and she rested her head on top of his, stroking his back and wrapping her arms around him to protect the child from the bitter breeze. Between both sails was a line of washing, rags hanging from a line. A man stood at the back of the boat and Romy could just make out that he was relieving himself off the deck into the filthy water.

'Orientals. No better than animals.'

Romy jumped with fright. The German first mate stood behind her in his freshly pressed white uniform, chiselled jaw clenched with disgust. Mutti gripped the handrail, saying nothing. Papa tipped his hat and nodded at the sailor, his mouth taut, face expressionless.

'No wonder it smells like a bloody sewer here,' he continued. The first mate pointed at the man, who now had his pants pulled right down and was squatting off the edge of the boat, trying to fashion a flapping sheet on the washing line as a curtain to preserve his privacy. 'They live on the river on these filthy sampans,' he said in disgust. 'Look at them.' The sailor waved his arm at the buildings onshore. 'Cotton. Silk from those filthy mills over there.' He pointed at the sheds dotted along the shoreline spewing grey smoke and filling the winter air with smog. 'They load up and come out here onto the water to trade. It's damn chaos.'

The smell of frying fish and some unfamiliar spices, warming scents that were cinnamon-like, drifted up to their deck. Romy tried to draw the scent deep into her lungs to drive out the cold. For her, unlike the other passengers retching over the railing, these strange sweet and spicy smells were a comfort.

'And their food . . . ugh.' The sailor wrinkled his nose and spat into the water, just missing the little boat. 'They are like animals,' he repeated. He turned to face Romy and her parents. 'You belong here,' he said before he turned on his heel, almost crushing little Nina, who was tiptoeing through the crowd to join the Bernfelds.

'Out of my way!' he boomed as the crowd shuddered in sympathy for the little girl.

Nina weaved quietly between the passengers to join Romy at the railing.

'Ah, Nina,' Papa said kindly. 'Come join us.' And he proceeded to point out the rice fields and cottages along the shore as if it were a giant adventure. As if Shanghai was just another port where they were docking to refuel on this endless crazy holiday.

Nina, with her pretty blue ribbons and smocked frock, had shared a cabin with Romy since the Suez Canal. Her pregnant mother had suffered pre-eclampsia and died in labour. Papa delivered the stillborn baby just before the mother died, but without proper medication he was at a loss to stop the seizures and the bleeding out. The captain had refused to help, saying, 'There are supply shortages, do I need to remind you, Herr Doktor? I'm not at liberty to waste valuable drugs.'

Romy hardly thought saving a dying woman was wasting drugs. The captain wanted to throw both bodies overboard immediately, but Mutti begged him to allow them to deliver a mitzvah with a makeshift sea burial. The bottom deck was full as passengers joined Mutti and Papa in reciting the Kaddish with low, breaking voices. Mutti and another lady a few cabins down had managed to find some spare cotton sheets to swaddle the bodies. Nina sobbed and held Romy's hand as her mother and her tiny baby sister who never took a breath were dropped into the ocean. The shrouded bodies slowly sank to the endless blue depths, swallowed by the waves.

Today, as the boat tipped and lurched through the filthy chop, Romy bent her knees to keep her balance, swaying as she reached out to clasp her friend's hand. She smiled to reassure Nina. Any nerves Romy had about what her life with Mutti and Papa would be like in Shanghai were overshadowed by Nina's loss. How would Nina adjust and survive when she set foot in this strange land? Nina's papa had been killed in a pogrom, like Benjamin. Who would love and care for her orphaned friend?

As they sailed into Shanghai, thin wooden jetties and pontoons jutted out from every available space along the riverbank, and people with jet-black hair, identically dressed in navy shirts with small round collars and matching pants, swarmed across every surface. Jumping on and off motorboats, sailboats and fishing vessels, and filling the air with loud chatter as they formed lines and unpacked barrels, crates and fishing nets, often carrying cargo on poles across their shoulders. The shouts and clanging were overshadowed by the vile undercurrent of diesel, sewerage, sweat and rotten fish mingling with the intriguing scent of spices, smoked meat and strange fruits and flowers.

As the *Conte Verde* slowed and released three deep blasts of her foghorn, they cruised beside a promenade in front of the grandest European buildings Romy had ever seen. Halfway along the promenade was the peak of a roof that soared upwards, an apple-green pyramid that pierced the soft grey winter sky.

Romy blinked three times to check she wasn't just tired and imagining it. Nina stood with her mouth agape and even Mutti managed to raise an eyebrow. These buildings were nothing like the shanty huts and factories along the filthy and muddy Yangtze. These buildings were grand yet modern, with soaring clock towers, shimmering domes, marble columns and wide balconies. But where Romy was used to marble statues of famous musicians, politicians and the occasional Greek or Roman god, out the front of these buildings were polished bronze lions and shiny oversized brass nameplates.

A giant billboard boasted the head of a glamorous blonde with bare shoulders in a ball gown, advertising *Castile Toilet Soap for Sensitive Skin* with Chinese characters running down the left-hand side. Another offered gold diamond watches and a third had a smiling Shirley Temple in puffy blue satin sleeves holding a white birthday cake with pink trimming, with *The Little Princess* over her head. Romy nudged Nina and they giggled with excitement and surprise. They certainly hadn't expected the latest American movies to be shown here. Perhaps Mutti and Papa would take them to see it?

What was this city, Shanghai? Papa had called it 'the Paris of the East', but Romy had never been to France. The grand stone buildings looked like they might be from Europe, but the glitzy billboards? They seemed straight out of Hollywood.

Between the row of buildings and the swampy riverbank were four lanes of traffic filled with bumper-to-bumper black, blue and dark green cars and sleek electric trams. Weaving among the traffic were wheelbarrows, or small carriages that were pulled by men instead of horses. Some were filled with flowers, melons or bamboo baskets, others with people in fine suits, fur coats and felt hats with colourful plumes.

Romy's little suitcase knocked between her knees as the *Conte Verde* nudged her nose into the dock. Mutti stood perfectly still, her neat brown suit nipped in at the waist, hat tilted, camel coat wrapped tight around a face so pale Romy feared her mother would fade into the paintwork. While the other mothers had laughed and played cards, smoking in the drawing rooms after supper while the men drank whisky or walked the decks, Mutti would stay in her cabin penning long letters to Daniel, promising him they would be reunited in Shanghai just as soon as she could manage it. She arranged for one of the cabin boys to post the letters when they went ashore for supplies at each port.

Sailors in starched white uniforms they must have been saving for Shanghai shore leave yelled at each other as they unfurled coils of rope, to be hoisted around the huge iron bollards sticking up from the jetty. There were dozens of angry grey warships bobbing around them, and Romy and Nina competed to see how many flags they could recognise: small gunboats from Britain and America, large British and American cruise liners anchored midstream, plus merchant ships from Holland and Italy . . .

Romy squinted at a white flag with a large red dot in the middle on a nearby warship. 'Papa—' she tugged on her father's sleeve '—tell us, which one is that?' She pointed to a larger version on a pole over a lean-to room. It had capital letters in English she could just make out.

'*Iz . . . Izumo*.'

'Japanese. They control some parts of Shanghai.' Papa's voice sounded resigned.

Romy hesitated. What if it was like the Italian border?

But she didn't get to ask Papa, as the steel gangplanks were wheeled out from the ship, screeching as they slid across the bottom deck to shore. The first mate gave a whistle with his thumb and forefinger, and the crowd obediently poured down the stairwells, men hitching their suitcases in front of them and women clasping their fur coats at the neck as if they might be ripped from their backs. No sooner had they stepped ashore than Romy and Nina were shunted with Romy's parents into a small tender smelling of rotten fish and diesel fumes, luggage piled around their feet, to make the short, choppy journey to what the deck hands called the Bund.

The tender pulled up at a rickety wooden dock and their luggage was tossed onto it as they clambered from the boat. Papa went ahead to clear their paperwork as Nina, Romy and Mutti gathered their suitcases and walked down the jetty.

As they stood on firm land for the first time in weeks, legs still swaying with the rhythm of the sea, they linked hands and waited for Papa to return and their new life in Shanghai to begin.